AT BLUEBONNET LAKE

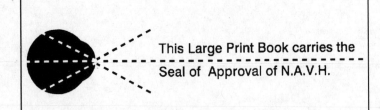

This Large Print Book carries the Seal of Approval of N.A.V.H.

TEXAS CROSSROADS, BOOK ONE

AT BLUEBONNET LAKE

AMANDA CABOT

THORNDIKE PRESS

A part of Gale, Cengage Learning

GALE
CENGAGE Learning·

Farmington Hills, Mich • San Francisco • New York • Waterville, Maine
Meriden, Conn • Mason, Ohio • Chicago

LIBRARY OF CONGRESS CATALOGING-IN-PUBLICATION DATA

Cabot, Amanda, 1948–
    At Bluebonnet Lake / by Amanda Cabot. — Large print edition.
        pages ; cm. — (Texas crossroads ; #1) (Thorndike Press large print Christian romance)
        ISBN 978-1-4104-7406-3 (hardcover) — ISBN 1-4104-7406-2 (hardcover)
        1. Life change events—Fiction. 2. Large type books. I. Title.
    PS3603.A35A95 2014b
    813'.6—dc23   2014033633

Published in 2014 by arrangement with Revell Books, a division of Baker Publishing Group

Printed in Mexico
1 2 3 4 5 6 7 18 17 16 15 14

For my readers.

Your emails brighten my day;
your support lifts my heart.
Truly, you are the reason I write.

1

It had to be an April Fools' joke. Any second, Sally would laugh and tell Kate to turn the car around, that they weren't really going to spend a month in a place that — if the front gate was any indication — was in desperate need of an extreme makeover.

The drive from San Antonio's international airport had been easy, the traffic no challenge for a woman accustomed to dealing with the Garden State Parkway and New Jersey Turnpike, and once they'd left the city itself, the scenery had proven to be even more beautiful than Sally had promised. The rolling tree-covered hills, the lush meadows, even the oversized prickly pear cactus all added to the pastoral beauty. No doubt about it: the Texas Hill Country was beautiful. All except for this particular spot. This was literally the end of the road.

After they'd left the tiny town of Dupree, they'd climbed a hill before descending into one of the prettiest valleys Kate had seen. Then the road had ended abruptly, leaving her with the choice of a U-turn or passing through this gate. Kate had seen similar gates on TV, and they'd always led to the estate of some millionaire. Not this time. She might be in Texas, but this wasn't Southfork. Far from it. This was definitely a joke, and now it was time to admit she'd been fooled.

Kate turned to look at her passenger. As she'd expected, Sally was smiling. Unfortunately, it wasn't a "fooled you this time, didn't I?" smile. To the contrary, Kate's grandmother radiated happiness. Genuine happiness.

Kate's stomach did somersaults at the realization that this was no joke. This was the place Sally expected them to spend the next month.

"Oh, Kate, it's just the way I remember. The beautiful iron gate with the rainbow on top, the trees — even the prickly pears are the way I remember them."

Kate tried not to sigh. The finish on what Sally called the beautiful iron gate was peeling; the rainbow's colors had faded; the ark that replaced the fabled pot of gold at one end was so bent it was almost unrecognizable. Though she knew that Sally's eyesight was no longer perfect, Kate was certain that the entrance to Rainbow's End hadn't looked like this when her grandmother visited it half a century ago. Sally was seeing what she wanted to see.

"The trees are beautiful," Kate admitted as she steered her rental car through the gate and onto the resort's private drive. Live oaks and cypresses shaded the badly rutted road and seemed to promise that even the hottest days of July and August would be bearable. Perhaps only the entrance needed work. Perhaps the resort itself would be better.

It was not. Kate parked as close as she could to what appeared to be the entrance and tried not to frown. Any resemblance to the Tyrolean cottage in the brochure was purely coincidental. The paint was faded; one of the shutters hung askew; and the flowers in the window box were cheap plastic, as faded as the paint. Whoever had designed the resort's brochure had both a vivid imagination and more than a passing acquaintance with Photoshop. Kate's colleagues would have laughed at this example of faux-tography. She wasn't laughing.

"Are you sure this is the right place?" Kate knew she was grasping at straws. There couldn't be another place called Rainbow's

End so close to this one.

"Of course it is." Sally's voice was uncharacteristically sharp as she ran a hand through her tightly curled silver hair in an equally uncharacteristic gesture. Kate felt more than a momentary stab of guilt. Her grandmother had asked very little of her over the years. It was unkind of Kate to even hint that she was less than thrilled to be here, especially given Sally's health. That was, after all, the reason Kate was taking an extended vacation, so that her grandmother could have the trip she'd dreamed of for so long.

"There's the door to the office." Sally pointed to a sign that appeared to be relatively new. "Let's see which cabin they've given us."

Waiting until Sally had swung her legs out of the car and stood, albeit a bit shakily, Kate extended her arm and let Sally grasp it. Though Sally hated any show of dependence, the path was uneven, making the few yards treacherous for a woman with poor knees that were already tired from the long trip.

Kate opened the door and ushered her grandmother inside the small but seemingly well-appointed office. A computer and printer shared space with a phone on a long credenza that housed six file drawers. There was even a vase of fresh flowers on the tall counter separating guests from the working area. There was, however, no sign of staff.

Kate smiled at Sally as she rang the old-fashioned bell on the counter. Her grandmother had had a similar bell at home and had never once complained during the weeks when it was Kate's favorite toy.

Within seconds of the bell's ringing, a tall, athletic woman whom Kate guessed to be in her midforties entered the office. Dressed in khaki slacks and a navy polo shirt with the Rainbow's End logo, she was undoubtedly an employee, and the way she assessed Kate and Sally made Kate suspect she was one of the owners.

"You must be our new guests," the auburn-haired woman said with a smile. "I'm Angela Sinclair."

Kate nodded as she recognized the name. According to the brochure, Angela and Tim Sinclair were the proprietors of Rainbow's End. "I'm Kate Sherwood, and this is my grandmother, Sally Fuller." Though colleagues found it a bit strange, Kate hadn't called her Grandma since Grandpa Larry's death when Sally had announced that Kate was old enough to drop the title.

"Ah yes." The woman's smile broadened

11

as she looked at Sally. Who wouldn't smile at a petite, silver-haired woman whose plump cheeks made her look like Mrs. Claus? "You mentioned that you were a guest here in the past." Angela Sinclair gestured toward the row of file cabinets. "I'm sorry, Mrs. Fuller, but I couldn't find the records."

Sally's laugh filled the room. "That's probably because it was such a long time ago. Dinosaurs were still roaming the earth then."

"I doubt that." Angela chuckled as she pulled a key from the rack over the credenza. "My husband and I have owned Rainbow's End for five years, but we have records going back another decade."

"Not far enough." Sally leaned forward and cupped her hand around one side of her mouth, as if she were about to impart a state secret. "I was here fifty years ago."

Her eyes widening in surprise, Angela nodded. "We get some repeat business, but you're the first from that far back. Welcome to Rainbow's End," she said, apparently realizing that she hadn't formally greeted them. "Tim and I are glad you've decided to return." Angela pulled out a map and circled a square. "I've put you in number 12."

For the first time since they'd entered the office, Sally's smile faded, making Kate wonder what was bothering her. She didn't have to wait long for the answer.

"The cabins have numbers?" Sally reached for the old-fashioned iron key and slid it into the front pocket of her purse. "When Larry and I were here, they were named for people from the Bible. We stayed in Joshua, right on Bluebonnet Lake."

Angela lowered her eyes, clearly uncomfortable with some aspect of the conversation. "I see. Tim and I made a few changes, and that was one of them. When we saw that the signs needed to be repainted, we decided it would be easier to replace them with new metal numbers."

Cheaper too. Judging from what Kate had seen so far, Rainbow's End was not exactly flourishing. She studied the map for a second. "I'm sure number 12 will be lovely. It looks easy enough to find."

With a quick nod, Angela handed Kate a second sheet of paper. "All the information is here. You know we're on the modified American plan. Supper's at 6:00. Breakfast is a buffet from 7:00 to 8:30. On Sunday we serve a midday meal instead of supper."

Her face once more beaming, Sally touched Kate's arm. "It's just the way I

13

remembered. Oh, Kate, I'm so glad we came."

And so was Kate, if it made her grandmother this happy. But as she drove the short distance to the cabin, Kate's doubts resurfaced. "Are you sure this will be all right?" she asked as she pulled into the parking space on the east side of the building and checked the odometer. "It's a tenth of a mile to the dining room."

Sally gripped her purse with both hands. "I'm not an invalid, Kate. It's true Dr. Morrison said my heart isn't as strong as it used to be, but I can certainly walk to meals."

Sally's cheeks flushed, and Kate wondered if it was from the realization that this story was significantly different from the one she'd told when she was trying to convince Kate they should come here. At that time, Sally had claimed that the doctor believed her heart was so weak that she might be unable to travel in another year.

Wondering if she'd been manipulated, Kate raised an eyebrow.

"Dr. Morrison told me moderate exercise is good," her grandmother said, sounding a bit defensive. "Besides, this cabin looks as delightful as Joshua, and it's bigger. I think I remember hearing that all the cabins along the lakefront had only one bedroom." Sally tipped her head in the opposite direction, her change of subject telling Kate she had ⟨…⟩ the discussion of ⟨…⟩ their cabin ap- ⟨…⟩ than the office, ⟨…⟩ constructed of ⟨…⟩ had seen only a ⟨…⟩ that each was ⟨…⟩ End a sur- ⟨…⟩ hodgepodge look. ⟨…⟩ cinder blocks, ⟨…⟩ peared to be ⟨…⟩ haphazard, ⟨…⟩ no idea what ⟨…⟩ but somehow ⟨…⟩ perhaps be- ⟨…⟩ metal roofs. ⟨…⟩ than most of its ⟨…⟩ boasted a front ⟨…⟩ or rocking chairs. ⟨…⟩ and Sally sitting ⟨…⟩ birds that Sally ⟨…⟩ area's attractions. ⟨…⟩ were lucky, they'd ⟨…⟩ fishers to gold- ⟨…⟩ gs. But first they needed chairs. Kate would ask for them as soon as she got Sally settled in the cabin.

"Let me take a quick look," she said to

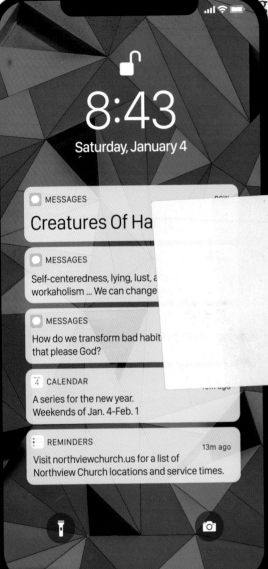

her grandmother, holding out her hand for the key. "There's no point in your getting out if we have to change cabins."

Sally pursed her lips. "I told you I'm not an invalid."

"Of course you're not, but you are the stubborn woman who refused a ride through the terminals. You can deny it all you want, but I know you're tired."

Her grandmother nodded. "All right. I'll let you be the boss this time." That was a first.

As images of the resort's dilapidated entrance sign flashed before her, Kate decided to examine all sides of the cabin's exterior before venturing indoors. The front and the east side looked fine. She rounded the corner to the rear and stopped abruptly, startled by the sight of a man on a ladder, doing something to the window screen.

There was nothing remarkable about him. Kate suspected that most of the men in this part of the country wore jeans and chambray shirts, and while many sported cowboy hats, a baseball cap like this man's wouldn't alert the fashion police. Even his height — at least six feet — and the dark brown hair that appeared in need of a good cut weren't uncommon here. As she and Sally had made their way through the airport, Kate had

16

spotted plenty of tall, dark-haired men who obviously saw no reason to spend a hundred dollars at a fancy salon.

"Is something wrong?" she asked after clearing her throat. The last thing she needed was to have the man tumble off the ladder and blame her. While Texans might admonish each other to "drive friendly," she doubted they were any less litigious than her New Jersey neighbors who'd been quick to sue their landlord when they tripped on a loose piece of carpet.

The man turned and shrugged, and in that instant, Kate revised her assessment. There was something remarkable about this man. It wasn't his green eyes, nor was it the square chin that kept him from being movie-star handsome. It was his attitude. Though his shrug was nonchalant, there was something about the tilt of his head and the way he regarded her that told Kate this man was used to being in charge.

What a ridiculous thought. That kind of guy wouldn't be working as a handyman at a rundown resort. Or would he? With the last recession, that was possible.

"Nothing's wrong," he said in a voice that bore no trace of a Texas drawl, "as long as you like flying insects and maybe a bat or two in your room." He pointed to a sizeable hole in the screen. "It'll only take a few minutes to patch this."

Though Kate knew that tourists flocked to Austin to see the bats that hung around — literally — on one of the bridges, she had no desire to see one up close and personal. "Thanks. We'd prefer bat-free accommodations." As she started to ask what else might be wrong here, she shook her head. That was one question best left unanswered.

She completed the circuit of the cabin, finding nothing to alarm her until she reached the front and saw Sally struggling to remove one of her suitcases from the trunk.

"Sally, I —"

"Let me help you, ma'am." The handyman must have decided that a woman who shuddered at the thought of bats needed assistance, for he had abandoned his ladder and was now approaching Sally, moving with an easy gait. Just as easily, he extracted the large wheeled bag from the trunk.

"Thank you, young man. I appreciate your help. I hate to admit it, but these bones aren't as young as they used to be." From Sally, that was a huge admission.

"My name's Greg, and I'm glad to help you, ma'am." His courtesy earned him a smile from Sally and Kate's admiration. The men she'd dated had not always been so polite to her grandmother.

When Greg reached the top of the stairs, he waited for Kate to unlock the door, then pushed it open. "Where would you like me to put the bags?"

Kate took a quick look around the cabin, feeling herself relax when she saw that it was spotlessly clean and seemingly free of bats and other winged creatures. Comprised of a small living area with a sofa and two chairs, a shelf filled with books and a few board games, two bedrooms, and a bath, the cabin was far from luxurious but would be adequate for their stay.

"Right here is fine," she said, pointing to an open area near the front door. "I'll let my grandmother choose her room." Though the bedrooms were of equal size and virtually identical with nondescript furnishings, Sally might have a preference.

"My, this is nice." To Kate's dismay, though there were only three steps leading to the porch, Sally was slightly out of breath. As images of heart attacks whirled through her brain, Kate forced herself to inhale deeply. There could be a less ominous cause. Sally wasn't used to flying. Perhaps that was the reason for her apparent fatigue.

Kate's grandmother flashed Greg a smile

that bore no hint of alarm. "Thank you, young man."

"Greg," he reminded her before he turned to Kate. As Sally began to explore the cabin, he asked, "Would you like me to bring in your bags too?"

His voice was low and well modulated. If Kate had had to guess, she would have said it was the product of an expensive education. That increased her belief that Greg had lost his job and was filling in here until he found another position. The question was, what had he done before? He didn't look like a lawyer or a financial planner — at least not the ones she'd met — but he moved with more assurance than most junior level managers.

Realizing that she'd been staring and hadn't answered his question, Kate shook her head. "The screen is more important." She reached into her purse and pulled out her wallet, intending to tip him.

Greg shook his head, then brushed back the errant lock that had tumbled over his forehead when he'd removed his hat. "No need for that. As I told your grandmother, I'm glad to help."

Though she doubted working at Rainbow's End paid more than minimum wage, Kate wouldn't insult Greg. She simply smiled and thanked him for his efforts. As soon as he'd left, she turned to her grandmother. Sally had given the bedrooms a cursory glance, chosen the one that faced the front of the cabin, then settled into one of the overstuffed chairs that flanked the large window.

"Are you sure you want to stay here?" Kate asked. Other than the helpful — and handsome — handyman, Kate had seen no reason to spend even one night, much less the entire month of April, here.

Sally ran her hand through her curls again as she nodded. "I'm as sure as I've ever been of anything. It's not just my heart and the feeling that time is short," she said, her expression as solemn as the day she'd taken Kate into the kitchen, given her a cup of hot chocolate, even though it was early May, and told her that Grandpa Larry had died.

"We need the time here," Sally continued. "I know you didn't want to leave your job for so long." She gave Kate one of those looks that always made Kate uncomfortable, because they seemed to see deep inside her. "You probably think your bosses will decide they don't need you. If this is the right job for you, it'll be there in a month."

"It is the right job." Kate was as convinced of that as she was that Rainbow's End was not a five-star resort. That was why she'd do whatever it took to keep Heather and Nick Maddox satisfied with her performance. Sally would probably disapprove, and so Kate had decided she wouldn't tell her grandmother that, although she was technically on vacation, she had agreed to check messages daily in case there was something Heather or Nick needed her to handle.

Though Kate had completed all of her projects, the advertising agency was small enough that one person's extended absence would make a difference in the daily running. Instead of having separate departments like larger companies, everyone at Maddox and Associates did a little of everything. That was one of the things Kate liked about the firm where she'd spent the past four years.

"You know I wasn't happy at the big agency." Even though it had been the one Grandpa Larry had claimed was the best, it hadn't been a good fit for Kate. "Maddox and Associates is perfect for me. Nick and Heather are great bosses, and everything they do is ethical."

Kate frowned as she wondered who had done Rainbow's End's advertising. The pictures in the brochure verged on deceptive. While it was true that any organization would choose photographs taken from the best possible angle, the ones for Rainbow's End were more than flattering. They were false.

"I love my job," Kate told her grandmother, "and they seem happy with me. Heather's even hinted that I'm being considered for a partnership." That had been Kate's dream for almost as long as she could remember. She'd grown up with Grandpa Larry's stories of the challenge of advertising, and they'd convinced her that was the career she wanted. Maddox, which combined business consulting with advertising, had turned Kate's dream into reality.

Sally smiled. "You see, I was right. They'll miss you while you're gone, but they won't replace you. They'll just realize how much they depend on you. Meanwhile, you and I will have a wonderful time here and then . . ." She paused, her expression once more solemn. "The future's in God's hands. Let's stay here."

"All right, Sally. You win." The truth was, Kate would do almost anything for the woman who'd raised her. If Sally wanted them to spend a month here, they would.

As she started to unpack her suitcases, Kate tried to put a positive spin on the day.

Perhaps Rainbow's End wasn't as bad as she thought. But though she gave herself a pep talk, her heart didn't believe it.

2

Greg gave the window screen one last tug, making sure the patch would hold, then began to pack up his tools. Nothing had been what he'd expected since he'd arrived at Rainbow's End, and the look in the new guest's eyes had simply confirmed his impressions. The elegant blonde had seen the problems as clearly as he had.

He slung the tool bag over his shoulder and headed for the office. When he'd left this morning, Greg had noticed a loose shutter on the front of the building. He probably should have fixed it right then. It would have only taken a minute to tighten the bracket. But when Angela had mentioned that new guests were expected, he'd wanted to ensure that they didn't have the same experience he'd had his first night at Rainbow's End. A leaky roof, particularly one that channeled water onto the bed, was not the welcome Greg had expected. Of course, few things here had been what he'd expected.

Taking a deep breath, he savored the clean air. That was one of the many attractions of the Hill Country. Smog-free air, cool breezes, tree-covered hillsides, picturesque rivers and streams, numerous lakes. Some might claim the Hill Country was the Garden of Eden. Rainbow's End, on the other hand, was not Greg's idea of paradise. Perhaps at one time it had been what it billed itself as — the premier Christian resort in the Hill Country — but that was no longer true. The advertisement he'd seen three months ago had painted a picture that was far removed from reality.

As his feet crunched an acorn, Greg shook his head, realizing that although the ad had been deceptive, he had no one to blame but himself. He should have left the minute he saw the dilapidated condition of the place. That was his first clue. The second was the realization that the new owners had eliminated the Christian focus that had been one of the resort's biggest appeals for Greg.

Angela and Tim Sinclair were clearly in over their heads. From what Greg had learned from Carmen, the one staff member who had been at Rainbow's End before the Sinclairs took over, Angela and Tim had

26

inherited a steady decline in occupancy. They'd made changes in an attempt to stop the cash drain, but those changes had been the wrong ones. They'd cut corners and delayed maintenance. They'd raised rates and reduced services. They'd even instituted heavy penalties for early departures. It was no wonder Rainbow's End was on its last legs. So why was he here?

When he reached the front of the office, Greg studied the shutter. It was worse than he'd thought. The bracket that secured it to the building wasn't loose. It was missing. He squatted and began to rummage through the dead leaves that had drifted against the foundation. His fingers encountered a plastic lid from a water bottle and an empty snack box, probably the result of the over-turned trash bin he'd seen last week.

No shutter bracket. He'd have to see if the hardware store in Dupree carried any. In the meantime, he didn't want to leave the shutter listing to the side. First impressions mattered. Of course, the pretty blonde and her grandmother had already formed their first impressions. The grandmother appeared to be happy, but the granddaughter had seemed to be on the verge of bolting. He couldn't blame her.

Greg considered the options for the shutter before pulling a long nail from the tool bag. It wasn't the perfect solution, but the nail would secure the shutter until he could find a replacement bracket. With a few swift taps, the shutter was once more in position.

He tossed the hammer back into the tool bag and entered the office. As was often the case, it was empty. As far as Greg could tell, Tim spent more time in the owners' suite above the dining room than he did working. From what Angela had said, he was as addicted to televised sports as Greg's father.

Biting back the sour taste that thoughts of the elder Vange always brought, Greg reminded himself that, contrary to Dad's predictions, he was a success. Look how easily he'd repaired the window screen and the shutter.

If only everything were that easy to fix. His life certainly wasn't. When he'd come to Rainbow's End, Greg had believed he'd find the answers he sought in a few days, no more than a couple weeks. The complete change of scenery and the slower pace of life were what he needed, or so he'd thought. He'd been convinced that once he was able to clear his mind, he'd know what the Lord had in store for him. He'd been wrong. He didn't know any more now than he had the day he'd arrived, and so he questioned his reasons for remaining.

Greg looked around, wondering where Angela was. The computer monitor no longer flashed screen-saver pictures, so she must be gone for the day, leaving the front desk unattended. That was one thing he'd change if he owned Rainbow's End.

Greg blinked. Where had that thought come from? It wasn't as if he had any intention of buying the place. Definitely not. He probably should have ignored the quiet voice deep inside him that had told him to come here in the first place. The truth was, Greg had tried. For more than a month, he'd closed his heart to the very idea of Rainbow's End, but try though he might, he could not forget the ad he'd seen and the sense that he was being led to this particular part of the Hill Country.

Why? Surely God had more in mind for Greg Vange, the man once acclaimed as a Silicon Valley wunderkind, the man whose computer software had streamlined the operations of so many small and medium-sized businesses, than repairing window screens and shutters in a struggling resort.

Greg spun on his heels and headed outside again. It was quitting time, at least for today. The new guest — the young one — had the right idea: hightail it back to wherever she'd

29

come from.

He narrowed his eyes as he pictured the pretty blonde. One of the coasts, he decided. East, most likely. She didn't have a California tan, and her clothes were more formal than Westerners'. Wherever she called home, it wasn't Dupree, Texas, population 597. There was nowhere in the town that called itself "The Heart of the Hills" where she could have gotten her hair cut like that.

Greg's sisters had given him more than one lecture on letting only the right stylist touch their hair. "It's got to flow," Ashley had explained when he'd questioned the bill that had been charged to his account. "When you shake your head, it's supposed to look like a piece of silk," Jessica had chimed in. Even Emily and Taylor had insisted on styles that cost more than he paid for haircuts in a year. So, it seemed, did the slender blonde.

As he hung the tool bag in the oversized closet that passed for a maintenance shed, Greg tried to guess what the blonde with those unexpected brown eyes did on the East Coast. He wasn't good at telling ages, but he thought she was a few years younger than his own thirty-two. That would mean she might be a junior executive somewhere. He dismissed the possibility of her being a stockbroker or an accountant. That silk blouse and those perfectly tailored slacks were too trendy for that. Perhaps she worked for a pricey boutique. Not that it mattered.

Though Angela had said the new guests were staying for a month and had made a nonrefundable payment, Greg doubted they'd last that long. He hadn't meant to eavesdrop while he repaired the screen, but the voices of the blonde and her grandmother had carried clearly. And, from what he heard, it was clear the blonde had a job to return to, a job she loved, a job with a future. Greg, on the other hand, lacked even a hint of what his future would hold.

He clenched his fists, then released them slowly. It wasn't supposed to be this way. He had never been one to dither. From the time he'd been a teenager, his future had been clear. At first he hadn't dreamt of having his own firm, but he'd known that writing computer software was what he wanted to do. And now . . . Maybe Drew was right that he needed him.

At the time, Drew had been touting his own skills and how they complemented Greg's. But maybe Drew had seen what Greg hadn't been able to. Perhaps Greg did need a partner.

The question remained: a partner to do what?

It will be all right, Kate told herself as she hung the last blouse in the tiny closet. Though the cabin would win no awards for decorating, it had what she'd heard described as good bones. The rooms, while small, were well proportioned with generously sized baseboards and door moldings. The closet doors were even real doors, not those accordion pleated vinyl ones that some hotel chains seemed to prefer. While the furniture was a bit rustic for her taste, it was in reasonable condition. What the cabin needed were things to brighten it: fresh paint and some artwork for the walls, colorful bedspreads and curtains.

Kate shook her head. It was silly to be thinking about redecorating the cabins. It wasn't as if this were her home. It was temporary lodging, with the emphasis on temporary. The only reason she was focusing on her surroundings was that it kept her worries relegated to the back of her brain.

She checked the pockets on the rollaboard for the third time, then, satisfied that they were empty, zipped it shut and slid it under the bed. As she did, she heard the creak of the bed in the other room. Sally.

The fears Kate had tried to block came rushing back, starting with the seriousness of her grandmother's heart condition. After Sally had played what Kate called the trump card to convince her to come here, Kate had called the doctor, but he'd refused to tell her anything, citing patients' confidentiality rights. The most Dr. Morrison would say was that he believed there was no reason Sally should not take this trip. That was good news. There was no reason to worry, and yet Kate did, because she didn't know what she would do without her grandmother. Sally had been the one constant in her life.

Three short strides took Kate to the window. If she craned her neck, she could see the next cabin. Constructed of painted cinder block, it appeared to be even larger than number 12. Perhaps that was the reason it looked unoccupied. This was, after all, not peak season. It was likely that the majority of guests were couples who might not want to pay for rooms they wouldn't use.

Kate and Sally might have shared a room had it not been for the length of their stay. When they'd planned this trip, they'd agreed that a bit of privacy would be good. Sally would read, and Kate . . . She paused, then chuckled. Kate would check her messages. It was what she always did.

She glanced at her watch. Sally had looked so exhausted when she'd announced that she was going to take a nap that Kate imagined she'd sleep for another hour. Perfect. She pulled her cell phone out of her purse and frowned. Not a single bar. Another strike against Rainbow's End.

Kate looked around her room, then walked into the living room and performed the same inspection. No phones, not even a phone jack. She hadn't been surprised by the absence of a television. The brochure had claimed that was one of Rainbow's End's advantages, a way of helping guests enjoy the natural beauty of the Hill Country without unnecessary distractions.

Kate could live without a TV. But cell service was a totally different story. She needed, she absolutely needed, to be able to connect. When she'd persuaded Heather that taking a month off wouldn't cause irreparable damage to Maddox and Associates, Kate had assumed she'd have cell service. It appeared that was a bad assumption.

She had seen a phone in the office. Surely she could use that, if only for today. While she wouldn't be able to check email or texts, at least she'd be able to call the office. Tomorrow she'd figure out a way to do all that she'd promised her employers. After sliding her phone into her bag alongside the laptop that she'd brought in case she needed to do heavy-duty computing, Kate scribbled a note for Sally and quietly closed the cabin door behind her.

As she stood on the porch, taking a deep breath, she glanced at the swimming pool on the opposite side of the road. An iron fence with the same design as the resort's entrance gates kept small children out. Not that there was much danger today. The pool was covered, and the diving board had been removed. Even in Texas, it was too cold to swim outside in early April. Kate didn't mind that, but she did wish there were chairs for the porch. She'd ask for them as soon as she resolved the phone problem.

Moving briskly, Kate made her way to the office and wasn't surprised when she found it empty. Though most hotels had someone at the front desk at all times, it was clear that Rainbow's End was not most hotels. Kate rang the bell to summon Angela Sinclair, then tried not to tap her fingers on the counter as she waited. Where was the woman? As tempted as she was to simply pick up the phone and place her call, Kate wouldn't do that without permission. She rang the bell again, this time pounding it a bit harder.

Still no response. The only sound was a woman singing. Though the melody was haunting, Kate could not understand the lyrics. With a sigh, she headed toward the sound. A short hall with three interior doors on the left and an exterior entrance on the right appeared to connect the office to the two-story building that housed the dining room. Though the first and third doors were closed, the singing came from the middle one.

Kate peeked in and found herself at the kitchen, where a woman a couple inches shorter and a few pounds heavier than her grandmother was crooning in Spanish as she sprinkled what smelled like oregano into a large bowl.

"Hello." Kate hoped the woman spoke English, because her knowledge of Spanish was limited to *por favor* and *gracias* with an occasional *hola* thrown in for good measure.

"Can I help you?" the dark-haired woman asked, her light accent as melodious as her singing had been. Kate guessed the woman, who was only an inch or two over five feet and a good ten pounds more than the recommended weight for her height, to be in her midfifties. If Sally were here, she would have described her as jolly, for her smile was more welcoming than the one Angela Sinclair had given them.

Kate nodded. "I'm Kate Sherwood, a new guest. I'm looking for a couple things." She might as well start with something that would benefit Sally. "Are there any outdoor chairs? Rocking chairs or maybe Adirondack? My grandmother and I would like to sit on our porch."

The woman nodded. "There are a few in the shed. I'll ask KOB to clean them up and bring them to you."

"Mr. Cobb?" Greg hadn't volunteered his last name, but he was the only other staff member Kate had seen.

A peal of laughter greeted her question, reinforcing the woman's pleasant disposition. "Sorry! We have three teenagers who help out here — Kevin, Olivia, and Brandi. I call them KOB for short."

"That makes sense. We use acronyms for almost everything, don't we?"

"TLAs according to my daughter." When Kate nodded, signifying that she recognized the acronym for three-letter acronyms, the woman raised a brow. "You said you were looking for a couple things. What else besides chairs?"

"I really need a phone. I've been trying to get a cell signal, but this must be a dead zone."

The woman ran her hands under the faucet and turned back toward Kate. "The only phone is in the office. We used to have a pay phone outside, but the phone company took it away."

Kate wasn't surprised. Though she hadn't actively looked for one in the past few years, she'd heard others bemoaning the fact that it was difficult to find a pay phone when their cell phone batteries died. "Do you think Ms. Sinclair would mind if I used the office phone?" The computer would be better, but she wouldn't ask for that. Not today.

"I can't say. Angela's gone for the afternoon. She and Tim go to San Antonio once a week. I heard them call it their date night."

Or their escape from Rainbow's End. Kate couldn't imagine what it must be like, living here permanently, especially now that she'd discovered there was no cell service. "Is there anyone else I can ask?" Even though she would charge the calls to her own line, Kate felt uncomfortable invading another person's office space without permission.

"I'm afraid not." The woman gave Kate another smile. "I should have introduced myself earlier. I'm Carmen St. George.

You've probably guessed that I'm the cook here."

Unlike the chefs Kate had seen on TV, Carmen did not wear a white jacket. Instead, she had a voluminous blue gingham apron tied over her navy polo and khaki pants. Perhaps that was why she called herself a cook and not a chef. Kate had never understood the distinction. What she did know was that the aromas coming from the industrial-sized range were making her mouth water.

"Whatever you're making smells delicious." And unlike the other parts of Rainbow's End that Kate had seen, the kitchen appeared to be in excellent condition. In addition to gleaming stainless steel appliances, it boasted two islands, one marble-topped for pastry making, the other with a butcher-block top and separate sink.

Carmen shrugged. "Tonight's spaghetti and meatballs. By the time you leave, you'll know the menu. Every week is the same."

The brochure hadn't mentioned that. It had waxed eloquent over the homestyle meals and promised genuine Western fare. Though Kate liked spaghetti, it was not her idea of Western cuisine. "Don't the guests mind?"

A wry smile lit Carmen's face. "Not many

stay more than a week."

Which might explain the punitive cancellation policy. "Isn't it boring, cooking the same thing every week? I don't claim to be a chef, but I enjoy trying new recipes. I made Thai chicken last week, and if I say so myself, it was delicious."

Carmen's smile turned into a chuckle. "You won't find any of that here. The Sinclairs like to keep things simple. The most daring experiment I've tried is changing the seasonings in the meat loaf. I added cloves and nutmeg once."

"How was that received?"

"Not well. It seems that one of the guests was allergic to cloves. I'd never heard of that allergy, but ever since, I've stuck to the basics."

"So I won't find any cloves in tonight's meatballs?"

"Definitely not." Carmen's glance at the clock reminded Kate that she had interrupted her.

"I'd better leave you to your work."

"Can I get you something to drink before you leave? Soda, lemonade? There's a small refrigerator in the dining room." Carmen pointed toward the door at the far end of the kitchen. "I keep it stocked with beverages, and at night I put out milk and cookies."

"Really? That sounds both delicious and decadent."

"And you sound like my daughter. She's always counting calories or fat grams."

Guessing that Carmen's daughter would be around her age, Kate asked whether she lived in Dupree.

A shadow crossed Carmen's face. "Atlanta. I don't see her very often. You know how it is with careers. You young people get so busy that there's no time for the older generation."

Kate heard the pain, although Carmen tried to hide it. She wouldn't tell her that, even though they lived four hundred miles apart, she visited Sally at least once a month. That would only hurt Carmen, and the kindly woman didn't deserve that.

"For the record," Kate said, infusing her voice with a light tone, "I would never describe you as old."

As she'd hoped, Carmen grinned. "For that, you can have an extra cookie . . . if you dare."

They both laughed as Kate feigned a look of horror.

3

The sound of women laughing drew Greg toward the kitchen. There was no mistaking Carmen's light chuckle, but the other woman's laughter was unfamiliar. Since school wouldn't be out for another half hour, it was too early for KOB to be here, and he hadn't heard any cars arriving. By process of elimination, he figured the woman with Carmen must be the new guest. The young one. Greg smiled at the thought that she'd found a reason to laugh. She'd seemed far too serious for a woman who was supposed to be on vacation.

"Do you mind telling me what's so funny?" he asked as he entered the kitchen.

Carmen gave the blonde a conspiratorial look. "You had to be here to appreciate it. Have you met Kate Sherwood?" Without waiting for his reply, Carmen turned toward Kate. "This is Greg Van—"

"I'm glad to meet you, Kate." Greg extended his hand, hoping she hadn't noticed that he'd interrupted Carmen. So far no one in Dupree other than Roy Gordon had connected his name with his past, but Kate Sherwood was different. She obviously had some sort of corporate background, so she might have heard of Sys=Simpl. It was possible she'd used the software he'd spent a decade perfecting.

While he had nothing to hide, Greg knew how quickly news spread in a small town. The last thing he needed was for the good folks of Dupree to learn that they had a billionaire in their midst. He'd had too much experience with the way attitudes changed when people viewed him as a walking dollar sign instead of a real person. Kate might be different, but there was no reason to take the chance.

She placed her hand in his, the firm shake confirming Greg's impression that she was accustomed to being in control. Her fingers were long and slender, her hand soft but strong, reminding him of that tired image of steel encased in velvet. It might be a cliché, but Greg suspected it applied to more than Kate Sherwood's hands. There was a strength about her that came from being comfortable in her own skin.

If he were a betting man, Greg would have

bet that Kate had been part of the in crowd in school, perhaps not the class president but certainly one of the girls who never had to worry about a date. And now she was here, shaking hands with him and smiling at him as if he were captain of the football team rather than the boy who'd always been picked last.

"If you won't let me in on the joke, at least tell me why you're in the kitchen," Greg said as he released Kate's hand.

"I was offering Kate cookies."

"I was looking for a phone."

The two responses came at the same time, almost canceling each other. Greg focused on Kate's answer. She'd probably already discovered, as he had his first day at Rainbow's End, that there was no cell service. The hills might be picturesque, but they also blocked signals.

"Angela won't mind if you use the office phone once or twice. I've done that myself," he told Kate.

"I'm afraid it will be more often than that." He'd been wrong about her eyes. They weren't the color of chocolate. They were more of a nut brown, with all the shading that nature provided. Right now those eyes were serious as they met his gaze. "I really need an internet connection."

"So this is a working vacation?" Greg was hardly an expert on vacations, working or otherwise. The twenty-four to forty-eight hours he spent at his parents' home each Christmas could hardly be classified as a vacation, and until he'd come to Rainbow's End, those were the only times he'd taken off from work since his college days.

"That's one way of describing it." Kate's tone was cool, as if she sensed his disapproval. It wasn't that Greg disapproved. Not entirely. He simply knew that there had to be better ways to live than focusing on work 24/7. That was why he was here, to discover at least one of those better ways.

Perhaps he was wrong to bait her, but Greg couldn't resist. He wanted to see if her eyes changed color when she became angry.

"What term would you prefer to 'working vacation'?"

As she raised one eyebrow, Kate's eyes took on an amber hue. He'd been right. Their color was as changeable as her moods. "How about keeping in touch with the real world?"

As Carmen chuckled, Greg feigned indignation. The truth was, he'd had a similar reaction when he'd first arrived, as if he'd passed through some invisible portal and been transported back in time. Either that or he'd stumbled into a living museum. "You don't consider Rainbow's End the real world?"

"Oh, it's the real world all right," Kate conceded. "The world of 1970 before anyone heard of smartphones and text messages."

He had to hand it to her. She was beautiful, smart, and sassy. This woman had it all.

Though Carmen had resumed her cooking and was now forming some of what Greg knew to be mouthwateringly delicious meatballs, he had no doubt that she was enjoying the conversation.

"That was before my time," he told Kate, "but I think I saw a rotary phone around here if you're feeling nostalgic."

"Let me guess." She tipped her head to the side, pretending to ponder the possibility. "It's stored next to the vinyl records."

Greg nodded. "With my favorite polyester leisure suit and white patent leather shoes."

What had been a smile turned into a laugh. "I can't quite picture you in that."

Nor could Greg. "You should be glad Rainbow's End doesn't have theme nights like some resorts. If they did, you might find yourself in a gold lamé jumpsuit."

"I'm afraid gold isn't one of my colors.

46

Now, to return to the subject, is there any way to get an internet connection other than using the office computer?"

They were back to business, and that was unfortunate. It had felt good to banter with Kate. "There's cell service in Dupree," Greg told her. "Since the only way to get to Rainbow's End is through Dupree, I know you saw it . . . if you didn't blink. At any rate, it's three miles down the road."

She nodded, the faint furrows between her eyes making him wonder if she'd noticed the number of vacant stores. Lone Star Trail, which was Dupree's main street, wasn't too bad. The grocery store, post office, bank, and Dupree's sole gas station were still in operation, and just driving by, Kate would not have realized that the smaller of the two churches held services only every other week because it was unable to support a full-time pastor. It was the side streets where Dupree's failing economy was most visible.

"The Sit 'n' Sip on Pecan Street has wireless," Greg continued, "but if you're used to Starbucks, you might not like their coffee. It tends to be strong and bitter."

"I'll order extra sugar and cream." Kate seemed to have made a mental note.

"Or you could turn this into a real vacation and forget checking messages."

A look of sheer horror crossed her face, but the smile that accompanied her words told Greg she was only pretending. "The next thing I know, you'll be telling me to give up caffeine." Her eyes were back to that lovely nut brown.

"Even I wouldn't suggest that." Although if he kept talking to her, he wouldn't need artificial stimulants. Greg felt as if he'd had an infusion of caffeine directly to his bloodstream. Though their topics of discussion were hardly on the level of world peace and eliminating the national debt, he was more energized than he'd been in months. Perhaps longer.

"Are you really determined to work?"

Her expression once more serious, she nodded. "You make it sound like a fatal disease."

"I didn't mean that. It's just that there's a time for everything, and that includes rest." As the words spilled from his mouth, Greg practically choked on the irony. He certainly hadn't done much resting since he'd arrived at Rainbow's End. After years of working almost 24/7, he'd found it difficult to do nothing. How could he blame Kate when he was guilty of the same misdemeanor?

"What do you do that needs daily connections?"

"I'm in advertising."

That explained the clothes that were neither too conservative nor too trendy. She would walk the middle line rather than risk offending potential clients.

"In New York?"

Kate nodded. "Lower Manhattan. Maddox and Associates is a small firm, but we've got some big-name clients."

"Any I'd recognize?"

"Possibly. Do you eat at Sid's Seafood?"

Greg shook his head. "Not often, but I've seen the ads on TV. The ads are better than the food."

A laugh spilled from those perfectly shaped lips. "Thank you. I was responsible for those ads."

She was good. More than good, and if there was one thing Greg appreciated, it was excellence.

"All right." He gave her a quick nod. "I can't get your phone to work here, but if you have a laptop" — and he'd bet she was carrying one with her — "there might be a way."

Greg had expected her to be pleased, but Kate's reaction exceeded his expectations. The smile she gave him was so bright you'd think she'd just been awarded the Nobel Peace Prize.

He was going to help her. Kate couldn't stop smiling. Perhaps the month at Rainbow's End wouldn't be as bad as she'd feared. The place might be a bit rundown, and there didn't appear to be much to do, but the staff, with the notable exception of Angela Sinclair, was pleasant. More than pleasant. Carmen had made Kate feel welcome, and Greg whatever-his-last-name-was was the most interesting man she'd met in a long time. He was smart and funny — handsome too — and he was going to help her, even though it was obvious he didn't approve.

It wasn't as if she were a workaholic. Admittedly, she worked long hours when she was preparing a proposal, but she also knew how to play or at least how to relax. Still, there was no denying that being able to use her laptop would make her days here easier. With access to her messages, Kate would know what was happening back at the office and wouldn't have to worry.

"Come with me." Greg led her back into the hallway and unlocked the first door, indicating that this was the supply room. Although the word *room* suggested something more impressive, the reality was nothing more than a medium-sized closet with floor-to-ceiling shelves filled with what appeared to be everything from lightbulbs to yellowing rolls of adding machine tape. Perhaps Greg hadn't been joking about rotary phones and gold lamé jumpsuits.

As Kate watched, he pulled out a stepladder and began rummaging on the top shelf. "Success! I thought I'd seen this." He handed her some sort of electronic component with a short cable attached and descended the ladder.

"What is it?"

"A modem." His voice was filled with satisfaction.

Kate studied the object in her hand. "It doesn't look like my cable modem."

"That's because it's not a cable modem." Greg chuckled, his voice warming her more than the Texas sun. "You don't think a place that doesn't have wireless would have cable, do you?"

It was a valid point, and yet . . . "I saw a computer in the office. It must be connected to the internet."

"It is. With a modem. A simple telephony modem like the one you're holding."

Kate wrinkled her nose, remembering the horror stories she'd heard about dial-up

51

connections. "I think I heard about them in an ancient history class."

"Have you also heard that beggars can't be choosers?" Greg closed and locked the door, then gestured in the direction of the office. "Right this way." The office was as empty as it had been half an hour before. "We'll go into the main lodge," he said with a nod at the door on the opposite wall.

Kate had paid no attention to it on her previous two visits, having been more focused on the work space. With a gallantry she thought had disappeared along with polyester leisure suits, Greg reached in front of her to open the door. She took a step inside, then stopped, amazed at the beauty.

Nothing in the office or her cabin had led her to expect this. The other parts of Rainbow's End were functional; this was simply magnificent. A soaring ceiling with exposed beams drew her gaze upward, while two walls with large windows overlooking Bluebonnet Lake beckoned her in their direction. A third wall held a massive stone fireplace where Kate could envision warming her toes on a cool night. Only the fourth wall, the one with the door to the office, was ordinary.

She looked around, her attention drawn to details. The upholstered furniture was shabby with threadbare spots; the tables' nicks and dings bore witness to too many years of use. And yet, despite the obvious need for maintenance, the room was spectacular.

"I wonder why this isn't in the brochure. It wouldn't need much photoshopping to make it look inviting." If she were planning the photo shoot, Kate would drape cozy afghans over the worst of the upholstered pieces and apply polish to camouflage some of the scratches in the wood.

Greg shrugged. "The whole place must have been something to see in its heyday."

"That's what my grandmother says. The funny thing is, I never thought she wore rose-colored glasses, but she doesn't seem to notice all that's wrong here."

"She must be an optimist." He gestured toward a low table flanked by three chairs on the wall next to the office.

"You might be right. *South Pacific* is her favorite movie. Maybe today's her cockeyed optimist day." Kate wouldn't tell Greg that her grandmother claimed love at first sight, à la "Some Enchanted Evening," was real. Kate had never experienced it, and she doubted that the obviously single man who was going to work some kind of magic on her laptop had, either.

"The limit of my optimism is that this modem still works. Angela dumped it in the storage room when her laptop died," Greg said, his voice so matter-of-fact that Kate knew he hadn't read her thoughts. Good thing, because her mind had taken a wild tangent, and she'd pictured herself standing on top of a hill overlooking the oh so romantic Pacific Ocean with a handsome man gazing into her eyes just the way Rossano Brazzi had looked at Mitzi Gaynor. The problem was, that man looked disturbingly like Greg.

Yes, he was handsome. Yes, he was intelligent. Yes, she'd enjoyed joking with him. But despite all those positive attributes, Kate had no intention of getting involved in anything like a shipboard romance. This was her time with Sally. When it ended, she'd go back to her apartment in New Jersey and her job in Manhattan, while Greg would remain here.

"Your laptop."

Kate blinked as she realized he was speaking to her. Hoping he hadn't noticed her daydreaming, she reached into her bag and handed the laptop to him. Greg plugged the modem cable into the laptop, then, pulling a phone cord from his pocket with the flourish of a magician producing a white rabbit from his top hat, he grinned. "Let's see if it'll work." He pointed to a phone jack on the wall. "As far as I know, this is the only one at Rainbow's End other than the one in the office. There's just the one line, so you'll have to use it when Angela's computer is off-line — normally before eight and after seven."

"And on her date night."

"So you heard about that. It's supposed to be a closely guarded secret."

"Someone forgot to tell Carmen."

Greg frowned, and for a second Kate thought he had misunderstood her joking. Then she realized that he was frowning at her screen. He'd booted up the computer. "No password?" he asked, his expression stern.

"I didn't think I needed one. The computer's never out of my sight." That was an exaggeration, but only a slight one. The truth was, between her smartphone and the laptop, she was connected for just about all of her waking hours.

"Put a password on it," Greg said in a tone that brooked no argument. "You never know what might happen." Though he did not raise his voice, it rang with authority, seeming to corroborate Kate's impression that whatever he'd done before he came to

Rainbow's End had been in a leadership role.

She nodded. It was good advice. "You sound as if you've had a lot of experience with computers." And that not all of those experiences were good.

To Kate's surprise, Greg appeared uncomfortable. It must be her imagination, because there was nothing exceptional about what she'd said. Most people would have taken it as a compliment.

"This is the twenty-first century," he said, his voice cooler than it had been a minute ago. "Who hasn't?" He busied himself keying information into the computer before looking up again. "All you need now is your credit card number. Then you'll be set."

When she'd entered the information and launched her email, Kate felt a rush of adrenaline. In seconds she'd have her messages.

"I don't know how to thank you," she said, extending her hand toward Greg while she waited for the first of her messages to download. There was no doubt about it. Dial-up was slow. "Are you sure I can't pay you for your time?"

As he shook his head, a mischievous smile twisted his lips. "There is one thing you could do."

Kate knew better than to agree without hearing the rest. "And that would be . . ."

"Work less."

She matched his smile. "Now you sound like my grandmother." But he didn't look like her. Or act like her. For that matter, Greg didn't act like anyone she'd ever met. He could be gruff; he could be funny. He seemed equally at home repairing window screens and upgrading computers. He wasn't the most handsome man Kate had ever met, and yet there was something about his face that was unforgettable. The truth was, Greg defied categorization. That must be the reason she found him so intriguing.

4

Sally looked much better. Kate smiled as her grandmother stepped out of her bedroom. The nap had done wonders; Sally's breathing was once more normal and she showed no sign of fatigue. Best of all, her smile left no doubt that she was excited about being here. Kate took a deep breath, exhaling slowly as she let the relief flow through her. Perhaps she was turning into a cockeyed optimist like her grandmother, but she was beginning to think it might not be so bad spending a month here.

Though the absence of alarming messages from the office had helped, the primary cause for her more positive outlook was Sally's happiness. Kate couldn't help but compare that to Carmen's obvious sadness when she spoke of her daughter. It almost sounded as if they were estranged, and that was a pity. A huge pity. Parents and children should not be estranged.

Unbidden, Greg's image popped into Kate's mind, and she wondered about his family. Neither of them had had any reason to discuss parents or siblings while Greg had been working on her computer, but she hoped he came from a stable and happy home. A home with two loving parents. As much as she loved Sally, Kate would have given almost anything to have had her parents with her while she was growing up. And if they were still alive, she knew she'd phone them every few days, just as she did Sally.

"I'm ready if you are." Sally smoothed the side of one of the floral print skirts she favored. When she'd seen Kate in the same clothes she'd worn for traveling, Sally had claimed it was only polite to dress for dinner and had convinced Kate to put on a broomstick pleated skirt and matching silk blouse. Though she'd acquiesced to the change of clothes, Kate had drawn the line at the strappy high-heeled sandals she normally wore with the outfit, having no intention of twisting her ankle on Rainbow's End's rutted roads. Judging from what she'd seen, those sandals would get no use here.

"Are you sure you don't want me to drive?" Kate asked as she hooked her arm with Sally's while they descended the front steps. True to her promise, Carmen must have enlisted KOB's help, because a pair of once-white Adirondack chairs had appeared on the porch. Since it had happened while Kate was in the lodge, she didn't know which teenager was responsible.

"Drive?" Sally flashed her a "you must be kidding" look. "And give up the moderate exercise that's supposed to be so good for me? Never! Let's go. I don't want to be late."

But, though Sally acted as if she were in a hurry, they walked far more slowly than Kate had when she'd gone to the office during Sally's nap. This was a leisurely stroll with the emphasis on leisurely.

When they reached the spot where the road curved to the left, Sally pointed to a second path on the right. "That one will take us directly to the dining room. Besides, it's prettier than the other one."

She was right, for this road provided glimpses of the lake along with views of the backs of half a dozen cabins. As was true of the ones Kate had seen before, each appeared unique. Whoever had built the resort had had a different vision than modern developers. The fact that the cabins were not cookie-cutter copies gave Rainbow's End a charm that set it apart from the competition, and yet the brochure made no mention of that. If Kate had been designing the marketing strategy, she would . . . She shook herself mentally. This was supposed to be a vacation, not a search for new clients.

"Larry and I stayed in the first one," Sally said, gesturing to the left as they approached the waterfront cabins. "We used to sit on the porch every evening and watch the sun set over the lake. It was so relaxing, not like some resorts that have activities planned every hour."

"That hasn't changed." Kate tried not to let her cynicism show. Relaxation was good, but a whole month of it? "What did you do if it rained?"

Kate glanced at the sky, and as she did, she smiled. There was no doubt about it: the Texas sky was beautiful, the air clear and clean. For all its shortcomings, Rainbow's End had a magnificent location.

Sally paused for a second, whether to catch her breath or simply think, Kate didn't know. "Everyone gathered in the main lodge. We'd sit around and talk, maybe play Monopoly or Clue."

"And you're still playing that." Kate had spent countless hours in her grandparents' kitchen calling Colonel Mustard and the candlestick into the conservatory.

Her grandmother chuckled as a lizard

scurried across the road. "We used to keep an eye out for armadillos too. I imagine all that seems pretty boring."

"Oh, I don't know." Recalling the three of them seated at the kitchen table, a board game and a bowl of popcorn between them, Kate smiled. "It seems to me you and Grandpa Larry got into some pretty heated arguments."

"That was only when we played Scrabble." A bittersweet expression crossed Sally's face. "The man insisted on inventing words. No matter how often I pulled out the dictionary and proved him wrong, he wouldn't stop."

"And you loved every minute of it."

"I did."

Within minutes, they'd arrived at the dining hall. From the outside, it appeared to be a simple frame structure, curiously devoid of windows on the first story. While the second floor had the normal complement of windows and boasted a deck overlooking the lake, the first floor was unusually plain. Kate had been inside several office buildings that had windows on only one side, but this was the first time she'd encountered a building without any on an entire floor.

She opened the door, ushering Sally

inside, and looked around. Her grandmother needn't have worried that they would be late, for there were no other guests in the room.

Like the main lodge, this room had a ceiling with dark wooden beams. The similarities stopped there. The lodge's ceiling was vaulted, while this one was coffered, and while the lodge's windows were its focal point, here the walls featured beautiful wood paneling. Correction. They featured what would be beautiful wood paneling if someone took the time to clean and polish it. As it was, darker squares where artwork must have once hung detracted from the ambience, making Kate feel as if she had entered a house whose owners had recently moved out, taking most of their possessions.

What was left were five round tables, each with a lazy Susan in the center and eight simple wooden chairs surrounding it. Only one was ready for guests, set with ironstone plates, commercial flatware, and heavy glasses. Two pitchers, one with ice water, the other filled with iced tea, were the sole items on the Susan.

Kate tried not to frown at the evidence that there were fewer guests here than she'd realized. With only a 20 percent occupancy rate, it was no wonder that the Sinclairs had neglected some maintenance. The wonder was that they were surviving at all.

As Kate and Sally approached the table, a teenage girl emerged from the kitchen, the tray she carried and the white apron she wore over the resort's apparent uniform of khaki pants and a navy polo shirt with a rainbow logo telling Kate she was part of the waitstaff. Since she obviously wasn't Kevin, she must be either Olivia or Brandi.

"Good evening," the teenager said as she started to unload salt and pepper shakers, a sugar bowl, and a butter dish from her tray. "I'm Olivia Hirsch. Welcome to Rainbow's End." A couple inches below average height, Olivia was an attractive girl with long brown hair caught into a ponytail, brown eyes, and a thin face.

Kate introduced herself and Sally. "Do we have you to thank for the porch chairs?" she asked.

Olivia nodded, seemingly surprised when Kate and Sally both thanked her and when Kate handed her a few folded bills. "Thanks," Olivia said. "I can definitely use that." Her eyes glowing with pleasure, she gestured toward the table. "You can sit anywhere you like. The others will be here soon."

As if on cue, two couples came through

the main door. One appeared to be in their early forties. The second was younger than Kate, and the way they looked at each other and had their arms wrapped around each other's waists made her suspect they were honeymooners. Sally would be pleased by the evidence that Rainbow's End still appealed to newlyweds.

The older woman, a tall blonde, smiled at Kate and Sally as she approached the table. "I'm glad to see we'll have a full table tonight. We're Janet and Bob Schwartz from Tampa."

The younger man gave his bride another smile. "And we're Jared and Alexa Tibbits, but we didn't come as far as the Schwartzes. We're from El Paso."

The foursome's casual attire told Kate there had been no reason to change clothes other than to please Sally. The other guests' jeans and Western shirts would have qualified them to serve as extras in a rodeo movie.

Kate introduced herself and Sally, explaining that they were from New Jersey and Buffalo respectively.

"I always wanted to see the Hill Country," Alexa announced to no one in particular. Like her husband, she was of medium height and had dark brown hair and eyes.

When she looked at Jared, those eyes radiated happiness, but right now they were somber, as if what she had seen disappointed her. Kate could identify with her. If she had had to choose one adjective to describe Rainbow's End, it would be disappointing. Only Sally seemed oblivious to the resort's shortcomings.

Her smile warm and welcoming, Sally took Alexa's comment as an invitation to respond. "The Hill Country is beautiful, isn't it?"

"I guess." The bride's voice held doubt rather than enthusiasm. She glanced around the room before focusing on the table she and her groom would share with six others. "This isn't what we expected."

Kate nodded in sympathy. Despite Sally's claims to the contrary, Rainbow's End did not seem to be a haven for honeymooners. Most newlyweds preferred private tables, and they probably sought more amenities than the resort appeared to provide.

"Here come the rest." Jared gave his bride a quick squeeze as he gestured toward the door.

A gray-haired man entered the room, followed by a tall, dark-haired one.

Greg? Kate blinked as the man she had thought part of the staff walked toward the table. Something was wrong, and she had the sinking feeling it was her assumption.

She narrowed her eyes, searching for clues. Greg had changed into casual brown slacks and a green polo almost the same shade as his eyes. A polo. Of course. That was the clue she'd missed. She should have realized Greg wasn't an employee when he wasn't wearing a Rainbow's End shirt. And yet, if he wasn't an employee, what had he been doing repairing her window screen, and why did he have keys to the supply room?

To clear her thoughts, Kate took a deep breath and focused on the man at Greg's side. Shorter than average with gray hair and wire-rimmed glasses that were years out of style, he appeared to be Sally's age. His deeply tanned and leathered skin made Kate suspect he'd spent a lot of time outdoors without the benefit of sunblock, while his broad grin when he looked at Sally left no doubt that he was pleased by the presence of another senior.

And then there was Greg. Kate wondered if he was enjoying her uneasiness. That didn't seem in character with the man who'd joked with her as he'd connected the modem, but at this point, Kate wasn't sure who Greg was. It was the first time she'd met a guest who doubled as a handyman.

When the two men reached the group, Greg directed his smile at Kate and Sally. It was a warm, easy smile, designed to put others at ease. It almost worked.

"Hello, again." He turned to the man at his side. "I had the pleasure of meeting these ladies this afternoon." Returning his gaze to Kate and Sally, Greg said, "It looks like everyone's getting acquainted, so let me finish the introductions. You already know I'm Greg. This is Roy Gordon."

And I'm embarrassed. Kate tried to recall everything she'd said to Greg. Had she sounded condescending, especially when he'd been working on the cabin? She hoped not. The man had been nothing but helpful, and she owed him an apology.

"We might as well sit down." That came from Bob Schwartz, who held out a chair for his wife. The honeymooners settled next to Janet Schwartz, leaving four chairs. Though Kate had expected Greg and Roy to sit together, they each pulled out one of the middle chairs, helping Kate and Sally into them, then took the remaining seats, with Greg on Kate's left and Roy on Sally's right.

It was time for an apology. Kate turned to speak to Greg but found him apparently engrossed in studying the far wall.

"Where are you from, Roy?" Sally asked as she settled into her chair.

"Dupree."

"Dupree as in three-miles-away Dupree?" Kate heard the mild surprise in her grandmother's voice.

"That's the one." The distinct Texas drawl left no doubt that he was telling the truth. "I don't stay over at Rainbow's End. I just take dinner here."

Before Roy could continue his explanation, Olivia arrived with a large tray. After placing half a dozen covered dishes on the Susan, she smiled at the guests. "One more trip, and then you'll be ready to eat."

"You can see that meals are family style," Roy said as Sally unrolled her napkin and placed it on her lap. Though Kate had expected several individual conversations to occur, it seemed that everyone was deferring to Roy, at least for now. "The Susans eliminate the need to pass food around."

"I remember."

"You've been here before?" Roy sounded surprised by Sally's response.

She nodded. "My husband and I came here the first year we were married. We weren't on our honeymoon like you two," she said with a smile for Alexa and Jared, "but we were still newlyweds."

"And you came back?" Jared's voice held more than a note of astonishment. It was clear that he was no more thrilled with Rainbow's End than his bride.

Kate saw Sally's back straighten. "Yes," she said firmly. "Larry and I planned to return, but it seemed there was always something else to do."

Like raising their granddaughter. It wasn't the first time Kate had realized how much her grandparents had sacrificed for her. Though they were not wealthy, they'd given generously of what they had, and — more importantly — they'd lavished her with love and attention. Not once had they taken a vacation without her. "There'll be time for that when Kate's out of college," Grandpa Larry had told friends. But there hadn't been time. Her grandfather had died the summer before Kate entered college.

"I'm glad you're here now." Roy smiled at Sally and then at Kate, as if including her in his statement. He didn't look at all like Grandpa Larry, and yet there was a kindness in Roy's expression that reminded Kate of her grandfather.

When Olivia had unloaded her second tray of dishes and returned to the kitchen, Roy looked around the table, meeting each

70

of his companions' gazes. "Let us give thanks," he said when he'd completed the silent greeting. Bowing his head, he offered a brief but eloquent blessing for the food, concluding with gratitude for Sally and Kate's safe journey and the opportunity to make new friends. "Amen."

It was the signal the others had been waiting for. As soon as Roy pronounced the word, the two married couples began to uncover the dishes, and soon everyone was piling food onto their plates, gently rotating the Susan so that the next person could take a helping. In less time than she'd expected, Kate found her plate covered with spaghetti and meatballs, corn, green beans, a green salad, two kinds of molded salad, and golden garlic bread. It was ordinary food, what some would call comfort food, and it smelled absolutely delicious.

As dishes rattled and silverware clinked on plates, the other guests began to converse. Kate noticed that, even though the table was communal, the two other couples were acting as if they were at tables for two, and Sally appeared to be engrossed in whatever Roy was saying. That left Kate with Greg and gave her the opportunity to make her apology.

"You don't work here, do you?"

Greg broke off a piece of garlic bread, shaking his head as he answered. "I'm a guest like you."

"I'm sorry. I thought —"

"There's no need for an apology," he said, interrupting. "I'd have made the same assumption if I'd seen you repairing my screen. It's not something you'd expect another guest to be doing."

"So, why did you do it?"

Greg shrugged. "The work needed to be done, and no one else was available." His explanation confirmed Kate's suspicion that the resort was understaffed. "I didn't think you'd want bats in your cabin."

Kate gave an exaggerated shudder. "Definitely not. We'd have left tomorrow."

"I thought about doing exactly that when the roof leaked." Greg's green eyes sparkled. "Murphy's Law was in effect that day. Or should I say, that night? The roof leaked right over my bed, and the power went out, so I couldn't do much other than move the bed."

That sounded as bad as bats. "But you stayed. How long have you been here?" Kate drizzled vinaigrette onto her salad, then forked a bite. Her impression of Greg was accurate. He was an intriguing man.

"Long enough to have the menu memorized."

An evasive answer if she'd ever heard one. "How long is that?"

"Three weeks."

No wonder Greg was helping repair the resort. With so few other guests here, there wasn't much else for him to do. Boredom must have set in quickly. Though Sally had assured her that there were many things to occupy their time, Kate wasn't sure what they'd do for a whole month. She might wind up helping Greg repair window screens. If he was still here, that is.

"Are you leaving soon?" Very few people other than teachers had more than four weeks' vacation, and since most schools were still in session, Kate doubted that Greg taught.

He scowled in feigned annoyance. "Are you trying to get rid of me? Be careful. I might take that modem back."

"Oh no! You wouldn't do that." Kate held up her hands in the universal sign of surrender. "Seriously, I was curious because Carmen said hardly anyone stays more than a week."

"That's true, but like Roy, I find it easier not to cook, especially when there's someone like Carmen providing meals. And, if you're wondering about the repairs, I figured that as long as I was here, there was no reason not to help the Sinclairs."

"It must be nice to have so much vacation." Kate was fishing for information and suspected Greg knew it, so she added an unlikely alternative. "Of course, you could have a trust fund and not need to work at all."

He twirled the long strands of spaghetti around his fork with an expertise that spoke of practice. "If I had a trust fund, do you think I'd be repairing window screens at a down-on-its-heels resort? I'd be sailing my yacht around the world or skiing on one of those slopes where you have to pay a small fortune to be helicoptered in." Greg raised his eyebrows, as if waiting for Kate's response. When she simply shrugged, he said, "The truth is, I'm between jobs, and this seemed like a good place to be."

He'd confirmed what she thought. Greg was unemployed. As for staying here, it made sense. The rates weren't exorbitant, and he probably got a discount because of the work he was doing, perhaps another one for staying so long. Still, it was a shame that Greg was unemployed. He was obviously intelligent, well educated, and willing to work. He could be doing so much more than odd jobs at Rainbow's End. "I hope you find a new job soon."

"Me too."

5

Sally took a bite of a meatball, chewing slowly, savoring the delicious blend of herbs and at least two kinds of meat. Being at Rainbow's End was even better than she'd expected. She had wanted more time with Kate than their normal one weekend a month. Even if Kate didn't realize it, Sally sensed that her granddaughter was at a crossroads in her life. Kate needed to step back, gain perspective, and reflect on what she wanted her future to be. That was why Sally had practically dragged her here, playing the trump card of her own health. She'd believed, and she still believed, that time away would be good for Kate. What Sally hadn't expected was finding herself next to a man like Roy Gordon.

He wasn't handsome by any definition of the word. With his gray hair and gray eyes, the predominantly gray plaid of his shirt was a poor choice, and yet it didn't matter.

Even those old-fashioned glasses couldn't hide the twinkle in Roy's eyes, and when he smiled, he made Sally feel as if she was the only woman in the world. It was an unexpectedly heady feeling.

"So tell me, beautiful lady, how long am I going to have the pleasure of your company?" Roy's voice was low, his Texas drawl more pronounced as he gave her a smile that was almost roguish.

Sally felt the blood rush to her face. Mercy alive! She couldn't remember the last time she'd blushed. Of course, she also couldn't recall the last time a man had flirted with her. "Kate and I have reservations for a month." Thank goodness her voice sounded normal, not betraying the fact that her pulse was racing. Sally picked up her glass and took a sip of tea, hoping the cool liquid would chase the blood from her cheeks.

Reaching for the pitcher to replenish her glass, Roy grinned. "Be forewarned. I'm going to try to keep you here longer than that. It's been five years since the Lord took Barb. I've been looking for a woman to laugh with since then."

Uneasiness welled up inside Sally, and she looked down at her napkin, trying to calm her nerves. A little flirtation was one thing, but Roy was moving too fast. Still, there was no denying that the admiration she saw in his eyes was flattering. It had been ten years since Larry's death. Though she hadn't been looking for another man, Sally had to admit that the years had been lonely, especially once Kate finished college and moved to the Big Apple.

"What makes you think that I laugh?" she asked, determined to keep the conversation light. The truth was, she used to laugh a lot, but for the past few years, reasons for laughter had been harder to find.

Roy laid down his fork and knife and stared at her for a second. "Those lines by your eyes tell the story."

"They're crow's feet."

He shook his head and frowned at her as if she were a contestant in a game show who'd just made a colossal mistake. "Laugh lines."

She couldn't help it. Sally chuckled. "You don't give up, do you?"

A shrug was his first answer. "I got you laughing, didn't I?"

"That you did, and I'm glad." It felt good. When she'd planned this trip, Sally had envisioned getting to know the other guests. Though she and Larry had been newlyweds, unlike Alexa and Jared Tibbits, they'd conversed with the others at their table.

Sally had hoped that she and Kate would meet some interesting people here. The change of scenery and the stimulation of new acquaintances would be good for both of them. Unfortunately, there were far fewer guests than she'd expected, and though she tried not to dwell on it, Rainbow's End was not the beautiful Christian resort she remembered. But neither of those was Roy's fault.

Sally smiled at him as she added, "I'm hoping I can get my granddaughter to laugh more too."

Roy's gray eyes turned serious. "What do her parents think about you bringing her to Texas for a month?"

Sally busied herself by cutting another meatball into pieces. This was one disadvantage of meeting new people. They didn't know her history. While it would be easy to slough off Roy's question with an innocuous reply like "They don't mind," Sally wouldn't do that. Roy deserved the truth.

"My daughter and her husband were killed in a drive-by shooting when Kate was seven. Larry and I were her only living relatives, so we did what anyone would do in those circumstances: we brought her to live with us." Sally raised her eyes to meet Roy's gaze. She'd expected pity. Instead she saw understanding and admiration. "I've never had a minute's regret."

"You shouldn't. It's obvious you did a good job."

Though Sally appreciated the vote of confidence, she wondered what Roy had seen in the few minutes he'd spoken to Kate to make him say that. She started to ask, but before she could get the words out, he continued.

"I think you might have some help with that campaign to get your granddaughter to laugh. Look at them." He tipped his head to the left. As Sally followed the direction of his gaze, she saw Kate and Greg chuckling as if sharing a private joke. "This could be good for both of them," Roy said, returning his attention to the mound of spaghetti still on his plate.

Sally forked a lettuce leaf. "What do you know about Greg?" He seemed like a nice enough young man, but she wanted a second opinion.

"He's between jobs, and he helps out around here." Though the story was plausible and Sally didn't doubt that it was true, the way Roy stared at his plate made her think there was more that he wasn't revealing. Although tempted to ask, Sally did not. Everyone was entitled to privacy.

Roy chewed a bite of spaghetti before he added, "We haven't talked about it, but I suspect Greg feels the way I do and wants to keep Rainbow's End alive."

Sally blinked, startled by the direction the conversation had taken. "Is it closing?" While she regretted some of the changes she'd seen, the idea of Rainbow's End shutting its doors saddened her.

"I don't know." Roy punctuated his word with a shrug as he spun the Susan around to take another piece of garlic bread. "I only know that if it goes under, life will be harder for the folks in Dupree. They get a fair amount of business from the guests, especially during peak season. People go into town for midday meals, souvenirs, and day trips. In the fall, it's hunting excursions."

He looked at the pitcher of extra spaghetti sauce, obviously considering whether or not to indulge in another helping, then shook his head. "Got to save room for dessert," he told Sally. "Fact is, when the inn is full, the townspeople are happy. I'd even give up having supper here if it meant that all the tables were filled with guests."

"Miss meals like this?" Sally forced a lilt to her voice, trying to lighten the mood. "That sounds like cruel and unusual punishment."

As she'd hoped, Roy laughed.

"Tonight's dessert is cannoli," Olivia announced as she cleared the dishes. "Does everyone want one?" She giggled as she looked at Greg. "Or more? The regulars know how good they are."

"Say yes," Greg urged Kate. "It's worth it." When she nodded in response to Olivia's question, Greg grinned. "Good choice. Carmen may not have a single drop of Italian blood, but I'd match her cannoli against any you can find in Little Italy."

"You've been there?" As they'd chatted during dinner, Greg had admitted that he considered himself a Californian, having lived there since attending Stanford. He'd also said that this was the first vacation he'd taken in a decade, unless you counted annual trips to Washington State to visit his parents. Though Kate had been surprised by the infrequency of those visits, she had said nothing. Perhaps as she learned more about Greg, she'd feel more comfortable asking about his family, but tonight his expression when he'd mentioned them had discouraged further questions.

"Who hasn't been to Little Italy?" he demanded. "Just because I've lived in California for almost fifteen years doesn't mean I haven't seen other places."

But he hadn't taken vacations, so either he'd been to New York more than a decade before, or he'd gone there on business. Kate was betting the second.

"Let me know the next time you're in New York, and I'll take you to my favorite Italian restaurant." Where had that come from? Kate had never invited a man who was practically a stranger to have dinner with her. But somehow Greg didn't seem like a stranger. They'd laughed, they'd sparred, they'd shared a few personal details, but though they'd spent less than two hours together, she felt as if she knew Greg better than even Chase and Brittany, two of her co-workers who had quickly become her friends.

If she and Greg were dating — which, of course, they were not — this would have been a first date. Kate had had plenty of first dates, but never before had she felt this sense of connection to a man she'd just met. Somehow it seemed right to invite him to visit her in New York.

"That's an offer I won't refuse," Greg said with a wide smile that made her think he knew he was the first to receive such an invitation.

As Olivia set plates in front of each of the

guests and a platter filled with the Italian pastries on the Susan, Greg placed one of the powdered-sugar-dusted pastries on Kate's plate. "Taste this and tell me what you think."

She cut a small piece of the ricotta-filled pastry and slid it into her mouth, letting the flavors rest on her tongue a little longer than she would have normally. When she'd swallowed it, she said, "It's . . ." Kate twisted her lips into a frown as if she'd eaten rancid meat, then relented when she saw Greg's expression. "It's sublime. You were right, Greg. I've never eaten a better one. No wonder you want to stay at Rainbow's End."

When she finished the last bite of dessert and declined a second helping, Kate turned toward Sally. By this time if she were home, her grandmother would be sitting with her feet up, watching television or reading a book. They'd gained an hour with the time difference and had traveled for half the day. Despite the nap she'd taken, Sally must be exhausted. But far from appearing tired, her grandmother seemed energized as she spoke to Roy.

"Are you ready to go back?" Kate asked.

To her surprise, Sally shook her head. "Not yet, but I'm afraid it's getting cold. Would you bring me my navy sweater?"

"Of course." Knowing how Sally would protest, Kate did not mention that she also intended to bring the car. Her grandmother did not need to walk those rutted roads tonight. Kate turned to Greg as she started to rise. "If you'll excuse me."

He rose and pulled out her chair in a gesture of old-fashioned courtesy. "Mind if I come along? The exercise will help me walk off that big dinner."

Delighted that she'd have more of his company, Kate wagged her finger at Greg. "You didn't have to take second helpings of everything, you know."

"And disappoint Carmen? She's insulted if there are leftovers."

"So it was your duty?"

"More or less." Greg held the door open for Kate, letting in the cool evening breeze. Though she hadn't thought the dining room overly warm, the breeze felt good as they started walking toward Kate's cabin. "That meal was incredible," she said. If Grandpa Larry had been here, he would have patted his stomach. "I can't remember when I ate so much good food. Of course, now I have to figure out a way to work it off. Dare I ask if there's a fitness room here?"

Greg grinned. "Dare away, but you know the answer."

"No cable, no wireless, no exercise equipment." It was not a surprise. "How about a gym in Dupree?"

"Same answer."

Again, not a surprise. Though she hadn't paid a lot of attention to the town as they'd driven through it, Kate's impression had been of a business district no more than two blocks long.

"So, what do people do for exercise here? The pool's not open, and I didn't see a golf course."

"There's one of those in Dupree. Nine holes, but it's not bad." Greg pointed to the right. "Closer to home, the tennis court is open year-round. Do you play?"

"Not well."

"Good. Neither do I. Much to my father's chagrin, I did not inherit the sports gene."

Kate was surprised, both at the bitterness in his voice and the admission. While she could not picture Greg on a football field, he had the lean build of a runner.

"If you really don't play tennis, this could be a pretty pathetic game. I haven't held a racquet in years."

"Excellent." This time Greg's voice was tinged with laughter. "We'll be well matched. What time shall we meet?" As if anticipating her refusal, he added, "There's no dress code, although I wouldn't suggest wearing that skirt, attractive as it is."

Kate smiled as pleasure rushed through her. Sally had been right when she'd advised Kate to wear a skirt to dinner. At least one person had noticed. But she hesitated to agree to tennis. When she'd asked about a fitness room or gym, she'd envisioned using it before Sally woke. There was no question of playing tennis on an unlighted outdoor court before the sun rose.

"I don't know if I should. I came here to spend time with my grandmother."

As a winged creature fluttered by, Kate shuddered.

"That was a bird," Greg told her. "The bats come a bit later."

"So you weren't joking about them?"

"No. I'm also not joking about the tennis invitation. Don't you think your grandmother would be happy to entertain herself for half an hour?"

She would. It was only Kate who'd feel guilty. "You're right. Sally likes to rest in the afternoon. She won't even know that I'm gone." The more she thought about it, the better Kate liked the idea. "Let's say 1:30."

"You've got a date."

But it wasn't. It was two people helping

each other get a little exercise. Nothing
more.

6

Kate grinned at the sound of Sally singing in the shower about beautiful mornings. Rodgers and Hammerstein, of course. There wasn't a single one of their songs that her grandmother couldn't sing, albeit a bit off-key. Sally might be a world-class Clue player and the best grandmother any girl could have, but her voice would never compare to Carmen's. While Carmen warbled, Sally croaked.

Kate's grin widened at the image of her grandmother as a frog. Knowing Sally, she'd laugh at the thought and then belt out another verse of "Some Enchanted Evening," insisting that Kermit the Frog would appreciate her voice even if Kate didn't. And if she knew that Carmen sang while she worked, Sally would probably want to join her.

Kate's grin turned to a chuckle as she slathered sunblock on her face and hands.

Though the sun had barely risen, she knew that by the time she and Sally finished breakfast and started their walk, she'd need the protection.

Even if it meant she might have to listen to more off-key singing, Kate would introduce Sally to Carmen. She knew her grandmother had been looking forward to meeting friendly guests, and neither of the couples at their table had qualified. Carmen might not be a guest, but she would be someone for Sally to talk to other than Kate. And Roy. Kate couldn't forget Roy.

Sally had certainly seemed to enjoy her conversation with him at supper. When they'd returned to the cabin last night, she had spoken of little besides Roy and how charming he'd been. Later, when Kate had brought two glasses of milk and a plate of chocolate chip cookies for what Carmen had called the essential bedtime snack, Sally had continued to speak of Roy.

He'd obviously captivated her grandmother, and while Kate wasn't sure how she felt about that, there was no ignoring the way Sally's face glowed. It might be an exaggeration to say there'd been a bounce in her step, but Sally had certainly seemed perkier and happier than Kate had seen her in a long time. If Roy could do that, who was Kate to worry? It wasn't as if they'd see each other again once April ended.

"Your turn." Sally emerged from the shower, toweling her hair as she stood in the doorway to Kate's room.

"I'm done." Kate had wakened early, taken a quick shower, then grabbed her laptop and rushed to the lodge to check her messages. There'd been none, nor had there been any sign of Greg. Though she'd felt a mild sense of disappointment at the latter, Kate told herself it was just as well. If he'd seen her with her laptop, Greg would probably have chided her and called her a workaholic. That wouldn't have been a great way to start the day, and yet she wondered what he was doing. Perhaps he'd be at breakfast when she was there. Silly Kate! Next thing you knew, she'd be like Sally, constantly talking about a man.

Kate looked at her watch. "We can go to breakfast whenever you're ready. They're already serving."

"Wear your walking shoes," Sally called from her room. "I want to explore the area after we eat." Kate decided not to mention that Sally had told her that three times last night. It had been one of the few non-Roy-related subjects of the evening.

"I already have them on."

"Good." For a few minutes, the only sound from Sally's room was the whir of the hair dryer. When she came out, she struck a pose worthy of a runway model. "What do you think?" she asked, gesturing to her outfit.

Kate stared. Sally was wearing a pair of jeans and a Western shirt, complete with pearl snaps. To complete the outfit, she dangled a cowboy hat from her fingers.

"Wow!" It wasn't the most eloquent response, but Kate could find nothing else to say. The woman with her hand on her hip had her grandmother's face, but those were definitely not her grandmother's clothes. "I didn't know you owned jeans."

Sally shrugged as if the habits of a lifetime were easily sloughed off. "Larry didn't like them, so I never bought any, but Larry's no longer here to complain." She shrugged again. "Besides, I always wondered how I'd look in jeans." She paused, and Kate sensed her uncertainty. "So, how do I look? The salesclerk said they were fine, but I could tell that she had her mind on making a sale."

"You look great, Sally." It wasn't flattery, either. The jeans and shirt were surprisingly slimming, camouflaging the extra pounds that Sally's doctor had urged her to shed, but the most dramatic difference was in her attitude. It seemed as if Sally had donned a new persona along with her new clothes. Kate looked down at her grandmother's feet, shod in sensible walking shoes. "All you need are some cowboy boots, and you'll be ready for the rodeo."

Though she'd been joking, Sally nodded. "I figured we could buy ourselves some here."

"We?" The boots Kate wore were fashion statements from exclusive Italian designers, not styles sturdy enough to be worn on a ranch.

"Sure." Sally slung her bag over her shoulder and opened the front door, refusing Kate's help in navigating the steps. "Remember how we had mother-daughter clothes when you were in grade school? We can do that again. Mother-daughter boots."

The smile on Sally's face was all the encouragement Kate needed. She'd gladly squeeze her feet into what was bound to be uncomfortable footwear if it made her grandmother happy. "Of course we can. The problem will be finding a store."

"It won't be a problem. Roy said there's a boot maker in Dupree. We can go there tomorrow." Roy again. It appeared he and Sally had discussed more than the loneliness of widowhood and the beauty of the

Hill Country.

Though Kate didn't hold out much hope for finding high-quality boots in a town as small as Dupree, she wouldn't disappoint Sally. Besides, it wouldn't matter if the boots were poorly made. They only needed to last a month. "Whatever you want. This trip is for you."

It took less time to reach the dining room than it had the night before, perhaps because Sally was more rested, perhaps because she was energized by her new outfit and the prospect of owning her first pair of cowboy boots. Whatever the reason, Kate wasn't complaining. It was good to see her grandmother obviously enjoying herself. On a morning like this, it was difficult to believe that Sally's heart wasn't as strong as Kate's.

The dining room was empty when they arrived, and Kate felt a twinge of regret that Greg wasn't there, but the delicious aromas of breakfast foods tantalized her. She walked toward the buffet, where an array of chafing dishes kept the food warm, and was about to lift one lid when Carmen entered the room.

"Good morning, ladies," she said in her lilting voice. "Just help yourself. There's a bell on the end of the buffet if you need anything else."

Kate turned toward her grandmother. "Sally, I'd like you to meet Carmen St. George. She's the woman who gave us last night's incredible meal." As Carmen smiled with pleasure, Kate continued, "Carmen, this is my grandmother, Sally Fuller."

"It's a pleasure to meet you."

"The pleasure is mine," Sally said as she shook Carmen's hand. "I've eaten a lot of meatballs in my seventy-three years, but I've never had any that compare to yours. Would you consider sharing your recipe?"

Carmen nodded. "Anytime. Just stop in the kitchen, and I'll write it out."

"Is there anything else I can get you?" Carmen asked when Sally had murmured her thanks.

Sally opened the chafing dishes, revealing pancakes, scrambled eggs, bacon, and oatmeal, and sniffed appreciatively. "If I eat all this, I won't need that box lunch I ordered."

"Some folks skip lunch." Carmen patted her ample hips. "I'm obviously not one of them."

Giving her a conspiratorial smile as she looked at her own hips, Sally nodded. "Me either."

"Enjoy your meal."

As Carmen started to leave, Kate touched her hand. "Sally's already told you how

95

much we enjoyed the meatballs. I wanted to say that your cannoli is the best I've ever eaten."

Her smile reflecting her pleasure at the compliment, Carmen nodded. "Thank you, but wait until you taste the peach cobbler."

"It can't be better."

Carmen raised an eyebrow. "Don't bet on that. There's nothing like Hill Country peaches."

"The state of Georgia might disagree." Sally's smile was wry. "They're mighty proud of their peaches — even put them on their license plates."

Carmen refused to be cowed. "It's all a matter of opinion. You can decide after dinner tonight."

When Carmen left, Kate and Sally filled their plates and carried them to the table, where insulated carafes of coffee and hot tea waited for them. After she blessed their food, Sally took a bite of pancake, then a sampling of the eggs. It was only when she'd tasted the bacon that she looked up at Kate, satisfaction on her face.

"The food is much better than it was fifty years ago. The Sinclairs are lucky to have Carmen cooking for them."

They were indeed. Though Sally hadn't voiced the thought, Kate suspected that

Carmen's meals were the only thing that had improved. The mattress had been surprisingly comfortable, but the sheets had worn spots and the towels were mismatched.

"The food may not be enough to save Rainbow's End." Her scrambled eggs were light and fluffy, and the oatmeal had a hint of spice — not cloves, Kate was willing to bet. If Rainbow's End were simply a restaurant, boosting business would be less of a challenge, but to be a successful resort, it needed an almost overwhelming amount of work.

Sally pursed her lips. "Please, Kate. No gloom and doom while I'm eating. Let's talk about something more pleasant, like Greg Vange."

"Vange." Kate swirled the name on her tongue as she had the cream filling from last night's cannoli. "So that's his last name." It suited him, a unique name for a decidedly out-of-the-ordinary man.

"Roy told me. He said he's a very nice young man." Sally looked up from the toast she was buttering and added, "Single too."

This was vintage Sally. "Please, no matchmaking. You know that doesn't work out for me." Though her grandmother had supported her move to New Jersey after graduation, acknowledging that Manhattan was the best place for Kate to start her career, she had never given up hope that Kate would move back to Buffalo and live near her. As an inducement, Sally had introduced Kate to a seemingly endless stream of supposedly eligible men until Kate had threatened to stop her monthly visits.

Sally shook her head. "Just because two men got cold feet doesn't mean everyone will. The right man is waiting for you." She gave Kate a long look. "I just hope I'm around for your wedding."

"Now who's talking gloom and doom?" Kate demanded. She took another spoonful of oatmeal, but it had somehow lost its savor. She didn't need the reminder that she'd had two steady boyfriends, both of whom decided it was time to marry someone else, and she definitely didn't need any reminders of Sally's health and advancing years.

"It's not gloom and doom," Sally protested. "I was simply being realistic. I've been a member of AARP for years." More vintage Sally.

Kate washed down the oatmeal with a swig of coffee. "It won't work, you know. You convinced me to come here, but you can't guilt me into marrying someone I don't love just so you can see me settled."

Sally took another bite of bacon, chewing slowly as she formulated her response. When she spoke, the words were so familiar that Kate could almost recite them. "God has a plan — and a man — for you. You just need to listen when he whispers to you."

"The bacon is delicious, isn't it? And Carmen added something special to the oatmeal."

Shaking her head, Sally gave Kate a stern look. "That wasn't even subtle."

"But it worked. We're not talking about prospective husbands anymore."

And they did not. Instead, Sally speculated on the types of boots that would be available in Dupree and how long they would have to wait if they wanted them custom-made. When they finished eating, she announced that she wanted to walk along the lake and gestured toward the right when they left the dining room. "We'll end up back here," she told Kate.

The grass, which had been wet with dew when they'd walked to breakfast, had dried, and as they left the shadow of the oak trees to approach the lake, Kate found herself wishing she had worn short sleeves. The air was much warmer than it had been less than an hour ago, making her wonder just how high the mercury would rise today.

"Look over there," Sally said when they reached the edge of the water. To Kate's relief, Sally showed no signs of either fatigue or breathlessness. Yesterday's episode must have been the result of travel.

Sally pointed to a small land mass to the northwest of the resort.

"An island?"

Sally nodded, her eyes glistening. "It's called Paintbrush Island, and it belongs to Rainbow's End, or at least it did. Larry and I took a rowboat there one day." She swallowed deeply, and Kate knew she was lost in memories. "It was the most romantic picnic of my life," Sally said softly. "A day I'll never forget."

Though Kate knew her grandparents had shared a deep and abiding love, it was unusual for Sally to be so emotional. "Do you want me to see if they still have boats? We could have lunch there today."

"Oh no, Kate. The island is not a place for two women. It's for couples." She shaded her eyes with one hand as she gazed at the site of her memories. "Legend has it that the island is the real rainbow's end."

"In the western sky? That's not very likely unless there were thunderstorms in the morning. Rainbows only occur when the sun is low enough, and they're most frequently seen in the east." The words were out before Kate realized that they might distress her grandmother. To her relief, Sally laughed.

"No one would ever accuse you of having your head in the clouds. If I didn't know better, I'd say you didn't have a romantic bone in your body."

That was what Pete and Lou had said when they'd broken off their relationships with her. "Maybe I don't."

Sally shook her head and started walking again. "I don't believe that. You just try to hide it."

They wandered slowly along the lake-shore, admiring the calm water, casting occasional glances at the cabins, most of which were unoccupied. Though Kate had wakened this morning hopeful that she'd been mistaken about the resort's condition and that the situation wasn't as dire as she'd thought the previous day, there was no denying that Rainbow's End needed a massive infusion of cash if it was going to attract enough guests to be profitable.

Peeling paint, broken railings, and holes in window screens were the most obvious effects of years of neglect, but Kate suspected they were not the only problems. The water heater in their cabin made ominous clunks, and the lights had dimmed when Sally turned on her hair dryer. In all likelihood, the cabins hadn't been upgraded in far more than the five years that the Sinclairs had owned Rainbow's End.

"Was the gazebo here when you and Grandpa Larry visited?" Kate asked as she and Sally completed their circuit and returned to the heart of the resort. Directly across from the main lodge, the gazebo was a fanciful white building that probably vied with the covered porches for shelter from the midday sun. When Sally shook her head, Kate realized that might be one reason why it wasn't as dilapidated as the other buildings.

"Do you want to have our lunch here?" Though it was still another hour until noon, Kate hoped that by introducing the idea, she'd be able to convince Sally to rest. Her grandmother would undoubtedly deny it, but she had become visibly tired, her early morning pep seeming to have evaporated along with the dew.

Sally sank onto one of the benches that lined the inside of the gazebo and smiled. "That's a good idea, but right now I'd like another cup of coffee. Do you think you can find one for me?"

Kate nodded, pleased that Sally had

agreed to rest. "Carmen said there's always some in the dining room. I'll get us each a cup."

When she returned bearing two covered paper cups, Kate found her grandmother staring into the distance, an enigmatic expression on her face. "Here you are."

Sally turned, obviously startled. "Thank you, Kate." She removed the cover and took a sip. "This is wonderful."

"Carmen's coffee is as good as everything else she makes."

Sally took another sip, then shook her head. "I wasn't referring to the coffee. It's wonderful being here. This is a special place."

A bird warbled somewhere in the closest live oak tree, then with a rush of wings flew to perch inside the gazebo. Kate looked up, wondering if she'd be able to identify it, but before she could form more than an impression of black-and-white feathers and a short beak, it flew away. Whether it was fanciful to think that the bird had checked out of Rainbow's End almost as soon as it had checked in, Kate couldn't help wondering if it was a metaphor for the resort's guests.

"It may be special, but it needs a lot of work."

Placing the cup on the bench next to her,

Sally nodded. "I won't deny that, but there's so much potential. Rainbow's End was once prosperous. It could be again." She sighed and leaned back against the gazebo's frame. "If I were forty years younger, I'd try to turn it around."

Forty years ago that might have been possible. Now Kate wasn't certain. "Everything's different now. I'm not just talking about the economy. People want different things when they take a vacation. Even when they go to national parks, they're looking for modern conveniences."

"Like flat-screen TVs." Sally's words dripped with scorn.

"And wireless access, not to mention refrigerators and coffeemakers in their rooms."

Sally straightened her shoulders and leaned forward, fixing her gaze on Kate. "You're missing the point. Rainbow's End is special precisely because it doesn't have those things. Look around, Kate." She gestured expansively. "Look at all it does have."

"I'll grant you that the setting is beautiful." Kate had been impressed with the Hill Country as they'd driven from San Antonio to Dupree. The rolling hills, the lush green of the trees and grass, the occasional patch of wildflowers had all been beautiful, and Rainbow's End seemed to have more than its share of that beauty.

"This is one of the prettiest lakes I've seen." Kate's first impression had been that it was a lake like any other, but as she and Sally had walked along its shore, she'd realized that Bluebonnet Lake was — to use her grandmother's term — special. The rolling hills that seemed to extend to the very edge of the water and the small island in the center made it look as if it were something from a fairy tale.

"The problem is, the brochure said power boats and jet skis aren't allowed on the lake. That doesn't leave much to do."

"Except enjoy the peace and quiet," Sally countered.

"That's all well and good." Kate wouldn't deny the appeal of peace and quiet in small doses. "Who'll pay for that?"

Sally shrugged. "You're the advertising maven. You figure it out."

7

Kate was still pondering her grandmother's challenge when she arrived at the tennis court. Though Rainbow's End needed much more than a new ad campaign, it couldn't hurt to —

All thoughts of slogans and jingles fled from her brain at the sight of Greg striding toward the court. Surely his claim of lacking the sports gene was bogus. With legs as muscular as his arms, Greg was the picture of a Wimbledon champion. He'd even dressed for the role. Kate had changed into shorts, a tank top, and her cross trainers — nothing special about them — while Greg was wearing what appeared to be new tennis whites. Furthermore, he carried two obviously new racquets. She was definitely outclassed.

"I'm impressed," Kate said when she saw the logo on the racquets. "I wouldn't have expected Rainbow's End to have such good equipment." Though she was only a casual player, she knew enough about the sport to know that these racquets were competition quality. It was odd that so much else had been neglected here, yet the resort had top-notch tennis racquets. But perhaps it wasn't so strange. Angela looked like a woman who enjoyed sports. Maybe she played tennis and wanted good equipment.

"Does Angela —"

Before Kate could finish her question, a man called out a greeting to Greg, then ambled over to the court.

"I'm Tim Sinclair," he said, extending his hand for a shake, "and you must be one of our new guests."

Tim Sinclair was not what Kate had expected. When she'd met Angela, she had formed a mental image of her husband. Tim, Kate had thought, would be taller than average with an athletic build. She was wrong on both counts. Tim was no taller than his wife, which put him on the short side of average, and though Kate wouldn't call him stocky, he was square. His face, his body, even his hands were square.

"Kate Sherwood," she said, noticing that Tim had a firm shake and that he looked her in the eye.

"Welcome to Rainbow's End. I hope you

enjoy your stay." He eyed the racquets but said nothing.

When he'd left, Kate turned to Greg. "Where did you get them?"

Greg shrugged, the movement tightening his polo shirt and accenting his shoulders.

"You bought them, didn't you?"

He shrugged again. "Guilty as charged. The ones I found in the shed were practically antiques. They had wooden frames and needed to be restrung. It seemed like a better idea to buy new ones. Besides, Ryan Wheeler was glad for the business."

"You found them in Dupree?"

He nodded. "Dupree might be a small town, but it has some top-of-the-line merchandise. Surprising, isn't it?"

What was surprising was that a man who was unemployed would spend so much money. The clothing couldn't have been cheap, and the racquets certainly were not. Surely he should be conserving money, since he didn't appear to be actively looking for a new position. Greg Vange was an enigma.

Kate took a deep breath, trying to slow her heartbeat. It was silly the way it accelerated when she was around this man. She hadn't felt this way around Pete or Lou, the two men she'd dated seriously. Being with them had been comfortable. They'd enjoyed the same activities, moved in the same circles. Not once had Kate considered playing tennis with them, and not once had either one made her breathless.

Greg was different. Though his name sounded vaguely familiar, Kate couldn't put her finger on the reason. Perhaps she should google him. At a minimum, she could check Facebook to see if he had a page. That was what she did for potential clients. But the simple fact was, Kate had never liked the idea of researching her friends. Even though they would go their separate ways and probably not see each other again when April ended, she hoped she and Greg could be friends for the month. No googling, no online sleuthing. She would wait to see what Greg told her.

He extended one of the racquets to her. "How does it feel?"

Kate wrapped her hand around it, somehow not surprised that it was a perfect fit. Greg had shaken her hand only once, but that seemed to have been enough for him to guess her hand size.

"I feel as if I ought to be at Wimbledon," she told him. "There's only one problem: the racquet is far better than I am."

The corners of his mouth twitched, and

she wondered whether he was downplaying his own prowess. "So, we'll practice. Let's get started."

Greg took his position on one side of the net, waiting for her to serve the ball to him. Within a few seconds, Kate realized that he hadn't lied. He wasn't any better than she was. Half the balls hit the net; the majority of the rest went out of bounds, but the few times they managed to volley felt good. There was an unexpected satisfaction in being able to return a serve, even though Kate knew that tomorrow her arms and legs would protest the unusual exercise.

Her regular workouts at the gym hadn't prepared her for tennis. Half an hour of running around the court, stretching to hit a ball and bending down to retrieve the ones she'd missed, had left her more winded than her usual routine. What she needed now was a hot tub.

Kate glanced around. There was plenty of space between the tennis court and the closest cabins to put a hot tub. If she owned Rainbow's End . . . but she did not.

"That was fun," she told Greg as she accepted the towel he pulled from his bag and dabbed at her face.

"Enough fun to do it again tomorrow?"

"Sure." Her muscles might protest, but

she wasn't going to give up the opportunity to burn calories in such an enjoyable way. Playing tennis with Greg was decidedly more fun than running on the treadmill at her gym.

He reached back into his bag and withdrew two bottles of water, handing one to her. Instinctively, she turned the bottle to read the label.

"Something wrong?"

Kate shook her head. "No. I just wondered what brands were available here. My firm does the advertising for a competitor."

A frown crossed his face, deepening the green of his eyes. "It's hard to escape work, isn't it?"

Greg sounded as if he understood, confirming her belief that whatever he had done before he'd come to Rainbow's End, it hadn't been a nine-to-five-forget-the-job-when-you-walk-out-the-door position. The truth was, Kate hadn't thought of the office once while they'd been playing. If anything, she'd spent more time today worrying about Sally and Rainbow's End than she had her clients.

"Work's an important part of my life." When Greg merely nodded, Kate continued her explanation. "I've worked hard to get where I am. If things go right, I may be made a partner by the end of the year. That's been my dream ever since my grandfather took me to work with him."

She and Grandpa Larry had left their coats in his cubicle, then had toured the office. Though ten-year-old Kate had been impressed by the drafting tables and the conference rooms lined with pictures of the firm's most successful ads, it was the end of the tour that had defined her life. When Grandpa Larry had shown her the partners' offices with their fancy furniture and the view of Lake Erie, Kate had known that was what she wanted. She hadn't looked back since.

Greg didn't appear impressed. "What happens after you make partner? What's the next rung on the ladder?"

Kate flinched. "I don't know." But she ought to.

Greg yanked the drawer open with more force than necessary, then stared at the socks, as if choosing the right pair would qualify him for an international award. He grabbed a pair of brown socks, then tossed them back and looked at the remaining ones.

Unlike Kate, he hadn't worried about climbing the corporate ladder. When you owned the company, there was no ladder. You were the top. But he'd done the same thing Kate was doing, setting increasingly challenging goals for himself. Unlike Kate's, his didn't involve titles or responsibility; they focused solely on money. One million, then the next, then the elusive billion. And when he'd reached that milestone, he'd taken Drew's advice and sold the company, netting himself more money than he'd dreamed possible. By any standard, Greg was wealthy. Filthy rich, some would say. The question was, what did he have to show for it?

He hadn't squandered the money. Most of it was invested, growing daily while he repaired buildings at a down-at-the-heels resort and played tennis with the most attractive woman he'd ever met. He'd spent some, but it had been wisely spent. Thanks to him, his family's life was a little easier. He'd set up trust funds to pay for his sisters' college expenses, and Mom had reported that his father seemed to enjoy the big-screen TV that had been Greg's Christmas present to them.

There was nothing wrong with what he'd done, either the accumulation of wealth or the way he'd spent a tiny fraction of it. Admittedly, the money hadn't bought him the one thing he'd longed for as he'd been growing up, but he hadn't expected it to. Though his sisters might disagree, there were some things money could not buy.

Greg was proud of what he'd accomplished. He'd worked hard, and he'd been rewarded for that hard work. But there was more to life. He knew that as surely as he knew that Kate Sherwood's eyes were brown. What wasn't clear was what that "more" was. That was why he was here: to discover what God had in store for him.

Abandoning hope of choosing a pair of socks, Greg slid his feet into sandals, then reached for his laptop. Shaking his head, he pictured Kate's expression if she could see him. Like her, he'd been thinking of work when he'd downloaded messages earlier today. It was time to read them.

Greg scanned the contents of his in-box. Only three new messages. The first two were from two of his sisters. Nineteen-year-old Taylor had been invited to a dance at some fancy country club and needed a new dress. Greg raised his eyebrows at the cost, then opened Jessica's note. The second oldest of the four girls had blown out a tire and had to buy a complete set. He'd transfer the money to them tomorrow. Fortunately, neither Ashley nor Emily had any requests.

That left the final message, the one from Drew.

He clicked it open and frowned. It was short and succinct, typical Drew. "We need to talk," it said. "Call me."

Greg wouldn't.

8

Once again, Kate and Sally were the first to arrive for dinner. Once again, only one table was set. But tonight there were only six chairs at the table, and tonight their server was a teenage boy. Kevin of the KOB trio, Kate guessed. Blond, blue-eyed, and tanned, he would have been the perfect model for the jeans ads she'd worked on last year. Too bad she hadn't seen him a year ago. Of course, a year ago she hadn't known that Dupree, Texas, existed, and even if she had, it wasn't a place she'd have considered scouting for models. That was why modeling agencies were in business, and why she . . .

Kate tried not to frown as she realized she was thinking about her job. If all it took was seeing a teen who could be a model, perhaps Sally was right. Perhaps Kate needed a vacation more than she'd realized.

"I'm Kevin Olsen," the boy said, extending his hand in greeting. "I'll be your server tonight."

Kate smiled as she shook his hand. "It's nice to meet you, Kevin. Is Olivia ill?"

"No, ma'am." He had no way of knowing that the courteous phrase, so common here, made her feel almost as old as Sally. No one in New York called Kate ma'am. Kevin unloaded his tray as he said, "Olivia and I alternate nights when there are so few guests."

The expression in his eyes made Kate sense that he regretted the reduced hours. If he were a typical teenager, Kevin was working so he could buy something his parents couldn't or wouldn't give him. In New Jersey, she would have speculated that special something was a car, but since Kevin lived in the heart of Texas, he was likely saving for a truck. She'd noticed that despite rising gas prices, trucks seemed to be the popular choice, especially once she'd left San Antonio. Ranchers needed them to haul supplies and pull horse trailers. Teenagers needed them for peer approval.

"What are we having tonight?" Sally asked as Kevin pulled out a chair for her. She hadn't minded being addressed as ma'am but had nodded in a vaguely regal gesture, as if it were her due. While Kate was still adjusting to the idea of a month away from work, there was no question that Sally was enjoying the slower pace and extra layer of gentility she'd found at Rainbow's End.

"Pot roast with vegetables and peach cobbler for dessert," Kevin said, keeping his eyes focused on Sally.

She tipped her head to one side and gave him a look that Kate recognized. *Tell me the truth,* it demanded. "Is the cobbler as good as Carmen claims?"

Kevin nodded vigorously. "Better."

He chatted with them for a few minutes, telling them that he was the middle of three children and that his older brother had offered to help him fix up his truck, once he found the right one. "I don't want just any truck," Kevin explained. "It's got to be special."

"You should never just settle for important things like trucks," Sally said with a grin. "Or boyfriends," she murmured so softly that only Kate could hear her. It appeared that Sally was back in matchmaking mode.

A minute later Roy entered the dining room and Kevin returned to the kitchen. Kate noticed that Roy's eyes rested on Sally as he crossed the room and took the seat at her side. He wore an obviously new shirt tonight, and the little nick on his cheek told

Kate he'd just shaved. It seemed Roy had taken as many pains with his appearance as Sally had. Kate's grandmother had spent the better part of half an hour debating which blouse was best with her denim skirt.

"You're looking beautiful tonight," Roy said, his eyes on Sally as he settled into his chair. Though they'd waited for everyone to arrive before taking their seats last night, the fact that Kevin had seated Sally had led everyone else to sit down as soon as they reached the table.

Roy looked at Kate as he added, "You too." It was definitely an afterthought, but Kate didn't mind. How could she when the pink in Sally's cheeks attested to her pleasure?

Seconds later, the Schwartzes arrived. "Did everyone have a good day?" Janet asked as she and Bob approached the table.

"I did." Sally's voice resonated with enthusiasm. "There's nothing quite like Rainbow's End."

"That's what Jared Tibbits said, but he wasn't smiling when he said it." Bob glanced around the table, apparently counting chairs. "They were checking out."

"There's not much to do here," Janet added.

Though it was nothing more than she'd

119

told herself a dozen times, Kate felt the need to contradict Janet. Perhaps it was the memory of Kevin's expression when he spoke of the lack of guests. "Sally and I enjoyed wandering around and having lunch in the gazebo. We made a mistake, though." She smiled at Janet. "We shouldn't have ordered two box lunches. There was enough food in one to feed us both." And that had surprised Kate. If the Sinclairs were trying to economize, they could easily ask Carmen to reduce serving sizes and still satisfy guests.

"I was thinking about something a little more active," Janet said. "Strolling around the grounds loses its appeal mighty fast."

Though Kate would have expected Sally to protest, she was engrossed in a discussion about boots with Roy. It was up to Kate to convince Janet that Rainbow's End was not totally lacking in activities.

"Greg and I played tennis this afternoon."

While Janet did not appear impressed, her husband nodded.

"Your day sounds more exciting than ours. Janet and I wandered around Dupree. There's not much to see there." Bob frowned. "Tennis sounds like a better bet. How did you do?"

As if on cue, Kate's opponent arrived. "I

beat her," Greg announced.

Kate couldn't help laughing at his apparent pride. "That means Greg scored one point. It was a pretty pathetic match, but we had fun."

"So you were fifteen-love."

Sally gave Kate her best matchmaker smile as she pronounced the last word. It appeared she and Roy had concluded their discussion of boots.

Refusing to acknowledge her grandmother's attempts to find her a husband, Kate simply nodded and said, "With aching muscles to prove it."

Greg took his seat as Kevin reentered the room. "Kate's either a real trouper or a glutton for punishment, because she's agreed to a rematch tomorrow."

"It's only because I plan to win," she announced, wrinkling her nose so no one would take her seriously. As she'd hoped, the others laughed.

When Kevin finished placing the covered dishes on the table, Greg bowed his head and offered a blessing for the food, ending with a prayer that the Sinclairs would find the path God had planned for them.

"They need all the prayers we can give them," Roy said when the chorus of amens faded.

"It's sad to see what's happening." As he spoke, Greg uncovered the largest casserole and held the lid so that Kate could help herself to delicious-smelling chunks of pot roast, carrots, onions, and potatoes.

Like last night's spaghetti, tonight's menu could be described as comfort food, the kind of meal she would have found in a diner, and yet Kate suspected that whatever Carmen had done to it, she had elevated it above ordinary diner fare. That was another reason why it was sad to see Rainbow's End deteriorate. The Sinclairs were blessed — it wasn't a word Kate used freely, but it was the only one that seemed to apply — to have Carmen, but even her talents weren't enough to attract guests and convince them to return.

"Tim told me they've had the place listed with a realtor since January but haven't had a single nibble," Roy said as he filled Sally's and his glasses with iced tea. On the opposite side of the table, the Schwartzes dressed their salads and seemed to be having a discussion about the merits of peach versus raspberry preserves for the hot rolls. Either they were not concerned about Rainbow's End or they realized there was nothing they could do to change it.

"Speaking of the Sinclairs, where are

they?" Sally asked. "When I was here before, the owners ate with the guests." She pointed to the gaps between each of the six chairs. "It might have been crowded last night, but there's plenty of room for them now."

"Maybe they're not comfortable socializing with guests that way," Kate said. Neither Angela nor Tim struck her as overly gregarious.

"Then they shouldn't have bought Rainbow's End." Roy frowned as he buttered a roll. "It's always been a friendly resort."

"It doesn't feel that way to me," Bob Schwartz said. Apparently he'd been paying more attention to the conversation than Kate had realized.

"Me neither," his wife chimed in.

"And that's a shame." The way Greg forked a chunk of potato with so much force that it broke into three pieces testified to his frustration.

"I'm afraid Rainbow's End will close for good." Roy shrugged as he added, "I never did understand that phrase 'for good.' It sure wouldn't be good if that happened here. The local economy doesn't need another hit."

The Sinclairs would move on. That was obviously their plan. But what about Carmen and KOB? Kate doubted there were other opportunities in Dupree for any of them.

Sally nodded as if she'd read Kate's thoughts. "Kate could fix it. People just need to know about Rainbow's End. A good advertising campaign is all it needs."

Kate knew better. Rainbow's End needed a huge infusion of cash to repair the cabins and improve the overall facility. While she'd never been a fan of the phrase "reinvent yourself," this was one case where it seemed to apply. A whole new image would help Rainbow's End.

"It's not that easy," she said, hoping someone would change the subject.

Though the meal was superb, no one seemed to enjoy it. Even the cobbler, as delicious as Carmen and Kevin had promised, did not boost anyone's spirits. The Schwartzes left as soon as they'd eaten the last bite of cobbler, leaving Roy and Sally deep in a discussion of how to improve the resort. Since she had no answers, Kate had no interest in joining that conversation.

"Can I interest you in another walk?" Greg asked when she refused a second cup of coffee.

"Sure." Kate tried to ignore the way her heart leapt at the thought of spending more time with Greg. Despite the fact that her matchmaking grandmother seemed to think they were well-suited, Kate wasn't romantically interested in him. Of course she wasn't. But he was the most interesting person at Rainbow's End, not to mention the one closest to her age. It was only natural that she had more in common with him than she did with Roy or the Schwartzes.

"What brought you here?" Kate asked as she and Greg strolled slowly along the lake's edge. The slight breeze had increased enough that it blew her hair off her neck and formed ripples on the lake. These weren't the crashing waves she'd experienced on Lake Erie or the pounding surf of the Jersey shore after a storm. Those spoke of power and majesty. These ripples brought a sense of serenity. Perhaps that was what Greg had sought when he left California.

"How did I pick Rainbow's End? You can blame it on an impacted wisdom tooth."

The response was so far from what she'd expected that Kate was certain Greg was joking. She tipped her head and tapped her ear, as if trying to clear it. "I must have something in my ear. I thought you said an impacted wisdom tooth."

"I did. And let me tell you that I don't recommend that particular experience to anyone." They'd reached the side of the lodge where the wide porch terminated in a dock. Greg extended his hand to help Kate climb onto the dock. "I was sitting in the dentist's waiting room, leafing through the usual magazines, when I saw a small ad for Rainbow's End. The image of Noah's ark at the end of the rainbow intrigued me. You don't see very many resorts advertising themselves as Christian." He shrugged and led her to a bench overlooking the lake. Though the sun had not yet set, it was low in the sky, backlighting the small island.

"I had no intention of actually coming here," Greg admitted when they were both seated. "The truth is, I had no intention of taking a vacation, but then my situation changed and I found myself being nudged in this direction."

Change of situation. It was one of the many euphemisms she'd heard for unemployment. Kate wouldn't ask about that. There was no point in reminding him of unpleasant circumstances, particularly when she had no way of resolving them. Instead, she focused on Greg's unusual choice of words. "Nudged?"

He nodded. "I tried to ignore it at first, but the idea wouldn't go away. When I woke at 3:00 a.m., having dreamt about the ark and the rainbow, I knew that God was sending me here. The problem is, I'm still not sure why. I just know I can't leave yet. How about you? What brought you here?"

Kate was silent for a moment, absorbing all that Greg had revealed about himself. In just a few sentences, he'd told her a great deal. If Sally had been here, she would have nodded and said this was additional proof that Greg was the right man for Kate. Sally wasn't here, but Kate was, and she was impressed by both the depth of Greg's faith and his willingness to be so open about it.

Though faith had always been an important part of her life, the men Kate had dated had been what she called Sunday Morning Christians. They attended church as regularly as a metronome ticked, but their faith didn't seem to have any impact on the other six and a half days of the week. Greg was different, and that was very appealing. But Kate wouldn't tell him that. Besides, it wasn't what Greg had asked about. He'd asked why she'd come to Rainbow's End.

"I thought it was pretty obvious that Sally's the reason I'm here." Kate saw Greg's eyes narrow and realized he deserved more than a curt response. He'd been open with her. Surely she owed him the same honesty. "Sally's not just my grandmother; she's my only family."

"Your parents . . ." Greg let the words trail off.

"Were killed when I was seven. It was a drive-by shooting, one of those senseless crimes that no one understands, much less a seven-year-old. We lived in Ohio at the time." Kate could still picture the small blond brick house that had been her first home and the kitchen where her mother had let her help make chocolate chip cookies. Of course, Kate's help had been limited to stirring the chips into the batter and licking the bowl.

"Both of my parents were only children, and my dad's parents had already died, so that left Sally and Grandpa Larry. They took me back to Buffalo and raised me." Kate stared into the distance, trying to control her emotions. "I owe them both so much. And now there's only Sally. When she told me it was her fondest wish to come back here, how could I refuse, especially when it turns out that her heart isn't as strong as it should be?"

"You couldn't." The sincerity in those two words told Kate that Greg understood, and that warmed her heart. When she'd told her boss, Heather had said she understood, but Kate still wasn't convinced of that. She had no doubts about Greg.

"I can't imagine life without Sally." There had been a time when Kate had thought that anyone over seventy was ancient, but that had been before her grandmother reached the milestone. Now, though she was realistic enough to know that Sally would not live forever and indeed did not want to, Kate was not ready to lose her.

"That's where we differ," Greg said, his voice a bit too hearty. Had she sounded so upset that he'd felt the need to comfort her? Before Kate could tell him that she was fine, he continued. "I'd like nothing more than to imagine life without my sisters."

"You're joking." His tone sounded ironic, but she wanted to be certain.

"Would I joke about four girls who've spent their entire lives expecting me to help them? I'm a year-round Santa Claus."

Kate smiled, her pensive mood chased away by Greg's lighthearted words. "I gather that they're younger."

"The oldest of them — that's Ashley — is ten years younger than me. Taylor's the youngest. She's thirteen years younger."

Kate did some quick math. "They must be close in age."

A chuckle was her answer. "My mom calls them the clockwork quartet. Just like clockwork, one arrived each September for four years. She won't admit it, but I suspect she and my father were hoping for another boy."

It was only the slightest change of tone. Kate might not have noticed it, but she'd been listening carefully, hoping to learn more about Greg and his relationship with his family. She kept remembering his comment about his father lamenting Greg's missing sports gene and wondered how that had affected him. The fact that his smile had disappeared when he'd pronounced the words "my father" told more than Greg probably realized he'd revealed.

"But you love your sisters dearly," Kate said, infusing her words with a smile.

Greg shrugged as a fish emerged, then plopped back into the water. "I'd love them more if they called me for things other than money. It seems one of them always needs something. A man can't think when his cell's ringing."

Kate looked out at the lake, once again silent except for the gentle lapping of water against the dock. "Then you came to the right place. Your cell will never ring here." That had to be a relief for a man who was unemployed. Kate was certain it was difficult for Greg to refuse his sisters' requests.

"You don't hear me complaining about

the lack of cell service," Greg said, "but I didn't realize that was one of Rainbow's End's attractions until I arrived. By then, I'd already taken other precautions."

Kate was intrigued. "Like what?"

"I told them I was going trekking in a South American jungle and would have only sporadic connectivity."

The idea was so preposterous that Kate laughed. "You're kidding, aren't you?"

"Absolutely not. I wanted some time to think."

And Rainbow's End was the perfect location for thinking, which brought Kate back to the dinnertime discussion. Rainbow's End was an anachronism, a place that offered solitude and serenity to a world that sought stimulation. It offered exactly what Greg needed right now, but it clearly did not meet either the newlyweds' or the Schwartzes' needs.

If there were more people like Greg, the resort might have a future, but Greg was one of a kind.

Rainbow's End was doomed.

9

The nightmare came again.

As he bolted upright, his body shaking in its aftermath, Greg switched on the light and tried to ease the pounding of his heart. It was always the same, coming without warning. He'd dream of something perfectly innocuous, and then all of a sudden he was standing on the edge of a precipice. In the throes of the dream, that seemed logical, although when he woke, Greg couldn't understand how a man so afraid of heights that he wouldn't visit observation decks had gotten to the top of that mountain crag. All he knew was that if he moved a foot in any direction, he'd plummet to his death.

And so he stood there, scarcely daring to breathe. He remained motionless, his heart throbbing as adrenaline coursed through his veins. One step. That's all it would take, but Greg wouldn't take that step. He wouldn't, he couldn't, for he wasn't ready to die.

And then, a second, a minute, an hour later — he had no sense of time, only that he stood on the edge for what seemed like an eternity — he would hear the voice. A man's voice. A familiar voice. One that he could never quite identify. Though he struggled to recall it when he wakened, Greg was unable to determine who had been calling him. He simply knew he'd heard the voice many times before.

"Jump! Jump!" the voice called to him.

Never. Though he made no sound for fear that even pronouncing a single word would send him over the cliff, the response echoed silently through his mind. He knew what awaited him if he jumped, if he so much as twitched. And then a large hand pressed the small of his back. It was always the same. Before he could stop himself, he was tumbling, a scream frozen in his throat.

Greg pushed himself to his feet and searched for a towel to wipe the sweat from his face. The dream always ended before he hit the ground, but that didn't stop him from remembering the sheer terror of falling into the unknown, all the while realizing that someone — probably someone he knew — had pushed him.

His logical mind told him that if the voice

was familiar, it must belong to whoever had pushed him. But who hated him enough to send him to his death? It was true that Greg had rivals. No one reached the position he had without them. But enemies who wanted him dead? That seemed far-fetched. Surely no one hated him that much.

It was only a dream, Greg reminded himself each time he woke in its clutches. Only a dream. A horrible dream.

It frightened him. It made sleep impossible. And yet it had positive effects. The days after the nightmares were different from all the others. Those days Greg worked feverishly, as if focusing every bit of his attention on the project at hand would keep the memories of the precipice and the terrifying fall at bay. It usually worked, but that was in California when he had mind-challenging projects. What could he do here to push from his brain the thoughts of that free fall into oblivion?

Greg blinked as the image of Kate's face appeared before him. It made no sense. She wasn't a project, wasn't even part of any project he'd ever worked on. She didn't need help. There was no reason he should be thinking of her. But he was, and that puzzled him.

Over the years that the nightmares had

plagued him, Greg had determined the pattern. Always before, when the nightmares had come, he'd been worried about some aspect of a project. He would feel as if he were deadlocked, faced with an insurmountable problem. He'd feared failure, and so he would gnaw on the problem like a terrier with a bone, approaching it from every possible angle. Nothing would help. At last, exhausted, he would fall asleep, and then the nightmare would come.

When he would waken, his only thought was to put the memories behind him, and so Greg would turn to the one thing that was virtually guaranteed to occupy every corner of his brain: his work. And, though he could not explain how or why it happened, somehow the terror of falling would become the catalyst he needed to turn his thoughts in a new direction. Those days when he would work maniacally in the aftermath of the nightmare, desperately trying to keep his fears at bay, he invariably found the breakthrough he needed.

Tonight was different. There was no reason for the nightmare. Greg no longer had a company to worry him. He had no thorny problem to solve. He should have slept dreamlessly. But he had not, and that made no sense. He'd slept well ever since he'd arrived at Rainbow's End. Fresh air, a bit of honest labor, and the absence of any serious worries had him sleeping like the proverbial baby. Until tonight.

Greg couldn't explain the nightmare any more than he could explain why he'd wakened thinking of Kate Sherwood. All he knew was that sleep was gone.

"Here we are." Kate smiled as she pulled the car into the diagonal spot in front of Sam's Bootery. She'd seen pictures of streets like these, but this was the first time she'd realized how much easier this was than parallel parking. It was too bad that the streets at home in New Jersey weren't wide enough to accommodate angled parking. There, rather than jockey her car into place, holding up traffic while she tried to fit it into a tight spot, Kate normally chose a parking lot, even though it meant walking several blocks. Dupree was different. Not only were the streets virtually devoid of traffic, but Kate hadn't seen a public parking lot anywhere.

Unfortunately, there was no need for one, with at least a third of the stores vacant. Even during the worst of the last recession, most of the shops near her apartment had remained open, the owners somehow managing to make it through the tough times. That obviously was not the case in Dupree. The Sip 'n' Sip appeared to be the only establishment still open in its block, and the store next to the bootery had a large closed sign in its front window. It was no wonder the Schwartzes had been disappointed. Dupree was not a thriving metropolis. Still, the bootery looked promising.

"You can't miss it," Roy had declared when he'd repeated the directions to reach the boot maker. He was right. Kate had turned from Lone Star Trail onto Pecan Street and two blocks later, there was Sam's Bootery, exactly where Roy had said it would be. If she'd had any doubts, the large fiberglass boot on the sidewalk in front of the plate glass window would have erased them.

"This is just what I was hoping for," Sally said, gesturing toward the huge boot.

"It's a little too big, don't you think?" Kate grabbed her bag and hurried around the car, planning to help Sally, but her grandmother had already swung her legs out of the car and shook her head when Kate offered her arm for support.

"I'm fine," Sally insisted. That seemed to be the case. Kate had noticed no shortness of breath when they'd walked to breakfast this morning, and Sally's cheeks had more color each day. Even if the changes were only temporary, it appeared that Rainbow's End was good for her. Kate offered a silent prayer of thanksgiving.

"The boot is wonderful." Sally stood next to it, chuckling at the fact that it was taller than she. "I need a picture to show the girls back home."

Kate nodded and pulled out her cell phone. "I'll mail them to you, so they'll be waiting when you return," she said when she'd taken several shots. Unlike Kate, Sally had not brought her phone, insisting that phones and vacations did not mix. Greg, it seemed, agreed with her.

Kate had spent hours last night thinking about Greg and his family. While there were two sides to every story, she couldn't help wondering about sisters whose primary interest in their brother was the gifts he could provide. Surely she had never treated Sally and Grandpa Larry that way.

"Let's go in," Sally said, her excitement visible in her heightened color. "I don't want to wait another minute." She might be in her seventies, but Sally was acting like a child at the first sight of snow. Kate smiled. It was wonderful to see her grandmother so enthusiastic.

As they opened the door to Sam's Bootery, a bell tinkled and a woman called out, "I'll be with you in a minute. I just need to finish this seam."

The shop was smaller than Kate had realized. Instead of the showroom she'd expected, the front of the store consisted of a five- or six-foot-deep waiting area with two wooden captain's chairs flanking a small coffee table. No pictures decorated the walls, and the room's sole ornament was an old-fashioned soft drink bottle with a purple hyacinth stuck into it. The makeshift vase stood on one end of the counter that served as a room divider and kept customers from approaching the door to the back room. It was what Kate would have called a distinctly masculine room, all except for the flower whose fragrance competed with the smells of leather and polish.

There was nothing else for them to look at, and so while they waited for the woman to emerge from the back room, Kate and Sally admired the half-dozen pairs of boots in the front window. Some were small enough to fit toddlers, while others would accommodate very large adult feet. Each was different in both color and design. What they had in common were intricate patterns and meticulous stitching. Kate might not know a lot about cowboy boot design, but she did know that these were as well constructed as her expensive Italian stilettos.

"Sorry for the delay."

Kate turned toward the woman's voice, blinking in astonishment at the sight of one of the most beautiful women she'd ever seen. Some might call her hair light brown, but Kate would have used the term caramel, with highlights that ranged from honey to molasses. Her blue eyes were as deep as the Texas sky, her nose and lips perfectly shaped, her cheekbones exquisitely chiseled. With her heart-shaped face and that glorious hair, the woman ought to be gracing a magazine cover, not working in a boot maker's shop in Dupree, Texas.

"How can I help you?" the woman asked.

"We're looking for Sam," Sally explained. "Roy Gordon sent us."

The woman's lips curved into a smile as she walked around the counter toward them. Though her jeans and shirt were ordinary, her boots stole the show. Bright red and intricately patterned, they were clearly meant to demonstrate Sam's expertise.

"I'm Sam," the woman said. "Samantha, actually. My father is the original Sam Dexter. When he retired and I took over the shop, some folks started calling me Sam."

Kate remained speechless, studying Samantha Dexter. Not only was her face drop-dead gorgeous, but her voice was melodic and her expression so engaging that Kate revised her first assessment. Why limit her to magazine ads? Samantha would be a natural for television. An instant later, Kate chided herself. Greg was right. It was difficult to stop thinking about work.

Extending her hand, Kate introduced herself and Sally, ending with, "We're hoping you can fit us in boots."

Samantha gave their feet an appraising look. "Six D and 7 1/2 AA."

"You're right." Sally's voice held more than a note of curiosity. "How'd you know that?"

"It's my business to know." A slight frown crossed Samantha's face. "I'm afraid I don't have any ready-mades in your sizes, but I can certainly create bespoke boots for you."

Kate smiled at the British term. She would have said custom, but perhaps boot makers had their own vernacular. "How long will that take?" She'd heard that people frequently waited months if not years for custom boots. Sally couldn't wait that long.

Samantha's blue eyes were serious as she said, "It takes me two days for each pair,

141

but you're in luck. My mom is in Austin visiting her sister, and my dad is bored at home. I wouldn't have to twist his arm too hard to convince him to help me. That way we could have both pairs ready by close of business tomorrow. You'll be able to enjoy them over the weekend."

Kate was virtually speechless over the time frame. Either boots were easier to make than she thought or Samantha and her father did not need much sleep.

But while Kate said nothing, Sally was not tongue-tied. "That would be wonderful," she said, her enthusiasm confirming that the boots were another part of her dream that was coming true.

The timing was perfect. Kate had only one other concern. "What price range are we looking at?" she asked. While Sally might tell her not to worry about money, there was no reason to spend a fortune on boots she'd wear for less than a month.

"That depends on the kind of leather you choose and how elaborate a design you want." Samantha pulled the largest boot from the window display. "This is ostrich. It's considerably more expensive than calf or shark."

"Shark?" Though Kate had a pair of snakeskin shoes, she had never worn shark.

"It's my favorite," Samantha told her. "It's virtually indestructible and will last a life-time."

Sally laid her hand on Kate's arm. "That's what you should get. You'll be wearing these boots for a long time."

Though Kate doubted she'd wear the boots once she returned home, she wouldn't argue. The price Samantha quoted was reasonable, and the quality appeared exceptional. Even if they remained in her closet once April ended, they'd be a souvenir of this time with Sally.

"I'm guessing these are your first boots, so let me show you what to look for in your next pair." Samantha pointed out the single-needle stitching and the wooden pegs that attached the sole, explaining that those were considered hallmarks of fine custom-made boots. "Doing it this way takes longer, but I think it's worth it. Now, let's pick a style." She reached below the counter and pulled out a photo album to show Kate and Sally some of the designs she'd made for other customers.

Kate stared at the pictures, marveling at the intricacy of the designs and the imaginative way Samantha blended multiple colors of stitching and leather to create one-of-a-kind footwear. These weren't just boots.

They were works of art.

"I don't want to pry, but I wondered . . ."

"How I stay in business here." Samantha finished the sentence.

Kate nodded, wondering how Samantha had guessed what she was going to ask. "Dupree isn't exactly a metropolitan area." It wasn't even on the road to anywhere. The fact that the highway that formed Lone Star Trail was a spur ending at Rainbow's End meant there were no casual visitors, no one just passing through. And with Rainbow's End attracting fewer and fewer guests, it was no wonder that Dupree's economy was shaky.

Samantha handed the book to Sally. "I have a website, and I've been written up in the Austin and San Antonio papers."

Kate's mind shifted into work mode. The website was essential, and the feature articles had undoubtedly boosted sales at the time they'd appeared, but neither was a continuing source of sales. Samantha needed more.

It had been relatively simple to increase repeat business for Sid's Seafood. One of Kate's recommendations had been that in addition to the core menu, Sid's would offer a special dish each month. The limited time availability and promotional price were designed to encourage patrons to make visits to Sid's at least a monthly event.

Boots were different. They were durable, and unlike shoes, Kate doubted many people felt the need for a closet filled with different styles and colors. Furthermore, the fact that Samantha was prepared to work on Kate's and Sally's boots immediately made Kate suspect that she had no other orders.

"Have you considered TV?" Kate asked. Whenever practical, Maddox and Associates advised a combination of print and television. "You'd reach more people that way."

Samantha nodded, frustration evident in her expression. "It's a good idea, but I doubt I could afford it."

"It might not be as expensive as you think." Kate's brain began to whirl as she searched for low- or no-cost ways to get Samantha and Sam's Bootery on TV. The woman had the poise and beauty to be a star, and her boots were — at least to Kate's untrained eye — exceptional.

"Listen to her," Sally said as she leafed through the book of photos. "Kate knows what she's talking about. My granddaughter is a hotshot New York advertising executive. And this is the design I want." She pointed to a pair of boots with entwined hearts.

"Only I want mine in shades of blue to go with my jeans."

When Samantha had made a note of the design, she turned to Kate. "I was going to show you my scrapbook. It's what I use for new customers in addition to the photos, but now I'm afraid you'll laugh. It'll probably seem amateur to you."

"Why don't I look at it while you fit Sally?"

Her hesitation evident, Samantha finally reached behind the counter and pulled out a large book. "Don't laugh too loud. Please." She motioned Sally to one of the captain's chairs and brought out an old-fashioned foot sizer, leaving Kate at the counter with the scrapbook.

Kate took a deep breath, inhaling the heavy scent of the hyacinth before she opened the book. Within seconds, she was engrossed, only dimly aware of the two women talking, finalizing the details of Sally's boots, while Kate turned page after page, studying the advertisements Samantha had included as well as the way she'd formatted the pages of FAQs.

"Pretty bad, huh?" Samantha stood only a foot away, obviously studying Kate as carefully as Kate was studying the book.

"It's not bad," Kate said, "but it could be

better." She pointed to the printout of one of the website pages. "If you switch the position of these two images and increase the font size, it would be more dramatic."

Samantha nodded. "I can do that. It's all on my computer."

"And you might want to darken these colors." Kate pointed to another page.

"Good idea."

Those were simple, no-cost changes. The one Kate was going to propose next wasn't. "What I really think you need is a new logo, one that incorporates your picture." Though Samantha said nothing, she seemed taken aback, so Kate continued her explanation. "I doubt there are very many women boot makers, and I'm willing to bet that even if there are others, they're not as photogenic as you. I think you should capitalize on both your gender and your looks."

Samantha was not convinced. Her brow furrowed as she said, "I don't know. My dad . . ."

The words triggered the memory of Greg speaking of his father. To Kate's relief, Samantha's voice held none of the tension Greg's had. Instead, she simply seemed concerned, perhaps not wanting to change something her father had done.

"It's your business now," Kate said firmly.

"Obviously, I've never met him, but the fact that your father turned the business over to you makes me think he'd approve of anything you do to make it stronger."

The furrows disappeared, and Samantha smiled. "You might be right."

10

"You look awful," Roy said as he pulled out his usual chair at their usual table. Like most of the stores in Dupree, the Sit 'n' Sip was narrow and deep. The primary seating area was the counter that spanned the width, but proprietor Russ Walker had installed a single booth in the corner next to the front window and two tables for four. For reasons he'd never explained, even when he came alone, Roy sat at the table closest to the door.

"Good morning to you too." Greg refused to rise to the bait.

Roy nodded when he'd called his order to Russ. The morning rush, as Russ described the half-dozen people who came to the Sit 'n' Sip for breakfast, was gone, leaving Greg and Roy the only customers. "My boys were like that too. Didn't want to talk about their problems. They figured it wasn't manly."

That wasn't the reason Greg hadn't confided in his father. After a few painful attempts, he realized that Dad didn't understand.

"It was a rough night," Greg admitted. "I didn't sleep much."

"Dreaming about Kate?"

Greg almost choked on his coffee. "What makes you think that?" The dream hadn't been about Kate, but thoughts of her had filled his brain as soon as he'd wakened.

Roy waited until Russ slid their meals in front of them and returned to his post behind the counter before he answered. "Not hard to figure out. She's a beautiful single woman. You're a healthy single man. Only natural you'd dream about her."

Greg slathered jam on his toast as an excuse not to meet Roy's eyes. "I didn't actually dream about her."

"But you thought about her."

Unwilling to lie, Greg nodded.

"I thought so." When he'd eaten the first of his eggs, Roy looked up again. "I figured you were like me — interested in the new guests."

Greg was interested in Kate, but not in the way Roy thought. He was realistic enough to know that while their lives might have converged for a month, they would diverge again. "Kate's an interesting woman, but I'm not looking for romance," he said, hoping Roy would take that as a signal to change the subject.

Roy's laugh turned into a guffaw. "Then you're a fool. Look at me. I'm seventy-three years old. I married and buried the most wonderful woman in the world, but that doesn't stop me from looking. I figure you never know. Lightning could strike twice."

Greg was still waiting for the first time.

"That was a nice thing you did," Sally said as she and Kate left Sam's Bootery.

Kate shrugged and pulled her car keys out of her bag, tapping the remote to unlock the doors. "Heather might not approve of my giving free advice, but I didn't see any harm in it. Who knows? Samantha might ask us to design a whole campaign for her." It was unlikely. Even if Samantha were interested, Sam's Bootery was too small a client for Maddox to care about. Heather and Nick sought national and sometimes international clients. But it had been fun helping Samantha.

"It was nice," Sally repeated. "You know what else would be nice? Checking out the other shops. Let's walk."

Though Kate doubted there'd be anything noteworthy, she and Sally had nothing else planned for the morning. Selecting boots had taken less time than Kate had expected, and though Samantha had appeared willing to chat with Sally, Kate had hurried her grandmother out of the store. Samantha needed to call her father and begin work on Kate's and Sally's boots.

As Kate had feared, the other shops on the same block as Sam's Bootery were either empty or temporarily closed. When they crossed the side street, Sally glanced at the store on the opposite corner. "Hill Country Pieces," she read. "Let's go there. You know how I love quilts."

Kate did indeed. Though Sally had never quilted anything, declaring that she had neither the patience nor the manual dexterity to make the tiny, evenly spaced stitches that the best quilts boasted, she attended every quilting show she could find.

They crossed the street and approached the store. Sally stopped abruptly to gesture toward the quilt hanging in the window. "Look, Kate. It's a rainbow."

Not just a rainbow but one of the most exquisite quilts Kate had ever seen. The artist had used hundreds — perhaps thousands — of tiny pieces of fabric to create a landscape. The Hill Country's green hills formed the background, while bluebonnets and half a dozen other wildflowers mingled with prickly pear cactus in the foreground. Above them all was a magnificent rainbow, each color blending into the next.

"That's incredible," Kate said softly. She'd accompanied Sally to a number of shows and had seen pieces that rivaled fine art. This was as good as any of the blue ribbon winners. "Incredible," she repeated. What was incredible was not simply the quilt but the fact that Dupree had at least two extremely talented artists in residence. Kate wondered what other surprises she might find if she and Sally continued their exploration.

"You should buy the quilt," Sally told her.

Kate tipped her head to the side, considering. "It's gorgeous, but I can't picture it in my apartment." Where she could picture it was at Rainbow's End. It would be perfect for one of the long empty walls in the dining room. The Sinclairs were unlikely to agree, especially since they were trying to sell the resort, but surely the new owners would realize the benefit of showcasing local talent. Kate began picturing quilts on all the beds and small wall hangings in the living areas of the cabins.

The new owners could . . . Kate's heart sank at the realization that there might be no new owners. It was possible that, if they couldn't find a buyer, the Sinclairs would simply close the resort. And that would be a shame. Kate focused her eyes on the beautiful quilt. That was much more pleasant than dwelling on the problems of a place she'd first seen less than forty-eight hours ago.

"I can tell you've fallen in love with the quilt," Sally said. "Let's go inside and buy it."

No matter how beautiful it was, Kate wasn't in the market for a quilt. She wouldn't buy that quilt, but she would look for a smaller version, perhaps made up as a pillow, as part of Sally's Christmas gift.

Soft music and the sweet perfume of scented candles greeted them as they entered the shop. While Sam's Bootery had a distinctly masculine feel, this shop was 100 percent feminine with pale mauve walls, a thick carpet in a deeper shade of mauve, and chintz covered chairs.

A woman whom Kate guessed to be in her midtwenties rose from behind the counter and approached them, introducing herself as Lauren Ahrens. An inch or so above Kate's own five and a half feet, Lauren was dark-haired and at least ten pounds lighter than Kate. Dressed in a denim skirt, boots that had undoubtedly come from Sam's

Bootery, and an intricately quilted jacket, she looked like a walking advertisement for Dupree. Though not strikingly beautiful like Samantha, she moved with assurance, as if she were comfortable in her own skin.

"Are you interested in anything specific?" Lauren asked when Sally had introduced herself and Kate.

Sally nodded. "I'm trying to convince my granddaughter to buy the quilt you have in your window."

A twinge of regret crossed Lauren's face and she shook her head slowly. "I'm sorry, but that's not for sale. I made it for my daughter. I sometimes make duplicates of a design, but not this one."

Though she had no intention of buying the quilt, Kate found herself battling unexpected disappointment. "It's a beautiful piece," she told the store's proprietor, "and perfect for a child. How old is your daughter?"

"Seven, although some days I think she's seven going on forty. Just this morning, Fiona told me it was time for me to start dating, because she wants a father." Lauren's face flushed. "Oh, listen to me, rattling on about my life when all you wanted was to look at a quilt."

Kate was getting used to the friendliness

of Dupree's residents and found that she didn't mind it. To the contrary, she — the woman who barely knew the other tenants in her apartment building — was intrigued by the willingness of both Samantha and Lauren to share part of their lives with strangers. Kate glanced at Lauren's left hand, the wedding ring suggesting that she was a widow rather than a divorcee. "Quilts and conversation. It's a great combination."

"That's what Patrick used to say." Tears filled Lauren's eyes. "I'm sorry. It's only been six months."

Sally, who'd been silent, reached forward to hug her. "You poor dear. It's hard to be a parent when you're dealing with your own sorrow."

She was speaking from experience, Kate knew. At the time, Kate hadn't realized how difficult it had been for Sally and Grandpa Larry to raise a child when their own was gone. The shooting had changed not just Kate's life but also her grandparents', thrusting them back into child rearing at a time when they'd been looking forward to a simpler lifestyle. It was only years later, after Grandpa Larry died, that Kate fully appreciated the sacrifice her grandparents had made.

Lauren brushed the tears from her eyes

and forced her lips upward. "It is hard," she admitted, "but each day is a bit easier. Now, can I show you any of my other quilts? I have other landscapes."

But none would compare to the rainbow. Kate and Sally admired Lauren's quilts and spent a few minutes looking through the album she had of her work, but though the pieces were beautiful, none touched Kate's heart the way the rainbow had. "We'll be back," Kate promised. She would bring Sally at least once, and she would definitely come alone to select her grandmother's Christmas present.

"Come anytime, even if it's just to talk." Lauren gestured to the empty chairs. "As you can see, I'm not overwhelmed with customers right now."

That, it appeared, was a common refrain in Dupree.

A burst of heat assailed Kate and Sally as they left the air-conditioned comfort of the store, and Sally teetered for a second.

"Are you all right?" Kate had seen the sadness in Sally's eyes when she'd comforted Lauren and knew she was reliving her own losses.

Sally nodded but refused to move. Instead, she stared at the quilt in the window. "It reminds me of you," she said, her voice filled with nostalgia. "Do you remember how you used to tell me you wanted to chase rainbows and see what was really at the end?"

Kate nodded, recalling how often she'd said that the first summer after her parents' death. Somewhere deep inside, she'd believed that if she found the end of the rainbow, her parents might be there. And so, every time the rain had stopped, she had rushed outdoors, searching for a rainbow. Most days she'd been disappointed, and the few times one had appeared, Kate had remained frozen with fear.

"You never did chase one. Why not?"

"I was afraid of getting lost." That had been Kate's worst nightmare, being as lost and alone as she had felt the night her parents were killed. Though the neighbors who kept her while Sally and Grandpa Larry made their way to Ohio had been kind and had seemed to understand when she'd screamed because she'd wakened and hadn't realized where she was, nothing they could say or do had erased the fact that Kate was alone. Even after Sally had arrived to comfort Kate, telling her she was not lost and that she would not be alone, the fear had remained. And so Kate had never once chased a rainbow.

"You're still afraid." It was a statement, not a question.

Kate shrugged. "That's why I have GPS. I can't get lost that way."

Her grandmother was silent for a moment, her gaze moving from the quilt to Kate and back again. "You might not be able to get lost literally, but it seems to me you're still afraid of taking risks."

Bristling at her grandmother's unexpected words, Kate countered with a question. "What's wrong with that? I don't see anything bad about security." That was one reason she wanted the partnership so much. It would give her an extra level of security, knowing that she couldn't be fired if one campaign failed. When she'd heard Grandpa Larry talking about colleagues being let go and how only the partners were safe, her determination to become a partner had deepened.

Sally shook her head slowly, her eyes filled with sorrow. "Oh, Kate, you're missing so much. If you don't take a chance, you'll never have the adventure of trying new things or the thrill of exploring the unknown." She gripped Kate's arm and stared into her eyes. "I know you think you're happy with your life, but I wish you'd chase rainbows. Just once. Promise me you'll do it."

"I can't."

11

"I think we're getting better." Greg leaned back on the bench and took a long swig of water. Though the sun was almost directly overhead and Kate could have sworn it was at least a hundred degrees in the shade, he appeared only slightly winded. She, on the other hand, could barely manage to catch her breath. Those hours at the gym should have prepared her for a little tennis, but apparently they hadn't. She was as out of breath as Sally the day they arrived. Could it have been only two days ago? Kate felt as if she'd been in Texas far longer.

She took a sip from the water bottle Greg had handed her before she responded. "Are you basing your statement on the fact that I actually scored in the last match?" Admittedly, she'd been proud of that accomplishment, even though it had felt like a fluke. It was difficult to believe she'd made any substantial improvement since yesterday.

Greg nodded, his green eyes dancing with mirth. "That and the fact that I managed to return more than one ball in ten. Another five or ten years and we might be passable players."

"Another five or ten years and my muscles might have recovered." Although that seemed about as likely as her playing at Wimbledon. Kate rubbed her upper arm, trying to massage out the pain in her biceps, triceps — some muscle. "Rainbow's End could use a hot tub."

His bottle empty, Greg tossed it back into his bag and reached for another. "I was thinking the same thing. As I recall, hot tubs are pretty good for soaking out aches. You don't have a patent on those, you know." He flexed his arms and let out a melodramatic groan.

"Poor baby." Kate gave him a patently false smile of commiseration as she added, "As I recall, tennis was your idea."

"But you were the one who wanted exercise."

"True, and now I want a hot tub. You sound as if it's been a long time since you were in one, but I've had a close acquaintance with them and their therapeutic properties."

"It's been almost fifteen years," Greg

admitted. That didn't surprise Kate. Somehow she couldn't picture him at a gym or spa. It wasn't simply that he claimed to have no natural talent for sports. More to the point, she imagined he had kept himself too focused on his college courses and then his job to have time for organized exercise. He struck her as someone who'd go for a long run late at night or early in the morning. Though Sally had accused Kate of choosing the sure path for her career — and Kate had to admit there was some truth in that observation — the path had included a gym membership. According to Grandpa Larry, gyms were good places to meet potential clients, and so she'd signed up for one as soon as she moved to New Jersey.

"I tried a hot tub my first year at Stanford," Greg said. "After that, I was too busy studying and working as many hours as I could to have time for much more than a nightly run."

It was what Kate had surmised. "So you worked while you were in college. I did too." When Greg raised an eyebrow, encouraging her to continue, Kate said, "I was lucky to get a job on campus. Nothing glamorous, I assure you. I worked in the stockroom at the bookstore, but that and two scholarships covered tuition."

"Which left just room and board."

Kate shook her head. "Not even that. I was a townie. I lived with Sally and Grandpa Larry and commuted to class. The only times I stayed in a dorm were when there was too much snow to drive home." Kate smiled, remembering those nights. "I didn't get much studying done then."

"That's because it was a novelty. You'd have settled into a routine if you'd lived there." As a bright yellow bird flitted by, Greg turned his attention to it, watching until it was out of sight. "Do you know what kind that was?" When Kate shook her head, he nodded. "Me, neither. I need to buy a field guide the next time I'm in town. But we were talking about school. It's interesting that you were content to stay at home while I couldn't wait to escape."

That made it sound as if she had no sense of adventure. If Sally were here, she'd probably say it was evidence that Kate was unwilling to take risks. Surely that wasn't true. There had been other, more important reasons why she'd stayed at home.

"I didn't want my grandparents going into debt for my education," she told Greg. It was what she'd told everyone at the time, and at the time she had believed it. Now, with Sally's words fresh in her mind, Kate wondered if her grandparents' finances had been her primary motivation. While no one would have called them wealthy, they weren't poor. Furthermore, Grandpa Larry had taken Kate aside and told her that if she wanted to live in a dorm, they'd find the money. Was Sally right that Kate had been afraid to take the risk of moving away from home? By the time she'd graduated and been offered her first position in Manhattan, it hadn't seemed like such an intimidating prospect, but when she'd been eighteen . . .

"I know what you mean." Kate blinked, wondering if Greg had somehow read her thoughts, but when he continued, she realized he was talking about college debt. "I couldn't ask my parents for money, but I didn't have a lot of choice. Even if I'd wanted to stay at home, there are no colleges within commuting range of Orchard Slope. Besides, I was determined to go to Stanford, so I wound up with enormous loans."

"That must be hard now." Kate couldn't imagine how stressful unemployment combined with substantial debt must be, especially since he had four sisters who regarded him as an open checkbook. And yet Greg showed no signs of worry. A man who was concerned about money wouldn't have bought top-of-the-line tennis racquets and clothes.

He shrugged and took another swig of water. "They're paid off. I was one of the lucky ones. And, no, I didn't win the lottery. I just worked really hard."

He must have, and it must have been lucrative. "What kind of work did you do?"

"Software engineering."

The pieces fit. Stanford. A job in Silicon Valley. The ease with which he'd helped her connect to the internet. Kate grinned. "No wonder you knew how to fix my laptop."

Greg met her grin, his eyes twinkling with amusement. "That's hardware, not software, but yeah, you could say I know my way around computers. When I was a kid, I used to stay late at school to use the ones there, and then I delivered papers and ran errands to buy my own."

Kate's grandparents had paid for her first computer. Compared to Greg, she felt like a pampered princess. While she'd worked as a teenager at one of the fast-food jobs that were practically a rite of passage, she'd never been as single-minded as Greg seemed to have been. He sounded like the definition of a workaholic. Perhaps that was part of the reason he was doing repairs here. "Do you miss it?"

"The work? Not really. Last year was . . . difficult." The long pause told Kate that Greg was choosing his words carefully. Before she had the opportunity to ask him about the job that had paid so well, he shifted so that he was facing her directly. "How about you? Have you adjusted to being on vacation?"

"I'm getting there." In Kate's experience, it took the better part of a week to relax enough to forget work, and by then, the vacation was over. But this trip was different. It marked the first time she'd taken more than a single week's vacation. It would be interesting to see how she felt next week. Right now she was definitely still in the adjustment phase.

"I'm really enjoying being able to spend more time with Sally, and Dupree has its charms." When she closed her eyes, Kate could still picture Lauren Ahrens's beautiful quilt and the exquisite tooling of Samantha's boots. "I couldn't imagine living there, though."

"You'd miss the Golden Arches that much?"

Kate shook her head. "It's the pace. Everyone here moves as if they have all the time in the world."

"Maybe they do."

■ ■ ■ ■

Sally chuckled as she switched on her e-reader, thinking about her granddaughter's reaction if she could see her. Kate thought she was napping each afternoon during those tennis matches. Admittedly, she'd done that yesterday. There was no denying that she'd been tired then, but today she felt energized and decided to read. She wouldn't tell Kate, of course. If Kate knew, she'd stop playing tennis, and that was one thing Sally didn't want to happen. Even if she didn't realize it, the matches were important for Kate. She needed them, and not just for the exercise. Kate needed time with a man who viewed her as more than arm candy.

Sally chuckled again. That was such a silly term. She couldn't recall where she'd heard it, but she'd found the whole concept ridiculous until she met Pete and Lou and realized that they regarded Kate as little more than arm candy. Greg was smarter than that.

Settling back in the comfortable chair, Sally scrolled through her books. Today Suzanne Woods Fisher would transport her to the seemingly simpler life of the Amish. And when she finished that, Sally knew she'd be caught up in a world of suspense, thanks to Irene Hannon's latest release.

Though she was deeply engrossed in the story, the knock on the door brought her back to Rainbow's End. "Sally, are you there?"

Her heart began to pound, and Sally felt her face flush as she laid the e-reader on the table and jumped to her feet. Her cardiologist might be alarmed, but Sally was not. She knew what was causing her to act like a schoolgirl. Roy. She'd recognize that voice anywhere.

"What are you doing here?" she asked as she opened the door and ushered him inside.

The man was too handsome for his own good. Kate might not agree, but Sally found his old-fashioned glasses and those gray eyes endearing. And then there were his lips. Right now they curved in a mischievous smile, setting Sally's heart to fluttering again.

"Is that any way to welcome the man who's come to play chess with you?" Though the words could have sounded harsh, they were spoken with good humor.

"Chess?" Her heartbeat accelerated again at the unexpected but very welcome invitation. Sally knew she'd never even mentioned the game, much less told Roy that it was her favorite, yet here he was, offering to play with her. The man wasn't just handsome; he was wonderful.

"Yes, chess. An ancient game with kings, queens, pawns, knights. I thought you might enjoy it." As Roy shook his head, a lock of hair tumbled over his forehead. He needed a haircut, but Sally would be the last to tell him that. Though Roy's hair might not be the latest style, it suited him, and the unruly locks gave him a boyish air.

"I know you like Clue, but it's not much fun with only two players." Roy's expression turned slightly sheepish. "I guess I made an assumption. I'd better ask. Do you know how to play chess? We can do something else if you'd prefer."

Sally grinned at the proof that chivalry was still alive. "Do I play chess? You bet your queen I do. There's nothing I'd rather do today." Especially since Roy would be her opponent. Though she played regularly online, there was nothing that compared to a real game, and one with an attractive man her own age . . . Sally felt her cheeks begin to flush again. "Prepare to be trounced."

"In your dreams." Roy nodded at the door. "I checked, and there's a nice set in the main lodge."

Sally looked for a pad and pencil. "I need to leave Kate a note."

"No, you don't. She and Greg are still on the tennis court. We can tell them what we're doing as we walk by."

When Roy had closed the door behind them, he bent his arm, placing Sally's hand in the crook of his elbow. Seconds later, they were walking toward the lodge, arm in arm, her heart singing with pleasure.

It was odd. When Kate had linked arms with her, Sally had bristled, knowing her granddaughter thought she needed help. It was different with Roy. His gesture was one of chivalry, not concern, and that felt oh so good. The way Sally felt right now, she could walk all the way to Dupree. Wouldn't that shock Kate?

"You are good," Roy said twenty minutes later when she captured another of his pawns.

Sally leaned back in her chair and smiled. There were so many reasons to smile — the beautiful lodge with its views of the lake, the ivory and ebony chess set with the fancy inlaid board, the challenge of the game, and Roy. Most of all, Roy. "Did you think I was exaggerating?"

The man who'd proven to be a worthy opponent shook his head. "It wasn't that. I know it's been awhile since your husband died. I thought you might be out of practice."

It was Sally's turn to shake her head. "Larry didn't have the patience for chess. I've been playing online."

"Me too, but this is more fun."

"It certainly is. Kate plays with me occasionally, but she's not much of a challenge." Roy was, but even if he hadn't been an expert player, Sally would have enjoyed the game. There was something exciting about being with a man her age.

"Roy Junior's the only one of my kids worth setting up a board for, but for the past few years, when we get together we're so rushed that there's no time for a game."

Though Roy had alluded to children before, this was the first time he'd mentioned a name. Sally took the opening. "How many children do you have?"

"Three. Roy Junior, Toby, and Will." Roy's smile was one of obvious pride. "They're all married, each with two kids. All boys. Barb was disappointed, because she wanted to buy dolls and frilly dresses, but I couldn't be happier. Think of all those boys just waiting to learn to fish."

Roy stared at the lake for a few seconds,

making Sally wonder if he was picturing himself and his sons in a fishing boat. "It's great to see them happy and settled. I only wish they were closer." His eyes darkened. "The truth is, I can't blame them for not staying here. There's no future in Dupree."

The number of vacant storefronts Sally had seen in downtown Dupree this morning seemed to confirm that. Though she hadn't said anything to Kate, Sally had found it alarming and wondered how much longer Samantha and Lauren would be able to stay open. "Have you considered moving closer to your sons?"

Roy studied the board for a moment before moving a rook. "They're all spread out. Birmingham, Poughkeepsie, Spokane. I won't play favorites and move near one of them."

That had to be difficult. It was no wonder Roy came to Rainbow's End for dinner. Even though there were few guests, the combination of superb food and some companionship must be a powerful lure. "I'm fortunate that Kate's only an hour's flight away and that I see her at least once a month," Sally told Roy.

"But you still worry about her."

"I do. I wish she were settled like your boys. I worry about what she'll do when

I'm no longer here." Though she hadn't thought that either Pete or Lou was the right man for her granddaughter, Sally hadn't given up hope that Kate would find the perfect husband or at least a close friend. Kate might think she was self-sufficient, but everyone needed emotional support occasionally.

"The worries don't stop when they marry. You just develop different ones," Roy said, his eyes once more meeting hers. "The funny thing is, at the same time that I'm worrying about them, I know the boys are worried about me. They want me to move to an old folks' home." Roy's laugh was strained. "Can you imagine that?"

Sally could. Though Kate hadn't said anything, the majority of Sally's friends had either downsized their homes or moved to a senior community. "Why do they think you should move?"

"They're convinced I'm lonely."

Sally gave up plotting her next move. This was more important. "Are you?"

"Sometimes."

"Me too." More often than she wanted to admit.

Roy grinned. "Let's see if we can work on that."

■ ■ ■ ■

Greg opened the door to his cabin and tossed his gym bag on the floor, giving it a kick for good measure. It didn't ease his frustration any more than blaming Kate did. There was no point in being annoyed at her. Her questions hadn't been intrusive, and it certainly wasn't her fault that their discussion of college had revived memories he'd tried to relegate to the back of his mind. The argument he and his father had had over Stanford hadn't been their first, and it wasn't their last, yet it was the one that was the most deeply etched in his memory.

"You think you're better than everyone in Orchard Slope, don't you?" Dad had demanded, his face flushed with anger. "You think that by being the first to go to some fancy school that costs more than most folks make in a year, you'll be accepted. You're wrong. Everyone knows what you are. That'll never change."

He'd clenched his fists, pounding one on the table that separated him from Greg. "If you think I'm going to take out a second mortgage to pay for it, you're wrong about that too. If you want to go to Stanford" — he spat the name as if it were an epithet —

175

"you're on your own. I won't give you a dime."

And he hadn't. Freshman year had been rougher than Greg had expected, mostly because he'd been working thirty to forty hours a week in addition to taking a punishing course load, but by his sophomore year, he'd grown accustomed to the schedule. Junior year, when he'd landed a job with a software firm that paid enough that he could work fewer hours, had been even easier.

The relatively light schedule had proven to be a godsend, because it had given Greg the time to think about other things, including his mother's complaints about the incompatible systems and paperwork problems at Orchard Slope's cannery. Her comments had triggered ideas, one leading to another. The end result was Sys=Simpl, the software product that had transformed Orchard Slope's nerdy misfit into a billionaire.

It had all ended well. There was no reason to dwell on a conversation that had taken place fifteen years earlier, and yet Greg could not dismiss the memory. Drew would have said it was because Greg had unfinished business with his father. Though Greg

didn't always agree with Drew, he wondered
if maybe — just maybe — Drew was right.

12

On Friday, Kate woke with a sense of anticipation. Today was the day she and Sally would pick up their boots, and — if she could find a way to distract her grandmother — the day that Kate would talk to Lauren about Sally's Christmas pillow. Inspired by the beauty of Lauren's designs, she had begun envisioning one that incorporated a cowboy boot, a rainbow, and a prickly pear. Though the elements might seem incongruous, Kate was certain that Lauren could find a way to turn them into a beautiful design.

Kate had practically jogged to the main lodge, smiling as she pictured Sally's pleasure on Christmas morning. She wasn't smiling now. She frowned as she opened her email and found an urgent message from Heather. It was the first time Heather had sent more than her daily "Are you ready to come back?" email. Today Kate's boss had a question about the Sid's Seafood campaign and was annoyed because she couldn't find the files.

Though Kate was confident that she'd put all the links to her files into the firm's database, there was nothing to be gained by suggesting that Heather wasn't looking in the right place, not when Kate had copies of all her work on her laptop and could send them to Heather. She attached the files to Heather's email and clicked send. They'd be in New York in seconds. Or not. Kate frowned again as she realized how long it would take to transmit half a dozen large files at the snail's pace of dial-up.

Realizing there was no point in being aggravated by something she couldn't change, Kate rose and walked to the window. Other than the momentary aggravation of Heather's brusquer than normal email, it was a beautiful morning. The sun was rising, gradually transforming the gray sky with fingers of pink and orange, while the lake cast off the shroud of darkness.

Though she'd spent most of her life near Lake Erie and never failed to be awed by the majesty of the Great Lakes, there was something almost hypnotizing about the calm of this small body of water. It had no waves. It was small enough that she could see the other shore, and yet Bluebonnet Lake seemed somehow mysterious, as if something unknown rested behind the tiny island. That was nothing more than fancy. The reality was, it was an ordinary lake in a part of Texas with more than its share of lovely lakes.

Kate stared at the water, surprised when she saw an object moving smoothly across its surface. At this time of the day with no wind, the lake should be perfectly calm. For a few seconds, she could not identify the object. Then as the sun rose, revealing additional details, she realized what she was seeing was a rowboat. Greg. He must have been on the lake before sunrise.

Kate smiled. Even though he'd claimed to have disappointed his father by not being athletic, judging from the ease of his strokes, it was clear that Greg had more than a passing acquaintance with oars. Perhaps his father believed the only sports that mattered were team sports like football, baseball, and basketball.

Reluctantly, Kate left the window to take a quick look at the email status bar and calculate how much longer the transmission would take. Knowing she had at least five more minutes, she returned to the window and sank into one of the wicker chairs.

Watching Greg was more entertaining than looking at the agonizingly slow progress of her email.

For what seemed like the hundredth time, Kate wondered exactly what he'd done in Silicon Valley. Most men were eager to talk about their careers, but Greg was reticent, almost secretive about his. There must be a reason. Perhaps he'd worked on some kind of high-security government contract. That would explain both his reluctance to share details as well as his ability to repay college loans in just a few years. Whatever he had done, Kate was glad he was here. Having Greg Vange at Rainbow's End made her life much more interesting.

She hadn't expected that. There were many things she hadn't expected, including the way she felt this morning. Rested, happy, and surprisingly content. Perhaps that was the reason why, despite Heather's email, her heart bubbled with pleasure at the sight of Greg in the rowboat. Perhaps that was why her mind was filled with images of the sun breaking through the clouds and coloring the sky. Kate closed her eyes for a second, savoring the rich aroma of coffee that had begun to filter into the room. Though it wasn't a term she normally used, today she felt almost peaceful.

Smiling as the status bar reached 100 percent and disappeared, Kate logged off and unplugged her laptop. It was no wonder Sally had insisted they come here. For all its shortcomings, Rainbow's End was a special place.

Ten more yards. He could make it. He knew he could. One foot in front of the other. That's all it took. One more step. Five yards. Now there was no question. He'd get there. Of course he would. One more step. His breath coming in ragged pants, Greg forced himself to sprint the final distance. Only when he reached the top of the small hill did he pause to pull his cell phone from his pocket.

Bouncing from one leg to the other to keep his muscles from tightening, he looked at the display. It was a good thing no one else was around to witness his daily battle with Ranger Hill. His father would scoff at the thought that Greg, the nerd who'd spent every spare minute studying computer code, the boy who'd been so inept on a football team that even the coach had admitted he was hopeless, was now rowing and jogging up a hill every day, not to mention playing tennis with a beautiful blonde.

Though he'd run for years, Greg had

quickly discovered that jogging on flat pavement was far different from climbing Ranger Hill. There was nothing pleasant about feeling as if your lungs were about to explode while your calves were shrieking for mercy. But there was a silver lining to the dark cloud, a pot of gold at the end of the rainbow. Greg grimaced at the clichés. The simple fact was, the first day he'd forced himself to jog all the way to the top, his phone had begun to ring. It wasn't a miracle, but the fact that he could get a signal here meant he didn't have to drive all the way to Dupree to check messages, and that gave him another incentive to put on his running shoes each morning.

He scanned the list. Two texts from his sisters, thanking him for the money he'd transferred. The expressions of gratitude were a bit belated, but that wasn't unusual. Three texts and two voice mails from Drew. The latter was unusual. Normally Drew preferred texting to actually speaking with Greg.

Greg played back the voice mails. "I've got to talk to you. It's important." Quintessential Drew. No greeting, no social niceties, just straight to the point. The second, delivered two hours after the first, repeated the message but with more emphasis. Greg could ignore them. He probably should ignore them. But if he did, he'd never know why Drew was so agitated. The man was normally unflappable.

Greg glanced at the phone's clock, calculating the time difference. He might wake Drew if he called now, but it was either now or not at all, since he had no intention of using Rainbow's End's phone. Angela wouldn't mind, but Greg would, because the caller ID would tell Drew exactly where he was.

Now or not at all? Now won.

"Hello?" Sleep muddled Drew's voice.

"It's Greg. I got your messages. What's up?" Greg heard the sharp intake of breath and realized his former partner hadn't expected him to call.

"Where are you? We need to talk." All traces of sleep had vanished, replaced by an unmistakable urgency in Drew's voice.

As he ran in place, determined to keep his muscles from tightening, Greg tried to imagine what was bothering Drew. "We can talk over the phone."

"No. It needs to be face-to-face."

Greg frowned. He'd heard that tone before, and he knew what it meant. Drew had something major in mind, and he wasn't certain Greg would agree. "What's

going on? Did you and . . ." He paused, trying to recall the name of Drew's latest
girlfriend. "Whatever her name is set a
date?"

"It was Shelley, and no, that's over. I realized she's not the one. This is more important."

"More important than entering the state
of wedded bliss?" Greg infused his voice
with sarcasm. "I distinctly recall you telling
me nothing was more important than finding the woman you wanted to spend the rest
of your life with."

Drew's search for the perfect mate had
resulted in a seemingly endless string of
dates and three broken engagements. It had
also convinced Greg that remaining a bach-
elor was not the worst thing that could happen. But that was before Kate Sherwood
had arrived at Rainbow's End. In less than
seventy-two hours, she'd made him recon-
sider the whole idea of dating and marriage.

"This is more important," Drew declared,
his voice harsh with urgency. "Just tell me
where you are, and I'll catch the next flight."

"Nope." Greg looked down into Firefly
Valley, his eyes resting on the rooftop of
Rainbow's End's main lodge and the small
lake. If there was one thing he knew, it was
that this was not the place for Drew. Not

only would he be out of his element here, but he'd destroy the fragile peace Greg had begun to wrap around himself.

"What do you mean, nope?"

"Exactly that. I'm not going to tell you where I am." The point of coming here was to put his former life behind him and start over.

"You're not really in South America, are you?"

Greg felt a prickle on the back of his neck. He hadn't told Drew where he was going, simply that he needed to take some time off to think. The only people who thought he was in South America were his family, and that meant that Drew had contacted them. Whatever he wanted must indeed be important for him to have gone to such lengths. Though he'd given Drew his parents' phone number as an emergency contact years ago, to Greg's knowledge, Drew had never used it.

"What's the matter?" Greg asked as lightly as he could. "Don't you hear those pythons slithering through the trees?"

"I can't say that I do. C'mon, man. Where are you?"

The hint of desperation in Drew's voice touched a sympathetic chord deep inside Greg. "Why exactly do you think you need me?" He emphasized the word *think.*

"I'll tell you when we meet."

Back to square one. Greg shook his head. The thought of Drew Carroll at Rainbow's End made his stomach clench. The thought of Drew between girlfriends was even worse. If Greg knew Drew — and he did — he'd latch onto Kate the minute he arrived. Greg couldn't let that happen.

"It seems to me we've reached a stalemate. So long, Drew." He ended the call and let Drew's calls roll over to voice mail.

Greg was working. When they'd met for tennis, he'd told Kate that new guests were arriving tomorrow and that he'd found a few things in their cabins that needed to be fixed. Sally was still playing chess with Roy. That left Kate at loose ends.

She glanced at her watch as she pulled on a pair of shorts. She'd change again for dinner, but the afternoon was too hot for slacks. Kate considered her options. There wasn't enough time to go into Dupree and talk to Lauren, then get back here in time to take Sally to Sam's Bootery. Though she could ask Roy to drive Sally into town to meet her, that would involve explaining why she was going alone, and that was an explanation Kate didn't want to offer. Instead, she'd stay here and find some way to while away the time.

She wouldn't go to the main lodge. That would be too much like spying on Sally. As far as Kate knew, this was the first time her grandmother had shown interest in a man since Grandpa Larry's death, and while she doubted it was anything more than a short-term friendship like her own relationship with Greg, Kate wanted her grandmother's stay at Rainbow's End to be as happy as possible. Chess and Roy appeared to make Sally happy, and so Kate would not interfere. In fact, if Sally's health continued to improve, perhaps she'd suggest they come back next year. If Rainbow's End was still in existence.

Unfortunately, Kate was not confident that would be the case. While she saw potential for the resort, she also knew that investors could find other places that would require less work and a lower capital expenditure with a higher probability of success. On the risk/reward chart, Rainbow's End was heavily skewed toward risk.

Kate closed the cabin door behind her. There was no point in dwelling on unhappy thoughts. She'd visit the kitchen, where Carmen could be depended on to put a positive spin on even a gloomy day. Besides, there was almost always something delicious that needed a taste test.

The pungent smells of onions and peppers greeted Kate when she opened the door to the building that housed the kitchen. She sniffed deeply, wondering what Carmen had in store for them today. Last night's chicken cutlets and butterscotch sundaes had been marvelous.

As she entered the kitchen, Kate saw Carmen patting out what appeared to be a cornmeal mixture while Olivia and a girl Kate hadn't met watched.

"Good afternoon, ladies," she said with smiles for the trio. Approaching the stranger, she extended her hand. "I'm Kate Sherwood, one of the guests, and you must be Brandi."

"I am. Brandi Lenhardt," the blonde, blue-eyed teenager said, "but how did you know?" She shot an accusatory look at Carmen. "Did you tell her about KOB?"

Carmen nodded. "Why not? Kate's going to be here for a month. That makes her practically part of the family."

"Like Greg." Brandi shook Kate's hand. "Welcome to the Rainbow's End family."

"Brandi and I are helping Carmen make tamales," Olivia announced.

No wonder the kitchen smelled so wonderful. Kate was willing to bet that Carmen's tamales would be the best she'd ever eaten. She smiled at the teenagers. "If you two are helping, I guess I'll just be the official taste tester. That's what I do best, isn't it, Carmen?"

The dark-haired woman nodded as she dipped a spoon into the pot of tomato sauce simmering on the back burner and handed it to Kate. Closing her eyes, Kate slid the spoon into her mouth and let the spicy mixture tantalize her taste buds.

"Delicious," she said. "I wouldn't change anything." Carmen chuckled at the predictable response. "So, what do you do here?" Kate asked, turning her attention to Brandi.

"Laundry. The last load is in the dryer now." When Brandi gestured to the right, Kate realized that the third door in the hallway must lead to the laundry room.

Olivia slung her arm around Brandi's shoulders and gave her a quick hug. "You probably already know this, but Brandi, Kevin, and I are the only staff other than Carmen," she said. "Carmen's the only full-timer. The rest of us come after school and work for a few hours. If there are enough guests on weekends, we get more hours, but even in summer, it's not full-time."

"They were asking for my advice," Carmen said as she laid a dozen wrappers on the counter, spreading a couple tablespoons of dough on each. "Maybe you can help them. I sure couldn't. It would be one thing if they wanted to know how to make masa," she said, gesturing toward the dough, "but that's not what they want."

"What do you want?" Kate asked the girls. They seemed bright and energetic, not the apathetic teens the media sometimes liked to portray as the norm.

"To go to college." Though Olivia answered, Brandi nodded her agreement.

Kate couldn't fault them for their goal. Though she couldn't pinpoint the reason, Brandi and Olivia reminded her of herself and her best friend from high school, Gillian. As teenagers, the two of them spent countless hours talking about college and their plans for the future.

Kate and Gillian had been fortunate. What had been daydreams had turned into reality. Kate was now working in advertising, and Gillian had graduated from Julliard and was quickly making a name for herself as a pianist.

"It's a good plan," Kate told the girls. "You'll have more opportunities with a degree." At least she hoped they would. The statistics of un- or underemployed recent college grads were appalling. "Have you thought about your majors?"

"I want to teach," Brandi said quickly, adding, "High school history."

Olivia was slower to respond, as if she were considering her words. "I want to be a veterinarian." She fixed Kate with her gaze. "Did you know there's not a single vet in this county?"

As someone who'd never owned a pet, Kate hadn't spent much time thinking about veterinarians, and she had no reason to know about the apparent shortage here. "No, I didn't."

Carmen handed Brandi and Olivia a few wrappers and showed them how to spread the dough. When they'd added the filling and rolled the tamales, tucking in the ends of the wrappers to secure them, the two teens grinned.

"There may not be any vets in this county," Brandi said, returning to the previous discussion, "but there are plenty across the county line."

"True, but they're overworked."

Kate was impressed by the fact that Olivia had done her homework. "It sounds as if you've thought it through."

Olivia nodded. "All except the money part. My parents can't afford to send me to school, and they're not excited about the idea of student loans."

"Mine either. That's why we're working. But now . . ." Brandi let her words trail off.

"Has something changed?" Kate directed her question to Carmen. It didn't take a genius to know that the resort was in trouble, but this sounded ominous.

As she spread meat filling over the tamale dough, Carmen nodded. "Angela called us all in to say that unless there's a miracle, she and Tim are going to close Rainbow's End no later than Thanksgiving weekend, most likely a lot sooner." Carmen looked up at Kate, her dark eyes troubled. "I probably shouldn't be telling you that, but you can see that we're not exactly overrun with guests."

Though it was nothing more than she'd surmised, Kate hated to have her fears confirmed. "What about summer? Isn't that peak tourist season?"

Carmen shook her head. "It seems advance bookings are really low."

"I can't blame folks," Brandi said, her lips twisted into a scowl. "For not much more money, they can go to a dude ranch in Bandera and have a lot more to do."

"Brandi's right. There's nothing to bring people here, but these are the only jobs we could find. We need them, and not just for the money. Our counselor told us that if we wanted to have a chance at financial aid, it was important to work."

"She claimed it showed initiative," Brandi chimed in. "We've got initiative, but it's not helping a whole lot."

Olivia stared at the floor, as if it held the answer to their dilemma. "Rainbow's End needs a miracle, and so do we."

13

"What kind of miracle are you two looking for?" Drawn by the sound of Kate's voice, Greg had approached the kitchen, only to discover that she was involved in a discussion with Brandi and Olivia, while an uncharacteristically silent Carmen assembled tamales as if her life depended on it. The teenagers looked glum, and Kate had furrows between her eyes. Even the mouth-watering aroma of Carmen's tamale sauce did not lighten the mood.

"We want to go to college," Brandi said, her blue eyes welling with tears. "That's why we're working here. If Rainbow's End closes, I don't know what we'll do." Her rapid blinking told Greg she was trying not to cry. "Did you go to college?" she asked.

"Sure did, and I had some impressive loans too. I used to joke that they rivaled the national debt." Greg kept his tone light, hoping to diffuse some of the gloom.

Though he'd come a long way from what he called the starvation days, he hadn't forgotten how financial worries had colored his life. He'd been determined and he'd been fortunate. While Brandi and Olivia might match his determination, there was no way of predicting whether they'd be as fortunate.

"Our parents don't like loans," Olivia told him. "We come from big families, and they're worried about the future."

Greg understood. When he'd mentioned college, his father had announced that he wouldn't give Greg something he couldn't promise to the girls. Not wanting his sisters to face the same hurdles, Greg had paid their college expenses.

"No one likes loans, but you shouldn't rule them out," he advised.

The girls did not appear encouraged. Though they snickered at the sight of their misshapen tamales next to Carmen's perfect ones, the humor faded quickly.

"There are other ways to pay for school." Greg flashed Kate a smile before he said, "Kate took a different approach."

To his surprise, her eyes widened, and her shoulders slumped. It was a momentary change, one Greg doubted either Brandi or Olivia had noticed, but it intrigued him. For some reason, Kate seemed uncomfortable having the spotlight on her.

"I kept expenses low by living at home," she said when it was obvious the teenagers expected a response. "That wasn't possible for Greg, and it might not be possible for you. College is tough enough without adding a long commute."

Though Carmen had started humming, Brandi's and Olivia's expressions remained glum.

"Kate's being modest." Greg wasn't sure why she hadn't volunteered the information about her scholarships when the girls had asked about ways to pay for school. "Tell them what paid for tuition."

Once again Kate looked uncomfortable. "I worked a lot of hours on campus."

"And . . ." If she didn't tell them, he would. It wasn't false pride or bragging to admit you were smart enough to land a scholarship.

"I had a couple scholarships." It must have been Greg's imagination that there was a hint of defiance in Kate's words.

As he had expected, the teenagers' eyes lit. This was the kind of information they'd been seeking.

"You must be smart." The look Brandi gave Kate reminded Greg of the way some people looked at him when they connected his name with Sys=Simpl, a mixture of awe and disbelief. The blatant curiosity had always made Greg feel as if he were an animal in a zoo on display for visitors.

"I had pretty good grades and SATs," Kate admitted.

"We do too," Brandi replied. "Especially Olivia. She's the smartest girl in our class."

Olivia blushed. "How'd you find those scholarships?" she asked, seeming to want to deflect the attention from her intelligence. "Our counselor mentioned the big ones but said we didn't have much of a chance."

Kate nodded and gave Olivia a look that said she understood. She probably did. Judging from her reaction, Kate had been the smartest kid in her class and had found it uncomfortable just as Greg had. Being born without the sports gene wasn't the only problem a teenager could have.

"The school counselors helped. I also did a lot of research online." Kate's uneasiness seemed to have disappeared. Her tone was matter-of-fact, as if she were reciting a list she'd memorized for a test. "I don't know what it's like here, but where I lived, there were a number of private endowments available to qualified students. Some were restricted to a specific county. Others were given based on the students' career plans."

Carmen's humming stopped, Olivia's eyes brightened, and Brandi's interest was obviously piqued. So was Greg's. Unlike Kate, he hadn't qualified for scholarships. "So you just googled for them?" Brandi asked.

Though Greg wondered why the school counselor hadn't advised the girls, he wouldn't ask. Perhaps the school was short-staffed and the counselor's focus was limited to seniors. Brandi and Olivia were only juniors.

Kate shook her head. "It was a little more complicated than that, but that's the basic idea. I'd offer to show you what I did, but it would take forever at dial-up speeds." She frowned and let out an exaggerated sigh, eliciting a giggle from the girls.

Greg couldn't help smiling at Kate's attempt to lighten the conversation. "I know a bit about looking for money too," he told them. Venture capital firms didn't offer scholarship funds, but perhaps some of the foundations he'd researched when establishing his own did. "What time do you have to be at work tomorrow?"

"At 7:30." Brandi raised an eyebrow as if to ask why he cared.

"The Sit 'n' Sip opens at 6:30. If you want

to meet us there tomorrow morning, Kate and I'll show you what we know."

He was being presumptuous, making an appointment for Kate and including himself, but the instincts that had served Greg well in the corporate arena told him this was the right thing to do.

As the teens gave each other high fives, Kate smiled. "Great idea."

He was glad Kate agreed. Though he might be able to muddle through on his own, Greg had enough experience with his sisters to know how beneficial having another adult could be. And when that other adult was Kate, well . . . the whole morning would be decidedly more pleasant.

As he headed back to his cabin to change for dinner, Greg reflected on the teenagers' dilemma and his own. He had the power to make Olivia's and Brandi's dreams come true. The question was whether he should. It was one thing to support his sisters and give his parents money for the luxuries they could not have afforded otherwise, but it was a far different thing to try to help everyone he met, no matter how worthy they were.

But maybe he wouldn't be called on to do that. Maybe he and Kate would find enough scholarship money to put both girls through school. And if they didn't, there was always Plan B. The foundation Greg had created when he'd made his first million had grown substantially over the past few years, the result of prudent investments and his continued funding. He and the other trustees were always looking for worthwhile causes, and this might be one. Or not.

Although it would be easy enough to create a scholarship for residents of this particular town or even the whole county, the question was whether it made sense or whether Greg was simply reacting emotionally. He had always prided himself on his cool, rational decisions, but since he'd come to Rainbow's End, he had found himself more concerned about people than bottom lines. He couldn't explain it. He wasn't even certain he liked the change. All he knew was that it had happened.

Unlocking his cabin door, Greg frowned. He wanted to ask Kate's opinion about possibly endowing a scholarship. After all, she was as involved with the teens as he, and he had no doubt she'd give him a thoughtful and honest answer. Still, he hesitated.

Kate wasn't the problem. He was.

It hadn't taken long to realize that once the women he met learned he was a billionaire, their attitudes changed. They no longer seemed to regard him as Greg Vange, the man. Instead, he became Greg Vange, the billionaire, their ticket to a life of luxury. They had no way of knowing that their attitudes brought back painful memories of his father's inability to recognize that Greg was more than Linc Vange's son, that he was an individual in his own right.

Money changed things. Drew claimed Greg was being cynical, but he was convinced that was the reason Drew had never made it to the altar. Drew called it cold feet. Greg suspected it was the realization, perhaps subconscious, that the women who were so eager to have him place a diamond on their left hands were more interested in Drew's net worth than in his happiness.

Kate was different. If he'd been a betting man, Greg would have bet on that. And yet, something held him back. The truth was, he wasn't ready to put her to the test.

Kate was practically dancing with delight. What a wonderful day this had turned out to be. Her new boots fit perfectly and were more comfortable than she'd thought possible. The red, a more subdued shade than Samantha's, was bright enough to be eye-catching but not so bright that Kate would feel self-conscious wearing them. Sally was so happy with her boots that she had insisted on looking through Samantha's photo album again to see if she could find a second design she liked. That had given Kate the opportunity to visit Lauren's shop. Unfortunately, when she'd approached the quilt store, she'd seen two customers inside and had realized that Lauren was busy.

But that delay had worked to Kate's benefit. She'd taken advantage of the town's cell service and had called her office. As she'd hoped, Heather had found what she needed in the files Kate had emailed her and was once more happy. She'd even complimented Kate on her fast response and had wished her a pleasant weekend.

All that was good, but the best part — the icing on the cake — was the way Greg had volunteered to help her help Brandi and Olivia. Perhaps it was silly, but Kate's heart had soared when he'd joined them in the kitchen, and it had threatened to burst through her ribs when he'd casually said "meet us." It wasn't a date. It was simply an early morning get-together to help two teens, and yet the prospect made Kate smile.

She glanced at her watch, calculating the hours until she and Greg would leave for Dupree. How silly!

"Can I interest you in breakfast?" Greg asked as Brandi and Olivia left, huge grins wreathing their faces.

Though the Sit 'n' Sip was nothing special, a small diner with a counter, two tables, and one booth, the past hour had been productive. The four of them had sat at the table farthest from the door and had searched the web for scholarship dollars. Once he learned what they were planning to do, the proprietor had not bothered them. Instead, he'd struck up a lively conversation with everyone who came through the door, whether they ordered food to go or lingered at the counter.

Kate looked at the menu propped in the middle of the table. "Is the food edible?" she asked Greg. The Sit 'n' Sip's coffee had proven to be as bad as he'd predicted. After one sip, Kate had pushed it aside and, following Brandi and Olivia's example, ordered a large glass of orange juice. Though not freshly squeezed, it was preferable to the dark brew. Kate would get her caffeine infusion when she returned to Rainbow's End.

"Surprisingly, yes." Greg drained his coffee, apparently unfazed by its strength. "The pancakes are amazingly light, and Russ serves real maple syrup."

Russ, Kate had learned, was the proprietor and, as far as she could tell, the sole employee of the Sit 'n' Sip. She judged him to be in his midthirties, an ordinary-looking man with brown hair, brown eyes, and a wide welcoming grin.

"You've sold me." Kate ignored the urge to glance at her watch. She was on vacation, not at work, and there was no reason to hurry.

When she'd heard what Kate and Greg had planned, Sally had said she'd spend some time with Carmen, who issued an invitation whenever she saw Kate's grandmother. "We've got lots to talk about," Carmen had declared. Kate didn't doubt that. It seemed that Carmen could talk to anyone about anything, and Sally was rarely at a loss for words. If she didn't return to Rainbow's End before lunch, Kate suspected neither woman would notice.

"That was one of the most productive hours I've spent in a long time," she told Greg after they'd placed their orders.

And one of the most rewarding. Kate had been surprised at how good it felt to work with the teenagers and how grateful they'd been. This morning's experience reminded her of how much she'd enjoyed giving Samantha suggestions for ways to improve her website.

Greg nodded. "I was surprised at how much money was available."

"And I was surprised at how many foundations you knew about." When she'd mentioned one and the work it did, he'd rattled off the name of six others that she'd never heard of. To Kate's pleasure, those six all had philanthropic arms that might be convinced to expand their original mission to include helping deserving students from rural Texas counties obtain higher education. Brandi and Olivia had taken copious notes and were planning to meet with their counselor to discuss the possibilities when they returned to school on Monday.

Greg shrugged as if his knowledge were of little account. "They were related to some work I did in California. I hadn't thought about them in years, but for some reason I have a good memory for names."

Kate had noticed that. Although he didn't live in Dupree, he greeted each of the customers who entered the Sit 'n' Sip by name. When she'd raised her eyebrow after the third greeting, Greg explained that he and Roy met here at least once a week and that everyone who'd come in so far was a regular customer.

"You'd be a good innkeeper," Kate told him. "Angela called me Kathy yesterday." She shrugged. It wasn't a big thing, and yet it had annoyed her. "You'd think she could keep her few guests' names straight."

Greg must have sensed Kate's feelings, because he said, "I alternate between being annoyed and feeling sorry for Angela and Tim. They're obviously in way over their heads. From what I can gather, they expected Rainbow's End to be a cash cow and never realized how much work is involved."

"Work that you're doing."

He shook his head. "That's only the tip of the iceberg. There's so much more they could — and probably should — be doing. I don't understand why they don't try harder."

Russ Walker slid two huge platters of pancakes in front of Kate and Greg. Though she doubted she'd be able to eat even half of the perfectly browned cakes, Kate had to admit they smelled delicious. She drizzled syrup over the top and took a forkful. After savoring the delicate blend of buckwheat and oats, she looked up at Greg.

"Maybe the Sinclairs don't know what to do." That was one of the problems Kate had uncovered on her first assignment for Maddox and Associates. The clients had thought they wanted an advertising campaign, but what they really needed was a better understanding of their core business. Kate had enlisted the help of a consultant who'd worked with the clients to develop a mission statement. It was only then that she'd started brain-storming ideas for telling the world about the clients' products and services.

"Possibly," Greg agreed, "or they're lazy."

"Or afraid."

He swirled a piece of pancake in the puddle of syrup that had formed on one edge of the plate, then looked up at Kate, his green eyes filled with an odd expression. "Afraid? That's an intriguing idea. What do you suppose they're afraid of?"

She shrugged. "Failure. Success. Everyone's afraid of something."

Greg's face darkened as he said, "That's true."

She'd obviously touched a nerve. As Kate debated whether or not to ask what Greg feared, the door opened and the opportunity was gone. Lauren Ahrens and a young girl whose resemblance announced that she was Lauren's daughter entered the restaurant.

As Lauren waved at Kate, the girl's glance skittered over Kate and rested on Greg. She looked up at her mother, then pointed at Greg.

"Look at him, Mom. He'd be a good daddy."

14

Kate wasn't sure who was more embarrassed. Lauren's cheeks were almost as bright as the one shocking pink sock her daughter wore, while all the blood appeared to have drained from Greg's face, leaving him with a distinctly unhealthy pallor. Judging from his expression, Kate realized that Greg had never met Lauren and that the idea of instant fatherhood was one he had not entertained.

"I'm so sorry, sir." Lauren looked as if she wished a sinkhole would swallow her.

Hoping to defuse the tension, Kate interrupted. When in doubt, she'd been taught, rely on the social niceties. She'd start with introductions. If that wasn't enough, she could always fall back on the weather. "Lauren, this is Greg Vange. He's another of the guests at Rainbow's End. Greg, I'd like you to meet Lauren Ahrens, who makes the most beautiful quilts I've ever seen. And this," Kate said with a smile for the girl who'd created such a stir, "is Fiona."

"My very outspoken daughter." As Lauren gave Greg an apologetic smile, Kate saw that her face was returning to its natural color. "Fiona's had a hard time since her dad died, but that's no excuse for rudeness."

Kate wondered how Greg would react. While it was true that he had four younger sisters, she suspected it had been awhile since he'd dealt with a girl Fiona's age. Furthermore, it appeared that Greg's father had not been the best of role models.

When Kate had mentioned seeing Greg rowing and that he appeared to have developed a sports gene, he had frowned. "Too little, too late," he'd said, leaving Kate no doubt that he was giving her the response he'd heard from the man who'd scorned his lack of athletic prowess. Kate had quickly changed the subject, but she'd lain awake wondering how any parent could be so cruel. It was obvious that although Greg had achieved some measure of success in his professional life, he was still suffering from the criticism he'd endured as a child.

Given that background, Kate wondered how he would deal with Fiona. Would he bellow or simply ignore her? To Kate's relief, Greg did neither. Though he'd risen to greet Lauren, he sat down again, putting himself closer to Fiona's height. He leaned forward slightly as he addressed the child, his focus so intent that neither Kate nor Lauren nor Russ Walker and the two men who were devouring pancakes at the counter might have existed. "I'll bet your dad was a pretty special man."

Fiona nodded. She wore her dark hair, so like her mother's, in braids, and as she nodded, they swayed.

"You know how I could tell?" Greg seemed to have expected the silent response.

Though she shook her head, Fiona's brown eyes radiated curiosity.

"Because you're a pretty special young lady." If she'd been a peacock, Fiona would have strutted at the praise of being called a young lady rather than a little girl. As it was, her shoulders straightened, and she held her head higher.

"I know you miss your daddy," Greg continued. "Your mom does too. I know you want to help her, but there are some things she has to do by herself, like picking out a new daddy."

Greg glanced at Fiona's feet, and Kate saw the hint of a smile. Who wouldn't smile at the mismatched socks — one pink, the other lime green — that clashed with the red shoes. "You wouldn't like it if your mom picked out your socks for you, would you?"

As Fiona shook her head, Kate had an inkling where Greg was headed. Like a snake charmer who wouldn't dare break his concentration, he kept his eyes focused on the child, as if there was no one else in the restaurant. "How would it be if you and your mom had an agreement? You can pick out your socks."

"Even on Sunday?" The eagerness in Fiona's voice told Kate this had been a point of contention.

For the first time Greg looked around. He gave Lauren a glance before confirming her nod. "Even on Sunday. In return, you'll let her pick out a daddy." He gave Lauren another look, and this time there was no doubt about it. Greg was smiling. "It might take a long time, though."

"But I can still pick out my socks."

"Yes."

Fiona grinned. "Okay." Turning to her mother, she held out her hand. "Shake?"

With a wobbly smile, Lauren let her daughter pump her hand, then ushered her to the counter to choose a muffin. When they left the restaurant, Fiona still grinning at her apparent victory, Kate leaned across the table to touch Greg's hand.

"You were amazing. How did you know what to say?"

He shrugged. "I don't know. I can't say I've had any experience dealing with death. Both my parents are alive, and my grandparents died before I was born. All I know is that when I looked at that little girl, the words started to flow."

"Like the nudge to come to Rainbow's End?"

Greg turned his hand over to clasp hers. He was silent for a second before he nodded. "Exactly."

Kate was smiling as she left the church. Though the building and congregation were smaller than either the church she'd attended while growing up or the one in New Jersey, the sense of peace and fellowship that she'd found in those churches was present here in Dupree. The minister had spoken of the miracles Jesus had performed before his final trip to Jerusalem, then challenged the congregation to search for the miracles in their lives. "They're there," he promised.

"My little miracle is happier than I've seen her since Patrick died," Lauren said as she approached Kate.

Although several members of the congregation had welcomed Kate, no one had lingered for a conversation. She hadn't minded. The day was beautiful, and it was pleasant simply standing in the shade of a live oak while she waited for her grandmother. But a few minutes with Lauren would be better. Kate smiled. This was her chance to talk to the quilt store owner. Sally appeared engrossed in a discussion with the pastor's wife, and judging by the animation on her grandmother's face, the conversation could be a lengthy one.

"Where is Fiona?" Though Kate had seen her seated next to Lauren during the service, she was no longer in sight.

"Sunday school. I used to teach it, but when Patrick was so ill, I took a leave of absence." Lauren tipped her head, gesturing to the left, where Greg and Roy seemed to be regaling a group of men with a story. "It's a shame Greg isn't a permanent resident. We could use him as a youth counselor. He was amazing with Fiona."

"You should have seen him with the teenagers. That's why we were at Sit 'n' Sip yesterday. We were helping Brandi and Olivia look for scholarship money." Kate had no doubt that in a town the size of Dupree, Lauren would know who she meant without introducing last names. "He made them feel as if they were adults."

Lauren nodded. "He's a special man, like my Patrick." She hitched her bag onto her shoulder and smiled. "You don't want to let him get away."

Though the morning was still relatively cool, Kate felt blood rush to her face, heating her more than the Texas sun at midday. "I'm not . . . He's not . . . We're not . . ." Kate was babbling like a child, all because Lauren had made a false assumption. "We just met," she managed to say. "We're both guests at Rainbow's End, and we play tennis together. That's all."

"If you say so." Lauren's smile said she wasn't buying Kate's protests. "It's just that when I saw you two together, you reminded me of myself and Patrick. For most of us, true love only comes once. Don't let it pass you by."

Kate was still thinking about Lauren's advice that afternoon when she returned to the dining room for another cup of coffee. Dinner, which had been served at noon since it was Sunday, had been a delicious meal of ham and scalloped potatoes with a molded salad, all followed by cherry pie à la mode. Though she had enjoyed every morsel, Kate couldn't keep her mind from wandering to thoughts of what Lauren had seen — or believed she had seen — between Kate and Greg.

It was true that Greg wasn't like any of the men Kate had dated. It was also true that she thought of him more often than she had either Pete or Lou, but that was simply because of their situation. They were in close proximity to each other, away from their normal lives. It was only natural that Kate's thoughts would turn to Greg. That didn't mean she was in love with him.

She wasn't even certain she'd recognize love if it took residence in her heart. She had thought she'd loved Pete, but those feelings had faded. A year later, she'd imagined herself in love with Lou. That had lasted a bit longer, but eventually she had realized that all she felt when she was with him was familiarity. Love, it seemed, happened to others, but not to Kate Sherwood. Maybe that was why Sally said she sometimes acted as if she didn't have a romantic bone in her body. As if bones could be romantic.

"I've had enough!" The angry words and the sound of footsteps storming down the outside staircase broke Kate's train of thought. A second later, she heard a door slam and a second set of footsteps descending the stairs. Whatever had happened, Tim and Angela Sinclair were not happy.

"There'd better be some coffee in here," Angela muttered as she entered the dining room.

Though her instinct was to flee and let Angela believe no one had overheard the outburst, Kate could see no way to do that. Instead, she would take her cues from Angela. She'd address the caffeine issue.

"The coffee is fresh," Kate said as brightly as she could.

Angela stopped in midstride, her embarrassment evident in the red splotches on her cheeks. She grabbed a mug and busied herself with the coffeepot. "I'm sorry you had to hear that, Kathy," she said as she added a splash of cream.

"It's Kate."

Angela nodded, her flush deepening. "That's right. I remember now. Kate Sherwood and Sally Fuller. You'd think I could remember the guests' names, especially when there are so few of them."

Though she'd been annoyed the first time Angela had forgotten her name, today Kate felt nothing but pity for the woman who looked so miserable. There must be something she could do to help her. Kate had never seen Sally and Grandpa Larry fight, but the few times her co-worker Brittany had come to work with a woebegone expression because she and Cal had argued, all she had wanted was a sympathetic ear. Perhaps Angela was the same.

"Do you want to talk?" Kate asked. "I've been told I'm a good listener."

Angela looked torn; then she nodded. "Let's go upstairs. That way we won't be interrupted."

And so Kate found herself in the owners' suite. Larger than her apartment in New Jersey, it showed no sign of the neglect that was prevalent elsewhere at Rainbow's End. Instead, the floor boasted what appeared to be a handmade rug, and a luxurious leather sofa and two matching chairs flanked a gas fireplace. An attractive oil painting hung on one wall, while another held an étagère with expensive-looking crystal vases. Though it wasn't her taste, there was no doubt that the Sinclairs had spared no expense in furnishing their own quarters.

Angela motioned to one of the chairs, then took the other, placing her mug on the chrome and glass table. "I don't know why I'm talking to you."

"Because I offered to listen." Kate recalled the way Greg had put Fiona at ease and wished she were as gifted. "Sometimes it's easier to talk to strangers."

"Like *Strangers on a Train*?" Angela's laugh was harsh. "I never used to consider killing Tim, but recently . . ."

Kate wouldn't let her continue down that path. "Why did you buy Rainbow's End?" Kate had wondered about that many times.

Angela let out a loud sigh, and her green eyes, a few shades lighter than Greg's, glittered. "We thought it would be an easy way to make a living. Boy, were we ever wrong." She sipped her coffee. "Are you sure you want to hear this? It's not a pretty story." When Kate nodded, Angela continued. "Tim and I worked for an insurance company in Austin. He was a claims adjuster, and I was in the underwriting department. When the company was bought out by a larger one, Tim's job was eliminated. 'Nothing personal,' they told him, but Tim took it personally. He got angry and hit one of the bosses."

Angela cringed, as if remembering. "You can guess what happened next. They didn't press charges, but there went Tim's severance package and any hopes for a recommendation. I knew it would eat Tim alive if I stayed there, so I quit my job. We sold our house and took all our savings to buy this place." Gripping her mug so tightly that Kate wondered if it would shatter, Angela stared at the wall. "It was a huge mistake, and now it's affecting everything, including our marriage."

Kate's heart ached for the Sinclairs. As Angela had said, they'd made mistakes — more than one, it seemed — and now they were facing the consequences.

"I wish there was something I could do."

"Find us a buyer."

Angela might as well have asked for the moon.

"Tonight's dessert is chocolate pound cake." Olivia had practically bounced to the table when she'd served the main course, and her enthusiasm did not appear to have diminished one iota since then. It was, she told Kate, the result of the morning Kate and Greg had helped her and Brandi investigate potential scholarships. Though both girls were still concerned about the likely closing of Rainbow's End, it no longer felt like a death sentence to their college dreams. They'd met with their school counselor earlier today, and she'd been impressed with their research and optimistic about their possibilities.

Kate was grateful she'd been able to help the teens, because her conversation with Angela yesterday had convinced her that

Rainbow's End was doomed. As much as she wanted to believe there was a happy ending, she couldn't envision it. Greg agreed.

"It would be hard to find two people less suited to be innkeepers," she had told him while they caught their breath between tennis games. "Angela and Tim may have had good intentions, but neither one had any experience in the hospitality industry. There's more involved in running a resort than serving meals and changing sheets."

Greg nodded. "It's even harder at a small place like this where guests expect the personal touch. That's probably part of the reason the Sinclairs are having trouble attracting buyers. The large hotel chains have no interest in acquiring a property like Rainbow's End, and there aren't too many individuals willing to make the commitment of time and money it requires."

Though the conversation had been depressing, Kate had welcomed it, for it had taken her mind off the way her heart had raced when she'd arrived at the tennis court and seen Greg waiting for her. It wasn't love, no matter what Lauren said. Discussing Rainbow's End had brought Kate back to reality, and she'd remained there, her feet firmly planted on the ground. There would be no more floating with her head in the clouds.

Greg had seemed unaware of her turbulent thoughts, both then and now at dinner. "So, are you going to have some pound cake?" he asked.

Kate groaned at the thought of the decadent dessert. "I wish I'd known. I wouldn't have eaten all that chicken fricassee." Delicious as it had been, she would have saved room for dessert if she'd known it was of the chocolate variety.

"There's always room for Carmen's chocolate cake." Greg spun the lazy Susan and picked up the pitcher of iced tea to replenish his glass and Kate's.

"You need to have at least one piece," Roy chimed in.

After the other guests agreed that they couldn't miss something that sounded so good, Olivia turned back to Kate. "It's even pretty healthy," the teenager declared.

"Right." Kate's response dripped with sarcasm. "Since when are eggs, butter, and chocolate anyone's definition of healthy?"

Olivia nodded. "Seriously, Kate. It's low fat and low cholesterol. Carmen developed it when we had a guest recuperating from heart surgery. He needed a special diet, and Carmen couldn't resist a challenge."

Though Sally had declined dessert, she tapped her fork on the table to get Olivia's attention. "I've got to try this."

"Me too." After that buildup, how could Kate resist? And when she'd taken her first bite, she was glad she hadn't. "Are you sure this is low fat?" she demanded. Surely nothing this moist and rich could be healthy.

Greg nodded. "You can ask Carmen for the recipe. I know she's willing to share."

"I think I'll do that." Sally turned to Kate and grinned. "You can guess what I'll be serving the next time you visit." Turning back to Roy, she asked if he was planning to eat the extra piece Olivia had left on the Susan.

Kate couldn't distinguish Roy's response, but a minute or so later, she heard him say, "I can't promise you healthy food, but you won't go hungry either. The last time I went, I ate more than my share of strudel and bratwurst."

"That's my kind of food." Greg leaned forward and looked at Roy. "Where do I find it?"

"The bluebonnet festival. It started on Friday and runs all this week. I'm trying to convince Sally to go with me tomorrow. It's only a couple hours' drive."

A prickle of uneasiness made its way down

Kate's spine as Roy expanded on his plans. There was so much to do, he said, that it would be an all-day event. And that was what concerned Kate. If her grandmother and Roy stayed for the evening concert, they'd be coming back after dark. Sally had trouble with night driving, and Kate feared that Roy might too. The ophthalmologist had told Kate she advised all of her over-seventy patients to avoid driving at night.

"Why don't I take you?" she suggested. "That way there won't be any rush to get back. I'll be your designated driver." Even though no one would be drinking, the term was still appropriate.

To Kate's surprise, Sally bristled. "I don't need a babysitter."

Kate blinked at the rebuke. That wasn't like Sally. Her grandmother was normally even-tempered. What was stranger was the fact that the woman who had declared she wanted to spend a whole month with Kate now proposed to take off on her own for a day.

"Of course you don't need a babysitter," Kate said, her tone conciliatory.

"But I could use a change of scenery, not to mention those brats," Greg interjected before Kate could remind her grandmother that the stated purpose of the whole trip to

Texas was for the two of them to be together. "Why don't I drive all of us? My SUV's pretty comfortable."

Sally and Roy exchanged a glance. "Okay," Sally said, apparently liking what she saw in Roy's expression. "You've got yourself a date."

Which meant that Kate had a date with Greg.

15

Greg stared at the road, thankful that the xenon headlights illuminated a wide swath. He'd heard that deer were common in this part of the Hill Country and that they were particularly active around sunrise and sunset. If he'd been planning the trip, he would have left an hour later to avoid potential collisions with wildlife, but Roy had been adamant that they reach the fairgrounds before the festival opened.

Greg wasn't certain Sally and Roy would last the whole day, but he reminded himself that he shouldn't underestimate their stamina. Sally had been looking healthier the past few days, and he had noticed none of the shortness of breath that had been so obvious when she and Kate arrived at Rainbow's End.

As for Roy, the man's energy levels seemed to have doubled since he'd met Sally Fuller. If Greg wasn't mistaken, Roy was hoping to convince Sally to stay in Texas for far more than a month. He couldn't blame him. Under different circumstances, Greg might have been trying to persuade Sally's grand-daughter to remain. But circumstances weren't different. Greg would be at Rain-bow's End only until he figured out what God had in mind for him next. And prob-ably well before that happened, Kate would return to her job.

Right now she was fiddling with the radio, trying to find a station she liked while Greg kept an eye open for Bambi's relatives. To his surprise, Sally and Roy had ignored the middle seat of the SUV and had headed for the one in the rear. That put them far enough away that he couldn't distinguish their words, although the occasional bursts of laughter told Greg they were enjoying their time together as much as he was enjoy-ing being with Kate.

She looked like a Texan today, dressed in jeans, a floral print shirt, and boots. She'd even tossed a denim jacket into the back of the SUV for the unlikely event of a cool evening. Greg had seen the clothes before, but something about her today — perhaps the tilt of her head, perhaps the fact that she'd done something different with her hair — had made his breath catch when she'd walked out of her cabin. The sophisticated, almost brittle woman he'd met that first day seemed to have disappeared. Or perhaps she had never existed. That might have been a mask Kate wore to keep others from seeing inside her, like the mask that had been part of his daily wardrobe in California.

"I give up," Kate said, switching off the radio. "Isn't there anything but country music?"

Greg couldn't help chuckling. The impatience was so typical of Kate. "This is Texas," he pointed out. "We're in the heart of country. A big heart."

Just like Kate. He'd discovered that the true Kate was a woman with a deep capacity for love and an equally deep vulnerability. There was no mistaking her love for Sally. That showed in everything she said or did. And it wasn't just Sally. Look at how she'd wanted to help the teenagers and the way her heart had opened to Angela Sinclair when she'd heard the woman's story. Kate might wear the façade of a cool businesswoman, but the reality was far different. She was warm and caring.

"What made you go into advertising?" he asked. Perhaps he was being foolish by reminding her of work, but Greg was curious.

The sky had lightened enough that he could see her smile. "It's what my grandfather did. I guess you could say I decided to follow in his footsteps. The truth is, Grandpa Larry enjoyed his work so much that I couldn't imagine doing anything else."

And Greg's father had hated his job so much that Greg had resolved he would never do anything like it. In the years since he'd left home, Greg had occasionally wondered if hating his job was one of the reasons his father had been so filled with anger, but by then their relationship had deteriorated to such an extent that he would not ask for fear of provoking another tirade.

"So your grandfather was a partner."

Kate shook her head. "He never made partner. I don't know why not." She shrugged. "That wasn't something we talked about."

Interesting. Another piece of the puzzle that was Kate Sherwood fell into place. Greg had wondered why she was so focused on the partnership. At first he'd thought it was a matter of money and prestige. Now he knew there was more involved. Kate was trying to meet her grandfather's expectations. He only hoped that the reality would be worth the sacrifices she was making.

■ ■ ■ ■

"This is wonderful," Sally said as she and Roy shielded their eyes to stare at the small plane pulling a banner. Not surprisingly, the banner was a promotion for the festival. As Roy had promised, the crowds were smaller than they would be on weekends or tomorrow when school was out to allow the children to attend, but there were still enough people to make the day feel festive.

Sally felt festive herself, and it had nothing to do with those marvelous boots Samantha had made. It was good to see her granddaughter looking so happy, but that wasn't the reason for Sally's mood, either. Her mood owed everything to Roy. As soon as they'd entered the fairgrounds, Kate and Greg had gone their own way, leaving Sally with Roy. Perfect.

First on the agenda was the parade. And, since it was midweek, they were able to find seats on the bleachers to watch the half-hour procession of floats, marching bands, and clowns, culminating with the all-blue float bearing the Bluebonnet Queen and her attendants. Sally had seen dozens of parades in her life, but she couldn't recall one she'd enjoyed more.

When the crowds had dispersed, she and Roy had abandoned their seats and wandered through aisles of craft booths. Exercising what Kate would call unusual restraint, Sally had bought nothing but a pale blue bandanna with darker blue bluebonnets printed on it, even though Roy had insisted that the matching sweatshirt was an essential addition to her wardrobe. They'd eaten certifiable junk food and drank enough sweet tea to make Sally's dentist cringe, and through it all, Roy had been at her side.

Not just at her side but touching her. He'd held her hand while they'd strolled, draped his arm around her shoulders when they were seated on the bleachers, placed his hand on the small of her back as they'd made their way through tight spaces. Roy was a toucher, and Sally liked it. Oh, how she liked it. It had been far too long since a man had touched her as if she were a desirable woman.

"I can't remember when I've laughed so much," she said with a smile. As wonderful as it had been spending time with Kate, this was better, for being with Roy filled a need deep inside Sally, a need she hadn't even admitted to herself.

Roy gave her shoulders a light squeeze.

"Those laugh lines at the corners of your eyes tell me you've done a lot of laughing in your lifetime."

"They're crow's feet," Sally said, reminding Roy of their first conversation. It was amazing to realize it had been only a week since she and Kate had arrived at Rainbow's End. "I used to laugh a lot, but not so much the past few years," she admitted as she and Roy meandered toward the midway. The rides had opened immediately after the parade ended and seemed to be drawing more visitors than the craft booths. "I can't stop worrying about Kate and the way she's throwing herself into her work. I shouldn't be surprised, because she always was single-minded, but I'm concerned. I want her to have more — a real life."

Roy nodded as if he understood, and Sally suspected he did. After all, he'd raised three boys and now had six grandchildren to worry about. "It's hard to make the youngsters listen, isn't it?" The corners of Roy's lips curved in a smile. "Not that Kate's exactly a youngster, but you know what I mean. The problem is, even though we want to save them from heartache, we can't. They have to make their own decisions."

"I know." Sally scanned the crowd, looking for Kate and Greg. The smells of popcorn and fudge mingled with sunblock and perfume, causing Sally to wrinkle her nose. "It's almost a miracle that Kate came with me. She had the hardest time convincing her boss the world wouldn't end if she took a month off from work."

"And look at her now." Roy pointed in the direction of the fortune-telling tent. Kate stood there laughing as Greg put his cowboy hat on her head. "Greg's good for her."

"And you're good for me. Thank you, Roy. Coming here was a great idea."

He held up a cautionary hand. "Don't thank me yet. The day isn't over. We haven't been on any of the rides. I have to admit that my roller-coaster days are gone, but can I convince you to ride the carousel?"

He stopped in front of a merry-go-round whose sign announced that it was a genuine Herschell carousel with fully restored wooden animals. Sally smiled, recalling the number of times she'd taken Kate to visit the Herschell Carrousel Factory Museum in Western New York and how Kate used to insist the sign was misspelled because of the double *r*. They'd both enjoyed the exhibits, and Kate had been thrilled when she was old enough to attend one of the annual Victorian teas, but the highlight of each visit had been the opportunity to ride the merry-go-round.

Sally studied the animals as they revolved, noting that although horses predominated, there were two pigs, a couple of goats, and four dogs in addition to two intricately carved chariots, one whose seat back was shaped like a peacock.

"A horse or a chariot?" she asked Roy. When they'd first been courting, Sally and Larry had chosen the chariots, simply because it gave them the opportunity to sit close to each other and steal an occasional kiss. When Kate had joined their family, she'd insisted that chariots were for babies and old folks and refused to consider riding in one.

"What's wrong with both? I think I can afford two rides."

"I like the way you think, Roy Gordon." As Sally mounted the painted pony next to him, she amended her opinion. *I like everything about you.*

"You'll never convince me that cotton candy is health food."

Greg tugged on Kate's hand, trying to draw her closer to the stand. "But it's fun."

"Messy," she countered. That didn't seem to bother the couple who had just bought a giant serving and were taking big bites, heedless of the sticky residue now decorating their faces. "There's no neat way to eat it."

"So, live a little. Take a risk."

The day was sunny and bright, the warmest since she'd arrived in Texas, but Kate felt as if a cloud had obscured the sun, chilling the air. It was nothing more than her imagination. Kate knew that. Greg was only joking. Kate knew that too, and yet the words hurt. "Have you been talking to Sally?" she demanded.

Her words came out more harshly than she'd planned, and so she tempered them with a shrug. "Sally's always saying that I should take more risks, only she has more in mind than cotton candy. If she had her way, I'd quit my job and join the circus." Though Sally was normally lavish with her praise when she saw Kate's ads, recently she'd told her she hoped Kate hadn't made a mistake in choosing advertising. And no matter how often Kate assured her grandmother that she was happy, Sally seemed unconvinced.

"The circus?" Raised eyebrows were Greg's first response. "I can't quite picture you as a clown."

"Are you kidding? I'd be the fat lady,

especially if I eat that." Kate pointed to the cotton candy, determined to steer the conversation away from risks.

As she'd hoped, Greg laughed. He held up both hands in surrender. "All right. I give up. Let's have caramel corn instead."

"Yes!" Kate pumped her fist in the air. Though it had little more nutritional value than cotton candy, caramel corn was something Kate enjoyed. It wasn't the flavor as much as the nostalgia. Caramel corn had always been part of her trips to the county fair and firemen's picnics, first with Sally and Grandpa Larry, then with her friends.

Greg purchased a box and offered it to her. "You won this round, but I'm warning you. You won't get away so easily next time."

"Are you going to expect me to eat pickled eel?"

He shook his head as he glanced at the midway. "Not food. Carnival rides. No self-respecting tourist would leave here without riding at least one."

The throngs milling around the ticket booths and queuing for the various rides seemed to confirm Greg's assertion. As two children who must have played hooky jostled them, Greg wrapped his arm around Kate's waist and drew her to the sidelines. "I saw Roy and Sally headed for the merry-go-round. Do you want to try that?"

Kate shook her head. Carousels might be beautiful, but they were tame, practically boring. "I thought this was supposed to be a challenge. If so, we need something a bit more exciting. What about the Ferris wheel?"

It had to be her imagination that Greg stiffened. "The line is long," he said as he let his arm drop to his side. "Pick another."

Kate looked around. The only short queues were for the kiddy rides. "The lines are long everywhere. C'mon, Greg. It's been years since I was on a Ferris wheel. It'll be fun."

"For whom?" Though he wrinkled his nose as if he were joking, Kate had the feeling his question was sincere.

"For both of us." It might lack the thrills of a roller coaster, but a Ferris wheel provided beautiful views. Kate always felt as if she were on top of the world when she rode one. "Let's go." She grabbed Greg's hand and tugged, urging him into the queue.

"This is a bad idea." He spoke so softly that Kate wondered if she'd heard correctly.

He must be joking. Just to be sure, Kate said, "I didn't quite catch that."

Greg shook his head. "Nothing."

Though the line had appeared long, it moved quickly, and within five minutes they were seated on the wheel. Seconds later, they were suspended a few feet off the ground as the operator filled the next chair.

Kate looked at Greg, and this time there was no denying it. Something was definitely wrong. His face was almost green, and he was gripping the safety bar so tightly that his knuckles were white. Kate gave herself a mental kick for having insisted. Why hadn't she realized that Greg wasn't kidding when he'd tried to discourage her? She didn't have to search far to find the reason. She'd been thinking of herself, remembering Greg's joke about taking risks. She hadn't considered anyone else.

"You really didn't want to do this, did you?" Short of jumping out, which would be foolhardy, they had no recourse.

"It's too late now." Greg's words came out in short bursts. "We're past the point of no return." As he pronounced the final word, Kate saw a flicker of something in his eyes — panic, enthusiasm, something else? She wasn't sure. All she knew was that something had changed.

A second later, Greg began to sing the famous song from *Phantom of the Opera*. She stared in astonishment, not quite believing what was happening. No one she knew had ever done anything like this. Greg could hardly carry a tune, and other than the title, the words he was singing bore no resemblance to Andrew Lloyd Webber's, but it didn't seem to matter.

"Past the point of no return, this Ferris wheel is climbing." As the car moved in fits and stops, Greg continued, improvising lyrics. He was singing as if his life depended on it.

Kate's heart began to pound. Though Greg might not admit it, this was his version of whistling in the dark, an attempt to overcome fear. It didn't even matter what the fear was. What mattered was that it was Kate's fault they were here. She should have known better. She should have listened more carefully. Kate wrapped her arm around Greg's waist and drew him closer to her.

"Are you trying out for *American Idol*?" she demanded, hoping to distract him enough that he'd forget whatever had made him turn green around the gills. Theirs had been one of the last cars to be filled. Now the Ferris wheel was full and had begun to revolve. "I can do better." She couldn't, but that was part of the plan. Before Greg could say anything, Kate started a terribly off-key rendition of "Don't Cry for Me, Argentina."

When she finished, Greg was laughing, and the color had returned to his face. As if he were suddenly aware of Kate's arm around his waist, he stretched out his arm and wrapped it around her shoulders, then slid it down to her waist. His movement released the tantalizing scent of his cologne, and the warmth of Greg's hand on her waist made Kate want to rest her head on his shoulder. Instead, she simply smiled and hoped her smile didn't look silly. She was the one who was supposed to be providing comfort.

"You were awful," Greg said, his smile taking any possible sting from the words. Though the Ferris wheel continued to revolve, he seemed not to care. Perhaps it was only those first few minutes when they dangled in the air as the other chairs were being filled that bothered him. Whatever the reason, Kate was glad that Greg appeared to have recovered.

"No worse than you." She didn't know how long the ride would last, but she did know that she couldn't let Greg's fears return. "We need to try a duet. What shall we do?" She thought quickly. "My grandmother sings 'Some Enchanted Evening' in the shower. Do you know that?"

Greg shrugged, the motion releasing more of his cologne. Though she had been trying to distract him, even without trying, Greg was managing to distract her.

"I know the melody but not all the words," he said.

"It doesn't matter. Whenever you don't know the words, just sing la-la-la. That'll work." Before he could protest, Kate started singing.

"Some enchanted . . ."

"La-la." Kate smiled as Greg joined in. The only prize they'd win would be for worst harmony, but she didn't mind. Greg looked almost carefree. That was what was important.

And then the Ferris wheel stopped, leaving them at the top of the arc. When Greg stopped singing, so did Kate. This was her favorite part of a Ferris wheel ride, the panorama from the top.

She caught her breath, amazed at the sheer grandeur of the Hill Country. The view was breathtakingly beautiful. As far as she could see, there were rolling hills dotted with clusters of trees. The varying shades of green against the deep blue sky begged to be photographed or captured on canvas, but what made the scene truly spectacular was the field of bluebonnets. A lighter blue than the sky and interspersed with patches of yellow and orange flowers, they looked as soft as velvet.

"Oh, Greg! It's incredible."

He made no response. Instead, he cupped Kate's chin, turning it so she could see that he wasn't looking at the landscape. For a second, he said nothing. His gaze met hers, his eyes a darker green than she'd ever seen, filled with an expression Kate could not identify. Slowly, his gaze moved lower, resting on her lips.

"So are you," Greg said as he leaned forward and pressed his lips to hers.

16

It wasn't the first time she'd been kissed. It wasn't even the first time she'd been kissed on a Ferris wheel. That "honor," if you could use the word, had gone to Jimmy Feneck the summer they turned thirteen. Neither one of them had wanted to repeat the experience. This was different. Totally different.

Greg's lips were tender; their touch sent shivers of delight down her spine, and his hand cupping her head made Kate feel cherished. The tangy scent of his cologne mingled with the sweet smell of caramel corn and the more pungent odors that the breeze wafted up from the fairgrounds. Carousel music blended with screams from the roller coaster and the shouts of delight when someone won a prize at one of the games. It was an ordinary day at the fair, and yet it wasn't. Today was the day Greg Vange kissed her. A wonderful, wonderful day. A wonderful, wonderful kiss. If Kate had her way, the kiss would never end.

It did.

As the Ferris wheel jerked into motion again, Greg pulled back, breaking the contact. Though the day was warm, the air seemed cool against Kate's lips, compared to the heat of Greg's kiss, leaving her feeling somehow bereft. How silly! It was only a kiss. But it wasn't only a kiss. It was the most wonderful kiss Kate had ever had. And, judging from the way Greg's lips curved in a smile, she wasn't the only one who felt that way.

"I don't think I'll ever hear 'Some Enchanted Evening' without remembering today." His hand dropped from her neck to circle her shoulders, drawing her closer to him. "You're an incredible woman, Kate Sherwood. You're the only person I know who could keep me from realizing I was sixty feet above the ground."

Though Greg's voice was low, Kate heard the note of amazement in it. "That sounds as if you're afraid of heights." She'd thought that might be the case, given his reaction, but it could have been something different, perhaps being in a confined space. No wonder he'd suggested they ride the merry-go-round.

Greg nodded. "I am afraid of heights . . . or at least I was." He kept his eyes focused on her, and the intensity in them made her wonder if he was considering looking down. Most acrophobics would not do that, but if there was one thing Kate knew about Greg, it was that he was not like most people. While few men would admit to any fear, he was open about his. And he'd gone along with her, even though he was uncomfortable. Kate knew no one else who would have done that for her.

"I'm sorry, Greg. I feel awful, knowing I forced you to ride the Ferris wheel."

"Are you really sorry?" He laid his finger on her lips and gave her a crooked smile. "I'm not."

As his finger caressed her lips, Kate shook her head. The ride with its silly singing and that incredible kiss had been more wonderful than anything she could have imagined. How could she regret the single most memorable event of her life?

"Me, neither."

The alarm rang, jolting Kate awake. Strange. She normally woke after six hours, but this time she'd slept for a full eight. She couldn't even blame oversleeping — for that's what it felt like — on a late night.

They'd returned from the festival several hours earlier than she'd expected, thanks to Roy's vigilance. He must have realized that Sally was more tired than she wanted to admit, because he claimed that his bunions hurt and insisted they leave after they'd all indulged in the chili cook-off.

Thanks to the early start, they'd arrived back at Rainbow's End without seeing any deer, and Kate had fallen asleep almost as soon as her head hit the pillow. Another first. Normally she was restless, tossing and turning for at least half an hour before sleep claimed her. Yesterday had definitely been different. Different in many good ways.

Kate splashed water on her face, dressed hurriedly, then rushed to the lodge, wondering if she'd be too late to watch Greg rowing. While she waited for her messages to download, she stared out the window, searching the lake for a man in a boat. Though the wind was creating small ripples on the surface, there was no sign of Greg. She was too late.

With a small sigh, Kate returned to her laptop and frowned when she saw three messages from Heather, one dated more than twenty-four hours ago. Though she'd been checking messages each morning, she hadn't thought about it yesterday, and she'd become so accustomed to not having cell coverage that she hadn't turned on her phone while they'd been gone.

It was amazing what a difference a week could make. At home her phone was practically an extension of her hand, but Kate wasn't at home. She was on vacation. For a second, she considered deleting the messages unread, but she couldn't, not when she'd promised Heather she would check them daily. As wonderful as this vacation was turning out to be, it was only a vacation, a temporary interlude. Work was permanent, and that made it important.

Kate clicked on the first message. *"Call me immediately. I need to talk to you about a new client."* The second and third had the same content but more urgency, with the final one, delivered two hours earlier, all in capital letters.

Kate tried not to frown. While the prospect of a new client meant extra work for whoever was assigned as the client executive, it happened often enough that no one at the firm panicked. There must be something special about this new client, because Heather was using the email equivalent of shouting, and that was unusual.

Kate glanced at her watch and frowned again. Though she could use the office phone, Angela would be arriving in five minutes. Knowing Heather, five minutes would not be long enough, and Kate didn't want her conversation overheard. She made it back to the cabin in record time and, when she heard her grandmother stirring, knocked on her door.

"I have to go to town for a few minutes," she said when Sally invited her in. Though she suspected Sally knew why Kate went to the lodge each morning, she did not want to engage in a discussion about working while on vacation. Perhaps Sally would think Kate was helping Brandi and Olivia again. "I should be back before breakfast is over."

Her grandmother was still lying in bed, her hair sticking straight up in back. "You don't need to rush. As long as you're going into town, could you bring me a carrot muffin from the Sit 'n' Sip? Roy said they're almost as good as Carmen's. If you get that and some of Carmen's coffee, I can have breakfast in bed."

Alarm speared Kate's heart, and she stared at Sally. Other than a few creases on her cheeks, the result of sleeping on a wrinkled pillowcase, she looked perfectly normal. But her request was not normal. "Are you ill?" Kate had never known her grandmother to linger in bed, and though she had given Sally a breakfast-in-bed tray many years before, planning to surprise her with a special meal and pampering one Mother's Day, Sally had declared that only invalids ate in bed.

"Not at all." Kate's grandmother shook her head as she pushed herself to a sitting position. "I'm feeling lazy. At my age, breakfast in bed sounds good."

As relief flooded through her, Kate smiled. "It sounds good at my age too. I'll be back as soon as I can."

"No rush." Sally switched on the bedside lamp and reached for her e-reader. "I've plenty to keep me busy."

So did Kate, although she suspected that her grandmother would enjoy the next hour more than she. She fished her car keys out of her bag and slid behind the steering wheel, feeling almost as if she were going to work.

Turning left out of the resort, Kate headed up the hill that separated Rainbow's End from the town, and as she did, she saw a jogger. Greg. The man who kissed better than any man she'd dated. Kate pushed that thought firmly out of her mind.

"Need a ride?" she asked, rolling down the window as she reached Greg's side. Like his tennis whites, his jogging attire appeared relatively new, and his shoes bore the logo of a top brand. The expense reminded Kate that while Greg might be currently unemployed, he had once held a well-paying job.

He stopped but jogged in place, panting as he said, "And give up the possibility of shin splints and torn tendons? Not on your life." Greg's eyes narrowed slightly, and Kate wondered if her hair was standing up the way Sally's had. "Why are you out so early?" he asked.

"Sally wants breakfast in bed." If that was only half the story, it was all that he needed to know. Kate had already heard Greg's thoughts on her working while she was supposed to be on vacation, and she didn't want an encore. The memory of yesterday was still too fresh for her to do anything to spoil it.

"You could have arranged that with Carmen," he pointed out, his tone telling Kate her subterfuge had failed.

"You're right," she admitted. "I need to make a phone call, and I didn't want to use the Sinclairs' line."

"Work." It was a statement, not a question.

"Unfortunately, yes." Two days ago, she might not have thought it unfortunate, but today she wanted to live "in the moment" as she'd heard someone describe it. Today she wanted to savor the memories of the time she and Greg had spent together, and — if she was fortunate — create some new memories.

Though he raised an eyebrow, Greg said only, "For future reference, you can get a cell signal at the top of the hill. You don't have to go all the way to Dupree."

"Thanks." Kate put the car back in gear and headed for the summit. When she reached it, she pulled to the side and called Heather.

"Where were you?" Heather demanded when she picked up the phone. To Kate's relief, she sounded harried rather than annoyed.

"At a bluebonnet festival."

Kate heard a brief intake of breath, followed by what sounded almost like a chuckle. Perhaps this wouldn't be as difficult a conversation as she'd expected. "I won't even ask what a person does at a bluebonnet festival," Heather said. "I'm not sure I want to know." Kate heard keys clicking and realized her boss was composing a message while she spoke to her. Heather prided herself on being able to multitask. "I know you're supposed to be on vacation, but something's come up."

"The new client."

"Precisely." The clicking stopped. "Aunt Ivy's Peanuts."

Kate thought for a second, trying and failing to place the name. "I've never heard of them." She switched off the ignition and leaned back in her seat. As she'd guessed when she'd seen Heather's messages, this was going to be a lengthy conversation.

"That's the problem. The company's been around for fifty years. The original owner, the real Aunt Ivy, died six months ago and left the company to two of her children."

Kate stared into the distance, wondering what role Heather expected her to play.

"The company makes a decent profit. In fact, they're doing pretty well," Heather continued, "but Ike and Hazel Preston — they're the new owners — want to change the image. They want to appeal to young, affluent buyers."

Kate smiled at Greg and waved as he reached the top of the hill, then turned around for the easier part of his workout. "When I think about young and affluent, peanuts aren't usually part of the same sentence," she told Heather.

"Precisely." That was one of Heather's favorite words. "That's why Hazel and Ike want to update their image. Their primary product is peanut butter, but they're considering expanding the line. They're looking for guidance as well as advertising."

"It sounds interesting." A change of management often led to new advertising campaigns and occasionally resulted in the company's choosing a new agency. That was one of the reasons Kate read as many business publications as she did. She wanted to be among the first to know when change was occurring at a company, because that was one way of identifying potential new clients. From what Heather had said, Aunt Ivy's had more potential than many.

"It is interesting, especially when you hear their budget."

Kate whistled softly after Heather told her the number. "We can do a lot with that." She pictured TV spots as well as print ads.

"*You* can," Heather corrected her. "They heard about Sid's Seafood and want you to handle their account."

This wasn't just good news. It was excellent news. Kate beamed at the realization that she had something to look forward to when she returned to the office. "Wonderful. I'll start on it when I get back."

Kate blinked. For some reason Greg had come back to the top of the hill. She almost chuckled when he pulled his cell phone out of his pocket. So he wasn't out only for the exercise. Interesting.

"That's not good enough." Heather's voice brought Kate back to her own phone call. "They want the proposal within two weeks."

And that was not good. Not good at all. "I'm in Texas, Heather. On vacation."

"You think I don't know that?" her boss asked, her voice totally devoid of humor. "If you were here, we'd already be running with this. As it is, Nick wants me to let Chase work on it."

"Chase is good." And he wanted to be the next partner, a fact he'd made perfectly clear to both Kate and Nick. "The problem is, he doesn't have any experience with food companies."

"Precisely. That's why I need you. That and the fact that Hazel and Ike Preston made it clear you were to be in charge of their account. It wasn't exactly an ultimatum, but pretty close. They want you, Kate."

And Kate wanted their account. It might not be a once-in-a-lifetime opportunity, but it was the most intriguing opportunity she'd ever had. The chance to do a complete revamping of a corporate image, perhaps helping determine how to expand the product line, was exciting. Kate knew from her own experience as well as Grandpa Larry's stories that projects like this were rare. She couldn't let it slip away.

"Maybe I can convince my grandmother to leave at the end of the week." Though it was unlikely Sally would agree, especially now that she'd be leaving not just Rainbow's End but also Roy, Kate was willing to try. So much was at stake.

The clicking of Heather's keyboard grated on Kate's nerves. So did her boss's next words. "That's not good enough. I need you to start right now. You know we can't put together a decent pitch in a week. It'll be hard enough doing it in two. You need to be on a plane to New York today."

The elation Kate had felt over the possibilities for Aunt Ivy's and the knowledge that Hazel and Ike Preston wanted her to run their account vanished, replaced by a sickening feeling deep inside her. "I don't see how I can."

Heather let out a huff. "I hate bringing out the big guns, but you've left me no alternative. The truth is, Kate, if you're serious about a partnership with Maddox, you'll figure out a way to make this work. I need your decision before close of business today."

"All right."
But it wasn't.

17

"What's wrong?" Greg stared at the woman on the opposite side of the net. They'd been playing tennis for ten minutes, and it was obvious her head wasn't in the game. If she hadn't looked so glum, he might have thought the reason for her inattention was that her mind was wandering back to yesterday and that ride on the Ferris wheel. His own had taken that particular detour more times than he could count. Greg hadn't been able to forget the ride. Oh, why pretend? It wasn't the ride he was remembering. It was the kiss.

He could have done without the ride, although — to his surprise — it hadn't been as bad as he'd expected. That was due to Kate. When Greg had been sitting next to her, he'd been able to concentrate on the light fragrance that always surrounded her. His sisters would be able to describe it, telling him whether it was floral or exotic, whether there were undertones of musk or jasmine. Greg didn't care. All he knew was that it was as much a part of Kate as that lovely blonde hair that had clung to his fingers when he'd touched it.

He'd wondered if her hair was as soft as it appeared. It was. He'd wondered if her lips were as soft as they looked. They were. But they were more than soft. They were sweet. He hadn't been tasting caramel corn when he'd kissed her. He'd been tasting Kate. Wonderful, unforgettable, and now obviously distressed Kate.

"What do you mean?" she asked.

Though he was certain she was aware of how poorly she'd played, Greg sensed that Kate wanted him to identify whatever it was that had alerted him to the problem. "You haven't returned a single volley, and you practically tripped over the serve. Even the first day, you didn't play like this." At least then she'd tried. Today he had the feeling that her body might be on the tennis court, but her mind was somewhere else. If he had to guess, he'd say that her mind was back in New York in her office.

"I guess I'm a little preoccupied."

Greg picked up the ball and nodded toward the bench. There was no point in continuing the match. "Let me guess. It's about the calls you made this morning."

"Yeah." She accepted the bottle of water.

Greg took a slug from his bottle as he considered his next move. He knew she checked messages each day, but this was the first time he'd been aware of her making a call. Something had changed, and her reaction told him it wasn't something good.

Yesterday Kate had been a happy, almost carefree woman. They'd laughed together, and then there had been that unforgettable kiss, a moment so wonderful that nothing had mattered beyond the fact that Greg had his arms around the most amazing woman he'd ever met. If it had been possible, he would never have let her out of his arms, he would never have ended the kiss. But the kiss had ended, and Greg had had to content himself with long gazes at Kate's beautiful face and those tantalizing lips.

The way she'd looked at him had made him believe she felt the same way. The way she'd smiled when he held her hand as they walked through the fairgrounds and the twinkle in her eyes when she'd wiped a speck of chili from his cheek had told him she cared as much as he did. And then she'd gotten those messages from her boss. This morning, Kate had seemed somehow deflated, as if the energy had been drained from her. Now she looked almost gray, as if her lifeblood was being leached away. He had to do something.

"Do you want to talk about it?"

She shook her head, then nodded. "No. Yes."

"If you add maybe, you'll have all the bases covered." Greg kept his voice light, not wanting to discourage Kate from confiding in him. As she'd told Angela only a few days ago, there were times when a person needed to talk.

"You're right. It's not like me to dither." Though Kate laughed, it sounded forced. "The short version of the story is that my boss wants me to work on a new account."

He had been afraid of something like that. "I'm guessing you mean right now, not when you return to New York."

"Yeah." Kate took a swig of water, then frowned as she recapped the bottle. "Heather wants me to cut my vacation short and go back, but I suspect she'd settle for my working while I'm here. It's not like I haven't telecommuted before. We all do that if there's a lot of snow."

Greg tried not to wince at the thought of how difficult telecommuting might be, given Rainbow's End's painfully slow dial-up connection and the limited amount of time

Kate could use it. "Did you agree?"

"Not yet. Heather needs my decision today." Kate glanced at her watch. "I have two hours and thirty-seven minutes left."

"But you're going to say yes." She might think she hadn't made a decision, but the tone of her voice said otherwise.

As a bird flew by, squawking at some unseen menace, Kate nodded. "Probably. My promotion is at stake."

"You know, Kate, there's more to life than a job."

She blinked, and the color that rose to Kate's cheeks told him he'd touched a sensitive nerve. "Says the man who doesn't have one."

"By choice." Greg saw the flicker of uncertainty in her eyes. Kate obviously thought he'd been laid off, one of the millions whose jobs had been lost to downsizing. Now that he'd started, he'd have to finish. It was time to tell her who he was. Correction: who he used to be.

"I left when I realized it wasn't fun anymore and that the only reason I was working was for the money."

Kate leaned forward, fixing her gaze on him. "That's not the only reason I'm working. I enjoy what I do." And she was trying to live up to her grandfather's expectations, to accomplish what he had not. Greg knew that was a powerful motive.

"I enjoyed my job too, until one day I didn't." It probably hadn't happened that suddenly, but it had seemed that way to Greg. One day he'd wakened, realizing that he dreaded going into the office. The thrill had disappeared, replaced by what felt like days of drudgery.

"What did you do then?"

Like the moment the Ferris wheel car had moved upward, Greg had passed the point of no return. He had to tell Kate the truth, and then he'd have to deal with the consequences.

"I took my partner's advice and sold the company."

Kate's eyes widened as she absorbed his statement. "You owned a company? A software company?" She had obviously remembered his comment about working for a software firm in college and had taken the not-so-large leap to assume that he'd continued in the same field.

Greg nodded. "I don't talk about it a lot, especially here, but Drew Carroll and I had a company. I was the majority owner with 60 percent of the stock."

Greg saw the speculation in Kate's expression, but unlike the speculation that normally surrounded him, he did not believe she was trying to calculate his bank balance. She looked more like she was trying to solve a puzzle. "Would I recognize the name?" she asked.

"You might. Have you ever heard of Sys=Simpl?" Employees referred to it as S-squared, but the public knew it by its full name.

"Of course." Kate's expression brightened, and she nodded vigorously, setting her ponytail to bouncing. "I read business magazines as part of my job." He must have looked surprised, because she added, "The primary reason is that I'm looking for trends and possible new clients, but I learn a lot of other things too. I read about the way your software revolutionized small business." She gave him an appraising look. "How did you get started? The articles never mentioned that."

Because he hadn't told the reporters. Though he'd known it would be impossible, he'd tried to keep his family from being involved in the frenzy that accompanied sudden success. His mother would have been embarrassed if reporters had descended on her home, and his father . . . Greg wasn't certain how Dad would have reacted, but he couldn't imagine that it would have been a pleasant scene.

"My parents both worked in the fruit processing plant in my hometown," he said slowly. "They complained about how none of the systems talked to each other. That caused problems and required a lot of duplicate work. I tried to fix that."

"And you did." For the first time today, Kate's smile seemed genuine. "I've never used your software, but from everything I've read, it's brilliant."

"It filled a niche." Admittedly a bigger niche than he'd expected, but it was still a niche.

"It did more than that. It made you and your partner billionaires." She said the words matter-of-factly, as if she knew dozens of billionaires. Perhaps she did. What amazed Greg was that there was no awe in her voice, no calculated gleam in her eyes.

Kate took another swallow of water, her expression serious as she asked, "So why are you here if you have all that money?"

It was a valid question, albeit not the one he'd expected. But nothing about Kate's reaction had been what he'd expected. Instead of looking at him as if he had suddenly sprouted dollar bills all over his body, she seemed genuinely interested in him, in what made Greg Vange tick, rather than what his money could buy. No one else, not even his family, had reacted so well.

As Kate raised one eyebrow, Greg realized she was waiting for his answer. It was simple and yet complex. "I'm trying to figure out what God wants me to do next." He wasn't certain what God had in mind for him, but he couldn't discount the possibility that he might have been led here to keep Kate from making the same mistakes he had.

She tipped her head to one side, reminding him of a bird listening for the soft slither of a worm. "Have you considered that your purpose might be to save Rainbow's End?"

It was clear that the tennis game was over. That was just as well, because this was more interesting and more important. "The thought has crossed my mind." More than once. The day he'd arrived and had seen the resort's deplorable condition, Greg had wondered if he ought to invest in it. Later, when he'd learned that the Sinclairs were anxious to sell, he'd considered buying it. But even though the thoughts refused to be dismissed, he'd never pursued them, because each time, he'd felt as if there were an invisible hand holding him back.

"If by saving Rainbow's End you mean buying it, I don't think that's the answer." Greg hoped Kate would understand. "Rainbow's End needs more than my money. It needs a whole new focus, and I don't have a clue what that should be."

Kate drained the bottle, then recapped it and tossed it into Greg's bag for future recycling. "There's a lot of talent in Dupree. You could hire some of them to develop theme weeks here. Lauren could teach quilting, and I saw a wonderful silversmith shop. The owner could probably be persuaded to share his knowledge with guests. Carmen could even offer cooking classes. Those would attract more people."

Greg hadn't thought of that angle, but it made sense. Other resorts and even cruise lines attempted to attract a specialized clientele using similar approaches. "They're good ideas, Kate. They'd probably work, but for some reason, they don't feel right to me. Maybe it's because they seem like temporary patches rather than a real fix. I don't know."

Greg hesitated, not wanting to burden Kate with his own problems, then realized she was waiting for the rest of his explanation. "Even if I wanted to buy Rainbow's End, there's another problem. I don't think I'd be good at running it. You've seen what a disaster the Sinclairs have created. They had good intentions, but they don't have the right background. I don't, either."

Greg looked up. A bank of clouds was moving in swiftly from the west, threatening a storm. It felt like a metaphor for his life. Yesterday had been the happiest day he could recall — the sun — but today the clouds of doubt had rolled in.

"Drew was the front man for Sys=Simpl." Greg continued his explanation. "He handled most of the people-related aspects of the company. Other than press conferences announcing new releases and meetings with venture capitalists, I was behind the scenes, designing the software. That's what I'm good at."

And, according to Drew, that was the only thing Greg was good at. "You may be brilliant, but you don't relate well to people," his partner had told him more than once. Though the criticism had bothered Greg, it wasn't unexpected. He had heard variations on that theme his whole life. According to his father, he lacked the basic elements for making friends as well as scoring a touchdown. It was only once he'd moved to Stanford and was surrounded by other equally smart and motivated students that he'd felt at ease. Still, running a resort and dealing with guests on a daily basis was far different from convincing venture capitalists to invest in his ideas.

As if she sensed Greg's turbulent thoughts, Kate laid her hand on his and squeezed it lightly. "I think you're selling yourself short. You may not realize it, but you're good with people. Look at how you handled little Fiona and the way you convinced Sally it would be a good idea for you to drive to the bluebonnet festival. You obviously understand what people need. If you didn't, your software wouldn't be so successful." Kate gave his hand another squeeze before releasing it. "I think you can do anything you set your mind to."

It was a good thing Greg wasn't a blusher. If he were, Kate's praise would have sent blood rushing to his face. As it was, he wasn't certain what pleased him more, her touch or her words. All Greg knew was that Kate had ignited a fire deep inside him.

He'd received accolades for his software. The company's success had given him the reward of financial security. And yet nothing had touched his heart the way Kate's approval had. She made him feel like one of those storybook knights who slayed dragons. If only he could live up to Kate's expectations.

"I appreciate your vote of confidence." More than she'd ever know. "But much as

I'd like to see Rainbow's End continue, I can't do it alone. It needs more than I can provide."

Kate shook her head, once again setting her ponytail to swaying. It was obvious she wasn't going to give up and that she didn't want him to, either. "You could hire people to do whatever you're not comfortable with. There are plenty of folks who could handle the finances and promotions, even the day-to-day running of the resort."

"Maybe." Greg hadn't thought about the details, mostly because every time the idea of buying Rainbow's End popped into his head, he heard a small voice saying no. "I like your ideas, Kate. In fact, I think they're really good, but . . ." He paused, wanting to choose his words carefully. "It's possible I'll change my mind, but it doesn't feel right."

Though Kate's face mirrored disappointment, she nodded. "You have to follow your instincts, and so do I."

18

"Let's slow down a bit."

Kate turned to stare at her grandmother. They were on their way to breakfast, following the same route they always did. The morning was no hotter than the others. If anything, the humidity had dropped a few points and the light breeze made it feel almost cool. It was a perfect spring morning, but not for Sally. She had her hand on her chest, her cheeks were flushed, and she sounded out of breath.

"Sure." Kate slowed her pace to little more than a crawl, while her own heartbeat accelerated. The fears that had been lurking at the back of her mind took front and center. For all Sally's claims that her condition was stable, it appeared that her health was more fragile than she would admit.

"Do you want to sit down?" They were close enough to one of the unoccupied cabins that they could sit on the steps.

"No need." Sally took a deep breath, held it for a couple seconds, then slowly released it in what she'd once told Kate was a good way to slow her heart rate.

Though her grandmother was starting to look better, Kate couldn't let the episode pass without trying to discover its cause. "Did you take your meds this morning?" Kate had been surprised by the number of prescription bottles her grandmother had arranged on her dresser, everything from low-dosage aspirin to blood thinners.

Sally nodded vigorously as she released yet another deep breath. "Of course I did. You were the one who always 'forgot' " — she put air quotes around the word — "to take her vitamins."

Relieved that her grandmother's breathlessness seemed to have abated, Kate forced a playful tone to her voice. "That's because you refused to buy chewable ones. My friends said they tasted like candy."

"Medicine's not supposed to taste like candy. You're just supposed to swallow it."

Kate nodded. Not only did that sound like the usual feisty Sally, but her grandmother's color was better. It seemed that whatever had been wrong had been only momentary. Perhaps they had been walking too fast. Though she had not been aware of it, it was possible that Kate's pace had been more rapid than normal. In fact, it was more than possible. It was probable. Kate had said nothing, but she was in a hurry to finish breakfast today so she could work. She hoped that Sally was intrigued enough by the book she'd started last night that she'd want to read for an hour or so after they ate. That would give Kate time to start reviewing the files she'd downloaded this morning.

Heather had sent copies of Aunt Ivy's most recent ad campaign, the corporate mission statement, product lists, even lists of ingredients. Kate wanted — no, she needed — to read them. Greg might disapprove of her working, but this was an opportunity she could not miss. The truth was, she suspected Greg would have made the same decision if he'd been at the same stage of his career. From the articles Kate had read about Sys=Simpl, she knew he'd been single-minded in his determination to make his software the best on the market. Perhaps that was the reason he wasn't married and didn't have a girlfriend.

Greg's marital status was not her concern, at least not this morning. She wrenched her thoughts back to the present and smiled at her grandmother. "You'll be glad to know that I take my vitamins regularly now."

"I am glad to hear that." Sally wagged a finger at Kate as they entered the dining hall and took plates from the end of the buffet. "I won't always be around to remind you, you know."

For the second time in less than ten minutes, fear speared through Kate. It was one thing for Sally to tell her that the doctor was concerned about her heart, quite another to have her talking like this, especially after being breathless and looking ill. "What do you mean?"

A mischievous grin creased Sally's face. "For one thing, I won't be able to have lunch with you today. Roy invited me to his house."

Kate caught herself before she bobbled her plate filled with scrambled eggs and sausage. Whatever she'd been expecting, it wasn't that. Though Sally and Roy had been, to use Sally's expression, thick as thieves at the bluebonnet festival, Kate hadn't realized that their relationship had progressed to this stage.

"That sounds like a date."

Her cheeks flushed with what was obviously a blush rather than a sign of illness, Sally shook her head. "I wouldn't call it that. We're just two friends sharing a meal."

Sally's blush said it was more than that. "Lunch at his house sounds like more than a casual meal. Definitely a date, if you ask me."

Though they spoke of ordinary things while they savored Carmen's breakfast buffet, Kate could not stop thinking about Sally and Roy's luncheon date. She ought to be pleased, since it would give her more time to work on Aunt Ivy's account, but still . . . Try though she might to dismiss it, there was something disturbing about the thought of Sally and Roy together.

She had shocked Kate, Sally reflected as she studied her appearance in the mirror. She hadn't been sure how her granddaughter would react. Though she hadn't said much, it was clear that Kate was disturbed. What Sally didn't know was whether it was because she was dating or because she was dating Roy.

She tucked the light blue shirt into the denim skirt, admiring the way the calf-length skirt showed off her boots. It was good but not great. The outfit needed something else. Sally held up several necklaces, shaking her head at each. The silver earrings added a nice touch, but they weren't enough. Opening the top dresser drawer, she pulled out the bandanna Roy had convinced her to buy at the festival and knotted it around her neck. Perfect. Even Kate, the fashionista, would have to approve of Sally's clothing, though she might disapprove of the reason Sally was dressing for lunch. Too bad. Kate's disapproval wouldn't stop her from spending time with Roy. This was something she wanted to do.

"They picked the wrong girl for Bluebonnet Queen," Roy said five minutes later as he opened the door to his truck and helped her in. "They should have chosen you."

The glint in Roy's gray eyes made Sally's heart skip a beat. Goodness, she hadn't felt like that in years and years. She managed a cool smile, not wanting to admit how much she was affected by Roy's words and — more than that — by the look in his eyes.

"If you think flattery will convince me to cook lunch, you're mistaken. I've been looking forward to your cooking." When he'd invited her, Sally had been both surprised and touched by the fact that Roy wanted to prepare a meal for her. Larry had never done that. He'd done many other thoughtful and loving things, but he had never cooked.

Roy turned the key to start the truck. "I wouldn't renege on that. I promised you a home-cooked meal, and that's what you're going to get. It's a good thing I did most of the cooking in advance," he said with a wink and a smile. "Having you in my kitchen is going to be mighty distracting, especially with you wearing that outfit. That blue blouse, shirt" — he shrugged — "whatever you call it, is the exact shade as your eyes: bluebonnet blue."

Roy had noticed not just that her eyes were blue but the precise shade. Sally felt a rush of pleasure at the thought that this man had done what no other had in many years. "You look pretty dashing yourself," she said, taking in his freshly cut hair and the shirt so new it still bore creases from the package. It was downright flattering to realize that he'd gone to so much trouble.

As the truck climbed the hill that separated Rainbow's End from the town, Sally turned around.

"Something wrong?"

She shook her head. "I just like the view from here. Rainbow's End looks like it's in a world of its own."

"It's mighty pretty," Roy agreed. "I can see why the first owners picked this spot."

"The first time I saw it, I knew it was special. That's why I wanted to come back."

Roy slowed the truck and turned to face

her. "Weren't you afraid it wouldn't be as good as you remembered?"

Sally shook her head again. "Kate was the one who worried about that. She told me I was making a mistake, trying to recapture the past. That wasn't the reason I wanted to come. I knew it would be different to come with my granddaughter instead of my husband, but I felt an urging. I can't explain it other than to say that I was convinced this was the time I was supposed to come here."

Pushing his glasses back on his nose, Roy smiled. "That's what Greg said too. He was convinced God wanted him to be here, but he hasn't figured out the reason yet. I suspect that's why he's stayed as long as he has."

"I probably sound like a matchmaking grandmother, but I wonder if the reason he's here is Kate." There was no mistaking the spring in Kate's step or the smile on her face when she was with Greg.

Roy shrugged. "Stranger things have happened. I can tell you one thing. Greg is a mighty fine young man. Now, let's have lunch."

When they reached Dupree, Roy turned left on the second street. Like the others Sally had seen the day she and Kate explored the town, this street was bordered by old oak trees, their broad branches forming a canopy over the pavement. Small but well-cared-for houses lined both sides of the road, the presence of plastic tricycles and wagons bearing witness to families with young children. It was very different from Sally's neighborhood at home. The trees, the shrubs, even the grass told her she was not in Western New York. And then there were the houses.

Roy pulled the truck onto a concrete driveway and turned off the engine. While she waited for him to open her door, Sally studied his home. Though she lived in a hundred-year-old two-story clapboard-sided colonial with black shutters, Roy's house was a simple one-story brick building that she guessed was a third smaller than hers. It also appeared to be of considerably newer construction.

As they walked through the front door, Sally saw that the differences were not confined to the exterior. Her home had a center hall, a formal living and dining room, a kitchen with a breakfast nook, and a separate family room. Roy's had an open floor plan with one huge multipurpose room visible from the front doorway. A small hall off the back led to what Sally assumed was the bedroom wing.

"This is very nice," she said. There was something reassuring about the large room, as if it had no pretensions to grandeur, preferring comfort over elegance.

Roy chuckled as if he'd read her thoughts. "Let me give you the grand tour." He took a couple steps into the room and gestured toward the right. "This is the living room." A stone fireplace highlighted one wall. "And the family room," he added. "To your left, you'll see the kitchen, dining room, breakfast nook, and general gathering area." A granite-topped counter separated the working kitchen from the rest of the room, but otherwise there were no barriers. Roy tipped his head toward the opposite end. "There are three bedrooms down the hall."

"It's very practical." And very homey, although Sally couldn't identify exactly what made her feel that way. It was simply that from the moment she'd walked inside the front door, she had felt as if she were returning to a place she had once visited, a place filled with happy memories.

"It was. Barb didn't have to leave the kitchen to keep an eye on the boys. They did a lot of homework at that table." Roy gestured toward the wooden table now set with two place mats and napkins.

"You miss her a lot, don't you?"

He nodded, his gray eyes more serious than they'd been a moment earlier. "Not a day goes by that I don't think of her. There were times when I didn't know how I was going to get through the day without her." Roy tossed his Stetson onto the hat rack. "It's better now that you're here."

He gave Sally a long look, as if trying to gauge her reaction. What could she say other than that she was incredibly flattered? Before she could form the words, Roy took a step toward her and cradled her chin in his hand, tipping it so she was looking directly at him. "For the first time since Barb died, I feel as if I'm living, not simply existing."

Tears sprang to Sally's eyes, and she dashed them away, lest he think she was sad. She wasn't. She was simply overcome by the realization that this man felt so deeply about her. Sally had known that he was special from the day she'd met him, but she had not let herself dream that what they shared was anything more than friendship. "That's one of the nicest things anyone's ever said to me."

"You're a special woman, Sally."

She caught her breath at the realization that he'd used the same word she had just used to describe him. Was it coincidence, or were they on the same wavelength?

Roy stared at her lips as if he were going to kiss them. They were definitely on the same wavelength. It would be wonderful, so wonderful, to feel Roy's lips on hers. But though he continued to stare, he made no further move, and so she said simply, "And you're a special man."

"Let's eat." Roy let his hand drop to his side and walked into the kitchen area, insisting there was nothing Sally could do to help with the meal preparation. Though she was disappointed that the tender moment had ended, Sally reminded herself that the day was not over. Perhaps he'd kiss her before they returned to Rainbow's End, or perhaps Roy did not believe in kissing on the first date.

Instead of pulling out one of the stools, Sally leaned on the counter and watched as Roy moved with brisk efficiency, removing a fancy bowl from the refrigerator, placing what smelled like freshly baked rolls on a small platter, pouring two glasses of sweet tea. "I hope you like the food," he said as he pulled out Sally's chair for her.

She did. Though Roy admitted that he'd bought the rolls and merely heated them, the salad was his own creation. It might be chicken salad, but it was unlike any Sally had ever eaten. In addition to succulent chunks of chicken, the salad boasted tricolor pasta, corn, black beans, and a spicy dressing whose ingredients Sally could not identify.

"This is delicious," she told Roy after she'd savored several bites. "What's in the dressing?"

He shook his head as he buttered a roll. "Carmen may give out her recipes, but I'm not that foolish. I want you to have a reason to come back."

Her heart skipped a beat. "All you have to do is ask." And there was nothing Sally wanted more than to have him ask. This was just lunch, she reminded herself, and yet it felt like so much more than a simple meal shared by two friends. The gleam in Roy's eyes made her feel as if she were the only woman in the world, the one he'd been waiting for. What a wonderful feeling!

Sally wondered what her eyes were revealing. She hadn't thought she was waiting for anyone. If someone had asked, she would have told them that, yes, there were times when she was lonely, but she hadn't expected the hole in her heart to be filled until she and Larry were reunited in heaven. That's what she would have said two weeks ago. She would have told anyone who asked that part of the reason she was coming to Rainbow's End was to relive happy memories. She had had no expectations of creating new ones with a man like Roy. Now . . .

Sally smiled at him, unsure what to say but wanting him to know that she hadn't been joking earlier when she'd told him he was special. Since she'd met Roy, her life had been different. She was different, she amended. She was happier. For the first time in ten years, she looked forward to each day, and it wasn't simply because Kate was with her. Kate was part of her happiness, but so was this man.

It was true that Sally had been apprehensive about coming here today. She had thought it would be awkward, being in another woman's house. She had expected to feel like a stranger, almost an interloper. Instead, she felt at home.

There was nothing familiar here, no reminders of Larry or her beloved granddaughter. At best, she should feel like a visitor. But though Sally couldn't explain it, she could picture herself spending the rest of her life in this house with this man.

What would Kate think of that?

19

Kate frowned as yet another serve went out of bounds. "I might as well give up. I just seem to be getting worse." She picked up another ball and tossed it over her head, this time failing to hit it.

"That's because you're not concentrating," Greg said as he walked to the net and handed her the first ball. "Tennis is like any sport. You need to give it your full attention. My guess is you're thinking about that new account."

"Partly." Kate nodded as Greg tipped his head toward the bench, silently suggesting they take a break. There was no question that she'd been distracted by the Aunt Ivy's account. She had even considered canceling tennis to give herself more time to work, but she hadn't.

Though at first Kate had rationalized her decision by reminding herself that exercise often triggered creativity, that was only an excuse. The truth was, she wanted to spend time with Greg. It was probably foolish. While she should have been focused on work, her mind had drifted back to the blue-bonnet festival and the kiss they had shared.

Kate sank onto the bench and accepted the bottle of water Greg offered. Though they hadn't been out long, she was still unaccustomed to the warmth of the Texas sun.

"I got an email from Gillian — she was my best friend in high school — saying she'd just received the invitation to our reunion and wondered if I planned to be there. They're planning a formal dinner-dance exactly ten years after our graduation day." Kate wasn't certain why she was giving Greg all those details. He didn't need them.

He took a swig of water before he spoke. "Are you planning to go?"

"I don't know."

"Do you want to?"

That was the problem. Kate wasn't sure. "I don't know," she said for the second time. "I have mixed feelings about high school."

Greg nodded as if he understood.

"I imagine my school was like most," Kate said. "We had a caste system. I wasn't on

286

the bottom rung, but the fact that I was what the teachers called a high achiever meant that I wasn't accepted into many groups. Gillian had the same problem, because even in grade school, it was obvious that she was a talented musician. Fortunately, we had each other."

"And I'm guessing she won't attend the reunion unless you do."

"Exactly." Greg did understand. "The thing is, I'm not sure why I'd be going. It's not like I've spent the last ten years wondering what happened to my classmates."

When Greg said nothing, Kate raised an eyebrow. "Did you attend your reunion?" He shook his head. "Why not?"

Greg's laugh betrayed bitterness. "Because unlike you, I was on the bottom rung. At Orchard Slope High, if you had a Y chromosome and couldn't play sports, you were nothing. I wasn't an academic success, either. My grades were average, because I didn't care about who fought in the Peloponnesian wars or why Shakespeare wrote both comedies and tragedies. My only interest was computers. Fortunately, my SATs and the software I'd developed convinced Stanford to take a chance on me."

And he'd been wildly successful. Kate did some quick arithmetic. By the time of his reunion, Greg was already a multimillionaire. "Didn't you want to show everyone how successful you were?"

He shook his head. "Why? I'm still the same Greg Vange who couldn't score a touchdown or hit a baseball. That'll never change."

Kate's heart ached for the man whose childhood wounds had yet to heal. She wished there were something she could do to help him, and just then Greg shook his head as if he'd read her thoughts.

"So tell me about your peanut butter company. That's got to be a happier topic than my high school years. What have you done so far?"

"I've looked at past campaigns. From what I've seen, it's no wonder sales are stagnant." Kate took another swig of water. "The product is good." Heather had overnighted her a box with every size jar of Aunt Ivy's peanut butter, and Kate had sampled one. "The problem is that the ads are twenty years out-of-date. Not just the ads but the labels too. They need to revamp everything."

"And you're not coming up with any ideas."

That was dangerously close to the truth. "I have some, but nothing that will work.

It's all organic peanut butter, so I thought about using the initials AOPB the way that TV chef did with extra virgin olive oil."

Greg's expression told Kate he did not watch TV cooking shows and made her wonder whether he cooked at all. She suspected he was like many single men and relied on takeout and frozen entrees. Peanut butter was probably not a staple in Greg's pantry.

"Using the initials isn't a bad idea," she continued, "but it's not enough. I need a visual." The TV chef wasn't promoting any specific brand of olive oil, so the acronym worked. Kate, on the other hand, was supposed to convince consumers that the only brand of peanut butter they wanted on their shelves was Aunt Ivy's. She could include Aunt Ivy's initials along with the acronym, but AIAOPB was simply too long to work as a slogan.

"What do the ads look like now?"

Kate wrinkled her nose, remembering. "It's a woman — the original Aunt Ivy — holding a jar of peanut butter." As Greg raised an eyebrow, she chuckled. "Did I say twenty years out-of-date? More than that. The labels remind me of something from the fifties or sixties, and the ads are almost as bad."

"I thought retro was good. Look at all the people buying vinyl records, even though digital sounds better."

When Kate wrinkled her nose again, Greg tugged her to her feet. "Let's walk. You need some exercise, and it doesn't seem that tennis is your game today." As they headed down the rutted road, he said, "So tell me why retro is bad."

That moment, Kate couldn't think of anything to say about retro. She could, however, tell him why holding hands was good. His was larger than hers, firmer and stronger, and the touch of his palm on hers made Kate want to soar at the same time that she felt grounded. Sally had once told her everyone needed roots and wings. At the time, Kate hadn't understood. Now she did. Walking hand in hand with Greg, she felt as if she had both. She was connected to a man who aroused deeper feelings than she'd ever experienced. Greg made her laugh; his past made her want to cry; most of all, he made her feel alive. But they were talking about peanut butter, not the way Kate felt when she was with him.

"The problem is that retro's only a small part of the marketplace." Though her thoughts were skittering in a dozen directions, fantasizing about Greg's hand cupping her face again, his lips capturing hers, somehow Kate's voice sounded normal. "I need something with mass appeal. I want hundreds of thousands of people to believe that Aunt Ivy's is not just the best peanut butter available but the only one they'd consider eating or feeding to their kids."

"That's a pretty tall order."

Kate nodded. Perhaps it was the fact that so much was wrong with Aunt Ivy's that made her feel almost paralyzed. Normally when she started on a new project, the problem wasn't a lack of ideas but a glut of them. She was accustomed to keeping a pad and pencil with her at all times so she could jot down ideas as they popped into her brain. Today nothing was popping.

"I wish I could help."

Greg quickened the pace so that they were practically jogging.

"That's not helping," Kate said as her ankle turned on a rough patch of road. "Tell me, what's the first thing you think about when you hear the words peanut butter?"

"Allergies."

It wasn't funny, and yet Kate laughed. "I don't think that'll be part of my ad."

Greg threaded his fingers through hers and slowed their pace to a walk. "If we're playing the word association game, what's your answer?"

"Sonograms."

As she'd expected, Greg's eyebrows rose. "Sonograms?"

"Yep. One of my co-workers was pregnant last year, and she shared a lot of stories with us. When she had her first sonogram, she declared that the baby looked like a peanut and started calling it that."

Greg's astonishment turned to curiosity. "Did you see the sonogram? Did the baby look like a peanut?"

"Yes and yes. And for the next six months, all of us called Brittany's baby Peanut. It turned out to be a girl that Brittany and her husband named Penelope." Kate smiled at the thought of the sweet baby she'd held in her arms only a few days before she'd left for Texas. "No one's supposed to call her Peanut, but . . ."

"You do."

Kate nodded. "And that's another idea I can't use to sell Aunt Ivy's. I'm back to ground zero."

"If I think of anything, I'll let you know." Greg glanced at his watch. "Meanwhile, it's about time to get back to your grand-mother."

"Not today." Kate looked at her own watch, surprised at how much time had passed. It seemed as if it had been no more than ten minutes since she'd arrived at the tennis court. "Sally's having lunch with Roy. She said she might not be back until three or four."

For a second, Greg was silent, though his green eyes narrowed as he looked at her. "You don't sound too pleased by that." He squeezed her hand, as if to take any possible sting from the words.

Kate hadn't realized that her feelings were so apparent, but she should have realized that if anyone would see below the surface, it would be Greg. Though he might believe he lacked interpersonal skills, Kate had seen no evidence of that. To the contrary, he appeared more than normally sensitive to others' feelings. Perhaps that was the result of his childhood. It was clear he'd been an outsider. Maybe that had given him the ability to empathize.

"I'm happy that Sally has friends," Kate said, hoping she didn't sound defensive.

"Are you, or are you worried about sharing her attention?"

If anyone else had asked that, Kate would have fired off an immediate denial. But the way Greg was studying her, she knew he'd see behind it. "You think I'm jealous?" she asked. "If anyone deserves happiness, it's Sally."

He nodded slowly. "I agree. The question is whether you do, deep in your heart. My guess is that the reason you're distracted isn't the reunion or the peanut butter company. It's your grandmother."

Kate nodded slowly, thinking about how worried she'd been this morning when Sally had seemed out of breath. That had triggered all kinds of unhappy thoughts of how different Kate's life would be without her grandmother. Sally wasn't simply her only family; she was Kate's rock, the person she knew would support her with her unconditional love. Kate didn't want to think of that ending.

"You're right that I'm worried about Sally," she admitted. "It's complicated. There's her health, and now there's Roy." Kate hoped Greg would understand. "Sally's been the one stable part of my life. I don't want that to change." And it would if Sally's health deteriorated or her friendship with Roy developed into something more serious.

The nightmare came again, but this time was different. As always, Greg stood on the edge of the precipice. The fear was there, as intense as ever, mingled with the knowledge of what would happen. As always, he felt powerless, but tonight he resolved that he would not fall. Somehow, some way, he would remain on the mountain. And somehow, some way, he would find his way back to sea level.

Start small, he told himself, and so he curled his toes inside his boots in a desperate attempt to keep from tumbling over the cliff. Even as he did it, he knew how futile the effort was. It wasn't gravity that would send him over the edge. It was that deadly push.

"Jump! Jump!" The voice came from behind him as it always did. "Jump!" He wouldn't turn to see his tormentor. He couldn't without losing his precarious balance. Greg knew that, just as he knew that he had to do something. And then he felt it, a presence directly behind him. For a second, he could not breathe. Never before had he felt his killer's presence. Never before had he smelled that sweet perfume. A woman's perfume. Mentally shaking himself, Greg inhaled a deep cleansing breath at the realization that whoever was behind him, it was not the killer. The killer was a man; he knew that as surely as he knew his own name. But why was a woman so close that he could smell her fragrance? Couldn't she see the danger?

With every fiber of his being, Greg wanted to turn, to warn her not to come any closer, but he couldn't. Any movement would be his death sentence and hers too, for somehow he knew that she would try to catch him and in doing so would tumble over the cliff with him.

She was closer now, close enough that he could feel her breath. *Go back!* he shouted, but no sound came out. Instead he heard her whisper, "Don't jump," as she wrapped her arms around his waist. For a second he felt nothing but relief. He was safe. She was safe. They were safe. And then it happened. Though the woman clung to his back, somehow he felt the shove. An instant later, he was catapulted off the edge, dragging the woman with him, and in that instant, he knew who she was. Kate.

Greg wakened, his heart pounding with terror, his mouth so dry he could hardly swallow. It was only a dream, he told himself. It meant nothing, and yet he didn't believe that. Dreams meant something. He simply did not know how to decode this one.

He'd always suspected that the nightmares were harbingers of danger of some sort, although not necessarily physical danger. While he was in California working on a new release of the software, the dangers Greg had faced had been the inability to find a solution to a bug or creating a clumsy design that took too much processing power and slowed his clients' systems to unacceptable levels. Those were no longer his worries.

That was good, but it also left Greg with more unanswered questions. What danger could he possibly be facing here, and — more importantly — why had Kate suddenly become part of his dream? Was the dream a warning to stay away from her? Though she'd comforted him, the comfort had exacted a terrible price. It was because of Greg that Kate had plummeted off the cliff. He couldn't let anyone or anything harm Kate. But what could he do?

Wiping the sweat from his brow, Greg swung his legs out of bed and stared at the clock. It was too early to run. Until the sun came up, there was too much danger of turning his ankle on a rough patch of road, but there was nothing stopping him from a long, hard row.

20

"I think I'll have her add purple stripes."

Kate blinked as the words registered. "What did you say?" She and Sally had been enjoying a breakfast of fluffy Belgian waffles with peach syrup made — naturally — from Hill Country peaches when Sally delivered her bombshell.

"You weren't listening to me," her grandmother said with a hint of asperity. "Your body might be here, but your mind is miles away."

The fact that the accusation was true and that it wasn't the first time she'd heard it disturbed Kate. She used to be able to concentrate, but for the past few days, she'd found her mind wandering. Kate could blame it on Heather and the new account, but the problem had started before then. Ever since the bluebonnet festival, she had found herself daydreaming, and it wasn't about peanut butter.

"I'm sorry. I was thinking about something else, and that was rude." Kate raised her eyebrows as she watched her grandmother cut another piece of waffle. "You aren't really going to put purple streaks in your hair, are you?"

Sally shrugged. "We'll see. If you'd been listening, you would know that I made an appointment to have my hair done tomorrow morning. I hope you'll take me to town."

"Of course." It was no hardship to drive Sally to Dupree, and while she was waiting for her grandmother, Kate could pay a visit to Lauren's quilt shop. "What time's your appointment?"

"Nine o'clock." Perfect. That was when Hill Country Pieces opened.

"Now, what was more interesting than the thought of your grandmother with Easter-egg-colored hair?" Sally sipped her coffee, never letting her gaze drop from Kate's face.

There was no reason to lie. "I was thinking of Greg." Though she'd also been reviewing the notes she'd made about Aunt Ivy's campaign, Greg had been foremost in Kate's mind. She'd wakened this morning with the feeling that something was wrong, that he needed her, but she couldn't identify the source of her concern, and she hadn't

299

been able to talk to him.

When she'd gone to the lodge for her pre-breakfast check of messages, Kate had looked for Greg, hoping to see him on the lake, but he'd obviously rowed earlier than normal today, because the boat was already on the dock drying. That might mean that he was jogging. Unless he had gone back to sleep after his early morning row, he wasn't in his cabin. Though it meant a slight detour, Kate had been worried enough that she had walked past Greg's cabin on her way back from the lodge. The absence of lights made her think he was gone.

"Did you know that Greg used to own a software company?" she asked.

Though Kate had meant it as a rhetorical question, Sally nodded. "Roy mentioned that. He said he'd been curious about him, so he did some checking online. When he saw Greg's name associated with some fancy software company, he asked him point-blank. Greg wouldn't lie, but he also asked Roy not to spread the story around."

Sally took another bite of waffle. When she'd swallowed it, she continued. "Roy didn't say anything more, but you don't have to be a Rhodes scholar to figure out that Greg must have had his share of people pretending to be friends just to see what they could get from him."

Kate had no trouble imagining that, and knowing what she did about his high school years, it wasn't difficult to imagine how wary he'd become. What she didn't know was why Sally and Roy had been discussing Greg in the first place.

"In case you're wondering, the story came out when I told Roy I liked Greg much better than the other men you've dated." Kate had been curious about that, but now a new worry assailed her: the possibility her grandmother could read her mind. Of course she couldn't. Matchmaker Sally was at it again.

Uncertain whether or not to be annoyed by her grandmother's discussion of her love life, Kate settled for a disclaimer. "Greg and I are not dating." There was no way she'd tell Sally that Greg had kissed her. If her grandmother knew about that kiss — that wonderful, unforgettable kiss — she would consider it a signal to begin shopping for wedding invitations.

Sally smiled over the rim of her coffee cup. "You and Greg are spending a lot of time together."

And Kate had told him things she had not confided to either Lou or Pete. Neither of them knew her mixed feelings about high school. The fact that she'd shared her past with Greg was another thing Kate would not tell her grandmother.

She shrugged, dismissing Sally's observation. "In case you haven't noticed, there aren't a lot of other people here."

"Don't get defensive, Kate. Greg's good for you." The gleam in Sally's eye told Kate she considered him a suitable candidate for grandson-in-law. And, knowing Sally, she had come to that conclusion before she learned that he was a wealthy man.

"Are you playing matchmaker again?"

"What if I am?" Sally stared at Kate, practically daring her to be the first to look away. "It's a grandmother's prerogative. I want to see you happily married. Is that too much to ask for?"

"No." Kate reached for the syrup pitcher and drizzled some on the rest of her waffle. "It's what I want too, but I need to find the right man."

Sally's grin resembled the famous Cheshire cat. "Open your eyes."

"Would you taste this and let me know what you think?" Kate asked as she strolled into the kitchen, trying to look nonchalant. With some luck, Carmen would be able to turn this day around. So far, it had not been one of Kate's best. The dark circles under Greg's eyes refuted his claim that nothing was wrong. Everyone had an occasional bad night, but Kate suspected this was something more than run-of-the-mill insomnia. Still, if Greg chose to pretend that everything was fine, there was little Kate could do.

Then there was her grandmother and her insistence that Greg was the perfect man for Kate. Sally had expounded on that subject all through their morning walk, leaving Kate feeling decidedly out of sorts. Greg *was* a wonderful man. She knew that, but she also knew better than to think that attraction, even an attraction as strong as the one she felt for Greg, was the same thing as love.

The only positive thing that had happened was that when Kate had walked through the office, she'd found Angela with a broad smile on her face. It seemed she'd received a last-minute reservation for the weekend, a party of eight. For the first time since Kate had arrived, there'd be more than one table set for dinner.

Greg was working to ready the cabins for the new guests, Sally and Roy were playing chess, and Kate was trying to find a concept for Aunt Ivy's. So far, the only ideas she'd come up with were duds, not worth discussing with Heather. In desperation, she'd come to Carmen, hoping that being in a kitchen might inspire her.

"I'd like your opinion." Kate held out a jar of Aunt Ivy's All Organic Peanut Butter with a sheet of plain paper covering the label. When she'd done test marketing in college, she'd been taught that it was critical not to prejudice an opinion in any way. It was a good precept made all the more important by the dated label. Stodgy, old-fashioned, blah. Those were the adjectives Kate used to describe the current label. What she needed was exciting, modern, maybe even edgy. But first she needed to know if the peanut butter was as good as she thought. That's where Carmen could help.

Carmen dug a spoon into the jar, closing her eyes as she tasted, then swallowed the peanut butter. "It's good," she said at last. "Better than the brand I buy."

That was what Kate had thought when she'd first tasted it. The problem was, she hadn't been able to pinpoint the differences. "Better how?" Other consumers might not be able to describe differences, but Carmen could. This was the woman who knew exactly how much cumin to add to tamale sauce to give it the special something that distinguished it from ordinary sauces.

"Two things." Carmen laid her spoon in the sink and turned back to Kate. "First, the chunks are a little bit bigger than most brands. That gives it more crunch. I like that, but some folks won't, even the ones who normally eat crunchy peanut butter. The second difference is the flavor. It's deeper than my old standby. It tastes more like freshly roasted peanuts than other brands."

Kate scribbled notes, not wanting to trust her memory. It was good that Carmen liked Aunt Ivy's, but there was one more critical question. "Would you buy it?" Kate removed the paper, revealing the label.

Carmen studied the jar. "If I hadn't tasted it, I probably wouldn't pick it up." Her candor confirmed Kate's belief that the label was a major deterrent to sales. "But now that I've tried it, I would buy it if it wasn't too much more expensive." Pointing to the label, Carmen added, "I like the fact that it's organic, but organic products usually have a higher price tag."

And price was important to the average consumer. While the affluent market that Aunt Ivy's sought was less sensitive to price, Kate didn't want to ignore a major market segment.

"What if it were the same price?"

"Then I'd definitely buy it." Carmen reached for a clean spoon and took another sample. When she'd tasted it, she nodded. "As I said before, the flavor is excellent. The label wouldn't catch my eye, though." Her gaze was filled with curiosity. "Why are you asking all these questions and where did you get that peanut butter? I never saw it at the Piggly Wiggly."

"I work for an ad agency, and Aunt Ivy's is a potential new client. I need to come up with an advertising campaign, so my boss sent me a box of the product."

Carmen's cluck reminded Kate of her grandmother when she was annoyed. "I thought you were on vacation," she said, her voice holding more than a hint of disapproval. "You're like my daughter. Marisa doesn't think of anything other than her job." Leaning back against the counter, Carmen continued. "She's an accountant, and she just passed the CPA exam. Now she's trying to decide whether to stay with her current firm, go into private practice, or join some corporation's accounting department."

Kate wondered why Carmen seemed almost disapproving. "It sounds like she has a lot of possibilities." That made her more fortunate than many people.

Carmen nodded. "She does. I know her job is important, but I still wish she'd think about dating." Carmen's face darkened as she added, "I hate the idea that what happened between her father and me soured Marisa on the whole idea."

Kate didn't know what to say. She had seen Carmen's wedding ring but knew that she lived alone in the stone lodge that Greg had explained was staff housing. Since she'd heard nothing about Mr. St. George, Kate had assumed that Carmen was a widow like Lauren. Now she wasn't so certain.

The question was whether or not she should ask Carmen about her past. Kate hesitated, then decided that the older woman had opened the door. "I don't mean to pry, but what happened?"

The pain that filled Carmen's eyes made Kate want to hug her, but something about the woman's demeanor made her stop. Instead, Kate stood stiffly and waited to hear Carmen's explanation. "Eric left us. He disappeared without any warning and without any word almost eight years ago." Carmen closed her eyes for a second before adding, "It was the day of Marisa's high school graduation. We haven't heard from him since."

Kate shuddered at the images Carmen's words evoked. "Oh, Carmen, I'm so sorry." This time, she followed her instincts and gave the woman a hug, dropping her arms when Carmen shook her head.

"It's not your fault. I'm not sure it was any one person's fault."

That might be the truth, but it did not lessen Kate's desire to help Carmen. "It must have been difficult for both of you."

Kate knew she would never forget those first few months after her parents had been killed. Despite the love Sally and Grandpa Larry had lavished on her, it had been a horribly painful time. In many respects, what Carmen and her daughter had endured was worse. Kate's parents hadn't chosen to die, but Carmen's husband had made the choice to leave his family. Kate knew where her parents were buried, but Marisa had no idea where her father had gone or whether he was still alive. Kate had had the example of her grandparents' marriage and knew that wedding bells could lead to a life of happiness. Marisa had no such role model. It was no wonder she wasn't convinced that marriage was the start of happily-ever-after.

Carmen tasted her tamale sauce, nodding

briefly before she turned to face Kate. "It was difficult," she admitted. "If I hadn't been working here, I don't know what I would have done. After Eric left, I couldn't make mortgage payments and pay for Marisa's college. I did everything I could, but I still lost our house."

The story wrenched Kate's heart. No wonder Carmen had been so interested in Brandi and Olivia's search for scholarships. She had firsthand experience with the challenge of paying for college.

"I was fortunate," Carmen said, her bittersweet smile surprising Kate. "The previous owners let me live here, and when the Sinclairs took over, they agreed I could stay."

But now Carmen's future was once more uncertain. If Rainbow's End closed, not only would Carmen lose her livelihood, she'd also lose her home.

"I should be done in an hour," Sally said as she climbed out of the car and headed toward Ruby's Tresses. The small hair salon was located on one of the side streets in Dupree, less than two blocks from Lauren's shop.

"That's fine." Kate turned off the ignition. She might as well leave the car here. "I'll wander around." It wasn't a lie. She planned to do exactly that after she talked to Lauren. If she was lucky, the exercise would help her brain focus. After talking to Carmen and hearing her reaction to the peanut butter, Kate had realized that flavor should be the major selling point in whatever campaign she developed. She'd sent Heather a note, suggesting the company consider free samples — not just coupons — to get consumers to try their product.

Though Kate was envisioning small tubs of peanut butter being sent to all households in a test market, she was also toying with the idea of inserting product in magazines the way perfume and face cream samples were sometimes marketed. The problem was the logistics. If the packaging broke in the mail, no one would be happy, not Aunt Ivy's nor the magazine nor the consumers. Heather had been receptive to the idea of samples but reminded Kate of what she already knew: that wasn't enough. Kate needed to devise a new concept and a new look for the aging peanut butter brand. But first she wanted to order Sally's Christmas gift.

"Going my way?"

Kate turned, startled by the sound of Greg's voice. "I didn't know you were in town."

He gestured toward the barbershop directly across the street from Ruby's Tresses. "It isn't just your grandmother who worries about her hair."

Kate chuckled at the thought of Greg worrying about his hair.

"What's so funny?" he demanded with false severity.

"I don't doubt that you worry about things." The dark circles under his eyes yesterday morning had been evidence that he did. "But I don't think haircuts are on the list."

Greg doffed his hat to let Kate admire his neatly trimmed hair. "Bob did a better job than the barber in Orchard Slope."

"What was it like?"

"Orchard Slope or the barber?"

"Orchard Slope." Kate had wondered about the town where

Greg had grown up, particularly now that she knew how unhappy he'd been there.

"Compared to Dupree, it's huge — about 5,000 — but it's still a small town with one major employer. My parents were like most of the other residents and worked at the cannery. Basically, it's a small town where everyone knows everyone else, and there are no secrets. I don't imagine it was like that in Buffalo."

Kate shook her head. "We knew our immediate neighbors, but certainly not the whole city. And now I don't even know all the people in my apartment building." She sighed, thinking of how she referred to her neighbors as Ms. 1-A and Mr. 3-C rather than learning their real names. "I guess we're all too caught up in our jobs to do more than wave at each other."

Greg was silent for a second. "Were you headed somewhere special when I so rudely interrupted?"

"You weren't being rude." Even though they were discussing ordinary things, Kate suspected they could be reviewing the menu at the Sit 'n' Sip, and she'd find the conversation fascinating, simply because she was with Greg.

"I was going to the quilt shop, but there's no rush." Kate realized how infrequently she said those words. At home, everything was a rush, trying to cram twenty-six hours of activities into a twenty-four-hour day. A week ago she had found Dupree's slower pace of life irritating. Now it seemed that she was embracing it.

When they reached Lauren's shop, Greg stopped. "Are we still on for tennis this afternoon?" He grinned as Kate nodded. "See you then."

"Are you sure you don't want to come in with me?"

"I'll pass on that. I don't know anything about quilts, anyway."

Kate nodded. Though she suspected that Greg was trying to avoid another potentially embarrassing scene with Fiona, she wouldn't say so.

Lauren had fewer inhibitions. As soon as the door closed behind Kate, she said, "Let me guess. Mr. Handsome was afraid Fiona might be here."

Kate simply shrugged.

"You don't have to tell Greg this," Lauren continued, "but he's off the hook. I told Fiona he couldn't be her dad, because he was going to marry you."

"You didn't!" Kate felt the blood rush to her face. Surely Lauren was joking, but why would she joke about something like that?

" 'Fraid so, but you're safe. Fiona knows it's a secret."

Kate was not reassured. After all, just minutes ago, Greg had said there were no secrets in small towns. Her blush faded, and she felt a chill creep up her spine. It would be horribly embarrassing if he heard the rumor and thought she'd started it. Unfortunately, it was too late to do anything about that.

She shrugged, trying to pretend that the thought of marrying Greg hadn't made her heart pound. "I actually came on business."

Fifteen minutes later, Kate had chosen a design for Sally's pillow, and two new customers had entered the shop. Bidding Lauren good-bye, Kate checked her watch. She still had half an hour before she was to meet Sally. She might as well take advantage of the free Wi-Fi at the Sit 'n' Sip.

As Kate entered the small diner and approached the counter, Samantha Dexter swiveled on her stool. "Kate! I'm glad to see you," she said with genuine enthusiasm. "Can I buy you a cup of coffee?"

Kate shook her head. "I think I'll try tea."

"You've obviously been here before." Samantha chuckled as she said, "Let me rephrase my offer. Can I buy you a cup of tea or any other beverage of your choice?"

"Tea would be fine. Thanks." Kate took the seat next to Samantha and placed her order, refusing the offer of an apple muffin that was, according to the boot maker, the best in the state. "I'm surprised you're not at work," Kate said as she stirred a packet of sweetener into her tea.

Though there were faint circles under them, Samantha's blue eyes were bright with excitement. "My dad's opening this morning." She took a sip of her coffee and smiled. "I can't believe you're here. I've been thinking about you all week, but I just never found the time to get out to Rainbow's End to thank you."

"For what?"

"For your help. I followed your advice and updated my web page." Samantha pulled her cell phone out of her pocket and touched the screen. "What do you think?"

Kate stared, amazed by what Samantha had done. "Wow! That really pops." Not only had Samantha made the font changes Kate had suggested, but the upper right corner now featured a boot with Samantha's face on it. "You must be a whiz at Photoshop. Your picture looks like it's part of the boot."

Samantha's grin widened. "It is. When I told my dad about your ideas, he made the boot as a surprise for me. I put it on my website as a test and couldn't believe what happened."

She took another sip of coffee, her grin telling Kate that she was delaying to increase the suspense. "I've never had so many clicks or so many orders. It's been less than a week since I updated the page, but we've gotten a normal month's worth of orders in five days."

Kate felt excitement well up inside her. "That's wonderful!" She looked down at her boots, which, contrary to her original plan, she wore almost every day.

"It's all thanks to you. I want to pay you for your help, Kate. Without your expertise, this wouldn't have happened."

Kate shook her head. "I didn't expect to be paid. You were doing my grandmother and me a favor by rushing our boots. The advice was my favor to you."

Uncertainty shone from Samantha's eyes. "That's very generous, but I still feel guilty about it. There must be something I can do for you."

Kate grinned as she pulled a jar from her bag. "There is. Tell me what you think about this peanut butter."

21

"It was a beautiful service."

Kate smiled at her grandmother as they made their way from the church to Kate's car. "Yes, it was. This is the first time I've had a palm for Palm Sunday." She looked down at the piece of palm tree that she and all the other congregants carried.

The pastor and his wife had gone to Corpus Christi earlier that week and had brought back fronds to share with their parishioners. "They'll lose their color," the minister had told them, "but not their meaning. When you look at your little bit of a palm tree, I hope you'll remember the crowds that cheered Jesus when he entered Jerusalem and how quickly they changed. Ask yourself what you would have done if you'd been there."

It had been a powerful message. Though Kate wanted to believe that she would never have turned against her Savior, she knew

317

how much influence crowds could have, how pressure from only one person could convince others to do things they wouldn't ordinarily consider. Wasn't that how she made her living, persuading consumers they couldn't live without things most people would consider luxuries? Her job was to create a perceived need, then find the words and images to convince tens of thousands of people that the only way to satisfy that need and make their lives complete was to buy her clients' products and services.

"Could I interest you ladies in a drive this afternoon?"

Kate turned at the sound of Greg's question, grateful not simply for the invitation but also for the diversion. She didn't want to think about her job today. It was Sunday. More than that, it was a beautiful Sunday morning, and she was on vacation.

She smiled at Greg, admiring the way the green in his tie complemented his eyes. Like most of the other men in the congregation, he wore no jacket, but he'd paired a dress shirt and tie with dark slacks.

"Sunday afternoon drives were a tradition in my family," Greg continued, "but I haven't taken one in years."

Kate noticed that the tension that often accompanied any reference to Greg's family was absent. Apparently Sunday drives — a tradition she and her grandparents had never established — had been enjoyable times in the Vange family. She was glad. While most people would envy Greg his lifestyle or at least his bank account, she realized that he was proof of the adage that money could not buy happiness. Greg had accomplished so much, and yet there were still holes in his life. Unlike Kate, he did not know what he wanted to be doing a year from now.

Kate looked at her grandmother, waiting for her response. Though Kate's pulse had accelerated at the thought of spending more time with Greg and possibly learning more about what made this fascinating man the way he was, she would not go without Sally. After all, the reason for coming to Rainbow's End had been for them to spend time together.

Sally smiled brightly as she shook her head. "I'm afraid I'm going to have to decline. Roy seems to think he will have a better chance of winning at backgammon than he does at chess, so I promised him a game today." She laid her hand on Kate's arm. "Don't let that stop you. You'll have more fun with Greg than you would watching two old people try to outplay each other."

As much as she knew she'd enjoy the time alone with Greg, Kate felt a twinge of jealousy. It was wrong. She knew that, and yet she couldn't seem to stop herself.

"Roy's welcome to come too," Greg said. "In fact, I pretty much assumed he would."

As if on cue, Roy appeared at Sally's side. "Did I hear my name?"

Sally nodded. "I was simply explaining that I was going to show you I was a backgammon champion and that nothing, not even a drive in the country with Kate and Greg, was more important than that." The look she gave Roy left no doubt that he was supposed to agree. Kate revised her opinion. Perhaps Sally's reason for remaining at Rainbow's End wasn't simply Roy. It appeared that matchmaker Sally was at work again.

Roy raised an eyebrow. "I thought you'd never played backgammon."

"So?" Smiling sweetly, Sally batted her eyes. "Some folks are born champs." She nodded at Kate and Greg. "You two will have a nice drive without us."

Greg gave Sally an appraising look, as if he also suspected she was matchmaking. Fortunately, he appeared amused rather than annoyed. "We'll probably be late. I thought we'd stop somewhere for supper."

"I'm sure Roy and I can take care of ourselves." Sally turned to him. "Can't we, Roy?"

The older man's smile left no doubt that he was grateful for the opportunity to spend more time with Sally. "It'll give me a chance to take my best gal out for an elegant dinner."

His best gal. Kate looked at her grandmother, whose attention was focused on Roy. Though Sally grinned, probably at the way he'd referred to her, her voice held more than a little skepticism. "An elegant dinner in Dupree?"

"Sure." Roy gave a self-deprecating shrug. "As long as you consider burgers and a shake elegant fare."

Though Greg chuckled, Sally did not. She nodded vigorously. "That works for me, unless Kate's going to be so rude as to refuse Greg's offer."

Kate had no intention of refusing. Besides the appeal of an afternoon with Greg, there was Sally's obvious desire to spend more time with Roy. Kate wouldn't disappoint her. How could she when she suspected that her grandmother would relish a meal of melba toast and water if Roy suggested it?

There was no doubt about it. Sally was happier and looked younger when she was with Roy. If thoughts of where that might lead bothered Kate, it was Kate's problem. She'd have to learn to deal with it.

"Say yes, Kate." Greg bent his head and whispered in her ear. "I know you won't be working on a Sunday afternoon. That's why I picked today for our outing."

"I'd love to go." It would be fun, and if she was lucky, the change of scenery combined with the relaxation a Sunday afternoon afforded would spark her imagination and give her an idea of how to promote Aunt Ivy's peanut butter. Kate knew from the past that concepts could come from anywhere at any time.

After a delicious meal of ham and scalloped potatoes, Greg helped Kate into his SUV and headed north. Though she asked more than once where they were going, he refused to answer, telling her it wouldn't be a surprise if she knew the destination. And so she leaned back in the seat and enjoyed the countryside.

"Sally would like this," Kate said, gesturing toward the tree-covered hills and the river that meandered next to the road. "The land is so beautiful here."

"What's it like where you grew up?"

"Much flatter, and of course there are no live oaks or prickly pears or bluebonnets in Buffalo." Kate smiled at the sight of the fields filled with expanses of the state flower in full bloom, the flowers' blue only slightly lighter than the sky itself. Mingled with the bluebonnets were orange and yellow flowers that Greg told her were Indian paintbrush and Texas dandelions. Though spring in Western New York was beautiful, thanks to the blossoms of countless fruit trees, there was something very special about this part of Texas.

"There are hills an hour or so from Buffalo," she told Greg, "and they're high enough for good skiing, but the city itself is bordered by Lake Erie and the Niagara River. The land is definitely flat there."

"With that famous lake-effect snow."

"Indeed." Kate nodded, remembering how much time it took to clear sidewalks and driveways. Even snowblowers were challenged by some of the storms. "New Jersey seems like the tropics compared to that. Of course, we have more hills there and freezing rain, so winter storms can disrupt commuting." She shrugged. "I guess no place is perfect. Spring in Texas is beautiful, but I'm not sure how I'd handle summer here. I've heard it's really, really, really hot."

Greg pulled the SUV onto the shoulder to let a truck pass. "That's the rumor. Summer in Washington was hot, but Roy tells me I haven't experienced heat until I've spent July and August in Texas." Greg drove back onto the road. "I wonder if either of us will be here to experience it."

Kate shook her head. "I won't. You know where I'll be in July and August — doing my job back in Manhattan."

"Ah yes, your job." Greg gave her a quick look. "I hope you don't wind up like me, asking yourself if it's worth all that you put into it — the time, the effort, the missed opportunities."

That was a question she had not asked. Just thinking about it made Kate uncomfortable and reminded her of her reaction to this morning's sermon. She shook her head again. Though the sun was still high, this section of the road was lined with trees, leaving the roadway dappled with light. Kate stared at the patterns, preferring to focus on them rather than explore the paths Greg's question had revealed.

"How long have you been doing that?"

"Every day for the past six months." Greg's light grip of the steering wheel suggested that, unlike her, he was not troubled by the idea. "I suppose most people would like to be in my shoes and retire at thirty-two, but I can't help thinking there's more to life than a bank account. I wonder what I missed by working so hard. I think I told you that other than the few days around Christmas when I visited my family, this is the first time I've had off in almost fifteen years."

He had told her, and though initially Kate had been surprised, when she'd learned that he owned the company, she had assumed that Greg, like many small business owners, worked harder than his staff.

"You must have enjoyed what you were doing, if you never needed a break."

"I did." The way Greg's lips curved into a smile left no doubt that he was remembering a particularly good moment. "It's satisfying when a program works, even more so knowing that Sys=Simpl software made people's lives easier. It isn't curing cancer or bringing about world peace, but there was satisfaction in what I did." He turned to look at her again. "What about you?"

Kate thought for a second, trying to frame her reply. She wasn't curing cancer or bringing about world peace, either. She couldn't even say that her work simplified others' lives. But as she thought of Samantha Dexter's delight in the increased sales her revamped website had brought, Kate knew that she was performing a valuable function. Yet that wasn't the only aspect of her job that brought satisfaction.

"I enjoy being with my co-workers. We're a team that works together to meet our clients' needs. We —" Kate broke off, startled by the sight of what appeared to be a large hairy pig lumbering through the field. "What's that?" Kate couldn't recall seeing one, even in a zoo.

"A javelina," Greg said without hesitation. "It's a kind of wild boar." He slowed the vehicle and put it into park as the animal approached the road. About two feet high and three feet long, the javelina was solidly built with short legs, small eyes, and a brindled coat. "I'm surprised it's out now," Greg said. "Normally they're nocturnal."

As the animal opened its mouth, Kate gasped. "Those teeth look dangerous." The canines were at least two inches long, and with their sharp points, she had no doubt that they could inflict a painful wound.

"It's not just the teeth. Javelinas are noted for their nasty dispositions." If Greg was trying to alarm her, he was succeeding.

The animal in question waddled across

the road, apparently undisturbed by the large vehicle and its passengers.

"Javelinas sound like a couple of clients I've had," Kate said as the animal made its way into the western meadow. "Nothing pleased them, and they weren't even polite about telling me exactly how unhappy they were. The best thing I can say is that they didn't bite."

With the road once more clear, Greg put the SUV back in gear. "So, what did you do with your javelina-like clients?"

"I kept trying until I found something they did like." It hadn't been a particularly pleasant experience, but at least the final result had made both the clients and Heather and Nick happy. Nick had even complimented Kate on her handling of that client.

Greg nodded slowly. "Your story makes me glad that most of my interaction was with computers. There's nothing personal there. A program works or it doesn't, and there are no nasty comments."

"Maybe so, but you miss out on seeing the people you've helped. There's a lot of satisfaction in that." Kate smiled as she recalled her encounter with Samantha. "Just yesterday, Samantha Dexter bought me a cup of tea to thank me for helping her."

Greg darted a glance at her. "I didn't know Sam was one of your clients."

"She isn't. I just gave her some suggestions the day Sally and I ordered our boots. Samantha took the idea and ran with it. Now she's seeing the results."

Greg slowed down as they reached the outskirts of a small town. "You probably could have charged her a lot more than a cup of tea."

Shrugging, Kate turned to study Greg. He looked as if he were trying to understand her motives. "There was no reason to do that. I was glad to help her, and it didn't take much time." The ideas had flowed quickly that day. Kate only wished that she were equally inspired by Aunt Ivy's campaign. The few ideas she'd had were so weak that she hadn't pursued them.

"You're a good person, Kate." Greg's words and the smile that accompanied them warmed Kate as much as Samantha's gratitude had. It had been such a simple thing, giving the boot maker a couple ideas, and yet it had brought Kate more pleasure than she'd found on any of the large accounts she'd serviced. Maybe it was because she'd helped Samantha on her own rather than being part of a team. Maybe it was something else. Kate didn't know. All she knew was that she had been so happy when she'd left the Sit 'n' Sip that she'd been tempted to skip down the street toward Ruby's Tresses.

"This is Kerrville," Greg said a few minutes later as they approached what appeared to be a fairly large town. "We're getting closer."

"And the excitement continues to build." Though Kate infused her words with irony, the simple fact was, she was excited about whatever it was Greg wanted to show her. It had been years since anyone had planned an excursion for her, even longer since she'd enjoyed an afternoon as much as she was this one.

Even though the conversation had touched on sensitive subjects, Kate felt more — she struggled to find the proper adjective — *alive* than any time she could recall. Being with Greg made her feel as if her nerve endings were on high alert, sensing things they would otherwise have ignored, enhancing even the simplest of pleasures. Kate didn't know whether Greg was similarly affected, but she did know that she would not forget today.

He turned northwest on highway 27 and drove for a few miles farther. Though neither one spoke, Kate did not mind. The silence was companionable, and it gave her time to speculate about the surprise Greg had planned. When the main highway veered to the right, he stayed straight. "Close your eyes," he said when they'd traveled perhaps half a mile, "and don't open them until I tell you. I don't want to spoil the surprise."

"We must be almost there."

Greg nodded. "Smart as well as beautiful. You're the perfect woman."

Kate felt her pulse accelerate. He was joking, of course. Matching his tone, she said lightly, "Only if I don't peek."

"True. Now close them."

Though she hated riding without being able to see where she was going, Kate complied. She felt the vehicle turn left, then slow. A few seconds later, Greg stopped, turned off the ignition, and walked to Kate's door. Opening it, he helped her climb down, then said, "You can look now."

She stared, amazed by the parklike setting with the standing stones. "Stonehenge!" There was no mistaking that circle of vertical stones and lintels. Kate had seen dozens of pictures and had told herself that her first European trip would be to England to see the famous monument along with the sights of London and Bath, but she'd never expected to find anything like this here. "I thought I was in Texas."

Greg wrapped his arm around her waist and gave Kate a little hug that sent frissons of delight down her spine. This was like holding hands at the bluebonnet festival, only better. "They call it Stonehenge II," he said. "It's not as large as the original, but you've got to admit that the trip was a lot shorter."

"With no need for a passport or airport security." She matched Greg's carefree tone. The truth was, she felt carefree. Carefree, relaxed, and happy. "It's not just closer. There's a bonus. I don't think the original has those." Kate pointed at sculptures whose distinctive shape appeared to have been inspired by Easter Island heads. Taller than the standing stones, the heads seemed to be either guarding Stonehenge or serving as an entrance to the monument.

"That's true. You won't find them in England, but this is Texas, and anything's possible."

Including an afternoon highlighted by a javelina, fantastical sculptures, and the most intriguing man she'd ever met. Kate darted a glance at the man who'd occupied so many of her thoughts. He was looking at her as if trying to read her mind. To cover her confusion, she studied the park. With the Guadalupe River on one edge and the verdant hills in the background, it was an ideal spot for almost anything, including a replica of one of England's most famous monuments.

"I want to take some pictures." Kate reached into her bag, then pulled her hand out, shocked to realize that the phone was not there. "I can't believe I forgot to bring my phone." That would never have happened at home. But then, if she'd been at home, she would not have neglected to turn it on the day she'd gone to the bluebonnet festival. In fact, there would have been no need to turn it on, because she never turned it off in New Jersey.

Greg appeared amused by her admission. "It must be contagious. I used to carry my phone everywhere — and I mean everywhere — but since I've been in Texas, I find myself forgetting to take it when I leave Rainbow's End. Fortunately, I remembered it today." Greg pulled it from his pocket and made a show of switching it on. "Let me get a picture of you next to one of those Easter Island heads."

Kate tipped her head to one side, pretending to ponder the idea. "Only if you let me take yours by the other."

"Deal."

When they and the large heads had been suitably photographed, Greg turned toward the circle of stones, taking Kate's hand. It seemed natural to be walking hand in hand, as if they'd done it a hundred times. Familiarity mingled with novelty as Kate savored the sensation of having her hand clasped in Greg's. His was larger, firmer, stronger, and when he laced his fingers with hers, she felt as if she were being protected. Since she'd become an adult, she'd never been conscious of seeking protection, and yet there was no doubt that this felt good. More than that, it felt so right that she wished the moment would never end.

"Who's responsible for this?" she asked, once again trying to mask her emotions.

Greg swung their hands lightly, as if he too enjoyed the link. "Two men," he said as they approached the standing stones. "Doug Hill gave his friend Al Shepperd a slab of stone he had left from a project. One thing led to another, and Al and Doug realized they could re-create Stonehenge."

"It's impressive, but it's a strange thing to see in the middle of the Texas Hill Country."

Greg stopped to take a picture of Kate standing by one of the lintel-topped stones. "Not as strange as Carhenge in Nebraska.

At least we're not staring at spray-painted old cars."

"I've seen pictures of that, and you're right. This looks like the original."

"Stand over there." Kate feigned a model's pose, not expecting Greg to take a picture. "You're going to regret that," he said as the camera whirred. "I'm going to give Sally an eight-by-ten glossy of her granddaughter pretending to be a cover girl."

"You wouldn't."

Greg grinned. "How much are you willing to pay me not to?"

"Unfair! You know I can't offer you anything you don't already have." Oh, how good it felt to be joking with this man. Kate amended her earlier assessment. She didn't simply feel carefree; she felt as if she were floating on air, and it was all because of Greg.

"Don't be so sure that you have nothing to offer," he said, "but since you refused to bribe me, you have to listen to the rest of my lecture." He straightened his shoulders and peered at her, as if he were looking over half-glasses. "This might resemble the real Stonehenge, but there are a couple critical differences," Greg said, as solemn as any professor Kate had encountered. "These are only 60 percent of the height of the original and 90 percent of the width. More importantly, only two are actual stone. The rest are made of plaster over metal mesh. In other words, they're hollow." When Kate raised a brow, Greg tapped one. There was no mistaking the sound.

"Definitely hollow," she agreed. "How did you learn all that?" There was a sign at the entrance, but neither of them had taken the time to read it.

Greg shrugged. "The internet. What else would you expect of a self-confessed nerd?" He slid his phone back in his pocket and linked hands with Kate again.

"This whole place is incredible." Almost as incredible as being with him. "How long has it been here?"

"Right here, only a few years. It was first built around 1989, but after Shepperd died, his land was sold, and the new owners wanted to tear the stones down. The local arts foundation decided it was worth salvaging and relocated it here."

"I'll bet that's one time they were glad the stones are hollow." Still, it had to have been a massive undertaking, even with the reduced weight. Kate looked around and smiled. "This was fun. Sally will be sorry she missed it."

But, as dearly as she loved her grandmother, Kate didn't regret the time she'd been alone with Greg.

22

Perhaps he was being selfish, but Greg wasn't sorry that Kate's grandmother hadn't come, with or without Roy. He had included her in the invitation because it would have been rude not to, but he'd been relieved when she'd refused. The twinkle in Sally's eye when she'd claimed that playing backgammon with Roy was more important than taking a country drive had made Greg wonder if she realized that he was hoping to spend more time alone with Kate. It was true that they were alone when they played tennis and on the nightly walks around Rainbow's End that he found so pleasant, but this was different. This qualified as a date, even though he hadn't phrased the invitation that way.

Greg almost laughed out loud, thinking of the other women he'd dated and the way they would have reacted to a walk through a Texas park, even if it did have a replica of

Stonehenge. Those women had expected to be escorted to trendy restaurants, preferably ones where paparazzi stalked the rich and famous.

After one particularly boring evening when a woman whose name he'd forgotten the next day asked him if he knew Bill Gates, Greg had announced to Drew that he was done dating. He was tired of being a meal ticket. That was humiliating enough, but he knew that the women had seen him as more than a meal ticket. In their eyes, he was the ticket to a life of leisure. They were shopping for rich husbands the way Greg's sisters shopped for shoes.

Kate was as different from those women as the Hill Country was from the California coast. Greg frowned at the comparison. It wasn't a valid one, because both the Hill Country and the coast were wonderful, each in its own way. The dating situation was different. While Greg's former dates might not have been wonderful, Kate was. She was warm and caring. She was . . . He struggled for the word, then nodded as he found it. Genuine. Kate was genuine. That was why she was able to enjoy a Sunday drive and a walk in the park.

"I'm glad you're having fun. So am I," Greg said, tightening his grip on Kate's hand. It felt so good, holding it, feeling the warmth of her palm against his. Holding hands might not be sophisticated — he'd never done it in California — but it felt more than good to have Kate's hand in his. It felt right. Everything about today felt right. The drive, the park, just being with Kate. Even though there were other tourists, laughing and snapping pictures of the stones, some attempting to climb them, Greg felt as if he and Kate were in a world of their own.

As if to prove him wrong, his phone chimed. Though he was tempted to ignore it, he pulled the phone from his pocket and glanced at the ID.

"Go ahead and answer it." Greg might be annoyed by the interruption, but Kate didn't seem to mind.

He frowned. "I'm not sure I want to. It's a text from my sister." He could guess the content. For the past couple of years, it seemed his sisters wanted only one thing from him: money. Even when they visited him in California, instead of savoring hot fudge sundaes at Ghirardelli or enjoying a trip to the Monterey Bay Aquarium as they once had, they had turned their visits into shopping marathons.

"Your sister?" Kate raised an eyebrow.

"That doesn't narrow it down too much. Which one?"

"Emily. She's the third." His favorite of the four, although Greg would never tell her that.

"The twenty-year-old."

Greg was surprised Kate remembered that. "You have a great memory." It was part of what made her unique, the fact that she seemed to care about who was who in his family rather than the size of his investment portfolio.

Greg opened the message and frowned. This was one time he wished he hadn't been right.

"Something wrong?" Kate asked.

"She wants me to send her some money. Apparently Emily is convinced that life as we know it will end if she can't go to the Caribbean with her friends." The message was couched in Emily's typically dramatic terms, including phrases like "absolutely must go" and "trip of a lifetime."

As a light breeze blew a few strands of Kate's hair onto her face, she brushed them back. "I probably shouldn't point this out, but I doubt the world's end will be triggered by your sister missing a trip."

Greg nodded. "I know. I just hate to say no."

"Why?"

Though they'd continued to wander around the circumference of the standing stones, Greg stopped and stared at Kate. No one had asked him that. It was, in fact, a question he hadn't asked himself. "I'm not sure. It's probably because I remember what it was like growing up and not having all the things the other kids did. My parents were struggling to make ends meet, so I wore no-name sneakers when everyone else had Nikes."

Kate nodded as if she understood. "Peer pressure can be rough. I remember when I was eight years old. I wanted a Barbie dollhouse more than anything I could imagine. I was convinced it was the most wonderful thing in the world and that I would be doomed to a life of misery if I didn't have it."

She sounded like Emily. The difference was, Kate had been eight, while Emily was twenty. "What happened?"

"I hadn't saved enough money to buy it, so I asked Grandpa Larry. He was always a softer touch than Sally." Kate's smile was fond, as if she were remembering happy moments she had shared with the grandfather who'd been a surrogate father.

"And he bought it for you."

To Greg's surprise, Kate shook her head. "He didn't. It was early September. School had just started, and one of my friends showed me her dollhouse. That was how I learned about it. Anyway, Grandpa Larry told me that if I still wanted it in three months, he'd make sure one was under the Christmas tree."

This time Greg thought he knew where the story was heading. "And by December you'd found something else you wanted even more."

"Exactly. My grandparents were firm believers in not spoiling children."

Something in her tone made Greg pause. He watched a boy and girl who didn't appear to be more than seven or eight chase each other around the stones. Though he was no expert on children's clothing, even Greg knew that what they were wearing was not the latest style, and yet they seemed happy.

"Do you think I'm spoiling my sisters?"

"Only you can judge that." Kate gave Greg's hand a little squeeze that made him realize she was confident he'd analyze the situation correctly. Instead of the disparaging remarks that had once been so common, she offered him approval. "What would your parents have said if you weren't in a position to write a check and Emily asked them for the money?"

"Get a job and earn it." The response came instinctively, a reminder of the many times his parents had said that to him.

"It's not bad advice. I think we all appreciate things we've worked for more than ones that are handed to us."

Kate's words triggered a new set of memories. "You're probably right. I still have the bicycle I paid for. I haven't ridden it in years, of course, but I wouldn't let my father give it away."

His father groused about the space it was taking up in the garage every time Greg was in Orchard Slope. Perhaps he should have it shipped to Rainbow's End. One of the guests might enjoy it.

Kate tightened her grip on his hand. "Do you want to talk about him?"

Greg blinked at the question. "Who do you mean?"

"Your father." The look Kate gave him was warm and reassuring. "Your expression changes every time you mention him. I don't claim that I can help, but I'm willing to listen if you want to talk."

He didn't want to talk about Linc Vange. Not today. Not ever. Greg started to tell Kate that and then reconsidered. With just

343

a few sentences, she had helped him reevaluate his relationship with his sisters. Perhaps she could help him deal with his father.

"There's not a lot to say," Greg told her as they continued to stroll around the standing stones. "I wasn't the son he wanted. In his day, my father was a sports star, and he expected me to carry on the Vange tradition. I didn't. It wasn't that I didn't want to or that I didn't try. I just couldn't. He never let me forget that I was a disappointment."

Greg wouldn't tell Kate that his father had called him a failure. Some things were best left unspoken.

Kate looked up at him, her eyes shining behind the dark lenses of her sunglasses. Greg hoped those weren't tears he was seeing. "He must be very proud of you now," she said, making it a statement rather than a question.

Greg shook his head. "If he is, he's never told me."

The way Kate's lips thinned told him she was upset. "Maybe he assumed you knew. I never heard Grandpa Larry tell Sally he loved her, but I never doubted it. I could tell from the way he looked at her and the things he did for her."

"My father's not like that."

"Are you sure?"

Greg wasn't. He stared into the distance for a moment, wondering if this was another thing he needed to reevaluate. Had he missed signals? Was it possible that he'd clung to the past and hadn't considered that both he and his father had changed? Greg wasn't certain. What he did know was that this woman was wonderful.

Impulsively, he wrapped his arms around Kate's shoulders and gave her a hug. "Thanks, Kate."

Kate could not recall a day she'd enjoyed more. It had had its solemn moments when she'd talked about her job and Greg had wrestled with his sister's request for money and his father's apparent disapproval. But even though they hadn't been as light and carefree as the rest of the day, Kate couldn't regret those moments, for they'd given her and Greg the opportunity to learn more about each other. And with each new facet she uncovered, Kate found herself more intrigued by him. He was a wonderful man who'd overcome so much. She said a silent prayer that he'd find a way to make peace with his father.

Kate smiled. The bluebonnet festival had been fun, but today was even better, because she and Greg were alone. Even though she knew her grandmother would have enjoyed Stonehenge, Kate was glad that she hadn't had to share the afternoon with Sally and Roy. It had been special, playing tourist with Greg.

They'd wandered around Stonehenge for an hour or so, looking at the stones from every possible angle, taking dozens of pictures, laughing at the antics of two small children who wanted their parents to place them on top of one of the lintels. Now they had found their way back to the Easter Island heads and the entrance to the park.

"If you're hungry," Greg said as they approached his SUV, "there's a little place I heard about on the outskirts of Kerrville. Don't tell Carmen, but it has a reputation for the best barbecue in the Hill Country."

"That sounds delicious." Kate would have said the same thing if he'd suggested sauerkraut on cinnamon rolls. It had been only a few hours since she'd thought Sally would be content eating melba toast and water if she was with Roy. Now Kate felt the same way. The menu didn't matter as long as she was with Greg.

Kate smiled at the realization that she'd never felt this way with either Pete or Lou. She'd gone to Broadway shows and A-list restaurants; she'd even been to black-tie receptions at prestigious art galleries and opening night at the Philharmonic. Those had been pleasant ways to spend an evening, but nothing compared to today. Simply strolling through a small park in Texas, her hand clasped in Greg's, was more exciting, more memorable than the elaborate dates she'd had in the past.

It took only a few minutes to reach the restaurant. As they pulled into the parking lot, Kate felt mildly disappointed. The exterior of the restaurant was unimpressive, a simple log cabin with one of the metal roofs that were so common in this part of the state.

"Don't judge a book by the cover, and don't judge this by the outside," Greg said as he helped her out of the vehicle. He draped his arm around her waist, drawing her closer to him.

Instinctively, Kate stretched her arm out and wrapped it around Greg's waist, bringing them even closer together. The restaurant might not be impressive, but it felt so good — so right — to be walking with Greg, matching her steps to his, listening to the soft sound of the breeze rustling through the leaves. Their boot heels clattered on the wooden ramp leading to the front porch, causing a bird to flap its wings and utter a warning cry as it flew away. Kate smiled. It was a typical evening in the country, and she was enjoying every minute of it.

As Greg opened the door, the aromas that wafted out erased her concerns and told Kate the restaurant's reputation was well-deserved. The interior was as nondescript as the exterior, with bare walls and rough-hewn tables covered with oilcloth. But the tantalizing aromas of spicy sauces and a wood fire combined with the contented sounds coming from the other patrons left no doubt that Greg had chosen well.

It took only a few minutes to be seated and an even shorter time for their orders to arrive. When Kate bit into the barbecued beef sandwich, she knew that Carmen had stiff competition. The food was simple but well prepared, with side orders of coleslaw and French fried sweet potatoes complementing the tender beef and tangy barbecue sauce. Washed down with sweet tea and followed by peach ice cream, it was a meal Kate knew she'd never forget.

"This was wonderful," she said as she and Greg emerged from the restaurant. "It was the perfect ending to a perfect day."

They stood on the porch, letting their eyes adjust to the near darkness. In a moment they'd descend the ramp. In another moment, they'd be inside the vehicle, headed back to Rainbow's End. The day had to end. Kate knew that, even as she wished it would go on forever.

Greg raised his hand to cup her chin and stared into Kate's eyes. "I'm glad you enjoyed the meal, but I can think of a better ending to our day." Slowly and deliberately, he lowered his lips to hers.

It was wonderful. Kate's perfume mingled with the scent of barbecue sauce and wood smoke. An owl's hoot and the scurrying of a small rodent in the dried leaves told Greg dusk had arrived. Ordinary things made extraordinary by the fact that he held this woman in his arms and pressed his lips to hers.

It was wonderful. She was wonderful. Greg had known Kate less than two weeks, and yet he knew her better than anyone he'd ever met. She was sweet; she was strong. She was pretty; she was principled. She was vulnerable; she was victorious. Most of all, she was Kate.

Wonderful, wonderful Kate. The woman he loved.

23

Sally had a secret. If it weren't more than eight months until Christmas, Kate would have said that her grandmother had just found the perfect gift and was trying her best not to spoil the surprise. But since Sally was not an advance shopper, something else was responsible for that mysterious smile.

"Do you want to tell me about it?" Kate asked as she sweetened her coffee. When she'd seen the rain sliding down the windows this morning, Kate had offered to bring breakfast back for Sally, but her grandmother had refused, saying she wouldn't melt, and so they'd both dodged puddles on the way to the dining room.

"Tell you about what?"

The innocent tone didn't fool Kate. "About whatever is turning you into Mona Lisa. I know that smile. It's the one you wore when you found that Barbie doll outfit that no one else had been able to get."

Sally reached for the peach jam and took her time spreading it on a piece of toast. "No Barbie doll dresses this time," she said slowly, "but I found something special for us. When I was getting my hair done, Ruby mentioned a spa that just opened in Blytheville. It's supposed to be the best one in the area, maybe in all of Texas."

A spa? To Kate's knowledge, her grandmother had never visited one.

"I've always been curious about them, and this one sounded so good that I knew it was time to find out what all the fuss was about." The smile Sally gave Kate was one of triumph. "They're normally booked up months in advance, so I didn't think there was much chance we could get in, but I decided to try. When I called them that afternoon, they had just had two cancellations. That's when I knew we were meant to go there."

Sally grinned as she broke off another piece of toast. "We're going to have the works, Kate: massage, facial, even a special pedicure with reflexology." Her grin widened. "I can't believe I've gone seventy-three years without a day at a spa, but now that it's scheduled, I can't wait."

Kate had to admit that it sounded like a wonderful day. "When are we going?" She'd tell Greg that she couldn't play tennis that day, and she'd make sure Heather knew not to expect her to work then.

"The Tuesday after Easter. Oh, Kate, I'm so excited. It'll be fun to do this, just the two of us."

"So this is where you're hanging out."

The hammer flew out of Greg's hand as he turned, shocked by the sight of his former partner. Greg had been so caught up in his thoughts that he hadn't heard anyone approaching. And now look what he'd done. The hammer had hit the porch step, making a small gouge. It wasn't a structural problem; no one else would notice it, but it bothered Greg because it was more proof that his world had been turned upside down.

He loved Kate. The thought had kept him awake for most of the night. Greg had never believed in love at first sight, and yet he knew that what he felt for Kate was love. True love, the real deal — it didn't matter what you called it. What Greg felt for Kate was genuine.

He'd spent the night and half of today trying to decide how and when to tell her. Thoughts of Kate filled his mind, even while he was repairing the loose porch railing for the new guest who was expected this afternoon. And now Drew was here. Drew, the man who considered himself an expert at love.

"How did you find me?" Greg demanded, rising to glare at Drew. Dressed in what passed for business casual at the S-squared offices, Drew looked as out of place as Kate had her first day. The difference was, Kate had adapted. Greg doubted Drew would. "What on earth are you doing here?" If there was anyone who didn't belong at Rainbow's End, it was Drew Carroll.

A self-satisfied smile was Drew's answer. He waited for a moment before he said, "You slipped up when you called me. There's GPS on your cell phone."

Of course there was. All cell phones had that. "That's not public information."

Drew shrugged. "True, but the sweet little thing I've been dating just happens to work for your carrier. She was more than willing to bend a few rules to help me track you down when I told her that your mother was on her deathbed."

Tamping back the anger that was starting to bubble up inside him, Greg gave Drew a long hard stare as he stepped off the porch. Though being two steps higher than Drew might be considered a power position, Greg had no desire to play the game. All he wanted was for Drew to leave.

"I would say I can't believe you told anyone a story like that, but I can." Drew had always maintained that his willingness to embellish the truth was what made him so successful. He'd derided Greg's belief in honesty, insisting that life wasn't as black-and-white as Greg seemed to believe.

Drew's only answer was another shrug. "All right," Greg said, recognizing the futility of changing anything about Drew, "now that you're here, what do you want?"

"To take you back to your mother's bedside or, more precisely," Drew said with the grin that many found charming, "to the S-squared offices."

So this was the reason for Drew's texts and voice mails. It was no wonder he'd told Greg they had to meet. Drew must have known there was no way Greg would agree if he'd raised the subject in a phone call, so he'd hoped that the personal touch would be more persuasive. He was mistaken.

"That's not gonna happen. I told you that the day I left." Though Greg had protested, the new owners had insisted on throwing a farewell party, and there had been more than one reference to the possibility of Greg rejoining the company in a new capacity.

When Drew had predicted that Greg would return by the end of the month, Greg had simply shaken his head, feeling freer than he had in years. Though his future had been and still was uncertain, he knew that his resignation was permanent.

"That was months ago," Drew said, giving Greg's tool belt a disdainful look. "People change their minds."

"I don't." Seeing Drew again had only reinforced Greg's belief that he'd done the right thing when he'd left Silicon Valley. The changes he'd made in his life had been positive. Though some might call his work at Rainbow's End menial labor, it gave Greg satisfaction. More importantly, coming here had brought Kate into his life. He didn't need Drew, who had seemingly majored in flirting when they'd been in college, trying to charm her.

"The least you can do is help me."

Greg kept his expression impassive, though he cringed inwardly, wondering how often he'd heard that particular refrain. "What do you need now?" If it was something easy, he might agree, simply to get Drew to leave, but Greg didn't hold out much hope for that. If it had been easy, Drew wouldn't have gone to the trouble of tracking him down.

Drew sank onto the top step and looked up at Greg, his lips curving into a half smile. "Ideas for a new release. Serge and Lisa want the next big thing."

Greg wasn't surprised. Though he'd been content to release one upgrade a year, when Serge and Lisa had taken over the company, they'd promised stockholders and current customers quarterly releases. What did surprise him was that they expected Drew to design the release. Though Greg had thought that Serge and Lisa understood Drew's role in the old S-squared, it seemed that his former partner had oversold his part in the creative process.

"Let me guess," he said, not bothering to hide his sarcasm, "you promised you'd give it to them when? Tomorrow?"

"Close enough. I thought I could do it. I did all the things you and I used to when we were brainstorming, but nothing worked. I'm fresh out of ideas. You've got to help me."

And let him take all the credit. As had happened so often in the past two weeks, images of Kate rushed through Greg's head. These were different from the memories of the time they'd spent together and the kisses they'd shared. This time Greg envisioned her staring at a jar of peanut butter, her brow furrowed with concentration. Kate was having a problem similar to Drew's, but she wouldn't pass off someone else's ideas as her own.

"I'm sorry, Drew. I can't help you."

Drew rose and glared at him. "Can't or won't?"

"I'm not sure there's much of a difference. The result is the same. You might as well head back to California."

"Not yet." Drew glanced at the cabin as if seeing it for the first time. "I thought I'd spend a couple days here, just in case you change your mind. The woman I talked to seemed glad for the business."

This was worse than Greg had feared. "So you're the new guest."

"Yeah. I wanted to see what the attraction was. So far I can't imagine what's keeping you here."

And he probably never would. He would see Kate, and he would assume she was the reason Greg remained. Drew would not search for the other, less tangible attractions. Wishing he could convince the man to leave but knowing that was impossible, Greg sighed. He had known that he and Drew were different, but seeing his former partner here made Greg realize just how deep those differences were.

"It's peaceful here," he told him.

Drew looked around, then shrugged. "That's a nice way of saying boring."

The man always had to have the last word.

Kate had never thought she'd be happy about rain, but today she was. It had started overnight and hadn't stopped until noon, which meant that the clay court was too wet for her and Greg to play tennis. And, as much as Kate wanted to spend more time with him, she knew this was for the best. One way or another, she needed to come up with a plan for Aunt Ivy's All Organic Peanut Butter. At this point, the only way she knew was brute force. She needed to spend every possible minute thinking about the company, trying to find a creative way to convince customers that they needed — absolutely, positively needed — to buy it.

Unfortunately, the ideas were not flowing. Ideas about peanut butter, that is. Instead, Kate found herself sketching Stonehenge and the restaurant where she and Greg had dined, devoting precious minutes to perfecting her drawing of the porch where they'd shared their second kiss, a kiss that somehow managed to surpass even the magic of the first.

And then there had been their good night

kiss on another porch, the one to this cabin, just before Greg had wished her sweet dreams. Her dreams had been sweet. In them she'd pictured herself and Greg walking through a field of bluebonnets, riding a gondola in Venice, gazing up at the Eiffel Tower. The scenes had changed, but what had not was the fact that she and Greg were together.

The dreams hadn't ended when she'd wakened. They'd simply changed to daydreams. The truth was, Kate was finding it difficult to think about anything other than Greg. Even Sally's surprise announcement about what she was calling their girls' day at the spa hadn't kept her attention once breakfast had ended. Kate had a dozen different ways to tell the world how special Greg was but not one that would convince even a die-hard peanut butter fan that Aunt Ivy's was somehow superior to every other brand.

"Oh, Kate. I didn't know you'd be here." Sally pressed her hand to her chest, obviously startled as she opened the door to their cabin and found Kate sitting on the floor, surrounded by piles of paper. "I just came back to get my e-reader to show Roy. Can you imagine? He's never used one."

When her breathing returned to normal,

Sally eyed the papers. "Are you working again?" Her slightly accusatory tone left no doubt of her opinion.

Kate wouldn't lie. "Maddox is pitching to a new client, and Heather asked me to help. You don't need to worry. I'll be done before our day at the spa. I'm looking forward to that as much as you are." When Sally did not appear mollified, Kate continued. "This is important. I wouldn't be doing it otherwise. My promotion depends on landing this client." Silence was the only response, leaving Kate feeling frustrated. It wasn't as if she was giving up time with her grandmother. Sally was spending almost as much time with Roy as she was with Kate. "You know how much I want to be a partner. It's what Grandpa Larry always wanted for me."

"Is that what you think?"

Kate nodded. "It's what I know."

Sally said nothing more, but she was unusually quiet when they walked to supper, not responding when Kate pointed out a mockingbird perched in one of the tree limbs and a small lizard scurrying across the path. When they reached the dining room, it was clear they were not the first to arrive, for an unfamiliar car was parked near the door.

As she and Sally entered the building,

Kate saw the young couple from Seguin who'd joined their table on Saturday, talking to a man. Though the stranger was about the same height as Greg, that was where the similarities ended. This man was blond with blue eyes, a golden tan, and a slightly arrogant tilt to his head. If Kate had been looking for a model for a California surfer ad, she would have used him, although his designer clothes and Rolex told her he probably had no need for another job. The man exuded wealth.

He broke off his conversation, apparently in midsentence judging by the Seguin couple's expressions, and strode across the floor.

"Good evening, ladies."

Kate gave him credit for including Sally in the greeting, even though his eyes barely flickered over her. Instead, he seemed to be studying Kate, cataloging her features. It was a decidedly uncomfortable feeling.

"I'm Drew Carroll," he said. "I'm going to be spending a few days here. Although," he added with a smile that did nothing to charm Kate, "if things work out the way I hope, I might extend my reservation."

"I'm certain the Sinclairs will appreciate that," she said. For a second, she hadn't recognized the name, but now she was almost certain that Drew Carroll was Greg's partner. Former partner, Kate amended, as she wondered why he was here. Despite the appraising looks he was giving her, she knew she was not the reason he'd come to Rainbow's End.

"What about you? Would you be glad?"

The voice was charming, although it rang a bit false to Kate. The smile was broad and seemingly genuine, and yet she did not trust it. Not for a second. Kate tried not to frown as her mind whirled. Surely this couldn't have been Greg's partner. The name was right, but not the personality. If Kate had been asked to pick someone who was the exact opposite of Greg, this would have been the man.

"I'm always happy to see more guests here, Mr. Carroll," she said, hoping her formality would tell Drew Carroll she had no interest in him. "Please let me introduce my grandmother, Sally Fuller. And I'm Kate Sherwood."

Before she knew what he was doing, Drew hooked arms with both of them and turned toward the table. "Shall we sit down?"

And so Kate found herself seated next to Drew instead of Greg. The man tried to monopolize the conversation, and when Sally pointedly turned her back and began to talk to Roy, Drew began what could only be called a blatant flirtation with Kate.

Short of being rude, she couldn't ignore him, so Kate kept her replies brief, hoping he'd take the hint and talk to Greg, who sat on his other side. But Drew did not take the hint. He seemed oblivious to Kate's lack of interest and continued talking about himself and his life in California, ending with an invitation for Kate to visit him there. When she told him she would be much too busy to even consider a trip, he acted as if she'd accepted the invitation.

Had no one said no to him before? Kate masked a frown as she took another bite of Carmen's delicious chicken fricassee. In all likelihood, ever since he'd become a multi-millionaire, Drew Carroll had gotten almost everything he wanted. That was sad.

24

Breakfast was quiet. The Seguin couple was leaving when Kate and Sally arrived, and there was no sign of Drew, a fact for which Kate gave thanks. She hadn't thought it possible that one person could upset the dynamics of a resort so easily, but Drew had done exactly that. He'd remained at her side after supper, interrupting whenever Greg spoke. Though the man was unspeakably rude, Kate did not want to descend to his level, and so, though she would have preferred her nightly walk with Greg, she had proposed a game of Clue with Sally and Roy.

Kate had smiled when they reached the main lodge and, though the night was far from cold by New Jersey standards, Roy suggested a fire. He and Greg built a roaring one while Drew tried to impress Kate and Sally with the people he knew. Though Sally did nothing more than nod politely,

Kate could see that she was not impressed. For her part, Kate was more impressed when Greg convinced Carmen that popcorn would be the perfect accompaniment to the gradual unraveling of a murder mystery.

"Unfortunately it's not caramel corn," he said softly as he handed Kate a bowl and a pile of paper napkins. The crooked smile that punctuated his words warmed her more than the fire, because it brought back memories of the bluebonnet festival and told her Greg shared those fond memories.

Kate watched the way Drew interacted with the others and marveled at the fact that he had been the customer contact for Sys=Simpl. What was even more remarkable was that he had somehow convinced Greg that he was the right man to handle all the personnel-related aspects of the company.

It was true that Drew was more forceful than Greg, quicker with repartee, but he also sounded glib. If her money had been at stake, she would have insisted on working with Greg. But perhaps customers had not realized they had a choice. If Greg remained in the background, Drew would have been their primary contact.

The man was handsome; some would call him charming, but he struck Kate as false.

Perhaps that was only because she was comparing him to Greg.

It had been an interesting evening. To Kate's surprise, although Drew seemed a bit ill at ease at the beginning, perhaps because he was unfamiliar with the game, his competitive nature overcame his misgivings, and he was soon an active participant, insisting that the candlestick was the murder weapon. Still, the glint in his eye when he smiled at her made Kate uncomfortable.

She had been equally uncomfortable when he'd insisted on accompanying her to her cabin. Sally must have seen Kate's uneasiness, because before she knew what was happening, the five of them had walked to Kate and Sally's cabin. It was a far cry from what Kate had hoped for. She had looked forward to some private time with Greg, perhaps an encore to the previous night's kiss. Instead she had had to listen to Drew compare Texas to California.

How had Greg managed to work with Drew for so many years? Kate resolved that she would ask Greg when they played tennis. Surely Drew's presence wouldn't affect that.

Kate was stirring sweetener into her coffee when Greg entered the dining room. She blinked in surprise, because this was the first time she'd seen him at breakfast. When she'd asked, he'd told her that he ate energy bars before he rowed and jogged, then grabbed a bowl of cereal and some juice at the end of the breakfast hour. The fact that Kate and Sally were usually the first to arrive meant that they missed Greg.

"Kate!" His smile was warm, friendly, and genuine, a marked contrast to his former partner's. "I was hoping to catch you here." Greg pulled out the chair next to her. "I hate to do this, but I need to cancel tennis again today."

Sally looked up from her pancakes. "The court must be dry by now." There had been no more rain overnight, and the sky was bright, sunny, and unseasonably warm.

"It is," Greg admitted, "but I want to show Drew around Dupree." He lowered his voice, though there were no others in the room. "I probably shouldn't say this, but I hope that'll convince him to leave."

"Then you obviously didn't invite him." Kate hadn't believed Greg would, but the thought still niggled at the back of her mind. She had had the impression that he had told no one he was coming here, but somehow Drew had found him.

"Never! I should apologize, though. I'm afraid you saw him at his worst yesterday.

Drew's a good guy. He's just out of his element here."

"If you say so." It would take more than that to convince Kate, especially since Drew's presence meant she had less time with Greg.

When Greg left, Kate turned to Sally. "Let's go rowing." It was one of the things they hadn't done, and since there was no need for Kate to rush back to play tennis, they'd have plenty of time today.

Sally nodded. "All right, but we're not going to Paintbrush Island. You know how I feel about that."

As it turned out, Sally needn't have worried. Rowing proved to be much harder than Kate had expected, leaving every muscle in her arms burning with the effort before they were halfway to the island. Greg made it look so easy, but it wasn't.

Disappointed that she hadn't been able to take Sally around the entire lake, Kate headed back. When she'd docked the boat and walked the short distance to the gazebo with her grandmother, she glanced at her watch. Still an hour until noon.

"I'm going to see if Carmen has lemonade ready yet." Her throat could use the cool liquid, and she suspected that Sally would be equally grateful for it.

As she walked down the short hallway to the kitchen, Kate heard Carmen's voice raised in anger. "The man has got to go. He's the scum of the earth. He cannot stay here another night." Her accent was heavier than normal, reminding Kate that English had not been Carmen's first language.

Though she was tempted to turn around and pretend she hadn't heard the shouts, Kate's instincts told her that Carmen needed her. Her words were angry, but Kate heard a deeper note, one that she might have described as anguish, in Carmen's voice. It reminded Kate of the day Carmen had spoken of her husband's desertion.

"What's wrong?" Kate asked as she entered the kitchen. Carmen was standing next to the sink, her hands fisted on her hips in a classic display of anger. Kevin stood a few yards away, one of his hands behind his back. Though Kate was surprised to see him here so early, she remembered that this week was school vacation.

"This is what's wrong!" Carmen strode to Kevin's side and yanked his arm, revealing a whiskey bottle. "Kevin found it when he emptied that man's trash this morning." Her face flushed with anger, Carmen continued. "Can he not read? The brochure says liquor is not permitted here. When I tell Angela, she'll boot him out."

"How can I help?" Kate wasn't certain what she could do other than put her arms around Carmen and tell her everything would be all right. But those could be empty promises. Kate doubted Angela would turn away a paying guest, even if he had broken one of the resort's rules, and she doubted that Drew — for there was no question he was the one who'd inflamed Carmen — would stop drinking simply because Angela or Carmen asked him to. The little time she'd spent with Drew Carroll had convinced Kate that the man did whatever he wanted, with no regard for others.

Carmen shook her head. "I will do it," she said as, bottle in hand, she headed toward the office.

"Carmen is really upset," Kate said to Kevin when they were alone in the kitchen. "I know guests aren't supposed to bring alcohol here, but her reaction seems over the top."

"There's a good reason." A hint of embarrassment colored Kevin's face. "You wouldn't know, because you never met Carmen's husband. Mr. St. George was the town drunk." When Kate flinched at the blunt term, Kevin shrugged. "No one was supposed to talk about it, but everyone knew. I heard more than one person say it was a good thing when he disappeared, even if it broke Marisa's heart."

This was worse than Kate had realized. Mr. St. George's disappearance was bad enough, but his drinking put a new perspective on Carmen and Marisa's lives. Though Kate had no firsthand experience with alcoholism, she knew that it could tear families apart. No wonder Carmen was so upset, and no wonder Marisa did not want to return to Dupree.

"That poor family." Kate's heart ached for Carmen and her daughter. She wanted to help, but what could she do? A snappy slogan wouldn't fix this.

"I can see why you're staying here," Drew said as Greg steered his SUV through the Rainbow's End gates and headed for Dupree. "With a chick like Kate around, I'd stay too."

Greg tried not to bristle. He'd known how Drew would react to Kate. She was an attractive, available young woman, and the fact that she wasn't Drew's normal type only added to her appeal. Drew had never been one to resist a challenge. But there was nothing to be gained by jousting with him, so Greg said only, "She's almost as bad a tennis player as I am." That might not discourage Drew, but it was worth a try. Drew preferred arm candy who could hold their own on a golf course or tennis court.

"The pro at my club could turn her into a star in a month or so. I just need to convince her to come to the West Coast." Drew grimaced as he looked around. "I don't understand why any of you are here. This place is in the middle of nowhere."

"We call it the Hill Country," Greg said mildly. "A lot of people think it's one of the most beautiful places on Earth."

"Sure thing." Drew pointed to one of the empty storefronts as they entered Dupree. "When I drove through yesterday, I didn't see a decent restaurant, and there aren't even any fast-food places. What do people do here? It looks like one of those towns where the most exciting thing is watching grass grow."

"It's definitely not LA or San Francisco." Since the object of this outing was to convince Drew that this was not the place for him, Greg did not point out the advantages of relaxation. "Let's get out and walk a bit. I'll show you around." Greg hoped the fact that Pecan Street was light-years removed from Rodeo Drive would be the final inducement Drew needed to return to

California.

"All right. I can invest five minutes, but when we're done here, I expect you to take me somewhere for a good lunch. The three-martini kind."

Drew was in for another surprise, because lunch would be at the Sit 'n' Sip, where the absence of a liquor license meant that Drew would have not even one martini.

Not wanting to tie up any of the spots in front of the Sit 'n' Sip, Greg parked on the opposite side of the street two stores away from the bootery.

"You have a boot maker in this Podunk town?" Drew stopped in front of the store, his incredulity almost amusing.

"This is Texas," Greg said. "Folks wear boots. Including yours truly." Though they weren't his normal footwear, this morning he'd donned the pair Samantha had made for him.

Drew glanced at Greg's feet. "You got those here?" When Greg nodded, Drew reached for the doorknob. "Maybe this place isn't so bad after all. I want to meet the man who made those."

The bell tinkled as they entered the shop, and Sam Dexter emerged from the back room. "Mornin', Greg," the tall, gray-haired man said. "Good to see you again. Did you bring us another customer?"

Greg wasn't sure why Samantha wasn't minding the store, but he wasn't complaining. Even though he was glad that Drew appeared ready to help the local economy a bit by ordering a pair of boots — maybe even two if he was feeling particularly competitive — it was just as well he didn't meet Samantha. She was at least as beautiful as anyone Drew had dated.

Drew nodded. "Those are nice boots you made for my friend. I'd like a pair of my own. A different style, of course. What's the best leather you have?"

This was vintage Drew, wanting to outdo Greg, to prove that he was more than the junior partner. It had never bothered Greg before, and it didn't now. "You probably want ostrich or sharkskin," he said. "Mine are ordinary calf."

Drew nodded. Turning to Sam, he said, "I assume you can ship them to me in California." The fact that Drew wasn't planning to extend his stay to wait for his boots was the first positive sign of the morning. Of course, he might have assumed that it would be months before they were completed.

"Sure can. We do a lot of mail-order business. Now, what kind of design would you like?" Sam pulled a binder from behind the counter. "This might give you some ideas. We can do practically anything."

Five minutes later Drew had chosen a combination of two designs and had his feet measured. "You're sure the workmanship will be the same as you put into Greg's boots."

Sam nodded, though his eyes narrowed at Drew's unspoken assumption that he might shortchange an out-of-town customer. "All of our boots are made to the same high standards," he said stiffly.

"Then you'll make mine exactly the way you did Greg's." When he negotiated, Drew could be as relentless as a badger chasing a scent.

This time Sam shook his head. "I think you misunderstood. I didn't make Greg's boots." He turned and called into the back room. "Samantha."

For the first time in all the years Greg had known him, Drew was speechless.

"Why didn't you tell me?" he demanded when they were once more outside the store. "Samantha Dexter is the most beautiful woman I've ever seen."

And like Kate, she had seemed immune to Drew's charm. When he'd announced that he wanted to get to know her better, her refusal had been polite but firm, leaving no doubt that she would not change her mind.

"She ought to be a movie star," Drew continued.

"From what I can see, she's happy right here making boots."

"It's a waste. A real waste." Drew looked up and down the street. Other than two women leaving the quilt shop, their bags overflowing with what appeared to be fabric, the sidewalks were empty.

"What other surprises do you have in store for me, or are you ready to help me?" Drew fixed his gaze on Greg. "You can't convince me you don't have some ideas for a new release. S-squared was your life for more than a decade. You can't just turn that off overnight."

But Greg had. Though a few ideas had flitted through his brain since Drew had made his demands, they were only wisps of concepts, nothing substantial enough to turn into a new software feature. Greg wondered if that was how Kate felt about her peanut butter campaign. The difference was, she was actively working, seeking a concept that would sell her client's product, while he had deliberately distanced himself from Drew and everything else connected to Sys=Simpl.

"Mr. Greg! Mr. Greg!"

Greg almost groaned as Fiona Ahrens left her mother's shop and scampered toward him, her face split by a huge grin.

"An admirer?" Drew's crooked grin left no doubt that he found the idea amusing.

Before Greg could reply, Lauren appeared in the doorway. "Fiona, you know you're not supposed to leave the store."

The little girl turned. "But I had to talk to Mr. Greg. It's important."

Her pleading tone touched Greg. He crossed the street in a few long strides and crouched next to the child, biting back a smile at the sight of her mismatched socks. It appeared Lauren was holding up her end of the bargain. He could only hope Fiona was doing the same and had stopped searching for a father.

"What is it, Fiona?"

She looked up at Drew standing at Greg's side. "Who is he?"

"He's Mr. Drew. He's a friend of mine." Unconcerned with the little girl, Drew was introducing himself to Lauren. "So what do you need to tell me?"

"I know a secret," Fiona said, her lips curving in a grin.

"That's nice, but you're not supposed to tell secrets."

Fiona nodded, setting her braids to swinging. "I know that. Mom said I couldn't tell anyone, but you're okay. You're the secret."

"I am?" The only secret Greg had was his connection to Sys=Simpl, and even if Lauren had discovered that, he couldn't imagine her sharing it with Fiona.

"Yes. It's a good one." Fiona leaned closer, cupping her hands around her mouth. Though Greg suspected she was planning to whisper, her voice came out as little less than a shout. "Mama told me you can't be my daddy because you're gonna marry Miss Kate."

25

"Do you want to go to Stonehenge?" Roy asked as he helped Sally into the truck. He'd invited her to join him for lunch again today, but she'd refused, claiming she needed to spend more time with Kate. And she did. Even though she knew that worrying accomplished nothing, Sally couldn't help worrying about her granddaughter. Kate seemed happier than she'd ever seen her when she was with Greg, but the moment they were apart, the happiness disappeared, almost as if it were a shield that Kate removed at will, and it was replaced with frowns and worry lines. The reason, Sally was certain, was her job.

For what seemed like the millionth time, Sally wished Larry were still alive. Kate had always listened to him where work was concerned, but it seemed she'd only heard half the story. Larry had filled Kate's head with stories of advertising, making it sound like the ideal profession. And it had been for him. He'd enjoyed the creative aspects, but he'd never let the job consume him. "It's how I make a living," he'd once told Sally, "but it's not my life." That was the part of the message Kate had missed.

When Kate had come to live with them, Larry had scaled back his hours so he'd have more time to spend with her. Both he and Sally had known that meant the end of his dreams of becoming a partner, but neither had cared. Kate was more important than a title, a fancy office, and a fatter bank account. Unfortunately, either Larry hadn't told his granddaughter that or she'd forgotten it.

"I've lived here all my life, and I've never seen Stonehenge." Roy's words brought Sally back to the present. Ashamed that she'd been so inattentive, Sally smiled. She wasn't going to let happiness slip through her fingers. Instead, she was going to grab it with both hands the way she had clutched the pole on the carousel, and she wouldn't let go.

Sally looked at Roy, trying to memorize the wrinkles and creases that made his face uniquely his. This was a man who'd lived, loved, and lost but who refused to be defeated.

"Stonehenge sounds interesting, but what I'd really like is to see more wildflowers," she told Roy when he climbed into the truck. "We don't have bluebonnets at home, and I can't seem to get my fill of them." The fact that April was peak bluebonnet season was the reason Sally had insisted on coming to Rainbow's End then. And though there were some around the lake that bore their name, there weren't the masses she longed to see.

Roy tipped his Stetson back a couple inches as he settled into his seat and switched on the engine. "If you want bluebonnets, you've come to the right place. Dupree isn't just the heart of the hills," he said, referring to the slogan on the partially faded sign at the town line. "It's also the heart of the bluebonnets. If you don't mind a little off-road driving, I know just the spot."

Sally matched Roy's grin. "That sounds like fun — a bit of adventure. Let's go." She was wearing jeans and her cowboy boots today, so there'd be no problem if they had to walk to reach Roy's special spot. She'd even brought a hat to shield her face from the sun in case the afternoon included outdoor activities.

Though they spent most afternoons at the

lodge, playing chess or backgammon or simply sipping lemonade in the gazebo, yesterday Roy had said he wanted a change of pace. Sally suspected he also wanted to avoid Drew Carroll.

The man might be handsome, but something about him grated on Sally. She had read that people's behavior sometimes changed dramatically when they were placed in uncomfortable situations — out of their comfort zone, the article had said. Perhaps that was the case with Drew. That made more sense than believing Greg had chosen to work with such a difficult man for more than a decade.

Pushing thoughts of Drew Carroll firmly to the side, Sally studied the man next to her. Each time they were together, she discovered a new facet of his personality. Today she learned that Roy was a careful driver, always stopping for pedestrians, never exceeding the speed limit. He slowed down a couple of times to greet friends as he drove through Dupree, seeming to take great pleasure in introducing Sally to them. Even if they didn't see any wildflowers, Sally knew that this was an afternoon she'd remember, simply because she was spending it with Roy.

"It's not too much farther," Roy said

when they reached the main highway. Turning south, Roy drove a couple of miles, then pulled onto a dirt track. The dirt didn't surprise Sally. He'd told her there would be some off-road driving. What did surprise her was the barbed wire fence and the white gate with the "no trespassing" sign. Though this was obviously private property, Roy hopped down from the truck, opened the gate, pulled through, then closed it again and returned to the truck.

"Do you know the owners?" Sally couldn't imagine this man who seemed so honorable intentionally breaking the law, and yet her discomfort with the situation forced her to ask.

Roy grinned and laid a hand on top of hers, as if to reassure her. "You could say that. This is my land. When we built the house in town, Barb and I figured it was a starter house, so we bought this acreage a few years later. We always intended to build a bigger house here, but the boys liked being in town and close to friends. There didn't seem much point in moving after they left home, and now . . ." Roy paused, his gray eyes serious as he gazed at Sally.

"It's beautiful." Though the terrain was similar to that around Rainbow's End, she could see that this land had had minimal disturbance. The rutted road led over a small hill and into a clearing surrounded by oaks, hickory, and mesquite. It would have been a beautiful setting at any time of the year, but now that the clearing was filled with a magnificent spread of bluebonnets, it was breathtaking.

"Oh, Roy," Sally said softly, not wanting to disturb the serenity of the scene.

Roy had no such compunctions. "Let's look at those bluebonnets up close and personal. That's why we came." He helped her out of the truck and walked at her side, his arm around her waist, guiding her until they were in the middle of the patch. "Think these are enough flowers for you?"

"Oh yes." Sally lowered herself to the ground, wanting to touch and smell the flowers, then bent forward to sniff the deep blue blossoms. The petals were tipped with white, while the palest of yellow centers provided a pleasing contrast to the vibrant blue.

Gingerly, she stroked one of the petals, smiling when it proved to be as soft as she'd thought. "These are incredible," she said. "I've dreamt about them for years. One year Kate found a calendar where every month had a picture of bluebonnets, but nothing compares to being here." Though the flowers were spectacular, what made Sally's heart beat faster was the fact that she was sharing them with Roy. Tears welled in her eyes at the sheer beauty of the scene.

Clearing her throat in an attempt to get her emotions under control, Sally pointed to a bright orange-red flower mixed in with the bluebonnets. "Is that Indian paintbrush?"

Roy nodded. His glasses had darkened in the sunlight, but Sally could see enough to know there were no telltale tears in his eyes. It was only she who was overcome by the beauty.

"Barb told me that if you look closely, you'll see that only the tips of the petals are colored. I guess whoever named them thought they looked as if they'd been dipped in paint." Roy fingered the brilliant flower. "I've heard there are other colors of paintbrush, including purple, but I've never seen them."

Sally looked from the floral beauty to the man who was sharing it with her. When she and Larry had visited Rainbow's End, it had been mid-June, and the bluebonnets were no longer in bloom, but other guests' tales of the flowers' magnificence had made Sally determined to return in the spring. Now she was here, and the flowers were even more beautiful than she'd expected. Or was it because she was seeing them with the most fascinating man she'd met since her husband? Roy was unlike Larry in many ways, and yet he shared one characteristic with her late husband: he made her feel beautiful.

It wasn't anything he said, merely the way he looked at her that made Sally realize that the wrinkles and gray hair she saw in the mirror didn't mean she was unattractive, at least not to this man. And that feeling was even better than the sight of bluebonnets, because unlike the flowers, it would not fade.

"What do you think about a house out here?" Roy asked as he helped Sally to her feet.

His voice was even, but her head was still spinning. Sally looked at the clearing and smiled. If Roy wanted to talk about houses, they would. If he wanted to talk about Mars, that was all right too. "I can't imagine a prettier site."

She turned around, studying the land. "You could put the house itself just inside the forest. It would be cooler there, and you wouldn't disturb too many of the bluebonnets."

Sally envisioned a single-width drive leading to the house and garage, with only a small expanse of grass around the house. If the majority of the trees were left standing, the house would require minimal landscaping. Its beauty would come from the meadow and the trees.

Roy nodded slowly. "That's what I was thinking too. The problem is, it's a ways out of town. Would you feel isolated if you were here? It would take first responders awhile to arrive in case of an emergency."

Studying his face, Sally tried to understand Roy's question. Was he asking if she personally would be comfortable living here, or was he simply asking whether she thought someone — some unspecified woman — would feel isolated? She wished she knew.

"It would be more practical to stay in town," she told him, "especially at our ages." Thirty years ago she hadn't considered ambulance response time. Now she did.

"That's what I thought." Though Roy nodded, Sally saw disappointment reflected in his eyes. She couldn't let that remain.

"On the other hand, there are times when it makes sense to throw practicality to the winds." Sally laid her hand on Roy's arm and looked up at him. "I never used those words, but that's what I told Kate. She can't always be a planner. She needs to take chances and chase rainbows."

"What about you?"

Sally took a deep breath, choosing her words carefully before she answered. "I'd love to live in a place like this." Though she wanted to cry out "I'd love to live right here with you," she wouldn't. Telling Roy that was more than taking a chance. It was stepping off a cliff without knowing what was beneath.

"So you'd sell your home and move to Texas?"

This time there was no need to hesitate. "If it weren't for Kate, I'd do it in a heartbeat. I'm not sure how she'd react. She's used to being only an hour's flight away from me. It would be more difficult for her to visit me here, and that would be hard on her." Sally looked at Roy, hoping he'd understand.

"What about you?" Roy wrapped his arm around Sally's waist and began to walk toward the spot where she'd suggested locating the house. "Would living here make up for not seeing Kate so often?"

"It might."

He stopped and smiled at her, his gray eyes once again reflecting enthusiasm. "That's what I hoped you'd say. Now, tell me about the kind of house you think I ought to build."

And so for the next hour, they discussed house plans. Plans for a house Roy might or might not build. But, though his smile warmed Sally's heart and his touch on her arm and waist made her feel cherished, never once did he ask if she would share that house with him. Sally didn't know whether to be relieved or disappointed.

26

Drew hadn't left. Kate frowned as she poured herself a cup of coffee and snapped on a lid. She was supposed to be concentrating on Aunt Ivy's peanut butter, not thinking about Rainbow's End's newest guest.

Drew had come to dinner last night, so apparently neither Greg's tour of Dupree nor Angela's reminder of the no-drinking rule had discouraged him. He'd been congenial at supper, and afterward he'd seemed to enjoy the game of Monopoly that Kate had organized. Perhaps that enjoyment was because he'd won handily. Somehow, Drew had never landed on the "go to jail" square, while the rest of them had spent more than their fair share of time behind bars.

Though Sally still regarded him with suspicion and had in fact told Kate he epitomized the rude younger generation, ignoring the fact that her granddaughter was part of that same generation, Kate had to admit that she was revising her opinion of Greg's former partner. Perhaps, as Greg had claimed, he'd simply been out of his element the first night and was adjusting to the slow pace at Rainbow's End.

But Drew Carroll was not Kate's concern. Aunt Ivy's was. She slung her bag over her shoulder and gripped the coffee cup as she opened the outside door. Though it was a bit farther than taking the indoor route, she had decided to avoid potential distractions by walking to the lodge on the less traveled outside path. She had already had enough distractions.

As soon as breakfast was over, Sally had returned to the cabin to rest. Though she'd claimed that nothing was wrong other than a bit too much sun and a bit too much walking the previous afternoon, Kate couldn't dismiss her concerns. She had wanted to stay in the cabin to be close by if her grandmother needed her, but Sally had insisted that all she needed was peace and quiet. And Kate needed to work.

Though Sunday had been wonderful, nothing had gone right since then. Kate looked around the lodge, satisfying herself that she wouldn't be bothering anyone if she worked here. The room was empty. Perfect. Something ought to be. Kate sighed as she opened her laptop, pressing the power button. She'd expected it to be different, but she and Greg hadn't had a single minute alone since they'd returned from Stonehenge, dinner, and the unforgettable kiss that had followed it.

Sunday had been a special day. In Greg's arms, Kate had felt as if anything was possible. Though she'd heard friends talk about being on top of the world, she'd never experienced that sensation. Sunday night had changed all that. For the first time, she'd felt as if she'd climbed Mount Everest and was ready to do it again. The world was at her feet, all because of Greg.

When she'd returned to Rainbow's End, Kate had felt happy, energized, and confident that everything was going right. The mental blocks that had plagued her would crumble, and she'd be able to create a campaign that would please both Heather and the client. It was a wonderful, heady feeling. Unfortunately, it hadn't lasted. Though the rain had given her extra time to work on Monday, all she'd developed was increasing frustration.

Perhaps it would have been better if she'd been able to spend some time with Greg. Kate wanted to talk to him. Oh, why mince words? She wanted to kiss him again, to feel the magic of his arms around her and his lips on hers. But there had never been the right moment, and now that Drew was here, it seemed there wouldn't be.

The man was like a barnacle. The only good thing Kate could say was that he no longer seemed to be clinging to her. Since he and Greg had returned from Dupree, although he'd given Kate a few puzzled looks, he had spent more time talking to Greg. It was almost as if he were trying to charm Greg, but that made no sense.

Then there was the ad campaign. Though she'd developed a few ideas, in her heart of hearts, Kate knew they weren't good enough, and so she hadn't discussed any of them with Heather. Time was running out. Heather wanted her concept no later than close of business Friday. Hazel and Ike Preston were expecting it on Monday, and though Heather hadn't said anything, Kate knew that if she failed to deliver, Heather, Nick, and Chase would spend the weekend coming up with something to present to Aunt Ivy's. If they managed to salvage the account, Kate might be given another chance. If not, unemployment was a distinct possibility.

Though distressing, that was nothing compared to Sally. She'd seemed unusually pensive this morning, and her insistence that nothing was wrong had rung false. Even their discussion of whether or not to have hot stone massages at the spa hadn't distracted her. Kate might have dismissed her concerns as an overactive imagination, but it wasn't like Sally to want to rest. Something was amiss, and that worried Kate more than anything else. If she had to, she could find another job, but her grandmother was irreplaceable.

Trying to push those thoughts to the back of her mind, Kate stared at the blank screen on her laptop. She had hoped that sitting in the lodge would spark her creativity. The problem was, she could wax eloquent about the lake. She could devise a catchy slogan for the lodge itself. But peanut butter? The ideas simply refused to flow.

She leaned back in the chair, sliding down to prop her feet on the coffee table. Sally would deplore the sloppy posture, but it felt good, and feeling good was the first step toward unleashing creativity. Kate had developed some of her best ideas sitting on the floor of her apartment, wearing her oldest clothes, listening to her favorite playlist, oblivious to the fact that the open carton of ice cream in front of her was melting. There was no ice cream this morning, but perhaps the relaxed position would help.

She closed her eyes, trying to envision a jar of peanut butter in an unexpected context. Could she float it on the lake? Perhaps, but what would that signify to consumers? Peanut butter was hardly a life preserver. Though potential customers might laugh at the idea, laughter wasn't what Aunt Ivy's needed. Sales were. Kate pursed her lips in concentration, wishing she could find a novel way to announce that Aunt Ivy's peanut butter was everything a customer had ever wanted in peanut butter and more.

"You've got to do it, Greg."

Kate blinked at the sound of Drew's voice. It seemed that the two men had entered the lodge, perhaps seeking solitude as Kate had. Realizing that they could not see her, Kate started to rise to announce her presence, but before she could do that, Drew continued.

"I promise I won't ask again, but I really need this. My job's on the line."

Kate winced. She didn't know Drew well, but what she knew was enough to make her certain that he would be embarrassed by her overhearing that particular admission. She slid back down, hoping the men would leave the room before she heard anything more.

"I already told you that I can't." Greg's voice held more than a hint of annoyance, as if this wasn't the first time they'd had this particular conversation.

"You *won't*. There's a big difference." And the angry note in Drew's voice left no doubt that he wasn't happy. "I know you, Greg. You could sketch out half a dozen new features for Sys=Simpl in an hour. I've seen you do it."

"That was then. It's not the same now. I'm not part of the company anymore. Just as importantly, it's no longer part of me. I don't eat and breathe it any longer."

Kate heard the sound of a fist connecting with wood and guessed that Drew was expressing his displeasure. "I don't believe you," he said. "You're just trying to pay me back for something. I'm not sure what that could be, but you're acting like a sore loser." He snapped his fingers, the sound echoing through the nearly empty room. "That's it, isn't it? You've realized that you're a loser and always have been. You know you couldn't do anything without me, and now you want to punish me for that."

Drew's voice was filled with anger, but there was something else, perhaps a hint of desperation. Though Kate felt a moment of sympathy for the man whose job was at stake, it evaporated with his next words.

"You're a loser, Greg," Drew continued. "You always have been, you always will be."

How dare he say such things? Kate shuddered at the thought that Greg's father might have used the same words. If he had, hearing them come from Drew would be like reopening a partially healed wound.

Kate had heard enough. Scrambling to her feet, she turned to face the men. "If anyone's a loser, it's you, Drew."

Both Greg and Drew stared at her, obviously shocked to discover the lodge wasn't empty.

Kate took a shallow breath before continuing. "You might have been the face of Sys=Simpl, but that's all you were: an empty shell. Greg was the brains of the outfit, something you're only now learning."

As Drew's face flushed with anger, Kate delivered her final salvo. "You're nothing without him. You're the loser, Drew."

Though she saw the shock on his face, Drew's voice was remarkably calm. "What makes you think you know anything?" His eyes roamed from the top of her head to her feet, his expression practically shouting "dumb blonde." At another time, Kate might have been annoyed by his attitude, but today she didn't care. What mattered was the way he was trying to destroy Greg.

"I have eyes. I have ears. And, believe it or not, I have a brain." She lifted one shoulder, feigning nonchalance. "I've read everything I could find about Sys=Simpl, and what I learned was that customers loved the software. Not the packaging, not the pretty speeches, not even the key chains you handed out at industry meetings. They bought it because it's great software that does exactly what they need. And we all know who was responsible for that software." Though Kate had been staring at Drew, daring him to be the first to break the gaze, she turned to smile at Greg. "Greg was the reason for Sys=Simpl's success. Face it, Drew. The company was successful *despite* you."

He took a step toward her, his stance menacing. "That's a crock of —"

"Enough." Greg clapped his hand on his former partner's shoulder. "It's time for you to leave Rainbow's End."

Drew swiveled to face him, his eyes burning with intensity. "With pleasure." A second later, the door slammed behind him.

Greg took a step, then another until he was only inches from Kate. His eyes had deepened to the shade of cedar needles, and his expression was serious. "Did you mean all that?"

"Of course I did." How could he doubt it? "Any idiot could see that you're worth a dozen Drews. You're smart, you're dedicated, and you don't need him. You can do anything you want all by yourself."

Greg stared at her for a long moment, as if he were trying to absorb what she'd said. At last he shook his head. "I don't know how I ever got so lucky as to have you on my side, but you're the best thing that's ever happened to me."

His lips curved into the sweetest of smiles as he pulled Kate into his arms. She stood there for a second, not daring to move lest he break the embrace. And then Greg began to stroke her back, his hand moving in lazy circles that sent ripples of delight through her body.

Kate moved a little closer, feeling the warmth of his breath, inhaling the tangy scent that was Greg's alone. This was wonderful, so very wonderful. The anger she had felt toward Drew drained away, replaced by pure pleasure.

Kate had no idea how long they stood there, neither of them speaking, their eyes locked in silent communication. At length

Greg's hand slowed and he leaned forward to feather kisses on her forehead, her nose, her cheeks. Kate closed her eyes, wanting to savor every sensation, determined to etch each instant on her memory. This was what she had dreamed of, what she had longed for. Greg, the man she loved, was holding her in his arms, making her feel like the heroine of every romance novel she'd ever read.

"Look at me," he whispered between kisses. And as Kate opened her eyes, Greg lowered his mouth to hers. She tasted cinnamon and coffee; her body tingled from the top of her head to the tip of her toes; every sense was heightened by the magic of Greg's embrace. Kate felt pampered; she felt protected; most of all, she felt loved.

Perhaps it was a minute, perhaps an hour, perhaps an eternity later that Greg drew back, ending the kiss, leaving Kate's emotions so tangled that she knew she would never unravel them.

"I don't know what I did to deserve you," he whispered, his lips only a breath away from hers, "but I thank God you're here."

27

Something was wrong. Sally wasn't acting like herself this morning. She hadn't sung in the shower, and she'd been quieter than usual as they'd walked to breakfast. Kate twisted the paper napkin between her fingers as she wondered if she had missed the signs yesterday. The day had passed in a blur, everything colored by her recognition that what she felt for Greg was more than friendship. Kate didn't know how it had happened, how love had grown so quickly. All she knew was that her feelings for Greg were deeper and more powerful than anything she had experienced. This was the real thing; she knew it.

But love, as glorious as it was, hadn't helped her find a concept for Aunt Ivy's. She and Greg had forgone their tennis match and evening walk so that Kate would have more time to work, but it had been to no avail. Though her brain was filled with thoughts of Greg and the wonder of his kisses, it was devoid of viable ideas for marketing peanut butter.

And while Kate had been daydreaming of white lace, gardenias, and happily-ever-after, she'd paid only cursory attention to Sally. How could she have been so selfish?

Kate watched as Sally spun the lazy Susan, bringing the coffeepot closer to her. Although she'd finished her breakfast a few minutes earlier, instead of preparing to leave as she normally did, Sally showed no sign of wanting to leave the dining room. Instead, she poured herself a third cup of coffee and turned to look at Kate. Her color was good, but there was an unfamiliar wariness in Sally's eyes that worried Kate.

"We need to talk," Sally said, her voice shakier than normal.

The oatmeal that had tasted delicious five minutes ago settled like a lump in Kate's stomach, but she forced herself to smile. "About what?"

Sally's smile looked equally forced. "I hope you won't be too shocked, but I'm thinking about selling my home."

Kate felt as if she'd been bludgeoned. She wasn't simply shocked; she was horrified. Growing up, Kate had heard both Sally and Grandpa Larry say that they hoped to live in that house until the day they died. Grandpa Larry had. If Sally was planning to sell, her health must be worse than she'd admitted.

"I thought you said the doctor wasn't overly worried about you." The words came out in a burst, propelled by fear.

Sally laid her hand on Kate's and squeezed. "I'm not dying, Kate. Not yet. That's not the reason I want to sell it."

"Then why?" Kate asked, no longer pretending to smile.

"It's larger than I need. Most of the time, I feel as if I'm rattling around there." Sally took a sip of coffee before she continued. "And then there's the weather. Those cold, damp winters are hard on old bones. Every year when the first snow falls, I tell myself that should be my last northern winter."

Kate took a deep breath in a vain attempt to stop her heart from pounding. Sally wasn't simply talking about selling her home. She was also planning to move, and when she did, Buffalo would no longer be Kate's refuge. Though she felt as if the world had tipped off its axis, she tried to keep her voice even as she said, "You're not old, Sally."

Her grandmother gave her an indulgent smile. "Of course I am. There's no denying it. I've already lived more than the three score and ten the Bible promises."

Though Kate was familiar with the psalm, she also knew that life spans had increased substantially from biblical times. Not counting Methuselah, that is. "That's old-fashioned thinking," she told Sally. "Lots of people live longer than that now."

"And others don't." Like Grandpa Larry, who'd been less than sixty-five when he'd suffered a fatal heart attack. The sorrow Kate saw in Sally's eyes told her that her grandmother was remembering her husband.

Though her heart might be heavy, Sally's voice was brisk when she spoke. "Don't worry, Kate. I'm not planning to die any time soon. I just want to spend my final years, no matter how many or how few they may be, surrounded by warmth and beauty. For me, that's here." She looked around the room, her smile broadening. "You know I always thought this place was special."

And it was. Though it needed a lot of work to restore it, Rainbow's End would always hold a special place in Kate's heart, because it was where she had met Greg. For Sally, the appeal must be even greater. She had spent a week here with her husband, and when she'd returned, she had met another man whose company she enjoyed. Though Kate doubted Sally was proposing to become a permanent guest at Rainbow's End, she suspected she was thinking about moving to Dupree to be close to Roy.

"It's not just Rainbow's End that's the attraction, is it? It's Roy."

Sally nodded. "I won't deny that I enjoy being with him. Roy makes me feel almost young again." The sweetness of her smile underscored the truth of her words. Just speaking of Roy chased years from Sally's face.

Kate was happy for her grandmother, but at the same time, she felt as if her world was crumbling around her. The foundation on which she'd built her life was shifting.

"Are you going to marry him?" The question escaped seemingly without conscious thought.

Sally was silent for a moment. "I don't know," she said. "Nothing's definite. Roy and I haven't discussed marriage. I'm not even certain I'm going to leave Buffalo. I'm just thinking about it."

Kate shook her head slowly as the words registered. Sally might say she hadn't made a decision, but Kate did not believe that. Sally would move to Texas, and when she did, both of their lives would change.

"You look like you lost your best friend."

Greg studied Kate. Though she'd waved her hand and smiled when Roy helped Sally into his truck to take her out for lunch, Kate's smile had seemed forced, and there was an unmistakable sadness in her eyes.

This Kate was a far cry from the woman he'd held in his arms yesterday. That woman had glowed with happiness when they'd finally broken apart. Before that, she had been the vision of an avenging warrior princess, her eyes flashing with anger at Drew and his accusations.

Greg had been almost speechless at the sight of Kate challenging Drew, all because she wanted to defend him. It was the first time in many years that anyone had done that. When he'd been a young boy, Mom had taken his side during his father's diatribes, but that had ended. Greg wasn't sure why, other than that she must have realized it made no difference. But yesterday when he'd believed he no longer needed a champion, Kate had taken on the role.

That had surprised Greg almost as much as little Fiona's assertion that he was going to marry Kate. Why on earth had Lauren told her daughter that? It was true that he loved Kate and that maybe in a year or so, if everything worked out, he might ask her to marry him, but how could Lauren know that? She hadn't, he told himself. She had merely wanted Fiona to understand that Greg would never be her new daddy.

Forcing thoughts of marriage away, Greg kept his eyes fixed on Kate.

"I've definitely lost something," she said, taking the hand he offered as he led the way to the gazebo. "I feel like my world is changing, and there's nothing I can do about it."

Greg knew the feeling. Though it had been his decision, once he'd agreed to sell the company, he'd felt as if events had spiraled out of control. He didn't regret the decision — seeing Drew again had convinced him that he'd been right to leave S-squared — but there had been days, even weeks, during the transition when Greg had felt distinctly uncomfortable with the changes the new owners planned.

"What happened?" Though Greg imagined that Kate was still worried about the peanut butter account, the way she had looked at Sally made him doubt that her concerns were related to her job. It was more likely Sally's health that made her look as if she had been abandoned.

"Sally's talking about selling her house and moving to Texas."

To Greg's mind, that was good news, because it meant that Sally was not facing any immediate medical crisis, but Kate obviously did not share that sentiment. There was something else at work here. Greg thought back to the first day Sally had had lunch with Roy and how Kate had tried to mask her concern. She appeared to like Roy, and she wanted her grandmother to be happy, but something about the situation bothered Kate. Greg wished he knew what it was.

"Is she moving because of Roy?" That wouldn't surprise Greg. He'd seen the sparks between the two of them. Still, they'd known each other only a couple weeks.

"Roy's one of the reasons." Though Kate confirmed Greg's supposition, her expression seemed to signal that Roy was not the reason she was upset. "Sally says the weather's a factor too. She claims Buffalo winters are hard on old bones."

Perhaps Sally's health was the issue after all. Greg couldn't change that, but perhaps he could lighten Kate's mood. "Tell her not to make any decisions until she's been here in July and August. Roy says Texas summers are not for the fainthearted."

Kate managed a weak smile. "Sally would say that's why air-conditioning was invented." As they sat down on one of the benches in the gazebo, Kate shifted her position so that she was facing him. Despite the smile, her eyes were serious. "I want Sally to be happy, Greg. Really, I do. It's just . . ." Kate stopped, as if unwilling to put her thoughts into words.

"Just what?"

"You're going to think I'm silly when I tell you that it's the house that bothers me. That's where I grew up. I never thought she'd sell it."

A house. Greg tried but failed to empathize with Kate. Maybe it was a female thing, or maybe it was another example of the disconnects in Greg's life. Unlike Kate, who seemed to still have roots in her grandmother's house, Greg had been eager to leave his childhood home and the town that had known him as an awkward geek. Home for him had been first a dorm, then a condo. Perhaps the fact that Kate rented rather than owned factored into the equation. Greg wasn't certain about that, but he did know that he had no emotional attachment to the house where he'd been reared.

"How long has it been since you've lived there?" he asked, trying to understand what linked Kate to her grandmother's home.

"Six years. I moved out when I graduated and got my first job."

And now she lived in a high-rise apartment. Greg wondered if it was the yard and the greater privacy she missed or whether her feelings were purely sentimental.

"Can you picture yourself moving back?"

Kate looked startled. "No, I can't. That's Sally's house. I . . ." She let out a chuckle. "Listen to me. I'm worried about a pile of bricks and wood. If Sally could hear me, she'd shake her finger at me and tell me I need to stop fearing change. She would say it was time to chase a rainbow."

Greg's confusion over the seeming non sequitur must have been obvious, because Kate continued. "That's Sally's shorthand for taking a chance. She's always telling me I need to take more risks and accept that change is part of life. I guess I never learned that lesson."

Greg nodded as he thought about what Kate had said and what she hadn't said. For her, the house was more than a pile of bricks and wood. For her, it was a symbol of continuity.

It didn't take a degree in psychology to realize that Kate's need for stability was the result of her parents' death and her being uprooted when she was so young. Close family ties were essential for her. When she'd talked about her job, Greg had formed the impression that Kate viewed the firm as her family. The threat of losing the pseudo-family might be part of the reason she was so worried about failing the new client. And Sally's announcement would only have aggravated a difficult situation, making Kate fear that she was losing her foundation.

"Change is harder than most people realize. I used to think I thrived on it, but look at me," Greg said with a grin that he hoped would encourage Kate. "It's been close to six weeks since I left California, and I still don't know what I want to do with my life."

Drew's visit had cemented his belief that returning to Silicon Valley would be wrong, but the future was still unknown. Admittedly, each day left Greg feeling more rooted here, but that could be because of Kate. She and Rainbow's End had become inextricably entwined in his mind, like a braid with three strands: Rainbow's End, Kate, and himself. Unfortunately, that was a dream with little likelihood of becoming reality. Even though he had begun to envision a future with Kate, Greg knew that Rainbow's End would not be part of a future he

411

shared with her.

Kate had no intention of staying in Texas, even if Sally did. Her career was in Manhattan, and though she could probably find an advertising position in San Antonio or Austin, it wouldn't be the same. Not only would there not be as wide a variety of clients, but it would mean leaving the group Kate considered a family. Greg would never ask her to do that.

Kate shook her head slowly. "You're being too hard on yourself. Six weeks isn't very long, not when you're talking about something so important." She sighed. "That's part of what bothers me about Sally. Her decision seems impulsive."

Sally hadn't struck Greg as impulsive. "It could be that she's been thinking about moving for years and simply hasn't told you." Sally obviously knew that Kate was resistant to change. It was likely that she hadn't wanted to upset her granddaughter until she had made a decision.

"You could be right. She sort of hinted that." Kate blinked rapidly, making Greg wonder if she was trying to hold back tears. He laid his hand on hers and gave it a quick squeeze.

"I'm sorry to dump all this on you. It probably wouldn't bother me so much if I weren't worried about my job."

That's what Greg had thought, that the combination was overwhelming Kate. "Still no ideas?"

She shook her head. "Peanuts are not inspiring me. It's strange. I like peanut butter, and Aunt Ivy's is the best I've tasted. The problem is, I can't figure out how to convey that to consumers. I need a compelling image, and the idea well is dry. I keep trying to prime it, but nothing helps."

That was a problem Greg had never had. Ideas for new features to be added to the Sys=Simpl software had come easily. In fact, until he left the company, the problem had been deciding which ones were the most critical.

"You sound like a writer suffering from writer's block."

Kate smiled as the bird that appeared to be building a nest in the gazebo rafters flew by, a few strands of dried grass dangling from its beak.

"I don't know any writers, so I can't say. All I know is that what used to be easy isn't this time."

Greg wished Blake Kendall lived close enough for them to visit him. Perhaps he could help Kate. After all, the man made his living with words. "One of my college friends surprised me and became a writer. Of course, he maintains he's never suffered from writer's block." Greg wasn't sure whether that was true, but given the number of books Blake published each year, it could be. The man was both prolific and popular, with his books consistently hitting the major bestseller lists. At the time, Greg had thought writing an odd change of career for a financial planner, but it had obviously worked out well for Blake.

If Kate had been a rabbit, Greg would have said that her ears perked up. As it was, he saw the interest reflecting from her eyes. "He's a lucky man. What does he write?"

"Thrillers."

She wrinkled her nose, again reminding Greg of the cottontails his mother tried to banish from her flower beds. "I never understood the appeal," Kate said with another nose wrinkle.

Greg wasn't surprised. Blake had said that the majority of his readers were men, perhaps because graphic descriptions of murders did not appeal to many women. "I'm not an expert on thrillers, but what I like about Blake's is that they tell the story of an ordinary man who is suddenly placed in extraordinary circumstances and needs to find a way to overcome evil."

"Like Superman or Spiderman?" Doubt clouded Kate's eyes as Greg watched her enthusiasm fade. Whatever had piqued her interest before was gone.

He shook his head. "Not at all. Blake's hero has no superpowers, and he's certainly not squeaky clean like Clark Kent. He's a hard-drinking man who's never far from a pack of cigarettes, but he's also a chameleon. He has the ability to fit in everywhere. For example . . ." Greg launched into a description of Blake's most recent release.

As she listened to his explanation, Kate's expression changed. Something he'd said, and Greg had no idea what it might be, had chased her doubts away. Her eyes shone, and her smile was radiant.

"You're a genius, Greg Vange. Thank you!" Her face flushed with excitement, Kate leaned forward and kissed him.

28

Kate barely heard Greg's voice. He was saying something about the hero of those thrillers his friend had written, but that no longer mattered. All that mattered were the ideas that whirled through her mind. She knew she'd never be able to explain how it had happened, but somehow the thought of Superman and the image of a chameleon had broken the dam that had blocked her creative thoughts as effectively as a real dam held back water. Now that the barrier had been breached, ideas were rushing through her brain faster than she could ever recall.

The image of Clark Kent changing from his mild-mannered, suited self into caped crusader Superman had triggered the idea of a humble peanut bursting out of its shell, transforming itself into a Thai-inspired main course, an elegant cake, a decadent mousse, or a succulent chowder. Kate closed her eyes, letting the images run rampant through her mind, and as she did, she envisioned the print and TV ads showing people savoring the dishes, while the tagline, "It's Aunt Ivy's peanut butter . . . naturally," ran across the bottom of the page or the screen.

"That's it," she told Greg. "I know what I need to do, and it's all thanks to you." She blew him a kiss as she raced back to her cabin.

For the rest of the day and all through the night, Kate worked feverishly, sketching designs, drafting a marketing plan, and trying to anticipate every question either Heather or the Prestons might have. By the time Sally's alarm rang, she had done everything she could. Now it was up to Heather.

Kate splashed cold water on her face and grabbed fresh clothes from her closet. Once Sally was finished in the bathroom, she'd take a quick shower.

Her grandmother emerged from her room, her hair tousled from sleep. She took one look at Kate and shook her head. "I don't have to ask what you were doing last night."

"Blame it on Greg. He's responsible for the breakthrough." Kate turned her laptop to show Sally one of the designs she'd been working on. "What do you think?"

As she had when Kate had been in school and had asked her to check her homework, Sally tipped her head to one side and scrutinized the screen. "It's brilliant," she said at last. "I'm not saying that just because you're my granddaughter, either. Larry was right when he claimed you had a flair for advertising. He'd be as proud as I am."

"I hope you're right." Grandpa Larry had never seen her professional work; Kate could only hope he would have believed that she had accomplished what he had urged and had lived up to her potential. "I hope my bosses and the clients like it too."

"They will." Sally nodded briskly and repeated, "They will."

"I'm going to Dupree right after breakfast to send everything to Heather." It was already too late to use the resort's phone line, and even if she had wanted to do that, Kate knew it would take hours to transmit all of her designs. She needed the faster connection of Wi-Fi. "Do you want to come along?"

"No thanks, but I don't think you should be driving." Sally headed toward the bathroom. "You'd better ask Greg to take you."

"I agree with your grandmother on both counts," Greg said an hour later when Kate

418

asked if he'd mind chauffeuring her into town. "The designs are great, and you shouldn't be driving. You've yawned at least a dozen times in the last minute."

It might have been an exaggeration, but he could see that Kate's adrenaline rush was fading and that she was too tired to be behind the wheel. She'd get her second wind once she sent the files to her boss and started talking to the woman, but in the meantime, he didn't want her driving. And, if he were being honest with himself, he was looking forward to spending time with her. He loved this happy, excited woman.

Greg smiled as she buckled the seat belt and leaned back in the seat, closing her eyes. Kate was more tired than she'd admit, but it was a well-earned fatigue. She'd solved the problem that had plagued her and had put her career back on track. She had found her direction. He only wished he could say the same.

When they reached the Sit 'n' Sip and had placed their orders, Greg waited until Kate started the transmission process, then took his coffee to the counter. She was still composing notes to her boss and didn't need him watching over her shoulder.

Settling onto one of the backless stools, Greg shot a smile at the proprietor. No matter when he'd come into the diner, he'd seen Russ Walker behind the counter. If the man had employees, Greg wasn't aware of it.

"Good morning, Mr. Walker." Greg turned at the sound of Kevin Olsen's voice. The teenager's grin was wider than normal, but the faint tremor in his voice told Greg this was no casual visit.

"What can I get you?" Russ Walker asked.

Kevin made his way to the counter, folding his hands and placing them on top. "Nothing right now. I wondered if you needed any help. Things are a little slow at Rainbow's End right now."

That was an understatement. Though Greg had thought the resort might be full for Easter weekend, he, Kate, and Sally were the only guests.

Kevin gestured toward the tables. "I'm good at waiting tables. I can wash dishes too. In fact, I can do just about anything you need."

The proprietor shook his head slowly. "I'm sorry, Kevin, but I'm afraid I can't hire anyone right now." His words rang with sincerity. "I'll call you if anything changes."

Kevin left, his shoulders slumping.

"I hate to discourage the kid," Russ said as he approached Greg with the coffeepot.

"I know how much he needs the money."
With a quick look around the almost empty
room, Russ added, "Don't we all? I promised my wife we'd do something special for
Easter, but there's only two days left, and I
don't have any ideas." Russ let out a sigh.
"What am I saying? I've got lots of ideas,
just not enough money to make them happen."

Russ's words touched Greg's heart as
deeply as Kevin's disappointment had.
"What did you have in mind?"

Russ shrugged. "A nice dinner for my wife
— one she didn't have to cook — a trip to
the movies for my kids. Simple things, huh?"

Simple things that Greg had taken for
granted for years. As he took another slug
of coffee, ideas began to whirl through his
mind, and he wondered if this was how Kate
had felt yesterday when the mention of
Superman and chameleons had sparked her
imagination. All Greg knew was that for the
first time since he'd left California, certainty
had replaced doubt.

"I imagine most folks in Dupree want
something like that," he said as casually as
he could.

Russ shrugged again as he held the pot of
coffee over Greg's mug. "Want a refill?"

Greg shook his head. "Not right now. I

need to make a couple phone calls." And he wasn't about to do that where he could be overheard. Seeing that Kate was still working, he pulled his phone from his pocket and gestured toward it as he walked past Kate's table. Seconds later, he was outside, grateful that for once there were no pedestrians in the immediate area.

"Have you ever considered renting out Rainbow's End for a daytime event — no room rentals involved?" he asked Angela when she answered the phone.

"Tim and I've talked about it," she admitted, "but no one's been interested."

"If someone were interested, what would you charge?" When Greg had answered her questions about how many guests would be involved and what kind of food he wanted, he heard her fingers clicking on the keyboard and guessed she was doing some quick calculations. A minute later, Angela gave him a number.

"That much, huh?" The figure she'd quoted sounded almost incredibly low, but that could be because Greg was used to California prices. "You drive a hard bargain," he told her, "but you've got yourself a deal if Carmen can pull it off. Can you transfer me to her?"

The length of the delay told Greg that

Angela was briefing Carmen on his request.

"How do you feel about throwing the biggest party of your life?" he asked when Rainbow's End's chef answered the phone. "Angela probably told you part of what I have in mind, including the fact that there'll be a bonus for you, but here's the important part." He outlined the menu — menus, to be more precise — that he wanted. When Carmen agreed that they would be appropriate for the event he envisioned, she asked the key question.

"When?" Greg repeated her question. "Easter Sunday. And before you ask, I do mean this Easter. Two days from now."

The lengthy silence was punctuated by a sigh and a volley of such rapid Spanish that he had no chance of understanding it.

"*Sí,*" she said at last. "I can do it."

Greg was smiling as he disconnected the call, but his face sobered as he opened the address book on his cell. This would be the most difficult call.

"Hey, Drew," he said as his former partner picked up the phone. "I hope I didn't wake you." Without waiting for a response, he continued speaking. "Didn't you tell me you had some contacts in LA? Here's what I need."

When Greg finished outlining his request,

Drew asked the question he'd expected: "Why would I help you?" Considering the way they'd parted, it was a valid question. "Because if you do this, Tuesday morning your in-box will have a list of possible features for a new release along with the names of the engineers who'd be the best bet to implement each one. Once you pick your top three, I'll send you notes on key functionality and ways to implement them."

Drew's intake of breath told Greg he'd hooked him. "I need everything by five tomorrow. I don't care whether you send it overnight or courier. Just get it here. And thanks, Drew. You won't regret this."

Nor would Greg. Though he had thought he'd severed all connections to the company he'd founded, believing the new owners were diluting Sys=Simpl's brand appeal, what he hoped to accomplish at Rainbow's End was more important than personal pride.

As Greg walked back into the diner, he found Kate sitting at the table, her laptop closed, her face wreathed in a smile.

"Your smile tells me everything went well."

She nodded. "It did. Heather needs to discuss the pitch with Nick, and she's going to have Chase do a quick cost estimate for the media buys, but she liked the idea. A lot."

Greg held out his hand and helped her to her feet. Giving her a quick hug, he said, "Wonderful! And now if you're ready, we've got some folks to invite to a party."

29

"You're planning to do what?" Kate stared at Greg as he took a sip of coffee. When he'd come back into the diner after making his calls, he'd looked like a kid on Christmas morning who'd just opened the gift he'd been dreaming of. His eyes had radiated enthusiasm, and his smile was one of pure excitement. When he'd heard her news and hugged her, Kate had thought Greg was ready to leave, but instead of heading for the door, he'd ordered more coffee and taken the seat opposite her in the booth.

"I want to invite the whole town of Dupree to an Easter party," Greg said, his smile announcing that he thought what he was proposing would be as simple as ordering another cup of coffee from Russ Walker. "There'll be a sit-down dinner for the adults and an outdoor barbecue for kids and teens. And to keep the kids entertained while their parents are eating, I thought we'd have a movie."

When Greg dreamed, he dreamed big. That was undoubtedly part of the reason he'd been so successful. He was what one of Kate's college professors had called a visionary. But vision needed an occasional infusion of reality.

"It's a terrific idea," Kate said, "but it's going to take a miracle to pull it off in two days." It wasn't as if they were in New York where almost anything was a phone call away. They were in Dupree, Texas, population 597, and on a holiday weekend to boot.

Greg shook his head. "O ye of little faith. I don't need a miracle, just some careful planning and a whole lot of help from my friends." The smile he sent in Kate's direction left no doubt that she was included in that group. "Trust me, Kate. We can do it."

Greg's use of the plural pronoun made her heart beat a little faster. He had offered her exactly what she wanted: a reason to spend the whole weekend with him.

"Count me in." Kate took a deep breath, savoring the relief that had settled over her like a warm blanket ever since she'd heard Heather's reaction to her campaign ideas. Though she ought to be exhausted from a night without sleep, she felt exhilarated, knowing that she'd hit the mark. That alone would have made today memorable, but now she and Greg had a party to plan. It might be crazy — it was definitely ambitious — but Greg's scheme excited Kate more than anything she could recall.

"What can I do?" she asked.

"Tell me what I've forgotten." Greg took a bite of cinnamon toast. Though Kate knew he wasn't particularly hungry, she suspected he'd ordered it to give Russ Walker a bit more income. That was classic Greg, seeing a need and trying to fill it. Even though she'd seen him wear them only once, he owned a pair of Samantha's boots, and Kate wouldn't be surprised if Greg had ordered a quilt he didn't need from Lauren. Now he was planning to help the whole town.

"What have you forgotten? That's easy. Logistics." Kate kept a smile on her face, not wanting to discourage Greg. "There are close to six hundred people in Dupree. There's absolutely no way Rainbow's End can handle them all. The dining room seats only forty."

Greg nodded as if he'd already considered that. "That's why the kids will eat outside. That'll also give the parents something that resembles a date night. They'll have close to two hours without any interruptions."

Kate had no trouble imagining how the

adults would welcome that idea, because Brittany had told her that she and her husband had craved time alone — what she called grown-up time — after Peanut Penelope's birth.

"I hate to point this out, but there are at least a hundred adults."

"Oh." Greg's face mirrored his dismay. More tellingly, he did not greet the customer who entered the Sit 'n' Sip.

Kate wouldn't let him stew, not when she knew the problem could be resolved with a little planning. "So we have different seating times. Three should work. It'll make it easier for Carmen too, because she won't have to have everything ready at the same time."

As Greg nodded, Kate continued. "Let's say we seat people at noon, three, and six. The middle slot will be the toughest to fill, but Carmen said some people have a big breakfast right after Easter services, so it could work."

"That sounds like a plan. I'd been thinking about an all-day event, but you're right. Rainbow's End isn't ready for that." Greg gave Kate an approving look as he finished his cinnamon toast and washed it down with a swig of coffee. "Any other problems?"

A dozen, but one stood out ahead of the others. "The kids. Who's going to watch them while their parents are eating? It would be disastrous to leave them alone."

Wrinkling his nose, Greg stared out the window for a second. "I don't suppose Angela and Tim would do that."

"I think you're safe with that assumption." Kate had heard Tim announce that children should be seen and not heard and that, when it came to Rainbow's End, they should not even be seen. "We definitely need adult supervision for them. Let me think about it." She drained the last of her tea. "Meanwhile, we'd better start spreading the word."

Greg beckoned the diner's proprietor who'd been standing behind the counter, waiting for customers to arrive. The last had taken coffee to go, leaving Russ alone. "Hey, Russ, come on over and pull up a chair. We need your help."

Though he looked skeptical initially, as Greg explained what he was planning, the man's face relaxed, the furrows that had seemed a permanent fixture between his eyes almost disappearing.

"So what you're saying is that Rainbow's End is going to host an Easter party for the whole town."

Greg nodded. "Exactly."

Not exactly. The party wasn't Angela and

Tim's idea. They were simply providing the locale and profiting handsomely from it. But Kate had no intention of contradicting Russ's assumption, not when it was clear that Greg didn't want anyone to know he was paying for the party. Her heart warmed at the realization that while almost everyone she knew would have wanted credit for such a generous gesture, Greg felt no need to advertise it.

"I was hoping you'd spread the word," Greg continued. "Kate and I will talk to the other merchants, but we need a central place for the sign-up. Would you handle that?"

"You bet." Russ wiped his hands on his apron in what Kate had come to realize was a reflex, having nothing to do with whether or not his hands were wet. "Wait until my wife hears about this. She won't believe her ears."

Samantha was just as enthusiastic, but it was Lauren's reaction that touched Kate's heart. The thin brunette's smile was so broad that Kate wondered if her cheeks hurt. "This is the answer to prayer," she told Kate and Greg. "I know Easter is supposed to be a joyous occasion, but I was dreading it. You see, my husband always made holidays special for Fiona. This will be our first

Easter without him, and I didn't know what to do. Going to Rainbow's End is the perfect solution." She wiped a tear from the corner of one eye. "How can I help you? Fiona and I'll do anything we can."

It was the opening Kate needed. "I'm a little worried about the kids. You know what happens when you get a lot of them together."

Lauren pretended to wince. "Were you thinking murder and mayhem?"

"At least the latter."

Nodding, Lauren glanced at her phone. "Why don't I organize a Mommy Brigade? I'll make sure there are enough adults there that you don't have to worry."

"Thanks."

Lauren shrugged. "It's the least I can do. I know the other mothers will say the same thing."

When they'd completed their circuit of the shops, Greg turned to Kate. "I thought I'd take a run into San Antonio. I need to arrange for a projector and screen."

That was one of the problems that had been nagging at the back of her mind. "I know you want to show a movie, and I think it's a great idea, but there's one not-so-little problem. It'll be daylight. That's not exactly ideal movie-watching conditions."

Greg shrugged. "So we'll get a tent."

"With black-out walls?"

"Sure, why not?" He seemed to believe that everything was possible. Perhaps it was, with enough money. "Want to go with me? I might even be persuaded to buy you some nachos."

"I wouldn't miss it for the world."

They headed back to Rainbow's End to tell Sally what Kate would be doing and to have a brief meeting with Carmen.

"Do you need anything — special food, more equipment, extra help?" Greg asked the chef.

Carmen shook her head. "I already took care of that. KOB will be the waitstaff for the adults, and they're enlisting some of their friends to serve the kids. I got a hold of one of the teachers, and she's going to send some food science students to help with food prep. They'll get extra credit instead of pay."

Greg shook his head. "I think we can pay them. After all, they're giving up a holiday."

Carmen flashed a warm smile at Greg. "It's a nice thing you're doing, Greg."

He shrugged. "Rainbow's End is throwing the party."

"Like I said, it's a nice thing."

Sally echoed Carmen's sentiment and

promised that she and Roy would help spread the word. "We'll go door-to-door if we have to, but we'll make sure everyone knows what's happening." Giving Kate a quick hug, she said, "You kids have a good time in San Antonio."

They did. As Kate had suspected, there were no tents available with room-darkening walls. Though Greg was clearly disappointed, once Kate discovered a fabric store that carried special fabric for making window shades, they developed Plan B. They'd already decided that the kids could sit on the ground to watch the movie, so they simply moved the event indoors. Into the lodge, to be precise. By moving the furniture out, they could accommodate a hundred people at a time, and if they tacked the black-out fabric over the windows, they'd have a relatively dark venue.

"It won't be elegant," Kate told Greg as the clerk began measuring the fabric, "but it should work."

"The kids won't notice anything once the movie starts."

"How did you manage to get it?" Kate had caught her breath with amazement when he'd told her the name of the film he planned to show. "I know it hasn't come out on DVD yet."

And, since Dupree's theater showed only older movies, unless the kids had gone to San Antonio, it was unlikely any of them had seen it. The third in an action figure series, this one was reported to be the best yet and had become a blockbuster. Kate knew that Greg had enough money to buy almost anything, but you needed more than money to score a coup like this. You needed contacts.

Greg shrugged as he handed the clerk his credit card. "Drew arranged it. He's got contacts in LA."

In a day of surprises, this might not be the biggest, and yet Kate was almost shocked that Drew had agreed, given the way the men had parted. Unless, of course, Greg was paying for the favor. "What did you promise him?"

Greg's shrug confirmed Kate's assumption. "What he wanted — some ideas for a new release. I should have given them to him when he was here." A frown crossed Greg's face. "Drew's on shaky ground with the new owners. I don't want him to lose his job."

Kate could understand that, and yet Drew's arrogance still rankled. "You're kinder than I would have been." She slid her sunglasses on as they exited the store.

Though Greg had apparently forgiven Drew for his harsh words, Kate could not forget the way he'd attacked Greg.

Greg tossed the bolts of fabric into the back of the SUV alongside the projector and screen. "Basically Drew's a good guy. He's just gotten his priorities a bit mixed up."

That was something no one would say about Greg. His priorities were crystal clear, or so it seemed to Kate. Right now his priorities were giving a small town in Texas an Easter to remember at the same time that he helped Angela and Tim Sinclair hold on to Rainbow's End for a little while longer.

Greg drove for a few minutes and was discussing where they should stop for lunch when he swung the vehicle into a video store parking lot.

"What are we doing here?" Kate asked. "Last time I checked, they didn't serve nachos."

"You'll see." He clasped her hand in his, swinging it as they walked through the parking lot. Once they were inside, Greg studied the overhead signs, then steered her toward the aisle marked "musicals."

"See if you can find a copy of *South Pacific,*" he said. "Drew's sending a new legal thriller along with the action flick, but I thought we could have a double feature after the last dinner seating, just in case anyone wants to make it a late night."

Greg was right. It would be the perfect ending to what promised to be a wonderful day. "I can guarantee at least two adults will stay for *South Pacific.*" When Greg raised an eyebrow, Kate answered the unspoken question. "Sally and me."

There was no doubt about Sally. Though she'd watched it often enough to have memorized the dialogue as well as the songs, she claimed she would never tire of it. Kate's reaction would be different. She knew that while the movie was playing on the big screen, her mind would be replaying the bluebonnet festival, that unforgettable ride on the Ferris wheel, and her first kiss with Greg. It would definitely be an enchanted evening.

Easter was as close to perfect as a day could be. Kate attended the sunrise service with Sally, then, when Roy declared that he was taking his best gal out for Easter breakfast, she returned to Rainbow's End, leaving Sally with the man who made her giggle like a youngster. Kate had planned to help Carmen but discovered that KOB and the food science students were already in the kitchen, peeling what looked like a hundred pounds of potatoes and basting more hams than Kate had ever seen.

"Are you sure I can't help?" she asked. Even though she'd never win a culinary award, she was confident she could apply pineapple glaze or dot pans of sweet potatoes with marshmallows.

Carmen shook her head. "You'd just be in the way. I suggest you rest up. Things are going to be hectic this afternoon." She stirred a dollop of mustard into the baked beans as she said, "I can't tell you how exciting it is to think of families here. Rainbow's End hasn't been a family-friendly place in decades. The last owners didn't allow anyone under sixteen, and the Sinclairs raised that to eighteen." Carmen turned and grinned at the teenagers. "KOB have been the kids." When they grimaced, she added, "It'll be good to hear children laughing."

"It will, won't it?" Kate could picture Fiona with her mismatched socks standing in line for a chili dog or rubbing her arms to chase away goose bumps during the movie. "If you're sure you don't need me, I'll see what Angela needs done."

Carmen laughed. "I guess you didn't get the memo. Angela and Tim went to San Antonio for the day. They won't be back until tomorrow morning."

And so Kate found herself and Greg serving as hosts, greeting guests, directing traffic, and accepting compliments. Of course there were a few glitches. Two boys dared a third to jump off the dock, with predictable results. Before his parents could learn what he'd done, Brandi hustled the soggy youngster to the laundry room. Half an hour later, he emerged wearing dry clothes and a sheepish smile.

Later someone managed to tip over a jar of lemonade, attracting an army of ants that fascinated the youngest guests until one tried to herd them and wound up with bites on his fingers. But overall it was a nearly flawless day. The children's excitement when they learned which movie they'd be watching more than compensated for the effort of creating makeshift shades, and Kate knew that her memories of the parents' relaxed expressions when they left the dining room would be indelible.

"I can't believe how well it's turning out," Kate said after she had ushered the last seating of adults to the dining room.

Greg nodded. "It's more work than I expected, but it's also more fun — thanks to you. I couldn't have pulled this off without you, Kate."

Though the warmth in his eyes made her

pulse race, Kate forced herself to remain calm. "You'd have done fine on your own, but I've had fun."

More than fun. Even during the day's most hectic moments, she had felt content and complete, as if this was exactly where she was meant to be. She had helped with Easter egg hunts and the delivery of lilies to nursing homes on Easter Day, but nothing had felt as fulfilling as welcoming guests to the Rainbow's End celebration.

"I can tell. You look more excited than you did when you came up with the idea for Aunt Ivy's." Greg put his arm around Kate's shoulders and drew her close for a quick hug. "You're a natural at this."

What felt natural was working with Greg. Though she had thought the team at Maddox worked well together, it was nothing like this. Planning and executing this party gave partnership a whole new meaning. There was no need for memos or status meetings. Instead, she and Greg seemed to anticipate each other's needs. Kate even found herself completing Greg's sentences, and he did the same to her.

He'd joked that they must be on the same wavelength. That was possible, but to Kate, what was happening was more than that. She felt as if she and Greg were two halves of a single whole, that when they were together, she was complete. And, as wonderful as that thought was, it was also more ·than a little scary, for she knew it could not last.

30

As the final strains of the *South Pacific* soundtrack died, Roy rose and extended his hand to help Sally up from the settee. Though Kate had told her that the children would sit on the floor to watch their film, someone — probably Kate and Greg with the teenagers' help — had returned the normal furniture to the lodge so that the adults would have more comfortable seating. Sally was thankful for that along with a million other things, including the man who stood so close to her.

"I can't ever remember an Easter like this," Roy said as he led her outside. "It was wonderful to see the town celebrating together."

Sally nodded. She had a lifetime of memories, but few could compare to those she'd made today. She and Roy had been together since the early morning service, and though they had spoken of nothing earthshaking, it had been a day of quiet comfort, of the simple pleasure of being with the man who made her remember what it felt like to be young and in love.

"Everyone looked so happy," she said softly, not wanting the day to end. "I'm glad I could be here to be part of it." Even though she hadn't made her final decision, Sally's instincts told her that she would not sell her home and that her days with Roy were numbered. As much as she'd come to care for him, in a choice between him and Kate, Kate came first.

"You sound as if you're planning to leave." Roy wrapped one arm around Sally's shoulders and drew her closer, then laid his other hand under her chin, tipping it so she looked directly at him. Though night had fallen, the light from the street lamps that illuminated the way to her cabin was bright enough that Sally could see Roy's eyes, and what she saw made her catch her breath. He was looking at her the way Rossano Brazzi had looked at Mitzi Gaynor, as if she were the only woman in the world.

"I was hoping you would stay." Roy's voice was low and deep, resonating with sincerity, while his eyes shone with an emotion so intense Sally wanted to believe it was love. In less than three weeks, what she felt for

Roy had changed from mild attraction to something much deeper. Now when she let herself dream, she dreamt about a life with Roy, the man she loved.

Sally could picture them living in his current house or building one in the midst of that incredible bluebonnet field. It didn't matter where they lived. What mattered was being together. But the dreams vanished as quickly as the soap bubbles Kate used to cherish for their rainbow hues, blown away by the winds of reality. Though she cared for Roy — Sally swallowed deeply and amended her thoughts — though she loved him, there was no happily-ever-after in their future.

Roy's lips softened into a smile. "We've only known each other a few weeks, but that doesn't change the way I feel." His hand caressed her chin before his fingers moved upward to feather across her lips. "I love you, Sally, and I want to spend the rest of my life with you. Will you marry me?"

Yes, yes! The words almost burst forth, but Sally bit them back. If this were a movie, she'd be in his arms, her lips pressed to his. But this wasn't a movie. It was real life, and real life included a granddaughter who longed for the security of a world that changed at no more than glacial speed. "Oh,

Roy, I don't know if I should."

He looked as if she'd slapped him. "I've got to say that wasn't the answer I was hoping for. Should? We should eat more vegetables and less red meat, but what does 'should' have to do with love?"

Sally's heart sank. She'd hurt this wonderful man, when that had been the last thing she wanted to do. "It's complicated," she said.

Roy lowered his hand but kept his eyes fixed on hers. "Then let's uncomplicate it. Do you love me?"

"Yes, I do." Sally infused her answer with every bit of the certainty she felt. Her love for Roy wasn't the same as the love she'd had for her husband, but it was no less strong. She and Larry had shared first love. This was different, a more mature but equally wonderful love.

"Do you want to marry me?"

Yes, yes, yes! Sally nodded. "I do."

A smile lit Roy's face. "Then that's all there is to it."

Though she wished that were the case, Sally knew it was not. "That might have been true fifty years ago, but now I have Kate to worry about. She was terribly upset when I mentioned possibly selling my home and moving here. I don't want to hurt her.

You know I'm her only family."

The silence hung between them, punctured by the hoot of an owl and the soft soughing of the wind through the cedars. At last Roy spoke, his voice firm. "I'd say that I could move to Buffalo to be with you, but I don't think that's the real issue. Kate's a grown woman with a life of her own. You've done a wonderful job of raising her, but it's time to let her go. Even if she doesn't want it, you need to push her out of the nest." Roy's eyes were solemn as he took both of Sally's hands in his. "Don't throw away our chance at happiness. Say you'll marry me."

Sally swallowed, wishing the lump that had lodged in her throat would disappear. "I can't," she said. The thought of leaving this wonderful place and never seeing Roy again made her want to weep.

"Not yet," she added.

Kate stared at her laptop as she opened her email. As she'd expected, there was a message from Heather. As she'd hoped, Heather said she and Nick loved Kate's concept and were confident the Prestons would too. Then came the problem. Heather wrote that she'd already spoken to Hazel and Ike, and they were eager to proceed. They wanted Kate to present the plan to them and would send their corporate jet to San Antonio to pick her up. Tomorrow. The day Kate and Sally were supposed to spend being pampered at the spa.

Taking a deep breath, Kate tried to marshal her feelings. She was happy — thrilled, in fact — that Heather and Nick were so enthusiastic about her idea. She was pleased that the client was close to signing a contract with Maddox. But she was more than a little annoyed by Heather's high-handed scheduling and the assumption that Kate would interrupt her vacation to go to New York. Hadn't she already done enough?

She powered off the laptop, then made her way into the office and picked up the phone.

Half an hour later, she was retracing her steps, this time with Sally holding on to her arm. Though her grandmother was visibly tired and her eyes held an unexpected hint of sadness, her voice was cheerful as she said, "Yesterday was wonderful, wasn't it?"

"It couldn't have been better," Kate agreed. "Everyone seemed to have a good time, and as far as I can tell, only Greg and I noticed the glitches. Even though all we had to eat were leftovers, the day ended well. I really enjoyed *South Pacific.*"

Sally warbled a few bars of "Some Enchanted Evening." "You know how I love that movie. Thanks for arranging it."

"It was Greg's idea." Kate wouldn't take undue credit. He was the one who'd expanded on Russ Walker's desire to treat his children to a movie, bartering his time and talent for an action flick that had delighted the children and a likely Academy Award contender for the adults. She also knew he'd chosen *South Pacific* specifically for Sally. "Greg thought we should have movies for grown-ups."

"But you must have told him it was my favorite."

Kate opened the door to the dining room and steered her grandmother toward their table. She wanted Sally to be seated when she broke the bad news. "I might have mentioned it once or twice," she said, hoping the pleasure *South Pacific* had brought Sally would compensate for tomorrow.

Sally squeezed Kate's arm as she sank into her chair. "Thank you. You're the best granddaughter anyone could have."

Guilt washed over Kate like a wave on the shore. "You may change your mind about that when you hear what I have to say." She took a shallow breath, then let the words tumble out. "Heather wants me to go to New York tomorrow. She's sure the client

448

will like the concept, and she wants me to present it."

"But tomorrow is our spa day." Sally's eyes radiated disappointment.

"I know, but it's the only day the clients can be in New York."

"It's also the only day the spa had time for us."

"I know." Kate had tried to convince Heather that the Prestons could wait a day, but she'd failed. It was tomorrow or never, at least according to Heather.

"I wish it were otherwise, but I need to go to New York tomorrow. My partnership hinges on this. If I don't go, I could lose my job."

When Sally said nothing, Kate continued. "I want to be a partner. That's what Grandpa Larry wanted for me."

"Oh, Kate, is that what you believe?" Sally appeared on the verge of tears. "Larry and I wanted you to find your place in the world, the one God has planned for you. It doesn't matter whether that's in advertising or chicken farming, and you certainly don't need to be a partner to please either of us."

Kate blinked as the words registered. Sally was mistaken. "Grandpa Larry wanted me to be a partner," she insisted. "He wanted me to accomplish what he hadn't been able to."

"Is that what you think?" Sally asked, and this time there was no ignoring the sorrow in her voice. "Do you think that Larry wasn't good enough to be a partner, that he somehow failed?" Without waiting for Kate's response, Sally continued. "That's not true. Larry was on the partnership track, but when you came to live with us, he took himself off the track because he wanted more time to spend with you. He knew he couldn't do both, and you were more important."

Kate closed her eyes and let the words settle in. If what Sally said was true, and she had no reason to doubt that, her world had shifted again. She thought she had known her grandfather, but it seemed she did not, at least not completely. Both of her grandparents had sacrificed for her, and now she was going to disappoint her grandmother.

Kate knew that Hazel and Ike Preston wouldn't wait. If she refused to come, Heather and Nick would lead the presentation. They'd make excuses for Kate, and those excuses might be strong enough to convince the Prestons that Maddox was the right agency for them, but even if that happened, Kate's partnership was in jeopardy. It would be delayed, perhaps permanently. Kate wasn't Grandpa Larry. She couldn't let that happen.

"I'm sorry, Sally, but I need to go."

"You don't need to go," Greg said when Kate explained her plans for Tuesday. He'd seen her leaving the dining room after breakfast and had hurried toward her to report that the phone had been ringing constantly with Dupree's residents calling to tell Angela and Tim how much they'd enjoyed the Easter celebration. The grin that had accompanied that announcement faded when Greg heard Kate's news. "You could do the presentation via videoconferencing."

Kate shook her head. "From the spa? I don't think so. And even if I could manage that, it's not the same. The client will be working with me. They want to meet me to be sure we click. The chemistry's important." Kate knew that from firsthand experience. That had been one of the reasons she'd left her first job: clients at that firm were assigned based on who was available rather than who would work best together.

"I think you could find a way that wouldn't disappoint Sally." Though Greg did not raise his voice, Kate heard the steel in it.

Anger flared through her. "It's easy for you to say that. You have plenty of money and a secure future even if you never work again. I don't. I'm sorry if you don't agree with me, Greg, but I'm going to New York. I have to."

31

So this was how the other half lived.

Kate settled into the comfortable seat, running her hands over the fine leather, noting that the trays were made from wood, not plastic or metal. And then there was the sheer luxury of being the only passenger in a cabin designed for ten. Her eyes took in the deeply piled carpet, the textured wallpaper, and the elegantly appointed seats. Here there was no locked cockpit, merely a heavy curtain separating the pilot and copilot from their passengers. Or, in this case, their passenger. Singular.

She fastened her seat belt as they began to taxi, reflecting on how different this had been from the day she and Sally had traveled to San Antonio. Because Kate was flying from general aviation rather than one of the normal passenger terminals, there had been no long line for security, no even longer walk to reach the gate. Instead, she had entered the small terminal and been greeted by the copilot, who introduced himself as Jake. Jake escorted her out the door, across a short expanse of tarmac, and up the stairs to the plane, pausing briefly to introduce her to Brad, the pilot. Within minutes, they were airborne.

Though Kate had never liked the word *surreal,* that was the only way she could describe the experience. Greg had probably done this dozens, perhaps hundreds, of times, but it was her first flight on a private jet. Pure luxury, even if she had left Rainbow's End so early that she'd had to skip breakfast.

She should have asked Greg for one of his energy bars, but Kate hadn't wanted to do anything that would remind him of the trip. He'd been quieter than usual when they'd played tennis, and though Sally had done her best to pretend nothing was wrong, Kate had felt the strain between them. When this day was over and she was once more back at Rainbow's End, she would do her best to make up for today, but first she had a pitch to make and a client to convince.

"Hungry?"

Kate nodded as she looked up. They'd reached their cruising altitude, and Jake had emerged from the cockpit. "Come up here."

He showed her the small galley stocked with an assortment of juices and pastries.

"We didn't know what you wanted for breakfast." Jake pointed to a drawer. "There's cold cereal there, and milk and yogurt in the fridge. And of course, there's peanut butter and bread. We even have a toaster."

Kate's eyes widened. "You did all this for one person?"

"The Prestons take good care of their guests. But don't worry if you can't finish everything. Brad and I'll eat whatever you don't want. It's one of the perks of the job. And if you let me know what you'd like for dinner, I'll arrange for that."

Feeling distinctly pampered, Kate wondered if Jake would expect her to order a five-course meal. "I'm not fussy," she told him. "Anything other than sandwiches would be good." Heather had said she was planning a working lunch with the new owners of Aunt Ivy's, and knowing Heather, that meant platters of sandwiches, salads, and cookies.

Jake nodded. "Fine. I'll see what catering suggests."

After helping herself to a container of yogurt and a Danish pastry, Kate settled back in her seat and opened her laptop.

Though she'd gone through the presentation half a dozen times, she wanted one last run-through before she reached New York.

She knew the clients would expect PowerPoint slides, and there would be some, but instead of the usual "why you should choose Maddox and Associates" introduction, she had created a short video to kick off the day. Her voice wasn't as dramatic as a professional narrator's, but the video would give Hazel and Ike Preston an idea of the TV spots she envisioned. Once they'd seen that, she would segue into the more mundane aspects of the proposal, including the other forms of advertising she was recommending.

When she'd watched the video for what felt like the hundredth time, Kate clicked through her PowerPoint slides, reminding herself of the points she planned to make with each one. At the end, she sat back, pleased with what she'd accomplished. It would be a good day. Greg was wrong; this wasn't a mistake. And, despite what Sally had said, Grandpa Larry would be proud that Kate was being considered for a partnership. He'd told her to aim high, and she had.

The flight went quickly, and before Kate knew it, she was once again buckled into her seat, waiting for the plane to touch down in New Jersey. Rather than confront the congestion that defined Newark airport, they landed at the smaller Teterboro field, and once again, nothing had been left to chance. A limousine was waiting to take Kate into Manhattan. It was a decidedly easier way to travel than her normal commute on the PATH trains under the Hudson followed by the New York subway system. And, fortunately, since the worst of the rush hour had ended, there were no delays.

"Good morning, Trudy." Kate greeted the receptionist as she walked through the main door to the Maddox and Associates offices.

The perky redhead nodded toward the larger of the firm's conference rooms. "The clients are here, but Heather wants to see you in her office first."

Kate had expected that. Either Heather or Nick always had a last-minute powwow with her before a major presentation. This was the first time neither of the partners had seen her full pitch, so it was only natural that Heather would want a few minutes with Kate to reassure herself that everything was ready.

Her dark hair sleeked into her signature French twist, Heather smiled as Kate entered her office. While Heather always wore the latest clothing style, her hairstyle never varied. She'd once told Kate she was convinced that an unchanging hairstyle was the best way of not dating herself. And if there was one thing Heather feared, it was looking old. At fifty-two she was at the peak of her career and determined to remain there.

"It's good to have you back, Kate. Three weeks is a long time. I wanted to see if —" Heather stopped in midsentence, her eyes widening as she looked down. "Are those cowboy boots?"

Kate bit back her smile at Heather's predictable response. When she'd chosen her clothing this morning, she'd debated over the boots, finally deciding to make a statement with them. "Genuine, hand-tooled sharkskin."

Heather stared at them for a second, then shook her head so vigorously Kate wondered if a lock of hair would dare to slip out of the twist. "I don't care if the shark himself did the tooling. You can't wear those. Ike and Hazel Preston are conservative."

Kate knew that from the notes Heather had sent her and from her own research. "But they want their products to appeal to young, affluent customers. Some of those customers wear boots."

Heather glanced at her watch, as if calculating how many seconds they had before the meeting was scheduled to begin. "I know you keep a change of clothes here. Surely that includes appropriate shoes."

It did. Kate had a pair of beautiful Italian pumps with stiletto heels that fairly shrieked "young and modern." But those were not going on her feet today. She'd worn the cowboy boots for a reason. They were her reminder of all that she had left behind in Texas, an incentive to give the Prestons her very best so that today's sacrifice would not be in vain.

"Look, Heather, I interrupted my vacation and upset my grandmother to be here. I'm here, and so are my boots. We're a package deal."

As if she sensed that Kate would not budge, Heather simply pursed her lips and rose from behind her desk. "Are you ready?"

Heather preceded Kate into the conference room, making the introductions to Hazel and Ike Preston. They proved to be a pleasant-looking man and woman in their midfifties. Hazel's suit was a bit frumpy by New York standards, but it was well cut and made of obviously expensive wool. Her brother Ike had a cheerful round face, and if he'd been given a beard and a red suit,

459

would have made an ideal Santa. Their light blue eyes shone with intelligence, making them exactly the kind of clients Kate liked best. They would ask penetrating questions and would be swayed by substance, not fluff. Perfect.

"I'm pleased to meet you," Kate said as she shook their hands. "I'm very excited about the possibility of introducing Aunt Ivy's peanut butter to a new segment of the population."

"Just how are you proposing to do that?" Ike asked when he and Hazel had resumed their seats and Kate had moved to the head of the table. Though he smiled, there was no doubt that Ike Preston was a no-nonsense man, and the look Hazel gave him confirmed that she was equally tough.

"That's what I'm going to show you in one minute," Kate said as she powered up her laptop and connected it to the projector. "I don't want to give you empty words. I want to demonstrate what I have in mind."

"Before you start the PowerPoint," Hazel said, pushing her chair back slightly, "I have a question that has nothing to do with peanut butter, but if I don't ask it now, I'll be distracted during your presentation." She looked at Kate's feet. "Where did you get those boots? I want a pair just like them."

Though Kate was tempted to flash Heather an "I told you so" look, she did not. Instead, she smiled at Hazel. "A friend made them, and I can tell you they're more comfortable than I thought possible. I'll give you her website later. But now, if you're ready, let's talk about the best peanut butter on the planet."

As she nodded, Nick lowered the lights and Kate began the video. She'd done everything she could to showcase her concept. Now it was up to the Prestons. They might love it; they might hate it. In sixty seconds, the length of two TV commercials, Kate would have her answer.

There was a moment of silence when the video ended, then as Nick flicked on the lights, Hazel and Ike began to speak at the same time, their words tumbling over each other's. "Wow!" "Fabulous!" "I wish I'd thought of that." Their reaction was everything Kate had hoped for. They loved the peanut bursting out of its shell; they liked the juxtaposition of ads featuring adults dining on gourmet dishes with ones showing kids ordering peanut butter sandwiches; they even liked the tagline.

The rest of the presentation seemed almost anticlimactic, but by early afternoon, Ike and Hazel agreed that Maddox was the only firm they trusted to handle their account and that the brownies that accompanied Heather's catered lunch needed only one thing to make them perfect: peanut butter frosting.

"This was more than I'd hoped for," Hazel said as Kate escorted the Preston siblings to the front door. Kate wasn't certain whether she was referring to the pitch or the slip of paper with the website for Sam's Bootery, but she didn't care. The clients were happy, and that was what mattered.

When she'd said her farewells, Kate returned to the conference room for the normal postmortem discussion. Each time someone at Maddox pitched to a new client, either Nick or Heather — sometimes both — attended the presentation, then critiqued it afterward. Today it appeared that though they'd both been present, Nick would take the lead in the critique.

He nodded at Heather before turning his attention to Kate. "You did a great job, Kate," he said, his voice warm with approval. "I know it wasn't easy, but you've clearly demonstrated both your talent and your commitment to Maddox. I liked everything you did today. More importantly, so did the Prestons."

Nick paused, perhaps for emphasis, then smiled. "We were going to wait until you returned from vacation, but Heather and I agreed there's no reason to delay. We are pleased to offer you a partnership in the firm."

Yes! The satisfaction that swelled up inside Kate was so intense that she was tempted to raise her fists in triumph. This was what she wanted. This was the reason she'd worked so hard. She'd wanted her talents to be recognized, and they were. The dream that Grandpa Larry had planted inside her had come true. It was wonderful, and yet . . .

Kate blinked at the realization that she felt as if she'd reached the end of the road. Greg had asked her what came after a partnership, what the next rung on the ladder would be. At the time, she had had only nebulous ideas. When she'd dreamt about a partnership, she'd seen it as opening new vistas. It would be a plateau on the climb to the top of the mountain. But now that she'd been given what she'd longed for, another analogy came to mind.

Kate felt as if she'd finished not a chapter but a whole book. She had that feel-good sensation that always accompanied reading the last page, and as happened with the best of books, she was now eager to find another story that would match or even surpass it.

It was time for a change. Unbidden, the image of herself and Greg greeting guests at Rainbow's End flashed before her. A few hours ago she would have dismissed it, but now she could not. Filled with a sense of urgency that she could not explain, Kate knew she had to return to Rainbow's End and Greg and Sally.

"Thank you, Nick. You too, Heather. This means a lot to me." Kate glanced at her watch, calculating the time difference. She needed to call Greg, but Greg would be at Rainbow's End, the land of no cell phone reception. Kate would have to wait until she returned to talk to him.

"I need to get back to Texas," she said, refusing the champagne that Nick wanted to open to celebrate her partnership.

Heather raised a carefully sculpted eyebrow. "Got a cowboy waiting for you?"

"Not exactly." Greg wasn't a cowboy, and Kate wasn't sure he was waiting for her. All she knew was that she felt as if something was tugging her back to Texas.

As soon as she settled into the limo, she turned on her phone. One message. Kate didn't recognize the number, and the caller ID said simply "wireless caller." She tapped the phone.

"There's no easy way to tell you this." The strain she heard in Greg's voice sent tremors of alarm up Kate's spine. "Sally's in the ICU. They think she had a heart attack."

32

"Can't you go any faster?"

When he'd seen the distress on her face and heard what had happened, Jake had assured Kate that he and Brad would get her to San Antonio as quickly as humanly possible. She knew that, and yet it seemed as if the plane was standing still.

"We've got some pretty strong headwinds," Jake explained. Nodding at the plate of food she'd barely touched, he added, "Better eat some of that. From what I've heard, hospital food is nothing to write home about."

Kate shuddered at the word *home,* hating to think of her grandmother in a hospital so far from home. She hated to think of Sally in a hospital anywhere, but somehow it seemed worse that she was in a place where she'd never been before. Alone. And that was Kate's fault.

Waves of guilt washed over her as she

remembered both Sally and Greg telling her she shouldn't go to New York. They were right, and now Sally was paying the price. A very high price.

When she'd returned Greg's call, Kate had learned that Sally had had severe indigestion right after breakfast but had blamed it on the extra piece of sausage she'd eaten. It was only when she'd collapsed on the way back to the cabin that anyone had realized how serious her condition was. Fortunately, Greg had been headed to his own cabin and had seen her sprawled on the path.

He'd assured Kate that the Dupree paramedics had arrived in record time, but though they'd done their best, Sally remained unconscious. There'd been no time to call Kate to see what Sally would have wanted, so Greg had authorized further treatment. Afraid that the hour's drive to the hospital was more than Sally's heart and brain could survive, the paramedics had called for an airlift.

"We're still waiting for her to come out of surgery," Greg explained.

"We?" Kate's brain whirled with images of Sally lying in an ER and now in surgery while Kate was surrounded by the luxury of the Prestons' private jet.

"Roy and I. When I called him, the poor man was distraught. I couldn't leave him in Dupree with nothing to do but worry, so I brought him with me." Greg managed a short chuckle. "He's trying to convince me to play chess with him. Says he needs to practice so he can beat Sally."

At least one of them was remaining optimistic. As she picked at what appeared to be a perfectly prepared plate of eggplant parmesan and savory green beans, Kate could think of nothing but the fact that her grandmother might not be alive when she reached the hospital.

"I love you, Grammy," Kate whispered, reverting to her childhood name for Sally. "Don't leave me."

At last the plane landed, and Kate sprinted toward her car. Grateful that she'd insisted on GPS for it, she followed the directions and found herself in the hospital parking lot less than half an hour after landing at the airport. *Please be alive,* she prayed as she rushed through the doors and headed to the ICU waiting room. There she found Greg and Roy bent over a chessboard.

"How is she?" Kate asked as she approached the two men, her boot heels clicking on the linoleum floor. They both rose. Though she longed to throw herself into

Greg's arms and be comforted by him, something in his expression kept her at arm's length. If he was blaming her for Sally's condition, he wasn't alone. Kate had spent most of the flight second-guessing the day. Would she have recognized the symptoms early enough to give Sally an aspirin and possibly avert the worst of the damage? She would never know.

Greg's frown made Kate wonder if he'd read her thoughts. "She's out of surgery, but her condition is critical. Her heart was in worse shape than they thought, and they had to do a triple bypass. Roy and I've tried to get in, but they won't let us see her because we're not family. They said until she's more stabilized, only relatives are allowed." Greg's expression softened as he said, "You'll be able to see her for five minutes each hour. You can probably go right now, if you're ready."

When the nurse ushered her into Sally's room, Kate realized she wasn't ready, that she might never be ready. It was as if she had entered a nightmare. The figure lying so still on the bed didn't look like Sally. Surrounded by machines that beeped and whirred, with tubes snaking from her body, the tiny woman bore only the slightest resemblance to Kate's grandmother. She looked pale and weak and oh so defense-less.

Kate pulled a chair close to the hospital bed and laid her hand on Sally's. "I don't know if you can hear me, Sally, but I'm here." There was no answer, no sign that her grandmother was aware of her presence. Kate closed her eyes, willing the tears not to fall. She had read that even when patients were in a coma, they could hear what was happening around them and that they sensed visitors' moods. Kate didn't want Sally to know how worried she was and how desperately she wished she had stayed with her. Blinking rapidly, she opened her eyes and leaned over to press a kiss on Sally's forehead. "I love you, Grammy."

Before she knew it, the five minutes were over. When Kate returned to the waiting room, she found that, at Greg's insistence, Roy had gone to the cafeteria. Though the story was plausible, Kate wondered if he'd wanted to spare Roy the sight of her after her visit. It was a good plan, for Kate was trying desperately to maintain her compo-sure.

"How is Sally?" Greg asked, his voice low and filled with concern. Perhaps she had only imagined his coolness earlier. This sounded like the Greg she knew and loved.

"Oh, Greg, it's awful! She doesn't look like my grandmother." Despite her resolve not to cry, tears began to flow. When Greg opened his arms, Kate ran into them, taking comfort from the way he enfolded her in his embrace. Greg was strong and warm and alive — all the things she feared Sally was not.

"I don't know what I'll do if she dies." It was the first time she'd voiced her fears, and hearing the words echo in the room deepened Kate's distress. She couldn't bear the thought of a world without Sally.

Greg stroked Kate's back, his motion rhythmic and somehow soothing. "You're stronger than you realize, and I suspect your grandmother is too," he said. "Whatever happens, you'll get through it. I know you will."

His words were like balm on an open wound, lessening the pain, making Kate believe that healing would come. She rested her head on his chest and let the tears flow. When at last they stopped, she murmured, "I should have been there."

This time there was no response. Though Greg did not pull away, Kate felt him stiffen and knew that she'd touched a raw nerve. She should have listened to him, but she hadn't.

As the elevator binged and Roy emerged, Greg let his arms drop. "I need to take Roy home, but I can come back if you want me to stay with you."

Though that was exactly what Kate wanted, she couldn't ask Greg to drive an hour to Dupree and then turn around, not looking the way he did. "You must be exhausted." And thanks to her, he had had a long, stress-filled day. If Kate had been here, Greg wouldn't have had to spend the day at the hospital.

"I didn't get much sleep last night. I was working on the stuff I promised Drew." Greg rubbed his forehead, trying to smooth the wrinkles, and as he did, he said, "I almost forgot to ask. How did your presentation go? Did the clients like it?"

Kate nodded. "They did, but that doesn't matter now." She gave Roy a brief smile before turning back to Greg. "You'd both better get some sleep. Why don't you call me in the morning? I'll be okay until then."

They were brave words. Perhaps saying them would make them true. When the elevator door closed behind Greg and Roy, Kate glanced at the clock. It would be another forty-five minutes before she could see Sally again. Though the waiting room was surprisingly pleasant, the chairs more comfortable than she had expected, she knew she couldn't remain here. If she did, she would simply replay the scene in the ICU, picturing Sally surrounded by tubes and machines.

Grabbing her purse, Kate wandered down the hall, her mind whirling in a dozen different directions. She saw herself reveling in the luxury of Aunt Ivy's corporate jet while Sally was in a helicopter, fighting for her life on the way to the hospital. While Kate was sharing sandwiches and conversation with the Prestons, nurses were monitoring Sally's vital signs as the surgeon tried to repair her heart. Even now, while Kate was debating which direction to turn, Sally was lying helplessly in the hospital bed.

If only Kate had been with Sally, but she hadn't, and nothing would change that. There was nothing she could do except pray, but though she'd offered countless pleas to God, she had received no answer.

Her thoughts continued to roil, her heart to pound with anguish. When she saw the sign for the chapel, Kate stopped. She knew that God would hear her wherever she was, but perhaps she could find the peace she sought within.

She entered the small room, dimly registering the stained glass window at the far end, and sank onto the last pew. As she closed her eyes, Kate waited for the comfort that she normally found in a church to settle over her. It did not. Instead, her thoughts grew more turbulent, pictures of Sally with those horrible tubes mingling with memories of the day they'd buried Grandpa Larry. As the images changed with the unpredictability of a kaleidoscope, Kate thought she heard an ominous cackling, like the sound of a Halloween witch but far more menacing.

Her eyes flew open, and she looked around. The chapel was empty. It was only her imagination, her guilty conscience conjuring both sights and sounds. Or perhaps it was Satan, preying on her vulnerability.

Kate pulled a Bible from the rack in front of her, and as she did, the evil cackling subsided and her pulse returned to normal. Drawing comfort from the familiar texture of leather and the simple gold lettering, Kate bowed her head and closed her eyes again.

"Oh, God," she whispered, needing to say the words aloud. "I was so wrong. I should have listened to Sally and Greg. I shouldn't have gone to New York." Tears welled in her eyes, and she dashed them away. "I know I couldn't have changed anything, but I should have been with Sally. I should have been by her side on the ride to the hospital. I should have walked next to her as they wheeled her into surgery. Please, God, don't let her die."

There was no answer. Though the terrifying images had faded, Kate was still filled with a sense of despair, as if she'd lost something infinitely precious and had no idea how to recapture it. Her fingers tightened their grip on the Bible. She needed to do more than hold it.

Taking a deep breath, she opened the book to Isaiah. When she'd been troubled as a child, Grandpa Larry had told her he found comfort in that book and had urged her to read it. Kate skimmed the pages, looking for a verse that would give her the comfort she sought. And as she did, her eyes lit on the sixteenth verse of Isaiah 42. "And I will bring the blind by a way that they knew not; I will lead them in paths that they have not known; I will make darkness light before them, and crooked things straight. These things will I do unto them, and not forsake them."

Kate stared at the words, committing them to memory. Grandpa was right. The answer was here. She had been blind — so blind. She had trusted in herself, not seeking God's plan for her life. She'd been so proud, so certain that she knew what she should do, and she'd been wrong. Horribly, horribly wrong. That was why she was now in the darkness, seeing only a crooked road that led to an unknown destination and feeling more alone than ever before.

"Please, God, don't let it be too late," she prayed, her index finger tracing the words that had embedded themselves in her heart. "Show me the path. Make my crooked ways straight, and if it is your will, heal my grandmother." She closed her eyes for a second, knowing there was more to be said. "Your will, Lord, not mine."

Kate wasn't certain how long she sat there, her head bowed, the Bible clasped between her hands. All she knew was that she felt the weight lift from her shoulders, and her heart filled with hope. She did not know what the future would hold, but she did know what was important: the people she loved. Sally, Greg, and her new friends in Dupree would walk the path with her. That much was clear.

33

"When are you going to stop running?"

Roy's question hit Greg with the force of a sledgehammer. Instinctively, he jerked the steering wheel. Wrong move. The vehicle began to swerve. Greg loosened his grip and guided it back into its lane. One person in the hospital was more than enough.

"What do you mean?" he asked when his heart had resumed its normal beat.

Roy chuckled, apparently unaware of how dangerous his question had been. "I've seen the way you look at that gal and the way she looks at you." He pressed his index finger against the bridge of his glasses, pushing them back. "I may wear glasses, but I'm not blind. Anyone can see that you're head over heels for her. Why'd you walk away?"

There was no good answer. Greg had asked himself the same question. As the day had progressed, his fears for Sally had mingled with frustration and disappointment — frustration that he couldn't reach Kate, disappointment that her decision to go to New York had meant Sally had been alone when she'd collapsed. By the time Kate arrived at the hospital, Greg had been simmering, and so, though his heart had told him to enfold her in his arms, his head had urged him to hold back. His head had won that round, but when Kate had emerged from the ICU, pain and anguish etched on her face, his heart refused to be denied.

There had been nothing romantic about the embrace. It had been a simple case of giving comfort, and yet when Greg had held Kate in his arms, it had felt right. Love was more than sweet kisses and moments of delight. Love also meant sharing the bad times.

Greg wasn't ready to confess all that to Roy, and so he settled for saying, "I was angry that Kate wasn't here when Sally needed her."

They'd exited the interstate and were on a two-lane highway where traffic was mercifully light. Greg glanced at his passenger. Roy had shifted in his seat until he was staring directly at Greg. "If that's not the pot calling the kettle black, I don't know what is." Roy made no effort to hide his disapproval. "You said your job kept you so busy you rarely visited your family. Don't you think there were times they needed you?"

Work was part of the reason he hadn't gone to Orchard Slope, but only part. On another day, Greg might have told Roy the whole story, but he was too tired to dredge up more unpleasantness tonight. "I send them money," he said shortly.

Roy shook his head. "That's not the same thing, and you know it. Writing a check is easy. Giving of yourself is much harder."

Roy's words were still echoing through Greg's head when he tumbled into bed, almost too exhausted to stand. He'd sleep tonight, no doubt about it. Bone-deep fatigue ensured that. But, though he hadn't expected it, the nightmare returned.

It began the way it always did. Greg stood on the edge of the precipice, once again paralyzed by fear, listening to the voice.

"Jump!" The voice that sounded so familiar even though he had never been able to identify it seemed closer than before.

"Jump!" But he wouldn't. He couldn't, for jumping would mean certain death. He stood there, not daring to move. He could never move, and yet Greg's heart began to pound as he wondered if the woman —

Kate — would come. He wanted her, and yet he didn't.

Greg was alone on the cliff's edge. He'd been alone before and it had never bothered him, but after he'd felt her close to him the last time, he'd realized what he was missing. It was wrong to want her to join him when he faced certain danger, and yet deep inside, Greg craved her presence. Perhaps the fear would not be so intense if Kate were here.

As had happened the last time, he smelled her perfume before he sensed her presence. As had happened the last time, she wrapped her arms around his waist. But this time was different. This time her embrace gave him more than a moment of comfort, and the terror began to subside. Perhaps this time would have a different ending.

"Jump! Jump!" The man's voice came again.

"No!" Greg cried out. "I won't!" For the first time, he could hear his words. They weren't trapped inside him the way they'd been in the past. Tonight they echoed as loudly as the unseen man's command to jump.

"I won't. We won't," he said to the woman who clung to him. They were brave words, akin to whistling in the dark. They would make no difference, for Greg knew what would happen next. He braced himself for the inevitable shove and the fall.

It did not come. Instead, the woman moved. Leaving his back, she came to his side and took his hand in hers as they stood together on the edge of the mountain. It was the first time he'd seen her face. It was Kate's face, and yet there was something different about it. Her brown eyes were filled with an emotion he had never seen, one he could not identify. She looked as if she wanted to speak, and yet she did not.

"Jump! Jump!" Before Greg could respond, Kate smiled at him, and in that moment he knew there was no reason to be afraid. That was what she had been trying to tell him. She was filled with courage, and he could be too. They would jump. Together.

It was time.

Greg gripped Kate's hand more tightly and pushed off the edge, leaping forward with her at his side. The fear that had always gripped him was gone, replaced by a sense of freedom. This had been his choice. He had jumped rather than waiting to be shoved.

He and Kate hung in the air for what felt like an eternity before they began to move. They should have plummeted to the ground. That was what he expected. Instead they were propelled forward by an unseen force, landing in the middle of a field of bluebonnets as gently as dandelion fluff carried by a soft breeze.

Greg wrapped his arms around Kate. "We did it!" he cried triumphantly as he whirled her in circles. She smiled, her eyes reflecting her happiness. As Greg started to lower his lips to hers, he heard the voice. Turning, he saw a familiar figure standing on the mountaintop.

"I always knew you could do it," his father said.

It was only a dream, Greg told himself when he wakened. Only a dream. And yet it had galvanized him as none of the other dreams had.

He knelt at the side of his bed, bowing his head and pouring out his heart as he begged for guidance. "Lord, give me the words I need." Greg wasn't certain how long he prayed. All he knew was that the doubt had disappeared, replaced by certainty.

After pulling on jeans and a sweatshirt, he headed for the office and picked up the phone.

"Mrs. Fuller is still in the ICU," the nurse reported. "Ms. Sherwood is asleep. Do you want me to wake her?"

Greg shook his head before he realized that the nurse could not see the gesture. "No," he said, "she needs her sleep." And if all went well, he would be back late tonight.

He pressed the disconnect button and dialed another number, nodding as the man on the other end confirmed his request. "We can do all that, Mr. Vange. The plane will be ready in an hour."

Greg sprinted back to his cabin, tossed a change of clothes into a bag in case the trip took longer than he expected, then grabbed his keys and headed toward his SUV. It was time to start running in the right direction.

Kate woke with a crick in her neck. The nurses had told her Sally's condition would not change overnight and had encouraged her to take a room at one of the local motels, but she'd refused to leave. Instead, she'd managed to get a few minutes of sleep between the brief hourly visits she was allowed.

She checked her watch. Another ten minutes before she could see Sally again. Leaning back against the wall, she closed her eyes.

"We're all packed, and if I know my kids, they're sleeping in their clothes so they'll be ready to head for the airport the minute I get home." Kate recognized the voice of the dark-haired nurse who appeared to be in charge of the night shift. "The next-door neighbors are taking care of the cats while we're gone." She paused, and Kate heard the shuffling of papers. "It may sound silly, but I feel almost guilty about this trip. The families on both sides of us have been unemployed for so long, I don't know how they're holding on to their houses."

"I know what you mean." The higher-pitched voice belonged to the blonde nurse. "A number of families from our church are in the same situation. The church does what it can and provides occasional meals and some clothes." Kate heard the resignation in the blonde's voice. "I know those are important, but I wish the families could get away."

"Vacations are such a boost to the spirit," the brunette said. "It may only be a temporary escape from reality, but vacations are my way of recharging my batteries."

"I hear you. It's too bad they're so expensive."

The conversation continued, but Kate paid no attention, because images began to whirl through her mind, triggered by the nurses' comments. Family. That was the answer.

Kate pictured the families from Dupree who'd spent Easter afternoon at Rainbow's End. Unlike the couples who'd come and gone, most disgruntled that the resort hadn't met their expectations, the families had been happy and relaxed. More than that, they'd looked as if they belonged there.

And it hadn't been only the guests who'd been happy. Carmen and KOB had sported smiles so broad that Kate had accused them of posing for a toothpaste commercial, while she couldn't recall when she'd had so much fun. The party had brought both Rainbow's End and its staff to life.

Her exhaustion forgotten, Kate grinned. Greg had said the reason he hadn't made an offer to buy Rainbow's End was that it needed a new direction, but that he had no vision for that direction. This could be the direction he'd sought for the resort. Rainbow's End could become a family retreat. Most of the cabins were large enough to accommodate small families, and with a few alterations, cabins like the one Kate shared with Sally could handle larger ones. It might even be possible to create a dormitory-like building for kids, to give their parents a chance to rekindle the romance in their marriages.

The ideas continued to whirl. Not even

when she'd been most inspired by an assignment for Maddox and Associates had Kate felt so energized. It had been less than a day since Nick had announced her promotion, less than a day since she'd realized she was ready for a change. At the time, she had had no idea what the future might hold, but now she knew what she wanted. She wanted to be part of creating a new Rainbow's End.

Kate looked down at the Bible that had been at her side all night. Rainbow's End needed to become more than a family resort. If it was going to achieve its full potential, it needed to become a Christian family resort, a place to restore guests' spirits as well as their bodies. Kate knew that idea would appeal to Greg. He'd told her that the Christian focus had been what had attracted him to Rainbow's End in the first place and that he'd been disappointed to discover the Sinclairs had eliminated it.

The ideas continued to percolate through her mind. Turning Rainbow's End into a Christian family resort was a good idea, but there was more that Greg could do to make it a special place. He could help families who were facing financial difficulties enjoy it.

Kate had read about philanthropic camps for needy kids. This would be similar and yet different, because the guests would include people across the economic spectrum. Those who could afford to pay would, while families who needed a break from what the nurses had called "reality" would pay whatever they could afford, with the rest of the cost coming from Greg's endowment. It would be a one-of-a-kind resort, just as Greg was a one-of-a-kind man.

Kate pictured him greeting guests, joining them for dinner, leading them in giving thanks for the food and the other blessings they had received. Drew may have told Greg he lacked interpersonal skills, but Kate knew better. If Greg took over, Rainbow's End would be a success, not just for him and his guests but for Dupree, the Heart of the Hills. The town would repaint their signs, and . . .

Kate's smile broadened as she envisioned a new logo for Rainbow's End. Not just a logo but a slogan too. Of course there would be a rainbow. She would keep the ark at its end, but instead of having animals peering out from the windows, the side of the boat would feature a heart with a cross in its center. "Rainbow's End: The Heart and Soul of the Hill Country."

Kate's heart began to race as she thought of the advertising campaign she could develop. It would be so much fun to work with Greg. She could update the website, create brochures, arrange the media buys. She could even help redecorate the cabins. Kate smiled, picturing Lauren's quilts in the rooms. There had to be some way to involve Samantha too. Perhaps Kate could add a display cabinet to the lodge to showcase local merchants. Samantha could provide a pair or two of boots, and the town's silversmith could display some of his goods. There was so much Kate could do if Greg agreed to let her participate.

After the way he'd left last night, Kate couldn't be certain that he would. There was only one way to know. She glanced at her watch. He was probably jogging, which meant he might be in cell range. She pushed "talk," but the call went directly to voice mail. She would have to wait.

34

Greg stared out the window, watching the puffy tops of cumulus clouds as the plane sped northwest. Roy was right. He'd been running away, first from his family and the expectations he could not meet, then from Kate and his fears. Both were wrong. He should have stood his ground. Admittedly, it would have been more difficult when he was a teenager, but he was a grown man now. There were no longer any reasons, only excuses.

He shouldn't have left his parents' home without at least trying to explain how his father's abusive anger had made him feel unloved, and he most definitely should not have left Kate last night. Not without telling her he loved her. Not without asking her to be his wife. Instead, Greg had walked away when she needed him the most. He should have taken Roy to a hotel, then returned to be with Kate.

He could have sat with her while she waited to be allowed back into the ICU. He could have told her how much he'd enjoyed the way they'd worked together on the Easter party. He could have told her that, even though he had started to dream of a future that included both her and Rainbow's End, she was the critical part of the equation. He could have told her that he would do anything, even move to New York, if it meant they could have a life together. But he hadn't.

He'd remained silent, and then he'd run away, grateful for the excuse she'd given him. That was a mistake, but God had been merciful. He had taken that mistake and turned it into something good. Greg knew without a doubt that Roy's question and the dream that could no longer be called a nightmare were gifts from God. They'd forced him to face himself.

If the dream was right, Greg's father was not the one-dimensional man he believed him to be. According to the dream, Kate had been correct in believing that his father had deeper, warmer feelings than Greg had ever acknowledged. Dad might refuse to admit them, but even if he did, Greg knew there were things he had to say and do before he could begin the next phase of his life, the life he hoped to build with Kate. The time for cowardice was over.

Greg took a deep breath before exhaling slowly. He loved Kate. He loved her, and he wanted her to be his wife. If they were blessed, he wanted her to be the mother of his children. Greg knew that with every fiber of his being. He should have told her, but he hadn't, because he was afraid of failing. It was bad enough when his father and Drew had called him a loser, but Greg couldn't bear to be a loser in Kate's eyes. And so he hadn't risked his heart. Until today. Everything would change today.

Greg rose and stretched, then helped himself to a cup of coffee from the pot the copilot had shown him when he'd boarded the private plane. He'd need caffeine — lots of it — if he was going to get through this day. Taking a sip, he headed back to his seat, reflecting on the things he hadn't done because he'd been afraid to fail. That was the reason he hadn't bought Rainbow's End. Even though buying it would have been the answer to Carmen and KOB's prayers, Greg hadn't done it, because he'd been afraid he couldn't make the resort successful.

He drained the cup and set it in one of the cup holders. As much as he'd come to love Rainbow's End and the Hill Country, he knew he would not stay there without Kate. He loved her, and that was more important than anything else. But that discussion would come later when they were together. Right now, all he wanted was to hear her voice.

He reached into his pocket for his phone, startled when his hand came back empty. Greg shook his head in disgust. Would he never learn? Somehow, he'd left his phone in the cabin. Now he'd have to wait to talk to the woman he loved. Fortunately, he had her number and that of the hospital memorized. All he needed was a phone.

It was a half-hour drive from the small airport where he landed to his parents' house. Though he tried to still the pounding of his heart, Greg couldn't help wondering about the reception he'd receive. This was the first time he'd arrived unannounced. In the past, Mom had made a special dinner, and Dad . . . Greg doubted it was coincidence that his father always had important engagements with his buddies the nights Greg was in Orchard Slope.

The town looked more prosperous than he remembered, but perhaps that was only in contrast to Dupree. There were no empty buildings in Orchard Slope, and the sign welcoming visitors was freshly painted. Even the food processing plant appeared to have new paint. But though downtown might sport a few changes, the house where Greg had grown up was the same.

The two-story white farmhouse with the green roof and shutters looked the way it always had. A bed of daffodils softened the lines of the porch, while a wreath of silk flowers added a cheerful note to the front door. The wreath and flowers changed with the seasons, but everything else was unchanged. Was it only Greg who was different?

He parked his car on the street and walked around to the kitchen door on the east side of the house. As a kid, he'd have gone in without knocking, but he no longer lived here, and so he rapped on the door. It took only a few seconds for it to be opened.

"Greg!" The blood drained from his mother's face, and she gripped the door frame as if she feared she would fall. The sweater he'd given her a couple Mother's Days ago had a spot of chocolate on one sleeve. That and the delicious aroma that wafted through the open door told Greg his mother had been baking. There was nothing surprising about that. What did surprise him was her appearance. Though it had been only four months since his last visit, Mom appeared to have aged several years. Her hair had more gray, and the lines on her face were more pronounced.

"What's wrong?" she demanded, alarm coloring her voice.

It seemed Greg had made yet another mistake. He should have called to warn his mother. "Nothing," he said, trying to reassure her. Judging from the way she was fussing with her hair, Greg guessed she would have colored it had she known he was coming. "I just wanted to talk to you and Dad."

His mother opened the door wider and wrapped her arms around him in a quick hug as he entered the kitchen. "I've got some brownies in the oven, and your father's watching sports. No surprise there." She shrugged. "It seems he spends more time with that big-screen TV and the sports channels than he does with me."

Nothing had changed since Greg's childhood other than the size of the screen and the number of channels available.

"Debra, what's going on?" Greg's father called from the living room, raising his voice to be heard over the roar of race cars.

"It's Greg," Mom shouted in return. "He's here."

A creak of the recliner and the thud of feet on the floor told Greg his father was coming. He stood in the doorway to the kitchen wearing one of his favorite plaid shirts and a worn pair of jeans. His hair might be a little grayer, perhaps a little thinner than the last time Greg had seen him, but his expression hadn't changed. The green eyes, so like the ones Greg saw each time he looked in the mirror, were just as cold as ever.

"Did you get tired of South America or wherever it was you went?" he asked. That was vintage Linc Vange. No greeting, nothing more than a question that sounded more like an accusation.

Greg shrugged. He wouldn't let the man intimidate him. Not today. "Actually, I was in Texas." He glanced around the kitchen, wondering whether there were any new pictures of his sisters on display, but the arrangement on the refrigerator door appeared the same as it had at Christmas.

"Texas?" Mom slid her arm around Greg's waist and looked up at him. "I thought you said you were going trekking somewhere there were pythons."

" 'Fraid not. The most dangerous thing I saw was a javelina."

While his father made a sound that could

have been a snort, Mom smiled. "I'm glad. I never did like snakes. Now, Son, how long can you stay?"

"Just for the day. I need to get back to San Antonio and the woman I hope to marry."

His mother's face brightened, and for a moment she looked as young and happy as the woman who'd cheered when he'd received his high school diploma. "Did you hear that, Linc?" she asked, turning toward her husband. "Our boy's getting married."

"If she'll have me," Greg cautioned. At this point he wasn't certain of anything other than the fact that if Kate refused him, he'd ask again and again until she agreed to be his wife.

"Why wouldn't she?" his father demanded. "You're a fine young man."

Greg blinked, astonished by the words of praise. This was more than he'd expected. It was the first time he could recall a compliment from his father, and it warmed his heart more than he'd thought possible, making him believe he'd been right to come here. Perhaps, as he'd hoped, the dream had been a portent; perhaps today could be a new beginning for all of them.

He looked from his father to his mother. "I'm here because there are some things we need to talk about, and it didn't seem right doing that over the phone."

As if she had some inkling of what Greg wanted to discuss, his mother pushed him toward the kitchen table. "Sit down, Son." She inclined her head toward her husband. "You'd better turn off the TV, Linc. It won't hurt you to miss a few minutes." When they were all seated at the round table that had been the scene of so many family meals, Mom smiled at Greg. "Tell us about your young woman."

He held up his hand in the classic gesture for stop. "First things first." He looked directly at his father. In the aftermath of last night's dream, he had tried to view his childhood from his father's perspective. "I want to apologize. I know I wasn't the son you wanted, and I'm sorry."

"What do you mean?" Mom asked, her voice shrill with emotion. "You're a good son."

Greg kept his gaze on his father. "I know you wanted someone who loved sports the way you do. Let's face it: I was the laughing-stock of Orchard Slope. I couldn't hit a baseball or dunk a basketball. As for foot-ball, my only chance would have been as a referee, but they wouldn't let kids do that. I know I was a disappointment."

Linc Vange, the onetime star of every sport played at Orchard Slope High, nodded. "You're right. I was disappointed. You weren't the son I wanted."

"Now, Linc." Mom laid a cautionary hand on his arm, the movement releasing a whiff of lavender that mingled with the aroma of brownies. The scents might be ordinary, but the situation was not. "There's no need —"

"Let him talk," Greg said, his voice harsher than he'd intended. It was too late for Mom to play peacemaker. "We should have had this conversation years ago. Go ahead, Dad. Tell me why you were disappointed." It wouldn't be anything Greg hadn't surmised, but he couldn't build a future until he'd put the past to rest.

"Sports were my whole life until I met your mother," his father said, his eyes bright as he smiled at the woman he'd married. "More than anything, I wanted a son to share that with me." And, though he didn't say it, Greg suspected he'd wanted his son to achieve what he had not: a place on a professional team.

Dad's eyes narrowed as he turned his gaze on Greg. "When you were born, I pictured us going to games together. I even figured I'd coach when you were old enough to play."

"And that never happened."

"No, it didn't. Instead, you turned into a brainiac. I don't know if you can imagine what it's like, having your kid know more than you do. My buddies never said much, but I could tell what they were thinking — poor Linc." He fisted his hands, then pounded one on the table.

"Linc." Mom's protest went unheeded.

"And then you started sending money. How do you think that made me feel? It seemed like you were rubbing my nose in the fact that I couldn't support my family."

That Greg had never considered this made him ashamed. He'd told himself his father had never understood him, but he was equally guilty. "You took it," he said softly.

"For her." Dad nodded at his wife. "I wanted her to have nice things."

Mom sniffed and pulled a tissue from her pocket. Though Greg hated the fact that she was upset, he couldn't stop now.

"Why didn't you say anything?"

"Would you have listened?" His father countered the question with one of his own.

"Probably not," Greg admitted. It hurt to think of how callous he'd been. Like father, like son was no excuse. He should have known better. "At first all I wanted was to

499

get away from here and stop feeling like a failure."

Mom laid her hand on Greg's arm and gave it a little squeeze. "You were never a failure."

"I was in Dad's eyes." He waited until his father met his gaze before he continued. "You talk about how your buddies made you feel. Did you ever think that once — just once — I wanted you to look at me and see me? Me, Greg Vange. Not Linc's son but a separate person. That's what I wanted, and you never gave it to me. Instead all you did was yell at me and tell me I wasn't good enough."

His father lowered his eyes to the table as if the scarred wood held the answers. Though Greg had hoped for a response, some acknowledgment of the pain he had felt, he knew he would not get it.

"I was determined I wouldn't come back until I proved to the world that I wasn't a failure, but I learned something along the way." And what Greg had learned had made an enormous difference in his life. "I discovered that it doesn't matter what the world thinks. It doesn't even matter what your parents think. All that matters is what God *knows*. He knows how I've struggled, and he knows how I've failed. But you know what? He loves me anyway."

Her eyes filled with tears, Mom tried to smile at Greg. "We love you too."

He'd always known his mother loved him. It had been his father's love he'd doubted. Greg looked at his father. "Do you?"

"Yeah, I do." The words were simple, but there was no doubting their sincerity.

"Then why didn't you ever tell me?" Greg demanded. All those years of feeling unworthy and unloved could have been avoided if only his father had uttered those three little words.

For the first time that he could recall, Greg saw confusion in his father's eyes. The mask of confidence had cracked, revealing the man behind it. "I don't know."

It was as if the dam had broken, releasing the words both men had held back for so long. They talked for hours, and as they did, Greg realized there would never be one of those made-for-TV-movie happy endings for him and his father. They were too different, their goals too diverse. But by the time his mother announced that supper was ready, Greg knew that even though he and his father might never become friends, for the first time, they understood each other.

"Won't you stay overnight?" Mom asked when he'd finished the second piece of apple pie she insisted he take. "With the girls away, there's plenty of room."

He hesitated, then seeing the longing in her eyes, relented. "All right, but I need to make a couple calls." He glanced at the wall phone. Since he'd forgotten his cell, he'd have to use it.

"Kate, it's Greg," he said a few minutes later when his father had headed for the lodge where he spent so many evenings, and his mother had left the kitchen, giving Greg the privacy he craved.

"Where are you?" He could hear the surprise in her voice, perhaps triggered by the unfamiliar number on her caller ID.

"At my parents' house."

"In Washington?" Surprise turned to confusion. He could picture the tiny furrows between Kate's eyes as she tried to understand why he had come here.

"It's the only one they have," he said with an attempt at humor.

She wasn't buying the casual air he'd tried to project. "But why? I thought . . ." Kate let her voice trail off.

"It's a long story. I'll tell you about it when I get back. If all goes well, that'll be tomorrow afternoon. We've got a lot to talk about. Now, tell me about Sally."

They spoke for a couple minutes more,

and when he hung up, Greg's smile was ironic as he realized that, like his father, he hadn't said what was on his mind. Not once had he told Kate he loved her. But perhaps that was for the best. Like the discussion he'd had with his father, a declaration of love was one thing that should be done in person.

35

It had been another difficult night, trying to sleep on the chair in the waiting room. Kate knew she'd probably crash the instant she got into a real bed, but in the meantime, it was important to be as close to Sally as possible. And soon Greg would be here.

Their phone conversation had been brief, but it lingered in her memory, as much for what hadn't been said as what had. Greg had sounded different. Tired, of course, but more relaxed, as if something had released the springs that had been wound so tightly inside him. It sounded as if the meeting with his father had been better than Greg had expected.

Kate said a silent prayer of thanksgiving that Greg was trying to resolve his issues with his father. It was good that he was trying to bridge the gaps between them. What puzzled Kate was why Greg had decided to fly to Washington yesterday. She had expected him to come back to the hospital, but instead he'd flown in the opposite direction.

Something must have happened to change his mind after he left the hospital Tuesday night. What? And, even more importantly, what did he want to discuss with her? Greg's voice had changed, growing warmer and more intimate, when he'd told her they had a lot to talk about.

Kate felt her cheeks flush as she remembered how Greg had sounded. If she were being fanciful, she would say that he sounded like a man in love. Perhaps dreams did come true. Perhaps Greg felt the way she did.

"Good morning, young lady."

Roy's words jolted Kate out of her reverie. "Good morning to you too, Roy." Kate smiled, relieved to see that another night's rest had restored his color and erased some of the shadows from under his eyes. "Your timing is perfect. They're moving Sally out of the ICU as we speak."

"I know." He sank onto the chair across from Kate, stretching out his legs and setting his Stetson on his lap. "I called to see what was happening before I left Dupree. Thanks for putting me on the authorized

list. I'd have worried the whole way otherwise."

"Then you know that she's doing remarkably well." While the doctors had hesitated
to call it a miracle, they'd told Kate her
grandmother's condition had improved
faster than they'd dared to hope.

Roy nodded. "Sally's a strong woman with
a heart as big as the whole state of Texas. Is
it any wonder I love her?" Kate hadn't realized that grown men blushed, but Roy's
cheeks reddened as the words came out. He
spun his hat on a finger, pretending to be
fascinated by the way it moved. A few
seconds later, he looked up, his expression
wary. "Did Sally tell you I asked her to
marry me?"

Kate blinked. The proposal wasn't a
surprise, but the fact that Sally hadn't
mentioned it was. "No, she didn't."

Though she saw disappointment in Roy's
eyes, he nodded. "She refused me." There
was no doubt of the pain the refusal had
caused him, and Kate's heart went out to
the man who loved her grandmother. Sally
was a fortunate woman to have found love
not just once but twice.

"She said she couldn't leave you," Roy
explained.

That was Sally, putting Kate's happiness

ahead of her own. Like Grandpa Larry, taking himself off the partnership track so he could spend more time with Kate, Sally was sacrificing her own life for her granddaughter.

Sally was right. A week ago, Kate had been worried about the impact her grandmother's marriage would have on her. But that was the old Kate. The new Kate knew what was important, and it was much more than successful ad campaigns and promotions. The new Kate no longer feared change. Instead, the new Kate realized that not only was change inevitable, but it could be positive, as long as she followed the right path.

Kate wouldn't let her grandmother give up her second chance at love. She would wait a few days until Sally had regained more of her strength, but then Kate intended to tell her that she should marry Roy. Sally deserved every bit of happiness she could find.

"Sally's already given me more than I deserve. It's time for her to think about herself."

"That's what I told her." Roy stopped twirling his hat and fixed his gaze on Kate. "What I'm telling you is that as soon as they let me see Sally, I'm going to ask her again, and this time I won't take no for an answer."

"Good for you!" If Sally was so misguided as to refuse him a second time, Kate would intervene. She wasn't about to let her grandmother allow happiness to slip through her fingers. This was one change Kate wanted to witness.

Roy raised an eyebrow. "Then you don't mind?"

"Absolutely not. I want Sally to be happy, and it's clear that you're the man who makes her happy." Kate leaned forward and dropped her voice to a conspiratorial level. "I just need you to promise me one thing."

"What's that?" Once again wariness filled Roy's eyes.

Kate smiled, hoping to reassure him. "No justice of the peace wedding. I want to be Sally's maid of honor and watch her walk down the aisle."

His eyes lighting with pleasure, Roy held out his hand for a shake. "You've got yourself a deal."

"Roy's here?" Sally looked up at her grand-daughter. Kate's face reflected both happiness and relief. Sally smiled, realizing she was probably displaying the same emotions herself, with the addition of fatigue. Though she didn't remember much of the past couple days, according to Kate, Sally was fortunate to be alive.

Triple bypasses might be routine to the surgeons, but they were anything but routine to Sally, nor was the fact that she had no memory of the past two days. From everything Kate had said, that was just as well. There were some things a person didn't need to remember, and heart surgery was one of them. Right now, Sally felt happy, relieved, exhausted, and very, very anxious to see Roy. There was so much she had to tell him. But first . . .

"Would you bring me a mirror?" A quick glance confirmed her fears. "He can't see me like this." Her hair was matted to her head, and without makeup she looked a hundred years old. That was no way to greet the man she loved and hoped to marry.

Kate's smile made Sally suspect she knew exactly why she was so anxious to see Roy. Perhaps she should tell Kate what she intended, but one thing Sally had realized was that Roy was right. It was time she thought about her future on Earth, however long or short it might be, and made the choices that would bring her the most happiness.

Kate was a grown woman, no longer a baby chick or even a fledgling. And if Sally's eyes weren't deceiving her, Kate was not the same woman who'd left Rainbow's End Tuesday morning. Though dark shadows under them betrayed sleepless nights, Kate's eyes reflected a serenity Sally had never seen. Something had happened to her granddaughter, and whatever it was, was good. Sally would ask about that later. First she needed to see Roy before her courage deserted her.

"The man has stars in his eyes whenever you're around," Kate said firmly as she laid the hand mirror on a small table. "He won't care that your hair is a little messed up."

"A little?" Sally couldn't forget what she'd seen. "It's worse than a bird's nest. You've got to help me do something with it." It was possible there might come a time when she didn't mind Roy seeing her at less than her best, but that time wasn't this morning.

Kate nodded. "Let me see what I can do." She returned a few minutes later, a couple small bottles in one hand. "This is the best I can do — dry shampoo. You're not allowed out of bed until the doctor sees you." The corners of Kate's mouth turned up in a mischievous grin as she added, "Of course, I could always ask Roy to wait until the doctor's made his rounds."

Her granddaughter was teasing her, and Sally couldn't think of anything that would please her more except seeing Roy. "You know I don't want to keep Roy waiting. Let's see what you can do." In less than fifteen minutes Sally studied her reflection in the mirror. It was amazing what clean — well, cleaner — hair and a bit of makeup could do for a woman's self-esteem.

"Thanks, Kate. I guess I'm as ready as I'll ever be." She took a deep breath, trying to settle her nerves when her granddaughter left. As dearly as she loved Kate, Sally didn't want her to overhear what she was going to say to Roy.

It seemed like only seconds later that the door opened and he entered the room. Just the sight of him made Sally's heart pound so fiercely that she was surprised she didn't set off one of the monitors.

"Hello, Roy," Sally said, her voice cracking with emotion. Had he grown more handsome or was it simply that the blinders had fallen from her eyes? Whatever the reason, she knew that she would happily spend the rest of her life gazing at this man. And if her heart beat faster when he walked into a room, that was okay too.

"You gave me quite a scare, young lady." To Sally's surprise, Roy's voice quavered as much as hers did. Though she wouldn't have thought it possible, he looked relieved and worried at the same time. She decided to defuse the emotion of the moment with a little laugh.

"If I'm a young lady, you must be a very young man." Sally's smile faded as she said, "The truth is, Roy, neither one of us is young. The fact that I'm here is proof of that." She glanced around the room that, while luxurious by hospital standards, was still a hospital room.

"You're going to be fine." Roy seemed to have recovered from his earlier display of emotion, because his voice was steady now. "The doctor said you'd be out of here in another day or two." He stopped, stared at the floor for a second, then looked back at Sally. Touching the bridge of his glasses as he often did when he was nervous, Roy said, "I probably should wait, but . . ."

Sally shook her head. "Stop right there, Roy. You're a gentleman, so you know it's 'ladies first.' "

He blinked in surprise but nodded slowly, letting her continue.

"Kate told me what a close call I had." Sally still shuddered to think of all that had happened after she'd suffered what she'd believed to be nothing more than a bout of indigestion. "It made me realize how precious life is and that I shouldn't waste a single day."

She took a shallow breath, never breaking her gaze. Her future happiness depended on this man and his reaction to what she was about to say. "I love you, Roy, and if your offer is still open, I accept. There's nothing I want more than to be your wife."

The happiness that shone from his eyes left Sally no doubt that he still wanted to marry her. "I know it's a cliché, but it's true. You've made me the happiest man on earth." Roy leaned forward and pressed his lips to Sally's. Minutes later when they were both breathless, he said, "If I had my way, I'd marry you today, but your granddaughter won't allow it."

Sally stared, shocked. The Kate of a week ago might have protested, but surely the one who'd fixed her hair and helped with her makeup so she could be pretty for Roy wouldn't object to the wedding.

"Let's get her in here. I've got a thing or two to say to that young lady."

"Now, Sally," Roy said, cupping her cheek, "it's not that bad. Kate gave me permission to court you. It's just the timing that's wrong. She wants us to have a proper church wedding, and she's insisting that she be your maid of honor. She'd be disappointed if we got married today."

"My maid of honor?" Sally smiled as she pictured herself in an ivory dress following Kate down the aisle. "Why not? We can wait a week or two."

"That's my girl." Roy leaned forward and pressed another kiss on her lips. "Now, here's what I'm thinking about for a honeymoon."

By the time Roy finished telling her his plans, they were both laughing. Tears of joy welled in Sally's eyes as she thought of all she'd been given: a loving husband, a wonderful granddaughter, and now a second chance at life and love.

"Life with you is going to be such an adventure," Sally said, clasping his hand in hers. "I can't wait to get started."

36

"Kate."

She turned, her heart skipping a beat when she saw Greg striding across the coffee shop. She'd spent the last hour here trying to compose herself but accomplishing little more than drinking two cups of coffee. There was so much she wanted to tell Greg, so much she wanted to know, but right now Kate's tongue was tangled and her brain frozen. She'd gotten so caught up thinking about Sally that her carefully rehearsed speech had evaporated. That was no problem, she'd assured herself as she'd stirred sweetener into the first cup of coffee. She had hours before Greg would arrive. But here he was, throwing her plans into disarray.

Kate glanced at the Bible she'd kept by her side and smiled. *I haven't learned, have I, Lord? I'm still worrying about my plans instead of trusting yours.* His plans had already proven to be infinitely better than anything Kate could have devised.

Look at Sally and Roy. They were in Sally's room, making wedding plans. Roy had come out long enough to announce that she had accepted his proposal and that the bride-to-be wanted to see Kate. While Roy scoured the hospital's gift shop for wedding magazines, Kate had hugged her grandmother and assured her that she did indeed want to be her maid of honor. And then Roy had returned, his smile as broad as Sally's, his face beaming with happiness. If Kate had had any doubts about the wisdom of the match, they would have disappeared when she saw the two of them together. Sally and Roy could have been poster children for love.

Sensing that they wanted time alone, Kate had stayed only long enough to congratulate them again and tell them how thrilled she was by their engagement. And Kate was. Though she had never imagined that their stay at Rainbow's End would result in Sally's moving to Texas, Kate saw God's hand in all that had happened.

Sally was meant to be here with Roy, just as Kate was meant to make changes in her life. Hers might not lead to marriage and happily-ever-after, but Kate knew that once she kicked off the Aunt Ivy's campaign, she would leave both Maddox and New York.

That much was definite. The rest depended on Greg. Kate didn't know what he wanted to discuss, but she had practiced her speech about possible changes to Rainbow's End, hoping she would be able to persuade Greg that was the right direction for the resort and, more importantly, for him. She had planned to review her points several more times, but Greg was here now, hours before she'd expected him.

"I didn't think you'd arrive until afternoon." Though she longed to throw herself into Greg's arms, Kate forced herself to walk toward him. His tone of voice when they'd spoken last night had made her hope they had a future together, but until she told him what had happened to her in the chapel, until she learned what had transpired with his father, she could not be certain.

Greg shrugged, the motion highlighting the fact that his shirt appeared to have been slept in. "I couldn't wait. I know my mom was disappointed that she couldn't fix breakfast for me, but the pilot was just as happy to fly at night. There's less air traffic then."

"So you took the red-eye." When she'd realized Greg had gone to Orchard Slope, Kate had doubted he'd flown commercial. His reference to the pilot accommodating his schedule confirmed that he'd chartered a plane.

"Pretty close to it." When they reached the hallway, Greg looked around, as if searching for someone. "How's your grandmother?"

"Out of ICU and happier than I've seen her in years now that she and Roy decided to get married." Kate pushed the button to summon the elevator. "It's not even ten o'clock, and it's already been an eventful day. They moved Sally to a private room, and Roy wasted no time proposing. He's with her now, making wedding plans and who knows what else."

The elevator dinged, and Greg ushered Kate into it. "That's wonderful news." His smile faded. "Or is it? How do you feel about this marriage?"

A week ago, Kate's answer might have been different. Now she could honestly say, "I'm happy for both Sally and Roy. They're meant to be together." When Greg raised an eyebrow, she nodded. "I've had a chance to do a lot of thinking these past few days."

"Me too. There's so much I want to talk to you about, but this isn't the place." Greg glanced at his watch as they emerged on Sally's floor. "Why don't we go back to Rainbow's End? Sally won't miss you if Roy's here."

"That sounds like a good idea." Other than a brief trip to buy a change of clothes and some toiletries, Kate hadn't been out of the hospital in more than thirty-six hours. "I can bring back some clothes for Sally." More importantly, the discussion she wanted to have about Rainbow's End would be best conducted there. The beautiful setting would ease any concerns Greg might have.

"I can pick up my phone." He shook his head in disgust. "I can't believe I left it there."

One question was answered. "So that's why I got voice mail when I called you."

"Yep. I should have bought a disposable phone when I was in Orchard Slope, but there wasn't time."

As Kate had expected, neither Sally nor Roy seemed bothered that she would be gone for a few hours. In fact, Sally's eyes twinkled when she saw Greg, and there was a note of amusement in her voice when she told them to have fun.

Kate could practically hear the wedding bells ringing inside her grandmother's head.

Now that she had her second chance at wedded bliss, she was undoubtedly hoping Kate would be the next to walk down the aisle.

"I guess your life will change when Sally marries Roy," Greg said as he opened the door to his SUV for Kate.

She waited until he'd climbed in and started the vehicle before she answered. She wouldn't talk about Rainbow's End until they were there, but she wanted to set the stage. "That's one part of my life that's changing. There are others." She kept her gaze fixed on Greg as she said, "I've decided I'm not going to stay with Maddox."

Greg seemed startled, as well he might, considering how many times Kate had told him this was the perfect firm for her. "They didn't offer you the partnership?"

"They did." Kate paused for a second as she framed the rest of her answer. "It was a dream come true. This may sound strange, but I realized that the *offer* was what I wanted, not the actual partnership. Even before I heard what had happened to Sally, I knew it was time for a change."

The morning commute was winding down, leaving gaps between vehicles. Greg looked at Kate, his expression filled with concern. "What will you do?"

She wanted to say, "That depends on you." But she wouldn't do that. Instead, Kate said, "I'm not sure. I'm still waiting to see where God is leading me." Behind his sunglasses, Greg's eyes widened in surprise. Kate laughed. "I told you I had a lot of time to think. Do you remember the day you said you'd been led to Rainbow's End?" When Greg nodded, Kate continued. "I was skeptical about the whole idea. You see, I had never felt as if I'd been led anywhere. I didn't think I needed to be led. After all, I was an adult."

Kate gripped the armrest as she tried to control her emotions. "I was wrong. I'd been going in the wrong direction, and it wasn't because God failed to show me the way. It was because I was too stubborn to listen. That's going to change."

Greg smiled. "It sounds as if we're in the same boat, waiting together."

Oh, how Kate liked the sound of that.

"Do you think you'll stay in the New York area?" Greg asked.

Kate shook her head. "I want to be close to Sally, and now that it looks as if she'll be moving to Dupree, that means a move for me too. I can probably find some kind of work in San Antonio." Glancing out the window, Kate smiled at the realization that in less than a month, this part of Texas had started to feel like home. "I've also thought about setting myself up as an independent consultant to small businesses. One of the things I realized was how much I enjoyed helping Samantha."

There were other things Kate wanted to say, like how she'd already begun envisioning a marketing campaign for Rainbow's End and how much she hoped she and Greg had a future together, but she'd wait until they arrived at Rainbow's End and she had Greg's full attention.

"I've been doing all the talking. Are you ready to tell me about your trip to Washington?" Kate asked, careful not to refer to it as home.

They'd left the city and were now on a two-lane highway. "I guess I am." Greg gave her a quick smile. "You were right. My dad and I needed to talk." His smile turned into a chuckle. "At times it was more like a shouting match, but I think we understand each other better now. I certainly do."

She could hear the difference in Greg's voice when he spoke of his father. The bitterness was gone, replaced by something else — not resignation, exactly — perhaps acceptance. Whatever had happened, it had brought Greg a measure of peace, and Kate was grateful. "Will you go back?"

He nodded. "Probably not as often as my mother would like, but it'll be more than an annual twenty-four-hour stopover. I want to spend some time with my sisters too. I want to hear about their dreams, and I want them to see me as more than a checkbook."

Greg was silent as they passed a slow-moving truck. Then he said, "It's a funny thing. I was even thinking about inviting the whole family to Rainbow's End."

Kate's heart leapt at the realization that Greg was mending his relationship with his family. The fact that he wanted them to see where he lived — at least temporarily — was promising. "That's a great idea." It would be even better if Greg agreed with her plan. Having the entire Vange family there would be the perfect way to open a family-oriented resort.

When they reached Rainbow's End and Greg parked the SUV in its usual spot, he turned to Kate. "What do you say to a picnic on the island? I remember you said you hadn't been there yet, and today seems like the perfect day. You don't have to rush back to the hospital; I could use the exercise, and I'm sure Carmen can rustle up something for us to eat."

Kate nodded. Today more than ever, she

wanted to see the spot that Sally claimed had the best view of Rainbow's End, because — depending on Greg's reaction to her idea — this might be her only chance to visit the island. She started to agree, then looked at the sky. "I'm not sure we should. The forecast calls for afternoon thunderstorms."

Greg glanced upward. "It doesn't look threatening now." Not a cloud marred the brilliant blue sky. "We'll be back well before the storms start. If they start," he amended. "You know Texas weather." He gave Kate an encouraging smile. "I move that we adjourn to the island."

"I second that motion."

Fifteen minutes later, Kate was ready. She'd changed into shorts, a sleeveless shirt, and sandals, and had slathered on sunblock. Grabbing a hat and her sunglasses, she hurried to the dock, planning to help Greg. It had obviously taken him less time to change into shorts and a T-shirt, because he already had the boat in the water, a picnic basket stowed inside it.

"I'm not sure what Carmen packed," Greg said as he helped Kate into the boat and untied the rope.

His grip was warm and firm, and surely it wasn't Kate's imagination that he held her hand longer than absolutely necessary to ensure that she was safely inside the rowboat. She wouldn't dwell on that. Instead, she looked at the basket, then made a show of sniffing the air as if to determine the contents. "Whatever it is, you can bet it's delicious."

"And there'll be enough to feed a troop of starving Boy Scouts."

Kate smiled, watching as Greg steered them past the dock. He was right. This was the perfect time to be out on Bluebonnet Lake. A light breeze kept the day from feeling sweltering but wasn't enough to make the ride rough.

"Carmen's a gem," Kate said, remembering not just the woman's superb cooking but also her motherly interest in KOB. "I can't imagine Rainbow's End without her."

"Or her without Rainbow's End."

Greg had given her the perfect opening. "I've got some ideas about that," Kate told him.

He shook his head. "Relax, Kate. There'll be time for serious stuff later. You need a rest."

It wasn't only the perfect day for a boat ride. It was also the perfect day for relaxing. A few puffy cumulus clouds had appeared and were drifting lazily across the deep blue sky. Kate let herself relax, lulled by the rhythm of the oars dipping into the water. Greg made rowing look effortless, his arms stretching and bending, the muscles flexing as he plied the oars. He might not have excelled at team sports as a boy, but there was no denying his prowess at rowing.

Instead of landing when they reached the island, Greg rowed around it, giving Kate the opportunity to study it. From a distance, she had seen trees in the center but hadn't realized they were growing on top of a small rise and that the land sloped down to the water, leaving only a narrow strip of flat ground.

That wasn't the only surprise. The grove was smaller than Kate had thought, a mixture of hickory and mesquite, while the grass was studded with wildflowers. Though she saw no bluebonnets here, the orange of Indian paintbrush was unmistakable and made a vivid contrast to the grass.

"That's the paintbrush." A lightbulb went off in Kate's brain. "Indian paintbrush."

Greg appeared amused. "Were you picturing an artist's palette and brush?"

"Exactly. Every time someone talked about Paintbrush Island, that's the image I saw. I wondered about it, especially since the lake is named for a flower, but I never asked."

"And now you know," Greg said as he slowed the boat. "This is the part of Indian Paintbrush Island I like." He emphasized the name. The area they were approaching was more private than the side that faced the resort, with no buildings in sight, and the trees were closer to the water, providing more shade. "I thought we'd have our picnic here."

Kate smiled at the idyllic location and wondered if this was why Sally had declared it a spot for lovers. Without a doubt, it was one of the most romantic places Kate had seen.

When she nodded her approval, Greg jumped from the boat and dragged it onto the shore, then helped Kate climb out. Within minutes, they'd spread the blanket and were exploring the contents of Carmen's picnic basket. As Kate had expected, the food was delicious, a welcome change from days of hospital cafeteria food. An assortment of barbecued chicken and roast beef sandwiches was accompanied by potato salad and coleslaw. Peach and apple fritters completed the meal, all washed down with a choice of lemonade or sweet tea.

"This is wonderful," Kate said when she

had repacked the basket and she and Greg were lounging on the blanket. The food couldn't have been better, but what made her heart sing with pleasure was being with Greg. No matter what happened, no matter how the day ended, she knew she would never forget this time. Since they'd arrived on the island, they'd spoken of nothing significant; they hadn't even shared a kiss, and yet Kate felt as if they were linked. It was almost as if they were communicating without words.

"I feel as if I'm a million miles from New York," she said softly.

Greg nodded. "Or California." He'd stretched out on one side and was watching her, his eyes intent. "Rainbow's End is a special place. I wish I knew what to do to save it."

Kate pushed herself to a sitting position and smiled when Greg imitated her action. They both seemed to have realized that the time for talking had arrived. Kate was thankful that Greg had given her the opportunity to go first.

"I have an idea for that," she said. "I overheard some of the nurses talking the first morning I was at the hospital." Quickly, Kate outlined her plan, watching Greg's expression. "I really think you could be successful. Probably not financially," she added when he started to frown. "Depending on how many families you have to subsidize, you might be lucky to break even, but you already know that success is more than money."

When Greg said nothing, Kate continued. "A new Rainbow's End would make a huge difference in so many lives. Besides the guests you helped, there would be more jobs for the Dupree teenagers, and the paying guests would help the local economy. You could even hold those theme weeks we talked about — cooking, quilting, jewelry making."

She had spoken quickly, almost as if she were delivering a pitch to a potential client. Now she was done. All that remained was Greg's reaction. Though Kate had hoped to see enthusiasm in his eyes or an occasional smile, Greg had kept his expression impassive while she'd spoken, giving her no way to gauge his thoughts. "What do you think?"

Kate had expected an instant response. Instead, there was a moment of silence, as if he were choosing his words carefully. "It's a good plan. It could work." There was no warmth in his voice, nothing but cautious approval. This wasn't the reaction she had anticipated, and it certainly was not the one she'd hoped for.

"You don't sound very enthusiastic." That was the understatement of the week. Kate tried not to let her disappointment show. The solution for Rainbow's End had felt so right that she had been certain she was on the correct road.

Greg stared into the distance for a long moment. When he spoke, his voice was as emotionless as his face. "I'm sorry, Kate. I know you've put a lot of thought into this." He closed his eyes for a second, then met her gaze. What she saw made Kate's heart ache. The Greg she'd known before, the one who'd kissed her, the one who'd made her believe in love and happily-ever-after, was gone, replaced by a cool stranger. Was this the way he'd been when he'd led Sys=Simpl?

"It's definitely the right direction for Rainbow's End," Greg said slowly, "but I'm not convinced I'm the right person to make it happen."

A tiny knot of hope made its way into Kate's heart. Perhaps this was simply a case of Greg's insecurities. Perhaps all he needed was encouragement. "You are the right person, Greg," she said firmly. "In fact, you're the perfect person to do this."

He crossed his arms, the gesture seeming

to distance him from her. "I appreciate your vote of confidence, but I know I'm not that person. I know my limitations even if you don't." Greg's lips tightened, and she sensed that he was trying to keep her from seeing his emotions. "You talked a lot about how *I* could do this and what a difference *I* could make. That's where you're wrong, Kate. I can't do it alone. Drew was right when he told me I needed a partner. I needed one for the company, and I need one if I'm going to turn Rainbow's End around."

Greg *was* insecure. Despite everything he'd accomplished, despite the fact that he and his father had finally begun to communicate, he didn't trust his own abilities. "I'm sure you can find a partner," Kate told him.

Greg shook his head. Unfolding his arms, he leaned forward, his eyes intense. "I don't want just any partner. I want a partner for life." He pushed himself off the blanket, and when he was standing, he reached down to pull her to her feet. "I want a very special partner. I want a wife."

Kate felt the blood drain from her face, then rush back, flooding her cheeks with color as her heart began to pound. She'd been wrong before, but maybe — just maybe — she wasn't imagining the love that shone from Greg's eyes.

His smile dissolved her fears, for it was the sweetest smile Kate had ever seen. Filled with love and promise, it made her want to smile back. When she opened her mouth to speak, Greg laid a finger on her lips.

"Please let me finish. What I'm trying to say is that I love you. I want to marry you and spend the rest of my life with you." Greg shifted his hand to cup Kate's cheek. "If you want us to live at Rainbow's End and turn it into a retreat for families, that's fine with me. If you'd rather live in a city, that's okay too. All that matters is that whatever we do, we do it together." Greg's smile broadened. "Will you marry me? Will you be my partner for life?"

Dreams really did come true. Her heart overflowing with a love that matched the one she saw reflected in Greg's eyes, Kate nodded. "I will, my darling, I will."

She cleared her throat, trying to dislodge the lump that had formed in it at the realization that this man loved her as much as she loved him. "You're the happy ending I've always dreamed of. You're the only person who can fill the empty spaces within me and make me complete. Oh, Greg, I love you with all my heart. Of course I'll marry you."

For a moment he grinned, a goofy grin that Kate suspected mirrored the one on her face. It was the grin of a man who'd climbed the highest mountain, slain the most ferocious dragon, battled the fiercest enemies, and won. It was the grin of a man who'd found his true love. And then the grin faded as Greg found a better use for his lips.

Slowly, gently, he drew Kate into his arms and pressed his lips to hers. An instant later, the flame that he'd ignited turned into a raging fire as they clung to each other and shared their first kiss as an engaged couple. When at length they broke apart, Greg slung his arm around Kate's shoulders and drew her close for one last kiss. "I suppose we should get back."

It was the practical thing to do, but Kate wasn't ready to return to reality. "Let's walk around the island first. I want to see it all." Sally had been right when she'd said this was a special place for lovers, and Kate wanted to savor every minute of her time here.

She and Greg strolled hand in hand, talking about their love, their plans for Rainbow's End, and how wonderful it would be to live here permanently. Oblivious to everything except the joy of their newfound love, neither of them noticed the approach of a dark cloud. They had reached the opposite side of the island when a loud clap of thunder announced a change in the weather. A second later, the cloud burst open, drenching them with cool rain.

Kate looked at the sky and began to laugh, her laughter increasing only moments later when the storm ended as suddenly as it had begun. She brushed the wet hair from her face and shoved her now water-spotted sunglasses on top of her head. Squinting, she glanced at the opposite side of the lake.

"Look, Greg!" Kate pointed to the perfect rainbow framing the lodge. It would disappear in minutes. She knew that, just as she knew that there would never be another moment like this. She was with the man she loved, the future spreading out before them with all the color and beauty of a rainbow. Grabbing Greg's hand, Kate tugged on it as she began to run.

"Let's do it. Let's chase the rainbow."

AUTHOR'S LETTER

Dear Reader,

Thank you for traveling to Rainbow's End with me. I hope you enjoyed your time there as much as I did and that you're looking forward to returning, because the story's not over. There will be at least two more Rainbow's End books. You'll have a chance to visit with old friends and meet some new ones as you see what happens after Kate and Greg restore the resort. No more leaking roofs or holey window screens!

Did you wonder what inspired Rainbow's End? It was a vacation my husband and I took to the Adirondack Mountains. The resort had received excellent reviews, but when we got there, it was obvious that it was in dire need of work. Like Greg, we experienced a leaky roof right over the bed, and the power wasn't reliable. The food bore no resemblance to Carmen's meals. But, despite all that, it was a memorable week. The location was beautiful, and though the boats leaked, it was fun kayaking and riding paddle boats on a lake ringed with beautiful mountains. Best of all, our time there started a game of "what-if" in my mind. *At Bluebonnet Lake* is the result. Writers, you see, can find inspiration almost anywhere.

Inspiration is exactly what Blake Kendall needs. Though his books have consistently hit the bestseller lists, for the first time in his career, he's facing writer's block. When nothing else works, he decides to visit his college friend Greg. Blake's expectations aren't very high — a change of scenery, a chance to see what Greg has done with his life, some of the good food Greg has raved about. Blake certainly doesn't expect to find a woman like Carmen's daughter, Marisa.

If there's one thing Marisa St. George knows, it's that she will never again live in Dupree. But when circumstances force her to return, she finds more than she expected — including an infuriating but intriguing man who seems to have more than his share of secrets.

While you're waiting for the full book

of Marisa and Blake's story, to be published soon as *In Firefly Valley,* if you like tales of love and faith in times gone by, you might enjoy my Texas Dreams and Westward Winds series. Information about them and my other stories is available on my website: www.amandacabot .com. My website also includes my email address and information about signing up for my online newsletter.

Were you intrigued by Carmen's "healthy" chocolate pound cake? It really exists. The recipe is one I modified to make it healthier by substituting applesauce for butter and egg whites for whole eggs. It's become one of my favorite desserts, and so I wanted to share it with you.

If you try the cake, I hope you'll enjoy it as much as I do. As always, I look forward to hearing from you. As the dedication to this book states, you are the reason I write.

Blessings,
Amanda Cabot

CHOCOLATE POUND CAKE

Please note that because this is low fat, all mixing is done by hand. It's important not to overmix the flour, since that will make the cake tough. Also, if you live at high altitude (over 5,000 feet) as I do, send me an email and I'll let you know what adjustments are needed.

Grease and flour a 12-cup Bundt pan. (I use a floured spray like Baker's Joy.)

Preheat the oven to 325 degrees.

Stir together until well mixed:

3 cups sugar
1 cup unsweetened cocoa

Add and mix thoroughly:

3 egg whites
1 cup applesauce

Combine:

3 cups all-purpose flour
3 tsp baking powder
1 tsp salt

Combine:

1 3/4 cups skim milk
1 tsp vanilla
1 tsp instant coffee crystals

Alternate adding the flour and milk mixtures, being careful to fold the ingredients rather than beating them.

Pour the batter into the prepared pan.

Bake at 325 degrees for 55 minutes or until a cake tester comes out clean.

Cool for ten minutes in the pan.

Turn onto a wire rack and cool completely before serving.

ABOUT THE AUTHOR

Dreams have always been an important part of **Amanda Cabot**'s life. For almost as long as she can remember, she dreamt of being an author. Fortunately for the world, her grade-school attempts as a playwright were not successful, and she turned her attention to novels. Her dream of selling a book before her thirtieth birthday came true, and she's been spinning tales ever since. She now has more than thirty novels to her credit under a variety of pen names.

Her books have been finalists for the ACFW Carol Award as well as the Bookseller's Best and have appeared on the CBA bestseller list.

A popular speaker, Amanda is a member of ACFW and a charter member of Romance Writers of America. She married her high school sweetheart, who shares her love of travel and who's driven thousands of miles to help her research her books. After years as Easterners, they fulfilled a longtime dream and are now living in the American West.